A
RANGER'S
JOURNEY

THE LAST ETERNAL
Book Four

by

JACOB PEPPERS

A Ranger's Journey: The Last Eternal Book 4

Visit the author website:
www.JacobPeppersAuthor.com

This one is for you, Gabriel
You're five now and growing up so fast—sometimes I think too fast
And while I am excited and privileged to watch you grow,
I cannot help but be a little sad at what is left behind
Let this then, stand in memory...
In memory of choo-choo-training around the house,
Of horsey rides and chicken nuggets,
Of monster faces and "I do's" that mean yes,

I love you, son.
To the moon and back.

Sign up for my VIP New Releases mailing list and get a free copy of
The Silent Blade: A Seven Virtues novella as well as receive
exclusive promotions and other bonuses!

Go to JacobPeppersAuthor.com to claim your free book!

CHAPTER ONE

Death was coming.

Standing as he was in the pleasant warmth of the wizard's cabin, with the appetizing smell of cooking rabbit filling his nostrils, it seemed hard for the wanderer to believe.

But death was coming just the same.

Staring through the small window and onto a world of rolling hills and snow-covered ground that seemed to sparkle in the sunlight like thousands of diamonds, it seemed impossible.

And yet...death was coming. It would be here soon.

That death came for him, he knew, for it had been coming for a long time. But he knew also that death was a hungry beast, one that would devour anyone or anything in its path. That included the sheriff of Alhs beside him, included the wizard as well as Dekker, his family, and all the villagers waiting at the boundary where the woods of the Untamed Lands gave way to the unnatural snowy dunes in which the wizard lived. The villagers who counted on him to save them.

"This should be impossible," the wizard said, frowning at him. "You should not be here. You should not have been able to find me."

"What do you mean?" the wanderer asked.

"The *Eternals*," the wizard hissed angrily. "A worthy name, though no doubt not for the reason your progenitors thought. When you are the last beings left alive, it will not be because of your long lives but instead because you have a way of getting everyone around you killed."

The wanderer frowned. "You know of us? The Eternals?"

The wizard snorted. "Of course I know of you—you and your kind are the reason I've spent the last few centuries hiding out in the middle of nowhere!"

The wanderer's frown deepened. "I...don't understand."

The other man watched him for several seconds, glancing at the sheriff who only shrugged, clearly confused, before turning back to the wanderer. "No," he said slowly, "no, it seems that you do not." He sighed. "No great surprise, I suppose. Your brothers and sisters always did love their secrets. They hoarded them the same way the ancient dragons were said to hoard gold. No doubt you do not even know why they sent you here to kill me."

"As I said," the wanderer said slowly, "I did not come to kill you."

The wizard watched him carefully, sniffing at the air as he did. "Truth," he said slowly, grudgingly. "Or, at least, it would seem so. But then, you Eternals always did enjoy your tricks, didn't you? And while your words might taste of truth, that means little. Some poisons, it is said, are sweet upon the tongue, but that does not stop them from claiming the life of any foolish or unlucky enough to swallow them."

The wanderer did not think that any speech was expected of him, and so he said nothing, only waited as the wizard continued to stare at him. "Well?" the wizard asked.

"Well what?"

"Aren't you going to answer?"

"You did not ask a question," the wanderer said.

The wizard frowned. "What assurances do I have that the Eternals did not send you here to kill me?"

"Well," the wanderer said slowly, "the first, I suppose, is that I have not yet tried to kill you."

"A state of affairs that you might choose to change at any moment," the wizard said, "though I warn you, Youngest of the Eternals, that a man does not live as long as I have because he is careless. I have expected this visit, and I have planned for it. Should you choose to attempt me harm, you will find me no easy prey."

There was a pregnant, tense silence then, as the three men stood regarding one another. Finally, the wanderer spoke. "The other assurance that the Eternals did not send me," he said, meeting the wizard's gaze, "is that they are dead. I am Youngest, yes, you are correct in that, but I am also the last. The Eternals are no more."

The wizard snorted. "Your first lie was better. But then that's the thing about lies, Youngest of the Eternals, the more you tell, the easier they are to spot."

"It is no lie," the wanderer said. "They are dead and have been for the last hundred years and more."

"I see," the wizard said. "You might be forgiven for assuming that here, so far from what you might consider the civilized world, I am clueless as to the goings-on of society, that I might be easily fooled. But I am no dull-witted farm boy to be tricked, and I make it a point to stay apprised of news from your world, particularly of the Eternals. After all, what better way for the hare to remain free of the lion's maw than to know, at all times, the disposition of the one who would make a meal of him? And so it is that I *know* you are lying, for while I admit that I may not be as knowledgeable as once I was, I would have no doubt heard through my sources had the Eternals—beings who nearly all the living saw as gods—been slain."

"Not if those who slew them took their place," the wanderer said.

The wizard frowned deeper at that. "Took their place."

"Yes."

"Then why *have* you come?"

"To help," the wanderer said. "To fix what I've broken."

"Don't you mean to get *me* to fix it?"

The wanderer winced but nodded. "Yes."

The other man snorted. "Well, you've traveled a long way to be disappointed, then."

The wanderer and the sheriff shared a look. "Please," the wanderer said, turning back to the wizard, "do not punish them for my sin, it is not their—"

"You Eternals," the wizard said with a sneer. "You think that the world revolves around you, as if my feelings for you are enough for me to condemn an entire village." He shook his head.

"That has nothing to do with it. The barrier that you destroyed so carelessly was long in the making. Unless those chasing you would be willing to grant you a few weeks' reprieve while I construct another we will all be dead long before it is finished."

"But there must be something you can do," the wanderer said, hearing the desperation in his own voice and unable to hide it, for he was thinking of Dekker and Ella, and Sarah, her most of all.

"*Fool,*" the wizard hissed. "There are consequences to our actions, Eternal, and the consequence for *your* selfish act is that an entire village of—"

"Excuse me," another voice said, and they turned to regard the sheriff. "Yeah," he went on, "I'm still here, in case you both forgot. Anyhow, while I appreciate this little history lesson or...argument or, well, whatever it is, I feel like maybe it could wait. You know, until we're out of reach of that army you just showed us, and that fella with the bow. I didn't much care for the look of him either."

The wizard turned back to the wanderer who shrugged. Then the other man frowned, giving his head a shake before turning and moving to a small bureau against the wall. He bent, grunting in pain as he did and bringing a hand to the small of his back. He frowned over his shoulder at the wanderer. "The hazards of old age," he grumbled, "but as bad as they are, I'd take them any day to the hazards of you Eternals. Better an aching back and knees that hurt when it rains than a viper in my bed."

"If it helps," the wanderer said, "I have no intention of getting in your bed."

The man grunted, shooting him a sour look. "No, it's not my bed you care about but my coffin."

The wanderer had nothing to say to that, and so he said nothing, only watching as the wizard withdrew a linen sack from inside the bureau and began to stuff clothes into it.

"Sorry," the sheriff said, "but...what's happening?"

"I'm leaving, that's what's happening, Sheriff," the wizard said.

"Leaving?" the other man asked, as if the wizard had spoken in a different language.

"Yes, *leaving,*" the wizard repeated, "fleeing if you prefer—if you haven't done it before, I'd suggest giving it a try and no time like the present."

The sheriff turned and regarded the wanderer with a mixture of disbelief and an almost child-like confusion. It was as if he was a young boy meeting his favorite childhood hero only to discover that the knight's faithful steed was not a horse but a bloodthirsty dragon and beneath the golden, shining armor lurked a visage more terrible even than those monsters he had thought the man would save him from.

The sheriff's mouth worked but no words came out. He could not find his voice for his disbelief, and so it was left to the wanderer to find it in his stead. "You mean to leave them," he said to the wizard's hunched back.

It was not a question, but the man chose to answer it anyway, spinning on him, his two bushy dark gray eyebrows drawn down in a frown to match the one on his mouth. "Don't you try to blame this on me—you are the one that brought the sheriff here, not me, just as it is you who are responsible for that which comes." The wizard's scowl gave way to a thoughtful frown, and he turned to regard the sheriff. "How *are* you here, anyway? The barrier I erected, it was meant to keep those dangers of the Untamed Lands away from your village, but it should have served just as well to keep those of your village from leaving." He sighed. "But then, I suppose nothing lasts forever. Tell me, how big is the gap?"

"The gap?" the sheriff asked.

"Yes, yes," the wizard said impatiently, "the one that has appeared in the barrier. How large? The size of a fist? Bigger?"

"Ah. Right. Well, the thing is," the sheriff said, wincing, "that is…" he cleared his throat, glancing at the wanderer with an almost guilty expression on his face.

"There is no barrier," the wanderer said, meeting the wizard's gaze, "and what the sheriff here is too kind to say is that it is my fault that it is gone."

"Why am I not surprised?" the wizard said. "What was it then, *Youngest?* Did you tire of torturing those in what you and your sisters and brothers like to consider the *civilized* lands and came here to do the same?"

"I did not mean to break it," the wanderer said. "I sought only to save a family, one I have come to care for and—"

"Save them," the wizard repeated. "From what?"

"The Accursed," the wanderer said. "They were coming for them and—"

"And for you too?" the man said, watching him carefully with a clever sparkle in his eye.

Perhaps the wizard expected him to lie. Likely he did, for while the wanderer did not know the reasons for the man's dislike for the Eternals, it was clear that they were strong ones. "Yes," he said. "For me as well."

"So you chose, in your benevolent wisdom, to risk an entire village in order to save yourself?"

"I did not know of the village, only that there was a barrier—it was not until after I found my way through it that I became aware of Alhs' existence."

"I see," the wizard said. "And if you had known about it before hand?"

The wanderer winced. "I would have done the same."

The gray-haired man snorted. "I thought as much." He shook his head. "You Eternals, so righteous, so *perfect.* Yet beneath all your gilding, beneath all your noble sculptures and pompous vainglory, you are selfish and cruel."

"And what of you?" the wanderer said, not in an accusatory tone but simply a question.

That caused the wizard to freeze, frowning. "What *of* me?"

The wanderer shrugged. "It seems to me that, by fleeing and leaving the sheriff—and the other villagers of Alhs—to fend for themselves, you are no better than we Eternals who you seem to so despise. After all, will you not be damning a village to save yourself, the same thing for which you hold me to blame?"

The wizard watched him for a moment then rolled his eyes. "Word games. You Eternals always have been good at those, but it is not the same thing, not even close. Your actions directly led to the villagers being in danger, and—"

"And your actions might save them."

"There *is* no saving them, you fool," the wizard snapped. "They are dead! *We* are dead! You speak falsely, as you have since you first entered my home, for the man who leads this army of soulless creatures is known to me. It is Ranger, one of the Eternals, one of *you.*"

"Ranger is dead," the wanderer said, though in truth he was not exactly sure how much of that was true, how much of the Eternals had been preserved by whatever spell Oracle had cast on the amulet about his neck. Either way, though, he decided that there was no need to mention that now.

"So you say," the wizard said, "yet I have seen him clearly. Tell me then, Youngest of the Eternals, how it is that a dead man is coming to kill us?"

"It is something else, something that took his place. His and the others. If you are as well-informed as you claim then you have no doubt heard the story—the story that I betrayed the others, the story that the enemy created to discredit me. It is a tale they fabricated once they took the others' place."

The wizard watched him, not angrily now but consideringly. Finally, he shook his head. "It doesn't matter. Even if what you're saying is true—and I'm not saying it is—it makes little difference. Whether he is Ranger or only an impostor, whoever comes is leading an army, that much is clear. An army that will find no difficulty in dealing with us. So, as I said, I am leaving."

"And the villagers of Alhs?"

"Will just have to make do for themselves, won't they?" the wizard snapped. He turned to the sheriff. "I am sorry, Sheriff, indeed I am, but there is a reason I have spent my life here, in the wilds. Now then, I wish you all luck."

The wanderer shrugged, turning to the sheriff. "Come, Sheriff Fred. It is time we left."

"Left?" the sheriff asked, blinking. "But...where will we go?"

"*You* will go back to the others," the wanderer said. "And tell them what has transpired—get them out of here. Save them, if you can."

"And...and you?" the sheriff asked.

The wanderer glanced at the wizard who had stopped packing and was now watching him, then he turned back to the sheriff. "It is I who has brought this doom upon us, and so it is I who must go out and face it. The wizard..." He glanced and the old man. "Do you not have another name?"

"None that I intend to give to you," the man snapped.

"Very well," the wanderer said, turning back to the sheriff. "The wizard was right about that much at least. Now go, while there is yet time—I will hold them for as long as I can."

The wizard snorted. "You can't be serious."

The wanderer glanced at the man, raising an eyebrow.

"You'll die," the wizard said.

"Then I'll die."

The wizard let out an exasperated growl. "Fine, damn you. Where are the other villagers?" he asked. "Where *exactly*?"

The wanderer schooled his features, not allowing his relief to show on his face. "We left them at the border of the snow—where the woods are yet warm."

"A good thing you did, or I do not doubt half of them would be dead," the wizard grumbled. He considered for a moment then shook his head. "Very well, damnit. We will go to them, and I will do what I can. But I warn you, Youngest, that should I die on the fool's errand you have set us, I will most assuredly haunt you for the rest of your days."

"Considering the likelihood that I'll survive, that is, perhaps, not as big of a threat as it might be," the wanderer said. "Still...thank you. For your help."

The wizard watched him for a moment, staring at him as if seeing him for the first time then rolled his eyes. "I'm sure your appreciation will be a great comfort when I'm breathing my last."

"But...but you'll help us then?"

The wizard turned to regard the sheriff. "If I were you, I wouldn't start the celebrating just yet, Sheriff Fred. Being born and raised as you have in the Untamed Lands, you may be forgiven for not knowing what it is that chases you, what it is that *this* one has brought to your doorstep...before knocking your door in and sending you...never mind. The point is that the one leading this army is a master of woodcraft, one who has forgotten, in his time, more than any other living soul has ever known about tracking, hunting, and capturing his prey. Although..." He paused, raising a gray, bushy eyebrow at the wanderer. "If some are to be believed, he is not that same man, yet he looks identical to him, so I would not hold out much hope on that score."

"So what can we do?" the sheriff asked, looking considerably sober and considerably paler after the wizard's brief speech.

"Run and hope...and pray, Sheriff. Pray to every god you have ever heard of and ask them each for their help." He turned, meeting the wanderer's gaze. "For I am quite sure that, before this thing is through, we will need it. Even then, I do not think it will be enough."

***

As the wizard prepared to depart, the wanderer walked outside to check on Veikr.

He was glad to see that the wizard had not lied about this much, at least—the horse did not look cold. He stood near the front door, and the wanderer saw that there was a small area including the door and part of the ground that was surrounded by a nearly invisible bubble. Nearly but not quite, for the air around it seemed to shimmer and shift as if he stared at it through water, similarly to the way the air looked when an Unseen moved through it.

While the blizzard continued its wintry war against the world outside the bubble, inside no snow fell. What little lay on the ground had begun to melt, revealing green grass beneath. It was also warm. As warm, or at least nearly so, as it had been inside the wizard's home, and the wanderer could not help but be impressed. Whatever else the wizard was—cantankerous and ornery came to mind—he was most certainly possessed of no small degree of skill in the Art, a skill, the wanderer thought, to rival that of the Eternals themselves.

"Okay?" he asked as he approached the horse.

Veikr gave a small nod of his muzzle, making a contented sound as the wanderer gave him a pat.

He heard the door open and was unsurprised to see the sheriff stepping outside and closing it behind him, a troubled expression on his face. The man moved to stand beside him, a far off, distracted look on his face.

"Everything alright, Sheriff?"

The man grunted, turning to him. "What's that?"

"I asked if everything was okay."

The sheriff nodded. "Sure, yeah, I think so. Only...it's strange."

"What's that?"

The heavy-set man gave a slow shake of his head. "I've known about the Wizard of the South since I was a lad, of course. Everyone does. But I've never said so much as a single word to him or him to me. Never thought to, to be honest. To meet him, that is."

"Why not?"

The man considered that, scratching his chin. "I don't know. I just didn't, I guess. He never struck me as a man so much as he did a sort of...well, a *force*, I guess. Like the wind or rain, that sort of thing. I wouldn't have ever thought to meet him, not anymore'n I'd have thought to meet the sunrise."

"And now that you have?"

"Well. He's just a man, ain't he?" the sheriff asked. "Like any other."

"No, Sheriff," the wanderer said, glancing back at the house. "Not like any other." In fact, the wizard was a mystery, one just about begging to be solved, but then he thought that the man could go on being a riddle. The Wizard of the South, as the villagers of Alhs knew him, could keep his secrets. After all, the wanderer had plenty of his own—he would not begrudge the man his.

"I s'pose you're right," the sheriff said. "Only...I can't help feeling a little...I don't know..."

"Disappointed?"

"Maybe that," the sheriff said, nodding slowly. "It's like...well. When I was a boy, my ma used to tell me stories, ones of knights and goblins and faeries and every other creature. And like most boys, well, I guess I thought the knights were just about the best thing in the world." He gave a soft, deprecating laugh. "S'pose I took it a bit further than most, though. See, it weren't enough for me to know that the knights were out there somewhere, to lie in my bed and listen to my ma's tales of them defeatin' dragons and slayin' goblins. No, I wanted—*needed*—to meet one. A knight, that is, not a goblin—met plenty enough of them in my nightmares to suit me for the rest of my life, if you want to know the truth. Anyway, I reckon that was about all I ever thought or talked about when I was a kid."

"There are worse things."

He grunted. "Maybe, though I'm not so sure my ma and pa would have agreed with you on that. I figure I probably drove them just about crazy with all my carryin' on. You see, I *had* to meet a knight, for any boy that ever listens to the stories knows that the only way to *become* a knight is to serve one, to be knighted by him when the time came."

"And you wanted to be a knight."

The sheriff gave a sad, almost whimsical smile. "'Wanted,'" he said, saying the word as if tasting it. "Sure, I s'pose you could say that, though it don't come close to the truth of the thing, not by half. I didn't just want to be a knight, I *needed* to be one. Needed it with every part of me, was desperate to go out and take on the world's dragons, all its monsters, to save the innocent and all that other tripe that those folks in the storybooks do."

"Is that why you became sheriff?"

The man blinked, as if he'd only just thought of that, then he gave a laugh. "Yeah, I think maybe it is. Anyway, I guess I loved knights the way only a little child can love things. After a while, I s'pose my parents realized that love wasn't goin' anywhere, then, maybe thinkin' to get it out of my system, my ma and da, they cooked up a little surprise for me. One day, I woke up for breakfast, was preparin' for my chores, when there was a knock on the door. My ma usually answered such knocks, sayin' she didn't want me botherin' the neighbors, but that day she asked me to do it, and I did, feelin' a mixture of pride and trepidation, feelin' like the man of the house as I went to see what villager of Alhs was visitin' and what they needed."

The wanderer smiled, thinking he knew where this was going.

"Only, it wasn't no villager on the other side of the door but a real-life knight," the sheriff said, smiling at the memory. "Golden-painted armor, sword and all."

"What did you do?"

"Froze is what I done," the sheriff said. "I was still froze when the knight reached out his sword and tapped it on my head, knighting me Sir Fred the Valorous. I guess I've never been so proud in my life, leastways until the knight's helmet slipped off. He caught it, tugging it back on but not before I saw his face, my *father's* face, and just like that the spell was broken. The man standing there weren't no knight at all but my father, and the golden armor was no more than thin slats of wood my dad had painted gold. As for the flowered circlet on his helmet, that was a small wreath my ma had fashioned—always good at such things, was my mother."

"Thoughtful of them," the wanderer said.

"Yeah," the sheriff said, giving a sniff. "Yeah, it was. Only, to a young boy who wanted to meet a knight above all else, it didn't seem so at the time. It seemed..."

"Like a tragedy."

"Yes, that and a betrayal besides." He shook his head, sighing. "I was so angry at them...angry because they, in their love, tried to give me what they could not...children can be little shits sometimes, can't they, Ungr?"

The wanderer, who did not know any children save Sarah and who had long since forgotten most of his own childhood, said nothing, only gave the man a small, commiserating smile.

"Anyway," the sheriff said, giving his head a shake as if to clear it of those old memories, those old ghosts, "that's a long tale for a short story, and that story is this—I feel about the same, now, as I did when that wooden helmet came off and I saw my da standin' there."

"You thought to find a wizard," the wanderer began.

"And found a man instead," the sheriff agreed, shrugging. "Stupid, I know, but there it is. Not sure what I was expecting anyway."

"Like a pointy hat and a wizard's staff?"

The sheriff gave him an embarassed smile. "Yeah, somethin' like that I s'pose."

The wanderer nodded. He considered leaving it there. True, it was clear that the man's faith—in the wizard, yes, but more than that, in the world—had been shaken, but it seemed arrogant to the wanderer to think that he had anything of value to say, anything that might begin to restore it. After all, he had lost his own faith long ago, had he not? Lost it somewhere along the dusty, blood-spattered trail that stretched out behind him, back through the years until the moment in which he had seen the gods meet their enemy in battle, had seen the gods lose, had seen them die.

Ever since then, he had been no more than a faithless wanderer, a vagabond traveling the face of the world alone. No faith or hope to sustain him but duty and that only, and what sustenance duty gave was dry, flavorless fare. So it had been since the day of their defeat.

But that isn't exactly true, is it? a part of him asked, and he was forced to consider. He had lost his faith, that was true enough, but he thought he had begun to regain it again, a process that had started when he'd first met Felden Ruitt and one which had continued as he'd traveled with Dekker, Ella, and Sarah.

They had helped him to find his way again, had given the vagabond a home, at least figuratively. "Perhaps there are no knights here, in this place," he told the sheriff finally, "at least not with golden armor, but I have met a few in my time."

"You have?" the sheriff asked, an eager, almost childlike note to his voice, a sparkle to his eyes that proved to the wanderer that while the journey to adulthood, the many worries and concerns and cynicisms that people accrued over the years, the wrinkles and stress lines, might hide the child they once were, that child was still there. Waiting to be inspired, to be awed.

"Oh, yes," the wanderer said, remembering his time training with Soldier in Celes, remembering the orders of knights that once lived there. "And while I do not know everything, I know that it wasn't their armor nor their swords..." he paused, glancing at Veikr—"not even their horses that made them knights. Instead, it was their code."

"The code," the sheriff said, smiling. "I remember it."

"Yes," the wanderer said. "More than a code...a promise, really. That they would protect the weak, would help those who could not help themselves."

"Yeah," the sheriff said, sounding a little confused now, clearly unsure of where the wanderer was going with this.

"There are some professions now that are very similar in what they do," the wanderer went on. "Professions, for example, that might lead those in them to shoot crossbow bolts into a giant serpent, stepping out of their cover in order to save those under their charge." The sheriff winced at that, clearly embarrassed. "Professions," the wanderer said, smiling, "that might lead a man to charge toward a farm to take on an unknown number of savages while others fled. You may not have the title, Sheriff, but there are many knights I knew who would be proud to have you beside them."

The man's expression was interesting to watch, embarrassed and pleased all at the same time. "Thanks...for that," he said.

The wanderer shrugged. "I speak only the truth as I know it."

"You know," the sheriff said. "The wizard, he might not like you Eternals, and while I can't say as I've ever met any of the others, if they're anythin' like you then I'd say the people of your lands could do far worse in pickin' their leaders."

It was the wanderer's turn to shift uncomfortably. He opened his mouth, not sure of what he was going to say, but was saved from the effort by the door of the house opening.

The wizard strode out, and the wanderer was forced to blink. A noise escaped the sheriff, one between a snort and a gasp, and the wanderer did his best to school his own features.

"What is it?" the wizard said, frowning from beneath the wide-brimmed, pointy hat he wore. "What's so damned amusing to the two of you?"

"Nothing," the wanderer said, "nothing at all. I like your hat."

The wizard's bushy gray eyebrows drew down into a frown. "It keeps the rain off."

"No doubt it does," the wanderer agreed.

"Is...is that a wizard's staff?" the sheriff asked, his voice sounding full of wonder.

"What, this old thing?" the wizard asked, glancing at the long length of wood he held in right hand. "This is just my walking stick."

The sheriff grinned widely, and the wizard frowned deeper, turning to the wanderer. "Has our sheriff been struck senseless while I was packing?"

"Something like that," the wanderer said, unable to keep the smile from his own face.

The wizard watched him for a moment then snorted. "Come on, the two of you—we have little time to waste, if we are to reach the other villagers before our death reaches us. I trust this horse of yours will not be averse to carrying my person upon his back?"

"You'd have to ask him," the wanderer said.

The wizard raised an eyebrow, glancing at Veikr who gave his head a shake, eyeing the wizard. The man turned back to regard the wanderer. "I am...not sure what that means."

"One way to find out," the wanderer said. The wizard did not like him, had made that very plain, and so the wanderer could not help but enjoy his obvious discomfort as he warily approached Veikr and, warier still, mounted the horse.

The wanderer grinned, nodding to the sheriff. "Hop on up, Sheriff. I will walk."

"You sure?" the man asked doubtfully. "I mean, that is, we only got here through that storm because of Veikr. Are you sure you can brave it again?"

"Braving will not be required," the wizard said. "Not yet, at least. The protective casting I have put around us will follow as we make it to your friends. Now, if we are quite finished chatting, I think we might well be on our way. I doubt if those creatures chasing us have decided to stop for tea."

"Very well," the wanderer said, nodding to Veikr. "Let's go."

CHAPTER TWO

The wanderer had lived far longer than all but a handful of people, and had thought, until meeting the Wizard of the South, that he was the oldest living being walking the face of the world. Yet he could not help staring around him in awe as he watched the wizard's magic at work.

He had seen magic before, of course, while training under the Eternals. Magic like that of Oracle who was able, on close examination, to divine much more about a creature than mundane means would allow. Magic like that of Shaman, a primal, elemental sort of magic which did not impose itself upon the world but instead chose to work naturally with those forces within it, offering no more than a nudge here, a suggestion there.

Both forms of the Art were effective, there was no doubt of that, but they had not felt to him, upon first seeing them, like *magic*. The wizard's use of the Art, though, was very different. As they walked, the protective barrier he'd cast melted the snow in a ten-foot circle around them, revealing blades of green grass poking up from beneath. But such was the power of the blizzard that a glance back showed him that no sooner were they past than the driving snow covered the grass once more.

It felt surreal, walking in that winter's landscape yet feeling as warm as if it were a pleasant summer day, and the wanderer found a smile coming to his face, one that, at a glance, he saw the sheriff shared. Veikr also seemed affected, moving with an alacrity and vigor that made it clear he was enjoying himself. Only the wizard himself seemed immune to the feeling of wonder his magic created, plodding on with what the wanderer was beginning to think was his perpetual scowl well in place, frowning out at the world as if it had personally done him wrong, and he was eager to find his recompense.

The wanderer did not let that bother him though, just as he did not let the knowledge that the creature who had taken Ranger's place, along with an army of Revenants and who knew how many Unseen were on their way affect his mood. There would be time for war, for violence later, after all—there always was. Sometimes it felt to him that life was little else.

Peace, though, was a far rarer sight, and so he would take this moment of relative peace in the storm, knowing full well that it would likely be a long time before he saw another. If, that was, he ever did.

With the wizard's spell protecting them from the storm's fury, they made far better time on the way back than they had on the way to the wizard's house and with considerably less chance of death.

Soon they crested the top of a hill, and the wanderer was able to see the forest in the distance, along with the villagers.

As they drew closer, the wanderer caught sight of Dekker standing at the border between the forest and the snow-ridden landscape. The man paced back and forth, obviously agitated, his hands opening and closing at his sides, looking as if he weren't walking on the ground so much as attacking it.

The big man was so focused on his assault on the dirt, in fact, that he didn't notice them approaching until those villagers that sat and camped beyond him began to point and shout words that the wanderer could not make out from this distance.

Dekker spun to regard them, and even from how far away they were the wanderer saw an almost comical look of surprise and relief on the man's face, one that was at once humorous and touching. Then, suddenly, the big man was hurrying forward, oblivious of the freezing temperatures as he strode out of the woods and a dozen feet into the snow-blasted wasteland.

He was covered in snow, his face red from the freezing temperatures by the time he reached them, but Dekker's grin reached from ear to ear. He stepped through the nearly invisible bubble of the wizard's spell as if it weren't there, striding forward. "By the Eternals, I thought you'd all died."

"Give it a bit," the wizard muttered.

The wanderer frowned at him before turning back to the big man. "Dekker," he said, offering his hand. "It's good to see you."

"You can stow that handshake shit, you bastard," the big man said, stepping forward and wrapping his thick arms around the wanderer in a hug that went a long way toward solving the being alive thing.

The man let go, and the wanderer did his best to hide the wheeze that threatened to come. "The villagers?" he croaked.

"Alive and well," Dekker said, apparently not hearing—or choosing to ignore—the strain in the wanderer's voice. "Or, at least, as well as can be expected."

"You know you might have waited only another few minutes and saved yourself a soggy, freezing trip," the wizard observed.

Dekker shrugged his massive shoulders. "I find the cold bracing."

"Most fools tend to find foolishness much the same, I'd think," the wizard said.

Dekker bared his teeth at the man in a smile that wasn't really a smile. "This is the wizard then?" he asked, glancing at the wanderer.

"This is him."

"Huh," the big man grunted. "Thought he'd be taller. Well, come on then—everyone's waitin', and if I keep you all from returnin' for much longer, I imagine Sarah'll have my head. She's been missin' that horse of yours somethin' fierce."

The wanderer nodded, his expression serious. "I am in the way of knowing that Veikr would like some more ribbons for his hair. If, of course, it isn't too much trouble."

The big man grinned. "Oh, I think that's a job Sarah'll be happy to take on."

And with that, Dekker turned and began walking back toward the woods where the villagers waited. The wizard started after him, but the wanderer grabbed his hand, halting him. The wizard looked at where he gripped him then met his gaze, frowning.

"Dekker is a good man," the wanderer said. "Better than me, and I'd hazard better than you. Say what you will about me—I don't care. But you will not belittle him. Do you understand?"

The wizard tried to pull his arm away, but the wanderer kept hold of it, not squeezing, just keeping a firm hold as he continued to watch the man. "Fine," the wizard said. "I did not mean it anyway. I am only frustrated, that's all—impending doom has a way of doing that to me."

The man tried to pull his arm away again and, this time, the wanderer let him. Then they followed behind Dekker and, in another few minutes, they were crossing over the boundary and traveling back into the forest of the Untamed Lands.

The villagers crowded around them, murmuring and talking excitedly, shooting glances at the wizard, mostly. Clint walked up to them, grinning and offering his hand. The wanderer took it.

"Ungr," the Perishable's leader said, "good to see you."

"It's good to be seen," the wanderer said.

"So," Clint said, glancing at the wizard who was currently scowling as villagers encircled him as if he were some famous bard. "The fella in the pointy hat—he's our savior, is he?"

The wanderer winced. "About that...something's happened."

"And this something, I don't suppose it's sweet cakes falling out of the sky? Or maybe that the wizard there's hiding a feast under that hat of his?"

"I'm afraid not," the wanderer said. "It turns out that the storm didn't take care of as many of the creatures following us as I'd hoped."

"Somethin' tells me that's not all," Clint said, watching him.

"I'm afraid it isn't," the wanderer admitted, "but come—we had best tell everyone. There is little time."

He glanced over at the sheriff who gave him a nod, then the two of them moved forward to where the villagers had gathered around the wizard. The villagers took note of them and grew silent, regarding them with grim, expectant faces, no doubt expecting more bad news, for the trip had been full of little else. The wanderer regretted, then, that he would not be able to disappoint them.

He had heard some people say, over the years, that bad news was best delivered quickly, while others claimed the kindest way to do it was to surround it on either side with something good in order to lessen the blow. He did not know which was right, knew only that each second they wasted here brought the impostor Ranger and those Revenants with him closer to the villagers of Alhs, and so he opted for the former strategy. "We can't go back to Alhs."

For several seconds, the villagers only regarded him in silence, clearly not understanding.

"But...but we found the wizard," an older woman said.

"Yeah," another villager, this one a man in his thirties, agreed, "you said...you said once we found the wizard, we'd be able to go back to Alhs. That he'd make the barrier again."

The wanderer glanced at the wizard, thinking that the man might take over and explain to the villagers, hopefully in a gentler way, what he had intimated to him back at his cabin. The man only looked at him though and after a moment the wanderer realized that the wizard had no intention of taking the brunt of the villagers' anger and disappointment. Not that he should have to— after all, it was the wanderer's fault they were here, his fault that the barrier was down, and so what burden there was, was his to bear. "Magic like that, it takes time," he told the villagers. "Weeks...months in the making. He would not be able to do it in time, particularly not with what's chasing us."

"Those things you call the Revenants?" the old woman who'd first spoken asked. "I don't see as that's so much of a problem— we've outrun 'em so far, haven't we?"

"We've been lucky so far," another voice said, and the wanderer turned, feeling a sense of relief to see the sheriff moving up to stand beside him. The man gave him a covert wink before turning back to regard the old woman. "I understand your frustration Alma, really I do. But the simple fact is that Alhs isn't safe—might never be safe again. We've got to push on."

"Push on to *where?*" another voice demanded, this one from a younger woman who held two small children pressed against her legs. "We've already gone farther than I ever thought to, farther than any of us ever *wanted* to," she went on, and there were murmurs and nods of agreement at that. "How much farther will we go? How much farther *can* we go? I say we take our chances back at Alhs. Those creatures, we've given 'em the slip before.

Perhaps we can outrun them back there, get the spell done before they're any the wiser and, if not, then the men folk could hold them off until the thing was done. They could do that," she said, a note of desperation in her voice as she looked at the wanderer, "couldn't they?"

"No," the wanderer said simply and with more than a little regret. "They could not." There were more murmurs of discontent among the villagers at that. "Even were it only the Revenants, we would all be dead within a few hours of their arrival. But it *isn't* only the Revenants that we need concern ourselves with. There is another who has shown himself, one who is far more deadly than any of the creatures we've encountered so far. He is coming, the one of whom I speak, and he will not slow, will not stop until he has accomplished his goal."

"One man?" a thin bald man from the crowd asked. "Is that what you're sayin'?" He regarded the wanderer, the sheriff, and the wizard in turn. "That you're all lookin' like you seen your own ghosts over one man?"

"The one who comes is more than just a man," the wanderer said.

"And so what if he is?" the thin man pressed. "Those damned Accursed were more than men, but we sent them runnin'. Those Whisperers or whatever they were, they were more than men, and we survived them too." He paused, wincing, as he glanced around him at the other villagers, an almost guilty expression on his face. "Leastways, most of us did. Even the giant serpent—I was in the village common, saw you put down that beasty myself. What is one man—even one that is more than a man, whatever that means—compared to all that?"

"Much," the wanderer said simply. "Believe me when I tell you that he who comes is the most dangerous foe any of us might ever face, and he is in his element. The woods, the world beyond civilization, the wilderness that lies outside the bounds of kings and kingdoms, of cities and towns, is *his* world, his more than any creature that might have ever been born to it."

"But...you can beat him, can't you?" This from the woman cradling the two children against her skirts, on her face a mixture of fear and hope. The wanderer saw that her hands, where she pressed the children against her, were trembling. "I mean...you beat all those other monsters. Surely...you can beat him?"

The wanderer realized something then. He was sick of bad news, sick of the truth when the truth was only that. He thought, in that moment, that while the truth was important—vital, for it was what gave the world and the people in it any shape—there was something just as important, if not more so. And that was hope. And hope, he thought, came not from staring at the naked truth but from staring at that truth and imagining what might be, what could be. The truth was important, yes, but that did not mean it needed to be used like a hammer, to beat someone down.

He might have told the woman the truth, laid it before her naked, bare of any artifice or hope, but he did not. Instead, he gave her a small smile, the best of which he was capable just then. "We need to leave," he said. "And know that, should the worst come, should he catch us, I will do everything in my power to stop him. To protect all of you."

"That ain't exactly an answer though, is it?" someone else asked, and the wanderer turned to see that it was the thin man, an almost malicious sort of joy in his eyes as he stared at the wanderer then at the woman with the two children. "Sounds to me like you don't think you could take this fella, whoever he is. Sounds like you think we're all goin' to die out here."

The wanderer knew that some people's reaction to fear was to try to make others more afraid and, in that way, they thought to cure themselves of their own terror. It did not work, but then people were very strange creatures and often did things whether they worked or not. "We need to keep going," the wanderer repeated.

"And just where are we s'posed to go?" the man demanded. "We listened to everythin' you told us already, and it seems to me all we've got to show for it is several dead and sufferin' untold hardships to find this wizard, and for what? It seems we're just goin' to die anyway."

Several of the villagers began to talk to each other in low, frightened whispers at that, and the wanderer winced. He opened his mouth, trying to find some words to reassure them—despite having no idea what those might be—but he was saved from the attempt as someone else spoke.

"Why don't you leave off, Curtis?" a voice growled.

The wanderer, along with everyone else present, turned to see that the man who'd spoken was none other than Daggett, father to Johnny, brother to recently deceased Elliot, and up until now, the villager of Alhs who had given the wanderer by far the most trouble on their journey. But just then, it wasn't the wanderer the man was scowling at but instead the old man, apparently by the name of Curtis. "You gonna flap your gums until that bastard catches us up, or are you goin' to let us get on doin' what needs doin'?"

Curtis blinked, clearly as surprised as the wanderer to find Daggett of all people coming to the wanderer's defense. "I didn't mean nothin', Daggett," the man said in a sulky voice. "Only wanted to know what the plan was, that's all."

"You want to know the plan, why don't you shut up and let him tell you?" Daggett said. "Ungr here's got us this far, hasn't he? Risked himself to save all of us, my boy included. I'd think you could at least show him the respect of keepin' your mouth shut while he tells you what's what."

The thin man opened his mouth as if to respond but, in the end, apparently decided that the wisest course—considering the scowl Daggett was shooting in his direction—was to hold his peace while he still had it to hold. Daggett turned to regard the wanderer and gave him a small nod.

The wanderer schooled his features to hide his surprise before returning the gesture. Then he turned back to the villagers at large. "The foe we face is dangerous, yes," he said, "and we must take the threat he poses seriously, but it is not yet time to despair. We still have a chance, one we must take, to escape."

"Yes," a woman asked, "but escape to *where?* We can't go back to Alhs—you've made that much clear, and it turns out that the wizard wasn't standing ready with a sanctuary for us all to go to. So what *are* we to do? Where are we to go?"

The wanderer frowned, thinking. He had been so wrapped up in dealing with the problems at hand, thinking mostly about the things they could *not* do, such as waste time, contemplating the places they could *not* go that he had spent very little time thinking of what they *could* do. They could strike out north toward civilization, he supposed, bypassing Alhs and the rest and aiming for the territory that had been Soldier's—or, at least, his impostor's, until the wanderer had killed him. But he'd had his reasons for leading Dekker and his family into the Untamed Lands, namely hundreds, perhaps thousands of creatures and troops hunting for them, and those reasons had not changed.

They could push farther into the Untamed Lands, but they would be venturing into the true wilds, territories known not even by the other Eternals, for none had traveled so deeply into the wilderness that was the Untamed Lands. He was stuck, without an answer, and the villagers began to mutter again. Another voice spoke, once again saving him, only this time it was not Daggett but instead the wizard.

"There is a place," the man said, almost reluctantly. "A place where all of you might be made safe from that which hunts you."

"Where is this place then?" Daggett asked. "Assuming you're not talking about our own graves. That ain't the sort of safe I'm lookin' for."

The wizard gave the man a small, humorless smile. "No, not the grave. It is...a sanctuary, of sorts. Protected by a barrier similar to that which served to protect your village from the dangers of the Untamed Lands until..." He paused, glancing at the wanderer for a moment before turning back to the villagers. "Well. Suffice to say that it should serve to offer the refuge you seek."

"Well, beggin' my pardon, sir," the sheriff said, "but that's good news, yet you're standin' there lookin' like you just ate somethin' that had gone off. Best case, we'd be able to get Alhs back, but if we can't, well, I s'pose I'd be alright with a bit of a change of scenery."

There were excited whispers of agreement at that from the gathered villagers. The wanderer, though, did not feel excitement, for he had noted well, as the sheriff had, the wizard's face, and on it was not an expression of hope or excitement to match that of the villagers but instead a grim countenance. A quick glance at Dekker where he stood with his family, as well as Clint and his Perishables, showed that the two men shared his trepidation.

"This place," the wanderer said slowly. "It will accommodate everyone?"

"Oh yes," the wizard said, nodding. "It is plenty big enough to accommodate all here and then some."

"Sounds great," Dekker said. "Why is it, then, that I'm getting the feeling there's a catch?"

"Well," the wizard said, licking his lips, "as to that...it will be a bit of a hike, but you will all be safe there once we arrive."

If we arrive.

The man did not say the words, but the wanderer heard them clearly enough. He opened his mouth but before he could speak Dekker asked the question he'd been wondering. "Just how far is a bit of a hike, in your mind?" the big man asked. "Just how far away is this paradise of yours?"

"Not so far," the wizard said, then considerably more quietly and with obvious reluctance. "A week. Or...maybe ten days. Certainly no more than that."

The villagers of Alhs reacted to that news with a variety of hisses and gasps and curses. "A *week?*" the man, Curtis demanded. "We haven't been out here a week yet and already we're nearly done in! You mean to tell me this salvation is a *week* away?"

"Or ten days," the wizard muttered.

"Well which is it?" the man said. "A week or ten days? That's a pretty damned big difference, particularly when we have a damned *army* chasing us."

"How should I know?" the wizard growled back. "I've never had to travel there with a whole damn village tied to my ankle like a lead weight, have I?"

That shut the man up quickly enough, for the wizard, as he spoke in anger, seemed to radiate a feeling of danger that was almost palpable, and the wanderer suspected that the man was augmenting his anger somehow, using the Art to add menace to his words. He wondered if the man did it intentionally or without even realizing it and suspected it was the latter, the power of his Art being shaped by his frustration.

"We will get there," the wanderer said. The villagers cut off their worried conversations and turned to him then, and he nodded. "We'll get there," he said again.

There was a hand on his shoulder, and he turned to see Dekker standing beside him. "Of course we will," the big man agreed, loud enough for the others to hear. "A week long jaunt in the forest, that's all."

"Or possibly—"

"Yeah, sure, or ten days," the man said, interrupting the wizard with a scowl. "Makes no difference—we'll do it because it's what needs to be done. I've come to know a lot of you durin' our trip," he said to the villagers. "Enough to know that you ain't no strangers to hard work. That's all this is—hard work that needs doin'. So let's get to doin' it, huh?"

The wanderer watched the big man, watched the reactions of the villagers to his words with a feeling of awe that was, in many ways, just as powerful as the one he'd felt when watching the wizard use his Art to protect them from the blizzard. And why not? After all, Dekker had his own kind of magic, one the wanderer had seen him use on more than one occasion. And like a spell, his words took root in the hearts and minds of the villagers. Faces that had been stricken with terror and disbelief began to harden, panicked expression giving way to purposeful frowns as they nodded at his words. Then, without being prompted, they all separated and began packing their belongings, making ready everything that might be made ready.

The wanderer glanced at the big man who met his gaze, then gave a small shrug, a look of surprise on his own face to match that the wanderer felt. "I think perhaps you missed your calling, Dekker," the wanderer said. "You would have made a fine orator."

"Screw yourself," the big man said, but he was grinning even as he said it.

"Fine words," a voice said, and they both turned to see the wizard moving up beside them, his walking stick—or wizard's staff, to hear the sheriff tell it—in hand. "But then, fine words will not get us where we are going, nor will speeches slow that which hunts us."

"For a man who has so much against talkin'," Dekker said, raising an eyebrow, "you sure do seem to do an awful lot of it."

The wizard scowled then reluctantly gave his head a nod. Then he turned to the wanderer. "I did not wish to say it before, for fear of scaring the townsfolk—"

"Yeah, seemed like you were takin' great pains to make everybody comfortable," Dekker said.

The wizard raised an eyebrow at Dekker. "You seem to be an...able man. But know this—you cannot begin to fathom the trouble and sacrifice I went through in order to retain my anonymity, And now," he continued, his gaze traveling to the wanderer, "that anonymity, that peace has been stripped from me. Not to mention that now I find myself—for reasons which appear to have nothing to do with me or the past I have tried so hard to leave behind—hunted by one of the most dangerous creatures in the world, one who has a personal army at his command. And on top of *all* of this, I am saddled with a village full of people to babysit."

"Yeah, well, shit happens, doesn't it?" Dekker said. "The world always hits a man, and it definitely doesn't stop just on account of he's down. In fact, I'd say that's when it really piles it on—a man's easier to hit, after all, if he doesn't have his feet underneath him. You ask me, you just got to learn to take the hits and keep goin'. Bitch about it if you want—but keep goin'. The hits are goin' to come, scowlin' or smilin'."

The wizard stared at him for several seconds as if seeing him for the first time. "This world," he said, slowly shaking his head, "it never ceases to amaze me."

"You think that's something," Dekker said, "you ought to see me juggle."

The wizard blinked. "Perhaps later, if there's time." He turned to the wanderer then. "For now, I think it best we get moving. It is a long trip, and many dangers lie ahead of us. Many of these I am able to avoid when alone, but such a task may prove trickier with so many."

The wanderer nodded, extending an arm to the front of the villagers. "Lead the way."

"As if I need an Eternal's permission to do anything," the wizard sneered then, without another word, turned and stalked away.

"Seems you've got yourself a fan," Dekker observed as they watched the man go.

"Seems so," the wanderer agreed.

"So, you goin' to tell me what you did to piss him off?"

"As soon as I find out," the wanderer said.

The big man shook his head slowly. "Gonna be a long trip, ain't it?"

The wanderer considered what they faced, what hunted them, then shrugged. "I hope so."

CHAPTER THREE

It did not take them long to get moving, for everyone present knew what was at stake. Soon they were venturing back into the perpetual blizzard, the wizard riding at the front, seated atop their last remaining wagon. The wanderer noted the reluctance of many of the villagers and Perishables when it came their turn to step over the boundary separating the humid forest from the freezing wilderness, and having experienced that cold for himself he could not blame them. This time, though, they needn't have worried, for the wizard, through his Art, had crafted another barrier similar in function—if not size—to the one he'd used when they'd traveled back to meet the villagers.

The footing was still treacherous—snow and ice were not easy to walk on in the best of times and melting snow and ice were even worse—but the temperature inside the protective spell was vastly different from that outside of it, and they at least did not need to count freezing to death among the many dangers they faced. In fact, the wanderer thought he could have done with it being slightly cooler inside the magic barrier—not that he was about to complain.

At first, there was much talk from the villagers. Many marveled at the snow, something as foreign, he suspected, to those who had been born and raised in the hotter temperatures of the south as a new pair of wings might have been for a fish. Next they marveled at the wizard's spell, casting amazed, awed, and nearly worshipful glances at where the gray haired man sat hunched at the front of the wagon, scowling out at the world as if it were all just a cruel trick.

The wanderer had lived a long time in the world, seen much of its people, its places, and so he was not entirely sure that the man was wrong.

But as the hours dragged on and weariness set on, the villagers' talk began to quiet, until in time, they traveled in silence broken only by the dragging *slush* of their footsteps in the snow, and their heavy breaths. Even with the wizard's spell it was no easy journey, and the wanderer was sure that many of the villagers who had first left Alhs with him would not have been able to endure it. But then, the wanderer knew that, like iron which passed through the fire only to come out stronger, people—assuming they survived—were toughened by the trials they faced, toughened in the same way that a man, not accustomed to manual labor and suddenly forced to endure hours of it for days and weeks on end, would find his hands toughening over time. They would hurt at first, but not forever. In time, they would become stronger, as the villagers had, for those who had survived the trials they'd faced were very different than the people they had been when they'd first been forced to leave their homes.

Pain was the flame, forging a man into something new, changing him.

Yes, he thought, *but into what?*

After all, the flames, the smith's hammer, they were good things. They gave the weapon its shape, its purpose. But if in being forged it took too much of a beating, it broke. People, he'd found, were much the same, and he feared, as he gazed at those people, saw several, noting his gaze, smile and give him a nod, that their trials were only beginning.

Ranger was coming. Or, at least, the creature who had spent the last hundred years impersonating Ranger, and if the one who'd been pretending to be Soldier was anything to go by the wanderer suspected that the similarities between the creature and the great woodsman would be more than just superficial.

But how *much* more? It was a question he could not answer, and that was too bad, for he suspected the answer would determine whether he, and all those he meant to protect, lived out the week.

The wanderer wondered at that, and as he walked, he replayed his encounter with the creature posing as Soldier over and over in his mind, thinking about the stance it had adopted, the same that Soldier had always used, thinking about the weak knee they had both shared. Soldier had acquired that weak knee from an injury during battle, a wound that had nearly cost him his leg. Healer had saved that much of it, at least, but the wanderer knew that while the man had rarely complained about it, the knee had often pained him.

The creature, in adopting his form, had also somehow adopted the man's weak knee—if not, the wanderer would have been long dead. And it had certainly fought like Soldier, possessed of the same speed, strength, and economy of motion that had made it impossible for anyone to stand against the man in true battle or sparring matches save Leader himself. Memories drifted to the wanderer then, memories of when he'd been newly chosen as an Eternal and he had been privileged to watch the two men meet in mock combat. And it *had* been a privilege, the same sort of privilege it was for any man to witness a master busy at his craft. The two men, individually, had been the best fighters he'd ever seen and, together, on the battlefield, it was said they had been all but invincible. An unstoppable force.

Only, they were stopped, a part of him said, *and you are avoiding thinking about what you should be thinking about.*

The wanderer gave his head a shake, and again began to think about how likely it was that the creature posing as Ranger possessed all the man's talents. He did not like what he came up with.

He was so lost in thought about this, so lost in trying to figure out some way that he might stand against such a man in his element—the very idea felt ludicrous—that he did not notice Dekker walk up beside him until the man spoke.

"I'd say a copper for your thoughts," the big man said, then paused until the wanderer blinked, glancing at him. "But then, judging by the expression on your face, I'm not sure I want to know. Everythin' alright?"

The wanderer opened his mouth to speak then noted that Ella, the big man's wife, and Sarah, their daughter, walked beside him. Instead of giving Dekker an answer—which, if honest, would do little to comfort the small girl—the wanderer asked a question of his own. "How are the three of you?"

Dekker raised an eyebrow but didn't push the issue further. "Better'n you by the looks of things," he said, giving the wanderer a small grin.

Ella rolled her eyes, slapping her husband on his shoulder. "What Dekker *means* to say, Ungr, is, if you need anything, we're here."

"That's what I said, ain't it?" Dekker asked, giving the wanderer a wink.

"That is," Ella went on, shooting a quick scowl at her husband, "if you're feeling a little...well...stressed...and you want to talk about it...we're here."

The wanderer blinked. "Thanks," he said, meaning it.

"So," she said slowly. "Are you?"

"Am I what?"

"Feeling stressed?"

The wanderer considered that question, considered the many answers to it and thought that each of them would be poor payment for the kindness the family was showing him so, in the end, he shook his head. "I'm fine."

"Sure you are," Dekker agreed, "just as fine as a man that don't know how to swim when he decides to take a plunge."

The wanderer winced and decided it was time for a change of subject. He glanced at Sarah, the little girl who was currently staring at her feet as she walked, watching her boots go in and out of the snow.

"And how are you, Sarah?" he asked. "What do you think of snow?"

She glanced up at him, surprised. "I'm sorry what did you say?"

Dekker grunted a laugh. "You'll have to forgive the wee one, Ungr. She tends to visit her own little world quite often."

The wanderer thought that with the real one being what it was, he couldn't blame her. "I asked what you thought of snow," he said.

The little girl's face screwed up in serious thought at that. Finally, she shook her head slowly. "It's wet," she said.

The wanderer nodded solemnly. "Yes."

"Cold, too," she said after a moment of reflection.

"Agreed," the wanderer said.

"But pretty," she said, nodding slowly as if even then just deciding it.

"I have always thought so," the wanderer said, reminded of his own childhood, long ago. He had lived far to the north and had been accustomed to snow storms, had always thought they were some kind of magic. That had been when he was young, young enough that he did not have to worry about all the troubles they caused and could only appreciate them for their beauty.

"And a pain, too," she finished. She glanced at her feet. "Difficult."

"Well, lass," Dekker said, glancing at his wife with a smug grin, "if it helps you any, I find that most pretty things *are* difficult."

The big man's wife's mouth opened in an "O" and she laughed. "You are aware that I am the one who fixes your meals, aren't you? It would not be so difficult a thing to add a dash of poison, next time."

"You haven't already?" the big man asked as if surprised. "I just figured that's what always accounted for the horrid taste."

Ella made a sound somewhere between a gasp, a growl, and a laugh, slapping the big man on the shoulder. Dekker accepted the blow with a wide grin, looking, in that moment, like a child who was particularly pleased with himself.

"You ox," she said, but the wanderer could hear the love for the big man in her voice even as she said it.

"Strong one too, to drag your ball and chain behind me all these years," Dekker agreed.

Ella rolled her eyes then gave the big man a hug and a kiss, and in another moment they were walking hand in hand, smiling at each other like two teenagers out on their first date and seemingly now in a world of *their* own. Which cemented two things in the wanderer's mind—one, he really did *not* understand women, and was no closer now after living more than a hundred years than he ever had been and, two, the husband and wife had a relationship, had built a *life* together that most people could only dream about.

Which, of course, got him thinking about how often he had put those lives in danger since meeting them, about how much they were in danger *now*. They had all been living happily in the woods together until he had arrived at their door, bringing death with him. They had survived that death, save for Felden Ruitt, at least, but it seemed that no matter how hard he tried to keep them safe, he found himself endangering the family over and over again.

Now, they were in the wilds of the world, one of the most dangerous places anyone could travel through, hunted by an army of creatures who did not feel pain, hunger, or thirst, who would never tire or grow weary or give up their pursuit, and yet they were able to smile and laugh and take joy in simply being together.

There was a magic there, he thought, and one he did not understand. One that he thought he likely never would, nor experience for himself. That got him thinking of Joan and Anne, and whatever good mood the family's antics had put him in quickly began to fade.

"It's okay to smile, you know."

The wanderer turned to regard the little girl who'd spoken, her mother and father still lost in speaking quietly to each other, Ella's head laid on Dekker's shoulder now as they walked. Then he glanced back at the girl. "I know," he said.

"Then why don't you? Ever smile, I mean?"

There were many answers to that, but they were all dark ones, not fit for a young girl who had not yet discovered just how cruel the world could be, and if he had his way, never would. So instead, the wanderer shook his head slowly. "I guess...I guess maybe I forgot how."

"You use your mouth," she said patiently. Then she nodded. "Don't worry—I'll teach you."

"I would appreciate that," he said, matching her serious tone.

"Good," she said. Then, abruptly, she turned to her parents. "Ma, can I go see Veikr?"

"It's alright with me," she said, glancing at the wanderer who nodded. "Go on then," she said, "but stay close."

"I will," Sarah promised. The wanderer expected her to hurry away then, and he was surprised when she spun back and gave him a tight hug, forcing him to stop walking. He stood there awkwardly for a second, then slowly found a smile spreading across his face.

The little girl stepped back, glancing up at him, her head tilted like a carpenter examining his work. "It's not bad, but it's not great either," she said. "We'll work on it."

Then, before the wanderer could answer, she was running toward where Veikr walked, carrying several wounded.

"I'd best go keep an eye on her," Ella said. She leaned forward, whispered something in Dekker's ear too low for the wanderer to hear, then shared a look with the big man before flashing the wanderer a smile and following after her daughter.

The wanderer glanced at the big man, raising an eyebrow, and Dekker sighed, shaking his head. "I'm meant to talk to you, figure out what's on your mind."

"An assignment, is it?"

The big man shrugged. "The latest. No doubt she'll have another for me soon enough."

"Well," the wanderer said. "I suppose there are worse things."

"And few better," the big man agreed. "Now, assignment or no assignment, I can't help bein' curious as to what put that dour look on your face, the one you were sportin' when me and the family come up. I've seen folks on their deathbed got more cheer in 'em than you. And don't think me and mine are the only ones who've noticed."

The wanderer glanced around at the villagers traveling by them and saw more than a few shooting glances in his direction. And those glances, without fail, looked grim, worried. He winced, turning back to the big man. "I...are you saying they're watching me?"

"Of course they're watchin' you," Dekker said as if it were the most obvious thing in the world. Which, to the wanderer, at least, it was not.

"Why?"

"Why?" the big man repeated. "Shit, it's obvious, ain't it? You're their worry ale."

The wanderer blinked. "I'm...I must have heard you wrong, it sounded like—"

"Worry ale," Dekker said. "That's what I said, and that's what I meant. You see, Ungr..." He paused, frowning. "Well. I've told you, a bit, haven't I? About my time...before Ella and Sarah, I mean?"

"A bit," the wanderer said. "You said you were a mercenary for hire."

The big man snorted. "I weren't no more a mercenary for hire than an assassin is a knight. No, I was a criminal, Ungr, that's the tall and short of it. A bruiser, no more than that. One that didn't do much thinkin', nor much talkin' really, save with his fists, and that was fine with the man I worked for as that was all he wanted me to do. I was a weapon, that was all, one to be turned against his enemies—or his friends, when it suited him—and the last thing a man wants of his weapons is for them to start thinkin'."

The wanderer nodded slowly. "I see, but that still doesn't explain the worry ale."

"Ah, that," Dekker said. "Well, the fella I worked for, he was only one man that fashioned himself a crime boss in a city full of 'em. A city *too* full of 'em, and that's a fact. So full that they started figurin' they ought to thin the ranks, as it were, just so long as those ranks didn't include them." He shook his head. "It meant a lot of killin', a lot of assassinations, poisonings, and stabbings in the dark. It also meant alliances—meant that the fella I worked for made sure to be in league with others. Made it safer for them, all around. And alliances mean meetings, plenty of 'em. Meetings in out-of-the-way taverns and alleyways. There was one particular tavern my boss liked. One where the barkeep and everyone in it was his man, bought and paid for. It's where he always conducted his meetings. Less chances of getting poisoned when you knew the man pourin' the ale, knew where his family lived."

"And the worry ale?"

"Ah, that," Dekker said. "Well, see, my boss wasn't keen on lettin' on that everyone in the tavern, all the way down to the bard singin' shittily, worked for him. But they were, and they all looked out for him, made sure the folks he was meetin' with were on the up and up. If they were, things proceeded as normal, the meeting happened. Everyone met, and then everyone left."

"And if they weren't on the up and up?"

"Then the bartender would bring my boss and his guest an ale. On the house, as it were."

"Ah," the wanderer said, nodding. "And that would let him know something was wrong."

"And that it was time to worry," Dekker agreed. "Which always involved a lot of running on most people's parts and a lot of violence on mine. See, to the villagers, shit, to Clint and his men and to me and my family too, you're our worry ale. They're watchin' you to see if they ought to be concerned, to see if they ought to worry."

"I see," the wanderer said, nodding slowly.

"So why don't you try on a smile or a laugh?" Dekker said. "It'd go a long way to put them at ease—might even go a ways to puttin' yourself at ease. After all, shit, we're still breathin' and in this life, that's just about all a man can ask for, ain't it?"

The wanderer tried a smile. It felt strange at first, as if indeed he *had* forgotten how, as he'd told Sarah, and Dekker snorted. "Looks like your lips are fightin' each other," he said. "Shit, Ungr, you got some talents but bein' cheery ain't one of 'em, and that's a fact. You could make a storm cloud feel dreary."

That made the wanderer laugh. A good laugh, the first he could remember having in a long time. Which, of course, was when the wizard decided to walk up.

"Having a laugh, are we?"

They both turned to look at the gray-bearded man who was frowning at the wanderer.

"A bit," Dekker said. "There some law against it out here?"

"In normal circumstances, no," the wizard said. "In fact, I guess I'd enjoy a good laugh just about as much as anybody. Only, it seems to me that it might be just a bit inappropriate coming from *him*," he went on, turning on the wanderer with a scowl. "You know, considering that he's the reason we're here in the first place, the reason why the entire village of Alhs is now being chased by an army of monsters."

"Now you just hold on a damn mi—"

"It's okay, Dekker," the wanderer said, holding up his hand. "He's right."

"Shit naw he ain't," Dekker said. "Fact is I'm the one that told Ungr here he ought to loosen up—you know, considerin' how grim everybody is."

"It seems to me that they *should* be grim," the wizard snapped. "How could they not be, with what they face? With what they've been *made* to face."

"And all that grimness, reckon it'll make them move faster?" Dekker demanded.

"Do you speak, *Eternal,*" the wizard said, making of the word a curse, "or do you only allow others to do so in your stead?"

"What would you have me say?" the wanderer asked.

The wizard stared at him for a moment, his face twisting with anger, then finally he gave a hiss. "There is nothing you can say, no answer you might give for the crimes committed by you and your companions."

"Somethin' he might do, then?" Dekker asked. "Crawl on his knees, maybe?" the big man went on, his own face grim. "Or maybe you'd have him bow down, kiss each of the villagers' feet for his terrible *crimes.* Crimes which, by and large, involve him doing his level best to keep them alive."

"It is not just what he has done to the villagers," the wizard sneered, "but what he and those others of his kind have done to..." He paused, taking a slow, deep breath, then shook his head. "Never mind." He turned to regard the wanderer, and while his expression was not twisting with anger as it had been a moment ago, the wanderer could see the man's hate clearly in his gaze. The wizard took a slow, deep breath, clearly attempting to gather himself. "I have come back here to tell you, Eternal, that in another hour, we will reach the edge of the snow and once more be into the woods of the Untamed Lands."

The wanderer glanced ahead of them and still could see nothing but snowy hills ahead. "So soon?" he asked, surprised.

"Do you think that I do not know my own land, the land which I have called home for so very long?"

"I did not mean any offense," the wanderer said. "I was only surprised, that's all. I'd expected it to take longer."

The wizard sneered. "Imagine, an Eternal being wrong. What would your fellows say, I wonder?"

The wanderer might have told him that they would be unlikely to say anything, considering that they were dead, but then he had told the man that already and he had clearly not believed him. Besides, while it was true that the Eternals were indeed dead, that certainly did not keep them from talking. In truth, they did little else. "Very well, we will reach the woods in an hour," the wanderer said. "Is there anything else?"

The wizard frowned. "I know your kind, Eternal. I have seen the work of your compatriots, and I need not see the two swords scabbarded at your back, nor feel the malevolent energy coming from the one to know that your solution to every problem, like those of your comrades, is murder. After all, to a hammer, every problem is a nail. But know this—I am leading you and those with us into parts of the Untamed Lands no man has ever traveled before. And—"

"*No* man?" Dekker asked.

The wizard frowned, glancing at him. "Excuse me?"

"Well, you're talkin' like you've been there before," the big man said. "And *you're* a man..." He paused, glancing up and down at the wizard, taking in his pointy hat and robe. "At least, after a fashion. So it begs the question..."

"*Fine,*" the wizard snapped. "Only I, among all mortals, have been there."

"Not that we can be sure of that," Dekker said quietly.

"My *point,*" the wizard went on, turning back to the wanderer, "is that you will see creatures no mortal has ever seen before, trod ground no mortal has ever trod. I ask that, in the case of the latter, you be respectful and understand that *this* land, at least, does not belong to you and your...compatriots. This land is free, and you are only a visitor within it—even calling you a guest would go too far. Trespasser is closer to the truth. As for the former, those creatures which we may encounter beyond are under my protection as much as the villagers of Alhs. So I will insist that you curb your tendency for violence and that you make sure that those swords of yours stay in their sheaths."

"So no choppin' innocent heads off?" Dekker said, his voice thick with sarcasm. "Well, that'll be tough as Ungr does love himself a good murder."

The wizard did not allow himself to be distracted by the big man's words. Instead, he only watched the wanderer, his expression deadly serious. "Am I clear, Eternal?

"You are clear," the wanderer said.

"Very well, then we will proceed."

With that, the wizard turned and walked back toward the front of the procession. The wanderer looked after him, trying to imagine, yet again, what it was that made the man hate the Eternals so much.

"Reckon he knows your real name or just thinks it's 'Eternal?'" Dekker asked from beside him.

"Oh, I believe he knows it," the wanderer said quietly. "In fact, I think he knows quite a bit." And that much was nothing short of the truth, for it was clear that the man was more than familiar with the Eternals as he spoke of them as if he had known of them for a very long time. Which made sense, for the wizard had said he'd been here, in the Untamed Lands, for many years, had made of himself an exile, an outcast. According to him, he had done so to keep himself safe. That left the wanderer to imagine, then, what it might have been that had driven the man here, to this place of untold mystery and danger in search of safety. Whatever it had been, it had been something that had made him hate the Eternals, that much was clear. To despise them with a hate so powerful that it included the wanderer and never mind the fact that they had never met before.

But however odd the man's hatred was, the wanderer decided it would remain a mystery, for the wizard didn't seem keen on sharing. Besides, it wasn't as if the wanderer and those with him didn't have enough to worry about already. An army at their back, led by the greatest woodsman to have ever lived—or, at least, a creature doing a good enough job impersonating him that it had not been found out in over a hundred years—and untold dangers at their front.

Yes, whatever issue the wizard had with the Eternals, with the wanderer himself, it would have to wait. It, after all, was unlikely to kill them anytime soon, and there were plenty of other problems facing them that were seeking to do exactly that.

"So what now?" Dekker asked, following the wanderer's gaze to the wizard's departing back.

"Why, we follow the wizard into the wilderness, of course," the wanderer said, turning and giving the man a small smile.

Dekker grunted. "The wizard and the wilderness. Sounds like the title of a book."

"If it is," the wanderer said, "then let us hope it's one with a happy ending." And with that, he started after the wizard and the villagers of Alhs.

CHAPTER FOUR

True to the wizard's word, nearly an hour later they crested the top of another snowy hill only to find that it was the last. At its base, the snow and perpetual blizzard of the place in which the wizard had chosen to make his home ended, giving way to thick trees.

A walk of no more than a few minutes would bring them down the hill and out of the snow, which was just as well as far as the wanderer was concerned. The wizard's spell might have protected them from the extreme temperatures surrounding them, but it did nothing for the cold, snowy slush they walked through, slush which had long since soaked into his boots. Already several people had complained about blisters, normally a nuisance but far more frustrating when they had untold miles left to walk before they reached a place that they might be safe.

Judging by the shouts and whoops of the villagers as they paused at the top of the hill, he was not the only one who was excited to bid farewell to the snow-blasted dunes. Even the wizard sported a small smile, though the wanderer did not think he had ever seen a smile appear so fragile.

"Won't be sad to be quit of that place."

The wanderer turned to see that Clint had walked up and was gazing back at the snowy land through which they'd walked, though the heavy snow-fall had already erased any mark their passage had left.

"You'll get no disagreement here," the wanderer said.

"Though, considerin' where we are," the Perishable's leader went on, "I s'pose it's possible we'll be missin' this place in another day or two."

The wanderer opened his mouth to answer, but before he could he became aware of agitated talk among a group of nearby villagers. He and Clint glanced over to them and saw that they were pointing back in the direction they'd come. The wanderer frowned, a sick feeling in his stomach as he followed their gestures.

The hill upon which he and the others stood was the tallest they had traversed or seen in the land of perpetual snow, affording them nearly a complete view of the land they had traveled through. Certainly one that was complete enough that they could see something on the horizon, at the other edge of the snow.

"What?" Clint asked. "What is it? Something's there, ain't it?" he asked. "Just...just looks like a blur to me. Maybe a sunspot or—"

"It is no sunspot," the wanderer said slowly, for his vision, better than any normal man's, was able to pick out an army of Revenants—the same army that had been following them for miles—as they emerged from the forest. And, at their front, walking with an easy, graceful stride, the kind normally reserved for the most dangerous predators of the world, such as some lithe jungle cat on the prowl, was Ranger.

"It...it's them, isn't it?" Clint asked.

The figure at the army's front raised its head, banishing any question the wanderer might have had about whether or not the enemy had adopted the enhanced senses of the Eternal whose place it took, as it met his gaze over that distance, looking up at him, and smiled.

The wanderer turned back to Clint and became aware that the villagers, who had been celebrating an end to the snowy landscape a moment before, had gone suddenly, deathly silent, and as one they watched him, all of them waiting for his answer.

"It is those who hunt us," he confirmed. "But they are still some distance yet. We still have a lead."

"One that's shrinkin' by the minute," Dekker said. "Best we be gettin' on. Besides," he went on, turning to the wizard who wore his familiar scowl once more, "they don't have a wizard with 'em. Probably the snow'll do for 'em, won't it?" The big man's gaze traveled between the wizard and the wanderer, who regarded each other for a moment.

When it was clear that the wizard had no intention of speaking, the wanderer did. "Some, perhaps," he said, though in truth he thought even that unlikely. Had their pursuers been normal men, he did not doubt that they would perish in the journey and in doing so would add their bones to the collection of those peeking out from the blanket of snow covering the rolling hills. But they were not normal men—they were Revenants. Revenants who did not feel pain or discomfort, Revenants imbued with hardiness and strength beyond that of normal men by those who had fashioned them. Most would make it, that the wanderer did not doubt. Likely, they all would.

He watched the oncoming army for another moment, looking for any tell-tale shimmer in the air that would be the sign of the Unseen. He did not see any, and he suspected that he knew why. The Revenants were made to be hardy, durable, to take a lot of punishment before finally being defeated. The Unseen, though, were made to be fast, and so they were considerably more fragile than their slower, more rugged counterparts. Which meant that, if he had to guess, they would have been ordered to go around instead of braving the elements that they would have likely not survived.

"How far away, do you think?" This from Clint.

"Six hours," the wanderer said quietly, "perhaps a little more." Less if the army chose to run, but he did not think they would, did not think that Ranger would risk any of his troops to make up a little bit of difference. After all, why bother, when it was clear that they were gaining on him and the others? Why bother when the Revenants didn't need to stop for rest or food in their implacable approach, when the lead he and the villagers enjoyed was destined to dwindle as time went on?

The wanderer was aware of the Perishables and the villagers watching him, and he turned his gaze back to regard them. "We'd best get moving," he said.

It was a quiet, somber group that made their way down the snowy hill, and even when they crossed the boundary into the woods, their feet lighting on forest floor instead of squelching snow, there was no celebrating. Instead, the villagers of Alhs only continued on, trudging after the wizard without so much as a word.

The sun slowly set behind them as they walked. The fading light gave the shadows life, and they seemed to huddle among the trees, watching the wanderer and villagers as they moved deeper into the woods. The trees themselves seemed malevolent to the wanderer, the shadows of their limbs like great hands reaching out to snare them.

He told himself he was being foolish, that the trees were trees and that only, the shadows things without substance or significance. Yet the feeling of being watched, of their progress being tracked, persisted.

The villagers continued on into the night without complaint, all of them well aware of the doom that stalked their footsteps should they falter. Yet for all their stoicism, the wanderer could not help but notice that their pace began to slow as the lack of rest and the exertion of the last several days began to take its toll.

He knew that, if they continued as they did, Ranger's army would catch up with them within a few hours, perhaps less.

He made his way to the front where the wizard sat atop their single remaining wagon, scowling out at the world beyond him as he rode with the reins of the mules loosely in one hand. The man took note of him and glanced over, his scowl deepening. "What do you want?"

"It isn't so long a list," the wanderer said. "For now, I thought we should talk."

"I can think of many things I would like to do or see done to you and your kind, Eternal," the wizard said, "but talking might not be counted among them."

"Nevertheless," the wanderer said, "we are both here, now, and you must realize, as I do, that the creature posing as Ranger and his army are gaining on us."

"Creature posing as Ranger, or more likely Ranger himself," the wizard said.

The wanderer gave a slight shrug of his shoulders. "I have told you the truth as I know it. If you choose not to believe me, there is nothing I can do to change your mind, and I will not try. Whether the one who chases us is Ranger or an impostor, I do not see that it changes our situation. Do you?"

The wizard watched him for a moment, frowning, then reluctantly shook his head. "It does not. So tell me, then, Eternal, do you have some plan, some way to save us poor doomed souls from our fate?"

"I do not," the wanderer said. "I was hoping that you might know of some means of doing so. Perhaps a less-traveled path we might take? One where we might gain some ground?"

The wizard rolled his eyes. "As if such a path might be created by magic, is that it?"

The wanderer said nothing, only watched him. It was clear that the man wanted to argue, to express yet again his hatred for the wanderer and the other Eternals, but the wanderer thought that, if he refused to be baited, the man might see his way past his hatred, at least for the moment. Indeed, in another few seconds the wizard sighed, seeming to deflate. "There is such a path," he said after a time. "One which would slow them, would force them to come at us no more than two at a time in the eventuality that they did manage to catch us up."

It sounded exactly like what they needed, an ideal situation, but then the wanderer could see by the man's grim expression that there was more yet to tell. "This path...it is too far away?"

The man shook his head. "No, it is close. An hour's distance, perhaps, if we deviate from our course and head west. Maybe a little more. Either way, we should reach it with time to spare before they catch us."

"This path, you did not mean to take it."

"No," the wizard said. "I did not. Nor did I mean to have some bumbling buffoon destroy, in minutes, what it took weeks to create and, in doing so, put an entire village that has lain safe for hundreds of years in mortal peril. In my experience, a man's plans matter very little when faced with reality. Perhaps a man might be bold enough to plan his breakfast but little more than that. And, in my experience, when the Eternals are involved, even that much planning is foolish."

"You do not like me," the wanderer said. The man snorted, but he ignored it, speaking on. "That's alright—so far, from what I've seen, I do not like you either. I suspect we will both survive our mutual enmity. However, we—and those with us—will most certainly *not* survive the army which comes for us, so if you know of another path we might take, now is the time. Unless, of course, you would prefer to stand around here insulting each other until the Revenants come and end our argument with finality."

The wizard gave him a silent sneer but, after a moment, he sighed again, showing that, whatever else the man might be, he was no fool. "Very well, Eternal. You will have it your way—as your kind so often do. There is a path we might take, one that might slow our enemy as much as us, but that path is not without its dangers."

"Nor is this one," the wanderer reminded him.

"And if those dangers, those that lie ahead of us on the path of which I speak, should spell your doom? Should spell the doom of all here?"

"Whatever doom they might represent, it can be no worse than that which awaits us should the creature posing as Ranger and his troops catch up with us."

The wizard watched him for a moment. "Spoken with the same arrogant confidence that all your kind seem to share," he said. "But know this, Eternal. A long life does not grant wisdom, and the world's truest fools are the ones who think themselves wise. It is a lesson that many men are forced to learn and always to their own peril. I can only hope that, when you learn it, it is not to the peril of us all."

And with that, he gave the reins a snap, clucked, and the mules started forward again, but the wanderer was gratified to see the man turn the wagon westward, in the direction of the path he'd spoken about.

"Have a nice chat?"

The wanderer turned to see Dekker walking up. "You could say that."

The big man grunted. "Saw the two of you talking, figured maybe I'd better come check it out, make sure you two didn't try to kill each other."

"Oh, you need not worry," the wanderer said. "We're becoming fast friends, the wizard and I."

Dekker said nothing, only raising an eyebrow at him, and the wanderer shrugged. "Well. Perhaps not so fast."

"Seems to be leading us in a different direction, though," Dekker observed glancing at the wagon.

"Yes," the wanderer said.

"A way to buy us some time before this army catches us up?"

"Maybe," the wanderer said. "He was not particularly forthcoming."

"So much for fast friends," the big man said, then sighed. "Fella's got a chip on his shoulder, doesn't he?"

"That he does."

Dekker nodded slowly. "Used to have a chip on my shoulder much the same, I reckon. Usually, such a thing comes from some past pain, some past loss. And sometimes, the chip's so big, the *burden's* so big a man can't get it off on his own. Sometimes..." He paused, glancing back to where his wife and daughter walked beside Veikr. "Well. Sometimes he needs help."

The wanderer nodded slowly, glancing at the wizard's departing back. He had allowed the man's anger to get under his skin, for anger, in his experience, was like fire. An angry man might easily ignite anger in others, the thing growing and growing until it was uncontrollable. Wars had been fought for reasons no better than that, wars that had left thousands dead. But now, in light of Dekker's words, he found himself considering the wizard in a different way. The wizard hated him, that was true, but hatred rarely appeared on its own. More often, it grew from a seedling, nurtured either by the man himself or by circumstances beyond his control.

The wanderer told himself he would try to figure out what it was that made the wizard hate him so, would not add to the man's burden if he could help it. *But first,* he thought, *we need to survive.*

***

As they followed the wizard, the wanderer found himself glancing behind them from time to time, half-expecting to see a Revenant moving in the trees. It was ridiculous, of course. They should still have two hours' lead on the creatures, likely more, yet he kept looking just the same. They were close now, that was the truth, far closer than he would have liked, and he could only hope that whatever path the wizard had in mind would be good enough.

It was a strange feeling, relying on someone else. The wanderer had spent the last hundred years alone, after all, at least save for Veikr, though it had to be said that he'd relied on the horse on dozens of occasions and that his journey, such as it was, would have ended long ago without his help. Still, it felt different, relying on a man.

Veikr was solid and beyond doubting. The wanderer would have entrusted his life to the horse without hesitation, but then animals were often steadier and more deserving of trust than humans. People, in their arrogance, considered them simple, but a thing did not need to be complicated to be of value. In fact, the wanderer had found that things generally only grew complicated because of the involvement of people, and often to serve their own purposes. Lies were often complicated, after all, but the truth rarely so.

It felt strange, then, to put his trust in a man, even one as long-lived and as clearly powerful as the wizard, for the wanderer had taught himself over the long years of his life to rely on no one, to make his way on his own without help or assistance from another. He had told himself, *convinced* himself, that he did not need anyone else. It hadn't been true, of course, Felden Ruitt had taught him that, but still it had to be said that he had made his way across the face of the world for a long time without any direct help from another person.

Yet now, he was forced to rely on another person to save not only his life, but the lives of those people he had come to cherish, people he would do anything—including sacrificing himself—to keep safe. And not only was he forced to rely on another, but the person upon which he had to rely had made no effort to hide how much he hated him.

But what choice did he have? None. At least none that he could think of, and he was still puzzling at that when the wizard led them out of the forest and into a wide, flat grassy plain. Yet it was not the grass, nor even the deer cropping at it in the distance, which drew the wanderer's attention. Instead, it was what lay beyond it.

A great stone wall that seemed to stretch into the sky forever, rising high, high above them. So high that the wanderer had to tilt his head back, craning his neck to see what might have been the top of it, though he could not be sure, for the upper part of the great stone cliff was largely obscured by the clouds.

There was a low whistle beside him, and he turned to see Dekker staring up at the great stone wall, his head tilted so far back he looked in danger of falling over. "I'll be damned," the big man breathed. "Now *that's* a mountain." He glanced at the wanderer. "You mean to tell me that wizard intends for us to climb that? Because if so, no offense, but I think I'll take my chances with those damned Revenants."

The wanderer couldn't blame him there, for looking at that enormous, giant slab of stone, he knew that such a climb would mean death and likely a quick one. Assuming, of course, that they even managed to get started on the climb, for what faced them was a sheer rock face, one with no path that might be walked. An impossible job, and as he stared at it, he wondered if perhaps the wizard had accidentally led them in the wrong direction. "I'll be back," he said quietly, then he started forward.

"You tell that bastard I'm not climbing that damned mountain," Dekker called after him.

The wanderer moved to where the wizard sat atop his wagon. The man watched him come, clearly waiting for him.

By the time the wanderer came to stand beside him, the wizard was gazing at the rock wall. "I call it the Wall Eternal."

The wanderer glanced at him, raising an eyebrow, and the wizard shrugged. "Your kind are not the only ones allowed to use the word. Anyway, perhaps it has another name, but I suspect that, if it ever did, those who called it so are long dead. So what do you think of it?"

"It is very large," the wanderer said. "And it appears to block our path."

"And *you* appear to be a man with at least some semblance of a brain," the wizard snapped. "Looks can be deceiving, Eternal. Ask any young suitor who, spurred on by a woman's smile, leans in for a kiss only to find a slap instead. A man who trusts his eyes and that only often pays a steep price, and a slap is the least of it."

"You do not mean to climb it, then?"

"*Climb* it?" the wizard asked, staring at him as if he were insane. "Damnation, I suspect there are few birds who could fly from the ground to the Wall Eternal's top without tiring and falling to their deaths. No, Eternal, I do not mean to *climb* it. If it's suicide you're after, I can think of better ways than that. Certainly ones that would require far less effort—not that it ever takes a man much effort to die. It's the staying alive that proves troublesome."

"So what, then?" the wanderer said.

"Ah, again, seen in the wild, an Eternal without answers," the wizard said, giving him a small, humorless smile. "It seems that you all are not quite so infallible as you would have people believe then."

"I have never claimed infallibility, nor would I," the wanderer said. "Do you mean to say there is a way beyond the wall?"

"No, I just thought it'd be a fine last sight before the army catches up and kills us all," he snapped. The wanderer said nothing, only watched him, and after a moment the wizard sighed. "Yes, of course there is a way beyond it. There is a path, largely hidden in that monstrosity of a wall. I have used it before, long ago, before I realized that there were far better ways for a man to die."

"You do not sound confident in this approach," the wanderer observed.

"I am not your nursemaid to pat you on the head, give you a sweet, and tell you that everything is going to be okay," the wizard growled. "I told you that the path was dangerous and so it is, yet probable death is preferable to guaranteed death, which is what we are facing thanks to you. Now, as I said, there is a path, hidden in the rocks, one I have used before. It should be straight ahead of us."

"And the dangers?" the wanderer asked.

"Take your pick," the wizard asked. "The Wall Eternal is home to all sorts of creatures, many of which would find us and our hapless villagers as no more than a morning snack. Not to mention the danger of rockfalls."

"Rockfalls?" the wanderer said.

"Make no mistake, Eternal," the wizard said, meeting his gaze, "you are not in civilization. You are in the wilds now, the *true* wilds, where nature has not been bent to the will of man. Here, any misstep might well be your last. And yes, rockfalls. The thin path— where no more than two might walk abreast—through which we will travel is a tiny crack in the great edifice of stone you see before you. A crack which I nearly died in, for the path is not sure and it spiderwebs out at least a dozen times before it reaches the other side, leading to dead end after dead end. I was lost for weeks inside and lost at least thirty pounds—of which I had scant extra to lose—before I finally crawled my way out the last time. Not to mention that I nearly lost my life at least a dozen times to the great rock showers that even a sound no louder than a whisper might occasion within the gorge. It is, quite simply, a place of despair and torment and pain. When I finally—and barely—managed to extricate myself from it, I promised myself that I would never dare venture inside again. But then the world does love to watch a man make his promises, knowing full well that, in time, it might make him break them. Now, are we done yammering? If so, I think we might well press on—I know it appears as if the Wall Eternal stands directly before us, but it's great size can be deceiving. We still have an hour of travel, at least, before we reach the path leading inside it."

The wanderer nodded. "I am ready when you are."

The wizard raised an eyebrow at him. "Are you, Eternal? Are you really?" he gave a small shrug of his shoulders, flashing the wanderer a smile that was all teeth and no humor. "I suppose that we will find out soon enough, won't we?"

In another hour they reached the rock wall. The closer they drew to it, the smaller the wanderer felt. It was strange, it being there, and he felt like some tiny insect with a giant boot hovering above his head, preparing to squish him at any moment and nothing in the world he could do about it if it chose to. The wizard rode his wagon up to the wall then stopped a few feet away, staring at the rock face. The wanderer glanced at Dekker and Clint who had been walking beside him, and the other men frowned, showing that they were wondering the same thing he was himself. Namely, where the path was that the wizard had told him about.

He gave the men a look and moved up to stand beside the wizard who was currently scowling at the wall. "I do not see a path," the wanderer said.

The man looked over at him, giving a hiss. "It is so very useful to have you along, Eternal. Who else, if not you, would point out the bloody *obvious?*"

"If it is the obvious you would like for me to point out," the wanderer said, "then know that we are running out of time. I suspect that the Revenants are no more than an hour and a half behind us, perhaps less. If there is a path, we need to find it. Now."

"Don't you think I *know* that?" the wizard demanded. "Now, still your tongue for a second and let me think."

He squeezed his eyes shut, muttering to himself. The wanderer watched him for a moment, then decided to leave him to it, turning instead to walk back to where Dekker and Clint waited with the villagers of Alhs—those of whom weren't staring wide-eyed at the giant stone wall before them—watching him to see what he would say. "There is an opening to a path somewhere here," he said. "Largely hidden, I'm told. We need to find it. Quickly."

The villagers and the Perishables, well aware of what was at stake, needed no more urging than that. They all started forward, the sheriff organizing them into groups which began moving along either side of the wall, searching through the loose bracken and occasional piled stone that littered the ground near the wall.

The wanderer began to search as well, the wizard offering no help, and after about half an hour he heard footsteps behind him and saw the sheriff jogging up. The man was red-faced, panting from the brief exertion of his run, but he was also smiling from ear to ear.

"Ungr," the man said, nodding.

"Sheriff."

"We've found it."

The wanderer found himself smiling in return. "Show me."

The man led him to a small opening in the rock. It was no more than five feet high, only six or so across, and in front of it the wanderer saw where one of the villagers had torn away some bracken and loose stones that had concealed the entrance. The wanderer knelt peering into the opening. It stretched on for as far as he could see and seemed to open up a few dozen feet in.

"Told you I'd find it."

The wanderer turned to see that the wizard had walked up behind him. He raised an eyebrow. "Yes, you did. Assuming this is the way?"

"It's the way alright," the wizard said.

"We'll have to leave the wagon," the wanderer observed.

The other man scowled. "I can walk just fine, thank you."

"How's your crawling?" the wanderer asked, glancing back at the opening.

The wizard said nothing. "Well. Best we get going then."

The wanderer gave the man a small smile. "After you," he said, gesturing to the small opening. The wizard gave another scowl then, with a huff, pulled up his robe, dropped to his hands and knees and started through the opening. The wanderer could mark the man's passage by the quiet—and sometimes not so quiet—curses he let out as he made his way through.

Then, after a few minutes, the wizard called back. "It opens up a little ways in. Go ahead and send in everyone else."

The wanderer didn't need to bother, for the villagers were already gathering around the opening. The children went first, thinking it all a game. Next came the women, following their children and calling their names, telling them to slow down and to wait as they passed through. Then were the wounded. Two of the men were healed enough to be able to crawl through, but another three had to be dragged. The wanderer stood with Dekker and Clint as the villagers disappeared through the opening one after the other.

Finally, there were only the three of them and Veikr. The wanderer turned, regarding the horse who looked askance at the hole. "It will be tight," he told his old friend, "but you can make it."

Veikr snorted as if to say he wasn't so sure, but in the end he moved forward, lay down and began to ease his bulk into the opening. The wanderer watched, his heart in his throat, for the truth was it was a tight fit, and there was no way to know for certain that Veikr would not get stuck. And if he did, the wanderer had no idea what they might do to free him. Finally though, after several close calls, Veikr reached the part where it opened up, and the wanderer released a breath he hadn't realized he'd been holding. "You're next," he told the two men.

They didn't argue, only started through. As he waited, the wanderer glanced back at the woods beyond the fields. He did not see any creatures emerging from the tree line, not yet, but he knew that they soon would. Sighing, he knelt and started into the hole after the others.

Soon he reached the spot where the pathway opened, and he was able to stand to his full height. As he did, he saw that the wizard had not been lying about this much at least—the path could accommodate two men standing abreast and little more than that.

"I can't say I like this," Clint said, glancing left and right at the two walls enclosing them, and the wanderer understood well the man's trepidation, just as he understood the pale expressions with which the villagers glanced at the two walls on either side of them. The wanderer had never been claustrophobic, had never felt any concern over tight spaces, but he felt so now. Those two great walls, so close that he could reach his arms out to both sides and touch them with the tips of his fingers, seemed to him like the massive stone palms of some giant, one who might, at any moment, bring his hands together and squish the wanderer and those with him.

"You got anything you want to say," the wizard called to all of them, "best get it done now. It's two days to reach the other end of the Wall Eternal, if I remember correctly, and anything more than a low whisper during that time pretty much guarantees us a stony grave." He gestured in front of them, high above their heads. The wanderer followed the man's gaze and saw immediately what he meant. Large groups of stones could be seen here and there, having landed in such a way that they had piled up between the two walls. There was no way of knowing how long that stone had stayed in those piles, but even as the wanderer—and everyone else present—stared up at them, he saw, a short way ahead, several stones come loose of one such pile in a cloud of dust.

The stones looked tiny when they fell, but as they plummeted through the sky, drawing closer and closer, the wanderer realized that what he had at first taken as rocks no larger than pebbles were actually the size of his head or bigger, and it had only been the vast height that had tricked his mind. The rocks struck the ground up ahead with the force of stones fired from a catapult and several whipcracks of sound echoed through the chasm like thunder.

"Huh," Dekker said from beside the wanderer, the man's voice sounding breathless. "Sure you don't want to get an ale instead? I know a nice little place back in Celes—not too crowded."

"Raincheck," the wanderer said.

Dekker grunted, gazing up at the dozens of piles of stone stuck between the walls of the stone crevice, lying in wait like traps and just as lethal as any manmade ones could hope to be. "Just to refresh my memory," he said, "what, exactly, is supposed to keep those piles where they are and not from falling on our heads?"

"Luck?" Clint suggested, the Perishables' leader looking decidedly pale as he, too, studied the stones.

"I stopped playin' dice a long time ago," Dekker said, "on account of the only luck I got is bad luck." He glanced at the wanderer, clearly having to pull his gaze away from the stones with a will. "Could we…I don't know, make shields, or something?"

The wanderer shook his head. "Even if such shields would do any good—which they would not, for stones falling from that height would tear through them—what would we make them from?" He glanced around at the ravine in which they stood, empty save for random piles of stone and small pieces of what appeared to be dried-out seaweed—though how such a plant might have gotten here the wanderer couldn't have guessed. "No," he said, "I'm afraid Clint's strategy is as good as any—luck. And a bit of hope."

"Luck. And hope," Dekker repeated. "If there's flimsier stuff to make a shield out of, I don't know it. Sure there's no other way?"

The wanderer glanced at the wizard but saw that the man was currently hunched in front of a few frightened children. Or, at least, they *had been* frightened. Just then, those children were busy watching as what looked like sparks of as many colors as those of a rainbow flittered off the wizard's thin, wagging fingers.

The children's sober, nervous expressions slowly gave way to smiles of wonder—much like the one the wanderer felt splitting his own face—and he came to the conclusion that the wizard was not a bad man. Obvious, perhaps, considering that he had created and regularly seen to a barrier around the village of Alhs to keep its denizens safe, and from the way he spoke, the wanderer did not think that it was the only one of its kind. But then, the man had been nothing but suspicious, snappy, and outright hostile to him since they had met.

But as he watched the wizard interact with the children, he was forced to admit that it was not people in general that the man did not like—and never mind that he'd apparently lived alone in the middle of a perpetual blizzard—but instead the wanderer specifically. "He said there was not," he said in answer to Dekker's question. "Or, at least, none that would keep Ranger and those following him from catching us. Besides, even if they do come upon us, their numbers will count for nothing here. Only two of them could come at us at once...it is the best chance we have."

Dekker grunted. "If you say it, I believe you. Still, I don't much care for it."

"Neither do I," the wanderer admitted.

"Do you suppose we might build up some rocks?" the sheriff asked, walking up and gesturing at the opening they'd all come through. "I don't think it'd take much to block the entrance. Who knows? Maybe they wouldn't see it at all or, even if they did, well, they wouldn't be able to make it through."

The wanderer noted the dubious expressions on Clint and Dekker's face, suspected he had a similar one himself. He could not fault the sheriff for the idea, of course, but then he had not seen the Revenants up close—the two men had, and so they knew just what it was they faced. "A good idea," the wanderer said, "but I think we would lose more time than we gained. The creatures who chase us, they are stronger than a normal man, and they do not feel pain. Whatever time it took us to barricade, it would take them less time to tear down."

"And what for concealing the entrance?" the sheriff asked. "So that maybe they won't know where we went."

"They will know," the wanderer said.

"How can you be sure?"

"The one who pursues us, he is the single greatest woodsman in the world, not just of this age but any age. He reads signs and marks of passage the way another might read a book. There is no way that we might evade him. Or, at least, not so easily as that."

"So if we're not planning on evading him, what do we plan on doing?" the sheriff asked.

"Running," the wanderer said. "As far as we can, as fast as we can."

"And when we can't run anymore?" the sheriff asked quietly.

There was no answer to that—at least no answer that would serve any purpose save to frighten the sheriff or those villagers around them—so the wanderer did not give one.

The sheriff shook his head, frustrated. "Just...it feels like a death sentence, walking through here," he said, his gaze going back to the stones. "Don't mind tellin' you, Ungr, I don't do great with tight spaces. Not at all. Don't you think we'd be better off outrunning them the way we did before, when you were leading us?"

The wanderer blinked, at once touched and surprised to see that the sheriff seemed to prefer him to the wizard, and he gave the question serious thought as he turned to regard the robed man. Finally, he shook his head. "No, I think we have to trust the wizard," he said, turning back to the sheriff. "He has something in mind—of that much I'm sure. And he's right. We cannot outrun them, not in the open. This is our best chance. Likely our only one."

"Alright, if you say so," the sheriff said, staring at those rocks gathered in clumps between the sides of the gorge as if they were death come to claim him. Which, of course, was not all that far from the truth, for anyone who was caught below them when they chose to fall would fare far worse than the rocks themselves when they'd smashed on the ground below. "Only....sure does look awful tight," the sheriff said. "Ain't even...ain't even sure we'll fit," he finished in a low voice, barely loud enough to hear.

The wanderer stared at the sheriff as the man gazed up at the rocks, thinking. It was clear that the sheriff wasn't lying—simply the prospect of traveling beneath those great stones, of walking between those two giant stone walls that seemed to stretch on to eternity, had him pale with fright, his hands trembling with fear.

The wanderer scolded himself for a fool. As they'd followed the wizard he'd noted some valerian and chamomile growing but had not thought to pick it. But the herbs, combined with a few others, would have done wonders for the sheriff's anxiety. That was when he remembered the herb woman, Clara. He hadn't spoken to her since they'd left Alhs—blame it on being busy trying to keep himself and everyone with him alive—but if she was like every other herbwoman he'd met over the years she would have been more likely to leave her head behind than her herb pouch on such an excursion as the one they were on.

And he had yet to meet a herbwoman who did not keep a remedy or two for stress on hand. After all, many of the problems people sought help from village herbwomen for, in the wanderer's experience, could not be "solved," at least not in the traditional sense, for they were more emotional than physical. And in such instances, the best cure, perhaps the *only* cure, was something to treat their anxiety.

Yet he had only recently regained the sheriff's confidence, and he did not want to risk insulting the man. "Sheriff, I wonder if you would do me a favor?"

"What...what's that?" the sheriff asked, still staring at the giant stone walls.

"Some of the villagers, they might be afraid. I wonder if you could check with Clara, see if she has anything that might calm their nerves a bit, if they need it."

The sheriff did turn to him then, a look that was a mixture of suspiciousness and relief on his face. "That's a good idea—I'll go talk to her. Be good to know if she has something, you know, in case anyone needs it."

"My thoughts exactly."

The sheriff nodded. "Alright then," he said, giving the wanderer a tight, nervous smile before turning and walking away.

"You know, might be I was wrong about you after all."

The wanderer turned to see Dekker standing beside him, the big man regarding the sheriff as the man moved away. "Oh?" the wanderer asked. "You mean I'm not an asshole after all?"

"Oh no, you're an asshole alright," Dekker said, giving him a grin. "In fact, until recent events, I would have been sure you were the oldest asshole still walking around on the face of the world." He paused, glancing at the wizard. "Now though, I'm not so sure. No, what I was wrong about was that I thought you were terrible with people—maybe from being used to your only company being a horse who could get along with anyone. But now, well, now I'm thinkin' you do know something about people after all—leastways something more than how to stick 'em with a sword, if it becomes necessary, anyway."

"You use the pointy end, don't you?"

The big man barked a laugh. "See, like I said—asshole. Anyway, all I'm sayin' is...well. Likelier'n not we'll all be squished beneath tons of stone come this time tomorrow, so I figure I'd tell you that, whatever happens, you've done a damn fine job. If it weren't for you, wouldn't a one of us have made it this far."

"Wouldn't have been here in the first place either," the wanderer offered solemnly.

Dekker shrugged. "Maybe. Or maybe me and my family would have been in the woods and lightnin' would have struck our house, or maybe—and this more likely—Clint and the other Perishables, including myself, would have been found out and made to suffer for our conspiracy. And knowing what I know now about that...that *thing* that called itself Soldier, I know we wouldn't have stood a chance, and I doubt very seriously if it would have been merciful enough to leave our families out of it. Shit, Ungr, without you, there's a good chance me and the other boys, my fam...well. There's a chance wouldn't none of us be alive today. And anyway, how long do you mean to punish yourself? If you're goin' to own the bad shit you cause—not to say that you even *did* cause it— then it seems only right that you own the good shit too."

"Put like a wise priest," the wanderer said.

Dekker grunted sourly. "I don't give two shits about those pompous, white-robed bastards with all their chantin' and starin' down their nose at folks like their shit comes out sparkling. Anyway, will you think about it? If the bad puts the load on your back, then the good ought to take it off, and Ungr, whatever else you done, you done plenty of good while you were at it. Why, if it weren't for you we'd all be dead thanks to that damned sword, so don't be so hard on yourself, alright? The world'll do that for you, and that's a truth I think you know already."

The wanderer frowned, nodding slowly. "Alright," he said.

"Good," Dekker said, giving a firm nod. He glanced ahead of them then let his gaze travel up to those waiting piles of rocks, some the size of wagons, some considerably bigger. "Now then, let's go get squished, eh?"

The wanderer grinned. "After you."

CHAPTER FIVE

The wanderer had started the morning thinking that he had never been claustrophobic, that he never would be. But after about an hour of traveling silently through the gorge, the great stone walls looming above them, he began to question that, to think maybe he was a bit claustrophobic after all.

After two hours, he knew it. After all, a man might not be afraid of spiders, but let him meet one the size of a wagon, and he would learn to be. It wasn't that he wasn't scared of spiders then, just as it wasn't that the wanderer hadn't been scared of tight places—only that he hadn't met the tight place that got to him yet. Now, though, he had.

His body was tense, a tightness in his shoulders and neck that he couldn't seem to loosen no matter how many times he stretched or rubbed them. Many of the villagers walked with their shoulders and backs hunched, moving in exaggerated, careful steps that were remarkably similar to the walk a child might use when tiptoeing past his parents' room and trying not to wake them.

The wanderer also had to fight the urge to walk with his shoulders hunched, as if preparing for a blow from above, and each time they walked beneath one of those great piles of stone caught between the gorge walls his gaze inevitably traveled upward, studying those rocks, *willing* them to stay in place until he and the rest of the villagers had safely passed.

The sheriff, at least, seemed to be faring no worse than the other villagers—not that that was particularly well. Their faces were pale with fright, their expressions tense. Even the usually stoic, unflappable Veikr was clearly uncomfortable.

The wanderer patted the horse's muzzle from time to time, muttering quiet, distracted words of comfort, but he did not think they did much good—the truth was that, at that moment, he did not have much comfort to give.

The path they followed wound its curving way through the gorge like a snake, the ground itself hard, packed, dry earth, littered here and there by stones. Some were small, but others were large enough that they had to climb over them in order to make their way past. Climbs that would have been challenging in the best of times. Add in the fact that they were terrified to make any sound above a whisper for fear of bringing the great piles of rocks crashing down on their heads, and the experience ranked up there with some of the worst of the wanderer's unnaturally long life.

In his examination of their surroundings, the wanderer also noted, as his gaze fell upon the rock walls on either side of the trail, that they were not nearly so sheer as he had at first thought. Perhaps they had been once, but the passage of time had done its work on the walls, eroding into their surface with wind and rain so that the stone face was riddled with pockmarks and indentations.

The wanderer walked at the back of the procession. Dekker and Ella walked a short ways ahead and, between them and the wanderer Sarah rode atop Veikr's broad back. Whenever the winding, twisting path straightened for any length of time the wanderer would check behind them but, so far at least, no army of monstrosities had presented itself.

Not that that gave him much comfort.

After all, they were coming—that much he knew. He was confident that by now, the army led by Ranger's impostor had already entered the gorge. The one thing for which he could be thankful was that the winding, rock-littered path would slow the army just as it slowed the villagers, for while the Revenants' unnatural endurance might help in many instances, it would not climb rocks for them, nor would it allow them to walk more than two-abreast through the ravine.

But slowed or not, they were coming. They had been set a task and nothing short of the accomplishment of that task or death would stop them now. The wanderer could only hope that no problems that would slow him and the others down presented themselves.

The first problem came about half an hour later.

The villagers' plodding progress slowed and slowed further still until they came to a halt. He and Dekker shared a frown, and the wanderer tried—and failed—to see past those in front of him to what had caused the stop. He could practically hear the sand running out of the hourglass—for them, very little sand and a very small hourglass—and he waited impatiently as he saw the villagers passing a message down the line until, finally, the villager in front of them turned to him. *"The wizard,"* the man said quietly. *"He wants to see you at the front."*

The wanderer didn't like the sound of that, for the man was clearly no fan of his—he'd made that evident—and it would take something significant to prompt him to seek the wanderer's company.

The villagers were slowly moving to either side of the trail, opening up a path for him, and the wanderer shared a glance and a shrug with Dekker before moving into the opening. It was strange, walking between those villagers, all silent, all watching him. He approached a turn in the trail then stepped around it. His breath caught in his throat as he saw the reason the wizard had stopped the procession, a reason that had been blocked from his view by the winding chasm.

He continued forward, painfully aware of the villagers watching him. Watching and no doubt hoping—unreasonably, but then hope *was* unreasonable, in fact that was the whole point of it—that he had a solution.

The wizard was standing with his hands on his hips, his familiar scowl on his face as the wanderer walked up. This time, though, the man's hateful expression was not for the wanderer but for what lay ahead of them. Or, more accurately, *above* them.

"How far does it go?" the wanderer asked quietly, finding it difficult to get the words past his suddenly terribly dry throat.

"How would I know?" the wizard responded angrily, his voice loud enough that a shower of small pebbles and dust rained down from high above their heads.

Pebbles that struck the path a few dozen feet in front of them and shattered. The old man took a slow breath at that, wincing. "I didn't check," the wizard said. "All I can tell you is that it wasn't here the last time I was here, but then that was many years ago."

The wanderer nodded grimly, staring up above his head. So far in their journey, they had walked beneath several large clumps of rocks that had managed to become wedged in the gorge, already and while those piles had been large, some as big as a carriage or even a bit larger, it had only been a few seconds' work to move beyond them.

What lay before them now, though, was something else entirely. Starting a few dozen feet farther down the trail, a great long line of rocks had become piled up in the ravine hundreds of feet above their heads. That line of rock stretched on as far as the wanderer could see, stacked so thickly between the great stone walls that it blocked the sunlight from reaching the ravine floor almost completely with only the barest shreds of light making it through.

But then the dark was far from the worst of it. The worst of it was that they would be traveling beneath that great overhanging of stone for an interminable length of time. Stone that might, at the slightest sound, shift and tumble down upon them, burying them all alive and doing the job of the creatures hunting him and the villagers for them.

"So what do we do then? Turn around?"

The wanderer and the wizard turned to see that the sheriff had walked up. The man was pointedly looking anywhere *except* at the hanging stone and there was more than a bit of relief in his voice at the prospect of escaping the chasm earlier than they'd thought.

The wanderer and the wizard shared a look. The man was not wearing an angry scowl now, but given the worry writ clear on his face the wanderer almost missed it. "No," he found himself saying quietly, shaking his head. "We cannot turn back, not now."

"You mean to—to walk under *that?*" the sheriff said, gesturing at the great length of piled stone stuck in the chasm and, as if it heard him, a shower of dust and small rocks chose that moment to fall a short distance away.

The wanderer looked up at the chasm walls, not seeming like inanimate stone, not then, but like great behemoths radiating menace and malice, waiting eagerly for them to step beneath that great weight of stone so that they might crush them beneath it. "We have no choice," he said, pulling his eyes away from those walls of stone to regard the sheriff. "I do not doubt that Ranger and his army have already made it into the ravine and are even now somewhere behind us."

"You mean we're trapped, then," the sheriff said.

"Not trapped," the wanderer said softly, putting a hand on the man's shoulder. "We have one way out yet."

"Had an uncle, when I was a boy," the sheriff said, his voice a dry rasp. "Uncle Jim. Jim loved to talk—fact is, he didn't care for doin' much else, particularly work. But he did a lot of talkin', had a lot of sayin's. Sayin's like, 'Work smarter not harder'—a favorite, I find, of those who don't want to work at all—or 'Measure twice, cut once,' though in my experience the only thing Jim ever sawed were logs durin' his afternoon naps. Oh yes, a lot of sayin's had Jim, but his favorite was 'A rolling stone gathers no moss.'" He grunted. "Funny, maybe, if you knew Uncle Jim, for the man despised nothing so much as getting up out of his chair and moving around."

"I see," the wanderer said. "Well, here, at least, his advice is right—we must keep moving."

The sheriff though, wasn't quite finished yet. "I'm sure you're right," the sheriff said. "Just as I was sure Jim was right, when I was a boy—I loved him fiercely then, always wished he were my dad instead of the harder, sensible, hardworking dad I had. Foolish maybe but then I find that boys—of any age—are little else."

"And what happened to Jim?" the wanderer said, aware that the sheriff was going to have his say, needed to, maybe, but aware also that they were running out of time.

"Talkin' was Jim's favorite pastime, but it weren't his only one," the sheriff said. "Jim also liked his drink. One day, he got to drinkin' and talkin', tellin' jokes. He was tryin' to explain to me and a friend of mine, Billy, the truth about a rollin' stone not gatherin' moss. He did so by turnin' a flip, one which took him in a drunken tumble off a hill and landed him on his head." He shook his head slowly. "He lived, did Jim, but he never was the same after that. Still did a lot of sittin', but he didn't talk anymore. And I learned somethin' that day, Ungr. A rollin' stone might not gather any moss, but if it ain't careful, it'll find itself on a cliff, and when you're on a cliff they ain't nothin' worse in all the world to do than to move forward."

"And you think we're on a cliff?" the wanderer asked.

The sheriff met his eyes then shrugged. "I don't know. But then that's the thing about cliffs, Ungr. Sometimes a fella doesn't know, not until he's already stepped off, and then it's too late. You say the way is forward, I'll follow you, but I'll say this and then I'll speak no more on it—if it's up to me, and I had to choose dyin' by bein' crushed by tons of fallin' rock or by men—or men*ish* creatures—with swords, well, that ain't a hard choice for a fella to make."

The wanderer nodded at that. "I understand, Sheriff, and I still believe that the right way is forward."

The man inclined his head. "You lead, Ungr," he said, glancing back at the villagers. "We'll follow you." And with that the sheriff turned and started away.

The wanderer glanced back to the wizard to see the man watching him, a strange expression on his face. "Everything alright?" he asked.

The wizard gave his head a shake. "Fine," he snapped. "Now, if you're done, I'd just as soon get this over with. Unless, of course, you'd like to find someone else to chat with, maybe keep right on chatting until Ranger and those damned monstrosities of his come upon us?"

"Think I'm all chatted out," the wanderer said.

"Good," the gray-bearded man said, gesturing forward. "Then, you lead, Eternal," he said with a sneer. "We'll follow."

***

The wanderer had thought himself tense before, when they'd traveled under the occasional pile of stone stuck between the two gorge walls. Now, though, as he walked underneath a ceiling of packed stone that stretched on as far as he could see, he realized just how easy they'd had it. Every noise, whether of a footstep behind him, a harsh breath from one of the villagers as they tripped over a rock not seen in the shadows, or the sound of pebbles and dust sprinkling from far, far overhead, was, to his anxious mind, the sound of the rocks beginning to tumble down upon them.

It was ridiculous to be worried, of course, for he knew that when a man could do nothing to change his fate one way or the other, there was no point in concerning himself with it. After all, if the great ceiling of stone lodged in the ravine above them did decide to fall there wasn't a thing the wanderer or any of those with them could do about it, no more than the bug who saw the boot descending might change its fate.

No, what would happen would, and there was nothing he could do about it. There was no point worrying over it.

But he worried nonetheless.

As they walked they came upon several piles of stone, ones that they were forced to climb over. The doing of it took more time than it normally would have, for they took exaggerated care, each motion slow and steady, all too aware that any sound might set off a rockfall that would bring their journey to a quick and definitive end.

They had traveled beneath the great weight of stone for nearly half an hour when a woman screamed behind him, and the wanderer spun, thinking that somehow the enemy and his army must have come upon them.

He caught sight of what the woman had been frightened of a moment later as a green mountain snake slithered its way into a tiny crevice in the rocks. But the snake was not their real problem. Instead, it was the sound that came a moment later, a low rumbling like approaching thunder, and the wanderer, along with every other person present, froze, staring up at the ceiling of rock overhead.

No one moved. No one even so much as breathed as the stones shifted, grating against each other. The wanderer stared as a giant boulder the size of some houses he'd seen came loose and fell. It struck the ground a few dozen feet behind them, hitting with such force that it broke apart and a man screamed as a shard of jagged rock, flying with incredible force, embedded itself into his thigh.

The rock above their heads began to rumble louder at that, like a giant annoyed at being roused and threatening to wake and bring a terrible punishment when it did. An old woman rushed forward, followed by a middle-aged man. The woman clamped her hand over the wounded man's mouth, silencing his screams and pulling him against her knees, while the man clamped his hands over the wound. The wanderer watched the rock above head, watched it shimmy and shake, threatening to give way.

Then, finally, it settled, and the only sounds were the harsh breathing of everyone gathered and the mostly muffled, pained moans of the wounded man.

The wanderer checked on Dekker and his family and saw the big man turning to him, his face ghostly pale. He gave the wanderer a shaky nod to show that they were alright. The wanderer moved toward the wounded villager. By the time he arrived the man was laid out on the ground, and he saw that the man who'd first moved to help him was Daggett who, along with two other men, was currently holding the wounded man's arms and legs down. Meanwhile, the old woman who'd moved forward was examining the shard of rock sticking out of the man's side.

The wanderer knelt beside the wounded man. As he did, he saw that the old woman was in fact Clara, the village herbwoman. He hadn't had an opportunity to speak with the woman since they'd left Alhs, but he'd seen her tending to the wounded as they traveled deeper into the Untamed Lands, and she had a reputation for being an effective—if slightly abrasive—healer.

"How bad is he?" the wanderer asked.

"Much the same as any other'd be if'n they got stabbed with a large chunk of rock, I imagine," the old woman said, giving him a small, tight smile to take the sting out of her words.

The wanderer nodded. "It was quick thinking, covering his mouth."

She shrugged. "I never have been able to countenance yellin'. Now, tell me, Ungr—it's what they call you, isn't it?"

"When they don't call me worse."

She gave him another smile. "The worse has been a lot quieter lately, I'll say that. Now then," she said, glancing at the two swords scabbarded at his back, "you seem like the type of fella that has seen a few wounds in his time, yes?"

"Yes."

"And durin' all that seein', did you happen to pick up any knowledge of healing?"

"Some," the wanderer said, thinking of his lessons with Healer.

"Good, cause we're goin' to need it. Do you know Shepherd's Purse by lookin?"

"Yes."

"Good. Reach into my herb pouch and grab some, if you would. We're going to have to work fast."

The wanderer did as she asked, and the woman jerked her chin at the ground. "Set it there. Now, I'm going to let go of the wound to make a poultice to slow the bleeding—I'll need you to apply as much pressure as you can, understand?"

"Yes."

The woman moved, and he moved with her, putting his hands over the wounded man's leg. The woman began preparing a poultice of several herbs, moving with an economy of motion that the wanderer had not seen in a very long time, not since his training sessions with Healer, and he watched in awe as the woman worked.

Violence had always come naturally to the wanderer. Even from a young age he'd always been stronger and faster than other boys. He'd always been good at hurting, at breaking things. But healing, putting things back together, always amazed him, and so he felt privileged to watch the woman work, following her orders the same as he would have followed those of Healer herself.

In ten, perhaps fifteen minutes, they were finished. The wounded man had passed out some time ago. The herbwoman finished tying the final bandage then sat back, using the back of her wrists to wipe a loose strand of gray hair back on her head, looking completely exhausted. The wanderer understood for he, too, was tired. A very different kind of tired than he would have been after a fight or a battle, but one that was no less powerful for all that—perhaps even more so. He thought that, overall, healers did not get near enough credit.

"He'll live?" he asked.

"He'll live. You did well," she said, watching him. "I've heard tale of you killin' that giant snake, and I've seen you fight with my own eyes, but it seems you're not all hard edges after all, and I'm sorry for thinkin' so. Turns out there's some softness to you, too."

"Don't tell anybody," he said, giving her a tired smile.

She winked. "Your secret's safe with me, dearie, though I think they all know it well enough, don't you?"

The wanderer had been completely absorbed in the task at hand for the last several minutes and only now became aware of all the villagers gathered around, watching them.

He cleared his throat softly, suddenly feeling very uncomfortable, and the woman gave him a small smile. "Not much good with gratitude, are you, Ungr?"

"I'm afraid not."

"Me neither," she said, giving him a wink. "But, comfortable or not, I want you to know that because of you this man's going to live."

"You saved him. All I did was what you told me."

"Probably that's why I like you so much," she said, returning the smile.

With that, she rose and motioned to two men. "Go on," she said, nodding at the villagers. "They're waitin' on you. I'll get him ready to move."

The wanderer bowed his head then rose and made his way to where Dekker waited with the wizard, the sheriff, and Clint. "Poor bastard," Dekker muttered as the wanderer drew closer. "He goin' to be alright?"

"Clara says so, and I trust her judgement in this matter far more than my own."

"Damn bad luck," Clint said. "Reckon he'll walk again?"

"Clara thinks he'll get full use of the leg—assuming he lives that long. Assuming any of us does. We've wasted time here, time we could ill-afford to waste. We need to get going—now."

"What about him?" Clint asked, nodding his head at the wounded man.

"He can ride on Veikr. It'll be painful, but there's no hope for it. There isn't time to build a stretcher and no materials to build it with even if there was."

The men around him nodded, each of their expressions grimmer than the last. Several village men helped secure the wounded man on Veikr's back and, within five minutes, they were moving again, making their way down the trail.

In another half hours' worth of walking they finally stepped out of the overhanging piles of rock and the wanderer breathed a heavy sigh of relief as he looked up at the sky for the first time in what felt like an eternity.

With that terrible shadow no longer looming over their heads, the villagers began to talk in quiet whispers again. The wanderer's own spirits began to rise as they moved on, the warmth of the fading afternoon sun a balm to his troubled mind.

The wanderer watched them from his position at the back of the line, their smiles and quiet, excited talk at this latest victory—for there was no greater victory that might be had than surviving in the face of likely death—comforting him even more than the warmth of the sun on his skin. The absence of that crushing weight of stone went a long way toward reinvigorating the villagers, and they made good time as they continued on through the chasm. Even the wounded man did not slow them down, for Veikr bore his weight as he bore all of life's difficulties—silently and without complaint.

There was a joke there, maybe, the wanderer thought. *Show me a man who doesn't complain, and I'll show you a horse.* Or perhaps not. He'd never been good at joking anyway, never been good at making light of things. He thought maybe the woman Clara had been wrong—maybe he *was* all hard edges, little more than a weapon. But then even a weapon had its place. For while it might not be a thing of value itself, he thought, glancing back at Dekker and his family, at the villagers, it might *protect* things of value and therein find its own worth.

They walked on.

The sun was sinking low on the horizon, darkness no more than an hour away when they stopped again. The wanderer craned his neck, looking beyond them, and once more he saw the news, whatever it was, being passed down the line of villagers, one whispering to the next, then the next, and on and on it went. As he waited, the wanderer felt that knot of worry begin to grow in his belly once more. After all, a weapon might protect against creatures of flesh and blood, but it was of little use against stone.

He glanced beside him to where Dekker stood with his family and the big man turned, his grim expression showing that he shared the wanderer's concern. After all, try as he might, the wanderer could not think of a single good thing that might cause them to stop. Meanwhile, he could think of plenty of bad things—specifically *one* bad, one bit of terrible news that he feared more than almost any other, one that had been preying at his mind since the giant boulder had come lose and fallen behind them, blocking a large section of the chasm.

As he watched those villagers whisper one to the other, noted their grim expressions as they first accepted the news then passed it on, the wanderer became more and more certain that what he feared the most had come to pass after all.

"You alright, Ungr?" Dekker asked in a whisper beside him, and the wanderer turned to regard the big man.

"That depends on the reason we're stopped," he said, trying for a small smile and not quite managing it.

A minute or so later the villager in front of them leaned forward, listening to the whisper of the one beyond him, then turned back and spoke to Dekker. The wanderer watched the big man's face, saw the grim expression grow grimmer still. By the time the man was finished and leaning forward to speak to the wanderer he thought he knew enough what the news was, what it *must* be.

"They say the trail's blocked up ahead," the big man whispered, his voice low and rough with frustration, putting the wanderer in mind of the giant rocks that had shifted above their head so recently. *"Ten feet high at least, packed pretty tight."*

The wanderer nodded, for he had expected as much. "Best we go figure out what can be done," he said.

"We?" the big man asked, raising an eyebrow.

"Sure," the wanderer said. "You said you worked on a crew repairing the wall, didn't you? Back in Celes?"

The big man gave him an incredulous look. "Sure, as hired help, haulin' stone from that pile and puttin' it in this one. I wasn't exactly the brains of the operation, Ungr. Shit, if I learned anythin' from it, it's that it's a job I'd never want."

"Let's hope you learned more than that," the wanderer said, then he turned and started toward the front of the line. After the time it took to hiss a curse, Dekker fell into step beside him. The villagers gave way before them, and in a few minutes he and

Dekker stood beside the wizard, gazing at the blocked passage before them.

The big man gave a low whistle. *"Damn,"* Dekker hissed.

"Yes," the wanderer agreed, feeling that tangled knot of worry solidifying in his stomach like a stone. The way was well and truly blocked, that was sure. He did not know much about rock, but he knew that much.

"This was not here the last time," the wizard said unhelpfully. "So, all-knowing Eternal," he went on, turning to regard the wanderer, "what solution do you have for us?"

"I don't," the wanderer said, turning to Dekker. "How bad is it?"

"Bad," the big man muttered distractedly as he gazed at the wall. "Could be worse. Could be a damn-sight better. The bad news is that there's a great big pile of damned rocks in our way. The good news is that, I think, we should be able to move them away— doesn't look like there's any piece in there too big to manage. Likely if there was it would have been broken up during the fall." He glanced at the wanderer. "How long before the army reaches us, you reckon?"

The wanderer considered that. "An hour. Perhaps an hour and a half. How long to remove the stones?"

"Too long," the big man said grimly.

The wanderer turned to regard the wizard. "Anything you can do?"

The man snorted. "And just what did you have in mind, Eternal? Do you wish for me to mutter a few words, waggle my fingers, and make the stones vanish?"

"I wouldn't argue," the wanderer said.

The old man rolled his eyes. "That is not how the Art works, Eternal, and I must admit that I am surprised to find one of your kind who has been taught so very little of it."

"Don't blame the teachers—I fear I was a poor student."

"Imagine my surprise," the wizard said dryly. "Anyway, trust me when I say that it cannot be done by the Art. Certainly, at least, not by mine. Another might be able to do it in my stead, perhaps, but unless you happen to have another wizard handy, we had best look elsewhere for our solution."

Dekker grunted. "Seems that Ungr wasn't the only student that ought to have paid closer attention."

The wizard's bushy gray eyebrows drew down in a frown at that. "What are you implying?"

Dekker shrugged. "Oh, I ain't much for implyin'. What I'm *saying* is that you're tellin' us another might could do it, makes me wonder why you can't. So what is it then, wizard? Too many late nights drinking and carousing when you ought to have been at home studying, that it?"

"That isn't how it works, you, *you*—"

"Go on," Dekker said, not smiling now but watching the wizard with an expression that was deadly serious, and even though the man was not looking at him the wanderer found himself feeling the sudden urge to back away. "You, what?"

The wizard paused, clearing his throat. "I only mean that the Art, and the ability to wield it, manifests itself differently in different individuals. To degrees, yes, but also in what way they might use it."

"Explain," Dekker said.

The old wizard gave a frustrated, impatient expression, but in the end nodded, showing once again, at least to the wanderer's mind, that he was no fool. "Imagine that the Art is a pool of water. A pool at which a man might kneel and, with cupped hands, drink, and that is the usage of the Art. Some mens' hands are bigger than others and so they might be able to hold more than others. And some men do not use their hands at all but a ladle, perhaps, or a spoon."

"What fool would use a spoon?" Dekker asked.

"One does not choose his own tools," the wizard said. "They are chosen for him."

"And who does the choosing?" Dekker asked.

The wizard glanced at the wanderer. "Some believed it to be the Eternals, but of course that is a lie. The *truth* is that no one knows. Some men and women are born with the ability to use the Art, that is all, the same way that some are born with red hair or green eyes. Some of it might be taught, to a small degree—little more than parlor tricks—but most are either born with it or not. There is a theory that many go through life, gifted with use of the Art, but never finding the mechanism by which they might use it, though that is of no importance to us now. As for my own gift, it requires intense preparation and concentration, and while capable of producing astounding—"

"You can't move the rocks," Dekker said.

The wizard gave a sour face. "No. I cannot move the rocks."

"Right then," Dekker said. "Then we'd best get started doing it the hard way." He glanced up, and the wanderer followed his gaze. They had left the worst of the great stone ceiling behind them, but still, at various heights above them in the chasm they could see other piles of stone. Nowhere near as large but certainly large enough to ruin their day, if one decided to fall. "And we'd best do it quietly. That'll slow it down more. Still," he went on, frowning at the pile of rock blocking their path, "I think, if we're careful, we can do it."

The wanderer nodded, thinking. He didn't doubt that, given time enough, Dekker could oversee the stones being moved out of the way. The problem, of course, was that they simply did not have the time. The enemy was coming, and at his back marched at least a hundred Revenants, perhaps more. At a certain point, the numbers really stopped mattering. What *did* was that there would be plenty enough to finish the job.

They were coming. Death was coming. Not just for the wanderer, but for the villagers, for Dekker and his family, too. Death was coming, and it would be here soon.

Unless someone stopped it.

But no one can stop death. His own thought and a true one, but there was another truth too, one connected to the first. People did not eat healthily, did not exercise or avoid risking their lives in an effort to stop death—that was beyond them. Even the Eternals were not beyond death's grasp, though it might be said that they had lain further from it. No, death came for everyone. That was a hard truth learned the hard way when he'd watched his companions butchered by the enemy one after the other.

No, death could never be stopped. Everyone learned that, sooner or later. But while it might not be stopped, it might be slowed.

"Ungr? You alright?"

He blinked, turning to glance at Dekker. "What's that?"

"I asked if you were plannin' on helpin' or just standin' around all day brooding. Not that you're not a good brooder—none finer, so far as I can see. But this rock ain't gonna move itself, is it?"

The wanderer nodded distractedly as an idea took root in his mind. A dangerous idea, a desperate one, but then that was as it should be, for he was a desperate man, and such men rarely had any other kind.

"I will help," he said quietly, "but there's something I need to do first."

He tried to keep his voice casual, but he saw the big man frown thoughtfully, and the wanderer knew at once that he'd failed. "Like what?"

"Just something I need to see to," the wanderer said. "I will be back soon. In the meantime, I'm sure the villagers would be happy to help you cle—"

"Bullshit."

The wanderer blinked. "I'm sorry?"

"And you ought to be," Dekker said. "A fella lies to his friend's face, I figure the least he ought to be is sorry."

"I'm not sure what you mean," the wanderer said slowly.

"Come on, Ungr," Dekker said. "I might not be a hundred years old, but I'm old enough that you can't piss on me and call it rain." He glanced around then leaned in, speaking quieter still. "Now, why don't you tell me what's on your mind? Maybe I can help."

For a moment, he was tempted. After all, what he planned was dangerous in the extreme, and Dekker had proven his resourcefulness and cleverness on more than one occasion. The wanderer did not doubt that, with the big man along, he would stand a far greater chance of succeeding, and that was before he even stopped to consider that Dekker had very particular knowledge that could prove useful if he was going to attempt what he meant to. But while Dekker's help would have proven invaluable, the wanderer refused to be so selfish as to bring him along. After all, it would be dangerous and if something happened to the big man because he accompanied him he would never forgive himself. Besides which, Dekker was needed here to oversee the removal of the stone. The wanderer shook his head. "It will be better if I do it alone."

"Why don't you tell me what it is," the big man said. "Let me judge that for myself."

"Perhaps better if I don't," the wanderer said. "Besides, they need you here. To oversee the removal of the stone."

"Anybody can—"

There was a threatening, rumbling sound, and they both looked back at the ten-foot-tall packed rock in front of them to see that a villager had stepped forward and started to pull a stone out. *"Not that one, damn you,"* Dekker hissed. *"Or do you want to bring the whole damned thing down on your fool head?"*

The man colored with a mixture of anger and embarrassment, jerking his hand back as if he'd been burned. "I didn't...that is, I only meant to help."

Dekker winced, sighing. "Sorry, man, I didn't mean that. Only, take that one there, instead," he went on, pointing. "It ain't load-bearin', so let's start there."

The villager nodded and set about it, another stepping forward to help him remove the big slab of stone that Dekker had indicated.

"It seems that you did learn a little bit during your time on the wall after all," the wanderer observed as the big man turned back to him.

Dekker cleared his throat, clearly uncomfortable. "What are you on about?"

"I think you know well enough."

"Aw, that?" Dekker asked. "That's nothin'. It was obvious."

"Not to me it wasn't," the wanderer said. "And not to him, either." The big man started to object, and the wanderer held up a hand, silencing him. "I know that you're not a mason, but you are the closest thing we have. The closest thing *they* have. It has to be done right, and it has to be done fast, for we have little time."

Dekker frowned. "And while I'm doing all this work, what will you be doing?"

"Oh, you know," the wanderer said. "Just relaxing. Maybe I'll take a nap."

The big man gave a quiet snort. "Act a fool if you want, just don't expect me to join in. You're meanin' to do something, aren't you? Something to slow them down?"

"Yes."

The big man nodded slowly. "And tell me. This something you've got planned, it ain't anything stupid like takin' on that army chasin' us, is it?"

"Of course not," the wanderer said.

Dekker watched him for several seconds then finally grunted. "Fine, you can go."

"Thanks, Pa," the wanderer said, giving the man a smile.

Dekker didn't return it. "Joke all you want," he said, "but if you end up gettin' your fool self killed don't come blamin' me."

"Impossible," the wanderer said.

"On account of you'd be dead," the big man said, frowning.

"That's right."

Dekker sighed, rolling his eyes. "Go on, you bastard. Get out of here. But *don't* get dead."

"I'll do my best," the wanderer promised. "Work as fast as you can but no faster, okay? It will not do anyone any good if you squish yourself."

Dekker raised an eyebrow. "Is Ungr, a man who carries two swords, one of which is cursed, and who I have personally seen charge at a giant serpent and invisible monsters telling me to be cautious?"

"Say that I am," the wanderer said.

"I'll try. Pa."

The wanderer smiled then turned and walked away, leaving the big man to it. He did so quickly, for he thought that, if he hung around, Dekker would see the worry that the smile tried to hide. He had not been lying when he'd told Dekker he did not mean to take the army on—at least not directly—but considering what he did intend he thought that doing so might have been the safer course.

He made his way past the villagers toward the back of the line where Veikr waited, for he would need the horse's speed if his plan was to have any chance of success. That meant that he and some other villagers had to take the wounded man, still unconscious, from Veikr's back, and the wanderer ignored the guilt he felt, telling himself that if he didn't do something, the wounded man would have far greater problems than being uncomfortable.

Once the wounded man was safely down, he climbed into the saddle. Veikr knickered softly, and the wanderer smiled, feeling good to be with his companion again, not having realized, until that moment, just how much he'd missed Veikr lately. There had been a time, after all, a very long time, when it had only been the two of them.

"I'm happy to see you too," the wanderer said, "but if I were you, I might wait on expressing that feeling until you've heard what I intend."

"And just what's this?"

The wanderer turned at the sound of the voice to find the wizard walking up, eyeing him with open suspicion bordering on hostility.

"Is everything alright?" the wanderer asked.

"Why don't you tell me?" the wizard said. He glanced at Veikr, let his gaze travel slowly up to the wanderer's face. "Going somewhere, are you?"

"Yes. I have to leave for a time, but I will return."

The wizard's upper lip peeled back from his teeth in a sneer. "Of course you will. You Eternals are all the same. Beneath all your supposed virtue, beneath your feigned kindness and noble words, you are all monsters, as bad as those creatures from which we run, as bad as the creatures inhabiting the Untamed Lands. *Worse,* in fact, because those creatures that chase us do so not of their own volition but because they are under the control of another, while those beasts which call these lands home do not do what they do out of cruelty but simply to survive. You, on the other hand, have chosen your evil."

"I don't know what you're talking about," the wanderer said, taken aback by the anger in the man's tone, for the last time they'd spoken he'd almost begun to think that he was making some headway with him.

"Don't you?" the wizard snapped. "You know as well as I that the way will not be cleared, not in time at least. You see the end coming, just as I do, and you seek to avoid it, a rat scurrying away at the sign of the approaching storm."

The wanderer blinked, confused, then, after a moment, he realized what the man meant. "You think I'm leaving."

"Of course I *think* it," the wizard said. "I think it in the same way that I think that the sky is blue, for I can see one as clearly as I can the other."

"You're wrong," the wanderer said, then winced. "I...that is, you are right in that I am leaving, but I do not mean to flee. I will return. Just as soon as I am able."

"Oh yes, no doubt," the wizard said sarcastically. "And no doubt you will return with a great army, one that will easily dispatch those who hound our steps."

The wanderer opened his mouth to say something, perhaps to try to convince the man that he would return, then decided it did not matter. The Revenants were coming. The enemy was coming, and there was no time to waste trying to convince the wizard that he meant well, even if the man might be convinced, a fact which he very much doubted.

So instead of saying anything, he gave Veikr a slight nudge, and the horse turned back in the direction they'd come.

"You will not make it out," the wizard said, stepping in front of him. "The army has already entered the gorge. There is no escape for you, Eternal. You will die here, like the rest of us."

"Maybe," the wanderer said, "but I am not trying to escape. Get them moving as soon as you are able—I will catch you up, if I can, but do not wait for me."

The wizard snorted. "As if I would wait for one of your kind," he said. "What treachery do you work, Eternal? Do you mean to go to them, to make some kind of deal with those who pursue us? Is that it?"

The wanderer found an anger kindling in him at that. "Get out of my way."

"I will not," the wizard said. "You are not leaving. You will remain with us and—"

"Let me be clear," the wanderer said. "I mean to do what I can to slow the enemy, to save everyone here. I do not care if you believe me," he continued, not giving the wizard the chance to utter the objection he clearly meant to. "You do not trust me, and that is fine. You can distrust me if you'd like, hate me if you must, but right now, you are in my way. You are slowing me down when speed is called for, and I will not let your hate keep me from doing what I can to save them. Now, move out of my way or be moved."

The wizard stared at him for a moment then, with an angry hiss, stepped to the side. The wanderer watched him for a moment, but only for a moment. Then he gave Veikr's sides a soft kick. "Come, Weakest—show me how swift you can be."

***

The sun set red, a crimson pool spreading across the sky, as the wanderer and Veikr made their way down the shadowed path before them. The wanderer stared out at that bloody sky as he rode, doing his best to ignore the growing trepidation he felt. Oracle had taught him about omens and signs, taught him to read dreams and portents, claiming that such were the secret language of the natural world. To those who did not know it, it did not seem like a language at all, not anymore than did the words of a man or woman speaking in a tongue they did not know. And yet, according to Oracle, it was a language just the same. And not just any language but the first, a language that had existed long before men had ever walked the face of the world, one which would exist long after the final man had taken his final step. It was the language of growing things and dying things, the whispers of millennia, the utterances of time itself.

Oracle had been an expert on such things, and she had taught him what she could, yet one did not need to be an expert, did not need to have spent decades studying that secret language to understand that bloody slash across the horizon, to know it for what it was. The same way that a man did not need to know the tongue of another to understand the meaning of a cry of rage. Some things, after all, could only be ignored with great effort and often not even then.

The thought reminded the wanderer of the ghosts. He had not spoken with them in some time, not since meeting the wizard. Often, in the past, he had avoided speaking to the ghosts but this time it had not been out of a desire to avoid their probing questions or their scornful reprimands. Instead, he had simply been too busy with the business of staying alive and trying to keep those with him alive as well.

Now, though, if he was to succeed at what he intended then he thought he would need their help. Even with it, he was far from sure of having any chance of success.

He opened the locket, tensing in expectation of the deluge of voices, the chorus of recriminations which nearly always accompanied such an act. But as the locket snapped open, the wanderer was greeted with silence and that only.

At first, he was relieved, for despite the fact that he'd suffered their scorn hundreds of times over the years he had never grown immune to their sting. But slowly, as one second stretched to two and two to three, that relief faded to be replaced by concern. "Hello?" he said aloud.

There was no answer, not from the world around him nor from the ghosts within the locket, and he felt his heart quicken in his chest. "Hello?" he said again.

Youngest? It was Leader's voice, but it sounded strange. Muffled and unsure, as if the man—or the ghost—had just woken from some deep and troubled sleep, sleep of the kind that left a man confused about his surroundings. *Is...is that you?*

"It is me," the wanderer said, frowning "Is everything okay?"

What? Hmm? The ghost asked, again sounding less certain in that moment than he had ever sounded in the time that the wanderer had known him, and instead of banishing the concern growing in the wanderer's belly it only increased it.

"Is everything okay?" the wanderer asked again.

Yes, sure. Yes, of course, Leader said, sounding more and more certain with each word he spoke until, by the last, he sounded like himself again. *We were...that is...Scholar?*

We...were sleeping, Scholar said, his voice sounding querulous and somehow frail, vulnerable in a way that the Eternal had never sounded before.

"Sleeping?" the wanderer asked, feeling confused himself. "I did not think that you slept. I...did not think you needed it."

We...have never slept before, Oracle said, her voice, too, sounding muzzy and unclear, perhaps even afraid.

"Then why now?" the wanderer asked, thinking that, at that moment, with all that he and the others faced, the last thing he needed was to find that the ghosts, upon which he had often relied over the last hundred years, were undergoing some sort of problem.

There was silence then, a tense silence, pregnant with dread, until finally Soldier spoke. *We do not know, lad,* he said in that gruff, casual way of his, yet the wanderer could detect a note of worry in the ghost's tone.

"I see," the wanderer said, but the truth was he did not, nor did he think he had time to worry about it just now. Ranger, or at least the creature in the guise of Ranger, was coming, and there was still much to be done. "Anyway, I need your help," he told the ghosts.

Of...of course, Youngest, Leader said. *What is it that we can do for you?*

Just then Veikr turned a corner in the path and the wanderer saw, in the moonlight, that which he had come to find. Or rather, he saw it not because of the moon's light but because the path before him ad grown suddenly dark, the light blocked by the line of giant stones and rocks stuck in the gorge far overhead.

Gazing at that line of tons and tons of stacked rock extending as far as he could see, taking in the massive walls reaching high into the sky, the wanderer began to doubt his plan.

Yes, we would be happy to help, as always, Youngest, Healer said. *Only...where are we?*

The wanderer had traveled a very long time with the ghosts since the real Oracle had given him the amulet, yet he had never heard them sound so confused before. In the early years following the Eternals' defeat, he had often wondered how long the spell on the amulet might last, had feared that the spell's power might fade, and that his link to the Eternals—however nebulous—would fade along with it.

Then, in the years and decades that followed, the ghosts had become more bitter—at least, he'd thought so, at the time, though now he wondered if it had been he who had become so. Either way, during those years of exile from the world, he had begun to *hope* that the spell would fade. Yet it had not, had continued on without failing or faltering for a hundred years and more, so long that he had taken it for granted, that some part of him had begun to think that it would last forever. Now, though, he was not so sure.

"The ravine," he said softly. "The one the wizard took us to."

Ravine? Leader asked. *What ravine, Youngest?*

And what wizard do you mean, lad? Soldier asked.

The wanderer blinked, beginning to think it unlikely that he would be able to get any help from the ghosts after all. "The wizard...the one we found in the snow. The Wizard of the South, they call him."

Listen, Youngest, Tactician said, not sounding angry or snappy as usual but instead sounding unnerved. *We know nothing of any wizard, nor any ravine. As we told you we have been...sleeping. The last thing we remember—the last thing I remember, at least—is seeing the house on the hill.*

There were murmurs of agreement from the other ghosts, and the wanderer frowned deeper. He had often wished for the spell Oracle had cast on the amulet to end, so that he might have some peace from the ghosts, his own personal spirits which haunted him, yet the thought of it now terrified him, for he did not think there had ever been a time when he was likely to need their help more. It was a worry for later, though. If he was going to do what he'd come to then there was no time to waste. "I need your help," he told them again. "I need to know everything any of you can tell me about rockfalls and landslides."

Very well, Youngest, Leader said. *As always, we are here to offer whatever assistance we may, but hear me. The wisest course would be to ride Veikr out of this ravine as quickly as possible—there is still time.*

"I hear you," the wanderer said.

But as is so often the case, you do not mean to listen, Leader said.

Perhaps it was because they had been "sleeping"—whatever that meant—or maybe it was simply that the wanderer was all too aware of the spell Oracle had placed on the amulet and how it might vanish at any moment, but the wanderer heard the weariness in the ghost's voice and felt a stab of guilt. Leader had never sounded vulnerable to him before, but he sounded so now.

"I can't," he said apologetically.

A sigh from the ghost. *Very well. Scholar?*

What? Oh, yes, landslides, the ghost said, his normally intelligent tone, with a confidence that bordered—and sometimes stepped wholeheartedly into—arrogance, sounding slightly bewildered. *A phenomenon in nature in which accumulated rock and stone slide or fall down a slope or decline. The largest such fall ever recorded was a mass of stone totaling in weight—*

He doesn't want a history lesson, you fool, Tactician said. *Nor to be bored to death with tonnage figures for stone that only mattered to those who found themselves underneath it. What Youngest* wants *is to know everything he can so that he can avoid being that poor, crushed bastard. He wants some advice on how to keep all that rock up there above his head from tumbling down on him and bringing a most abrupt end to his heroics.*

"That's not...*exactly* accurate," the wanderer said, his gaze taking in that great shadow of stone stuck in the gorge above him.

*What do you—*Tactician's words cut off for a moment. *Wait a minute, you* want *it to fall!* he finished accusingly.

"Yes," the wanderer said, "though you were not completely wrong. I want all this stone to fall, but if at all possible I'd much prefer not to be underneath it when it did."

You mean to block the pass, so that the army chasing you and the creature leading them cannot follow you.

"Yes," the wanderer said.

It is madness, Tactician said. *You will die in the attempt and what will become of your precious villagers, Youngest, when you are no longer there to protect them? Sheep without a shepherd do not last long in the wild, particularly the wilds of the Untamed Lands. The evils of this place are not the kind to sit and wait—they are hungry evils, ones that will come for your newfound friends. And without you, these villagers will stand no chance against what pursues them.*

He is right, Youngest. This from Ranger, the man's taciturn voice sounding gruff and stern as usual. *These who travel with you are civilized,* he continued, uttering the word with undisguised contempt. *And civilized man expects the world to bend to him instead of giving way before it. He looks at nature and thinks only of what he can gain from it, how it might be made to better suit him. And in doing this, he forgets—if he ever knew—how to work within it. For by considering himself superior to nature he sets himself apart from it and the world. And nature does not long tolerate those things which are unnatural. They cannot survive here. They are not even sheep, for sheep, at least, are part of nature and understand their place within it. Those villagers are like children walking in the dark, only aware of what is around them by the light that you cast. But without you to guide them, they walk blind, and soon, very soon, they will stumble into one of the many traps that lie in wait for them. They are a parasite, a disease, and nature will find a way to cure itself of them.*

The wanderer was surprised by the bitterness, the hatefulness he heard in the Eternal's tone. He'd heard Ranger speak on his opinion about civilization before but never at such great length, for the man normally spoke no more than necessary, if that. "I do not mean to die," the wanderer said.

No one does, Youngest, Leader said sadly. *Everyone, every man and woman walking the face of the world thinks, deep down, that they will live forever and each of them, in time, is proven wrong.*

"Nevertheless, I intend to try. Now, will you help me?"

A weary sigh from Leader. *Scholar?*

Impossible. What you mean to do is impossible, Youngest, Scholar's wizened voice said. *Perhaps, if you had weeks, we might be able to discern some method of causing the effect you wish without—*

"Pretend that I don't," the wanderer said, beginning to lose his patience and all too aware that time was running out. Assuming he managed to do what he wanted, it wouldn't be of much use if the creature posing as Ranger and the army it led had already passed beneath him.

Impossible, Scholar said again. *It is not a question of moving the stone—vibrations might do such a thing. The vibration of voices or something else—it is how such events often occur naturally. The problem, of course, is with the lack of tools available to you, any method you use to produce the effect you seek will inevitably have the unfortunate result of leaving you far too close to the event. You would perish.*

"Let me worry about that," the wanderer said. "Just help me with how it might be done."

I must advise against this, Youngest. This from Soldier, his voice sounding reluctant. *A long time ago, I led some troops out to deal with bandits that had been harassin' mountain villages on the fringes of my territory. Dealt with the bandits easily enough but on the way back we got caught in an avalanche. Fifteen of us set out from Celes, and fifteen of us left the bandit camp after they were dealt with, yet only myself and five others made it back to the city. We were camping on the mountainside when the avalanche struck.*

*Still not sure what caused it—one of the lads being too loud singin',
maybe, or maybe Ranger's right and the mountain chose that
moment to tell us, in no uncertain terms, that we were not welcome.
I don't know. All I know for sure is that it was one of the most
terrifying moments in my life—perhaps the most terrifying. All that
snow and ice and rock comin' crashing down on us. Felt like the
whole world was against us, and those of us as made it out did so not
out of any talent or skill on our part but out of pure luck. I wouldn't
wish such a thing on anybody, lad, not even Tactician when he's bein'
a prick, which as you know, is most times.*

I'll have you know— Tactician began, but the wanderer didn't
let him finish.

"I am going to do this," he told the ghosts, "with or without
your help. But I believe I'm right in thinking that, with it, I stand a
far better chance of not being crushed to death. So I would prefer
it if you help me—but either way, this is happening."

Very well, Youngest, Leader said. *I see that you are set on this
course, no matter where it will inevitably lead. Help him, Scholar. If
you can.*

As you say, the old man's voice came. *I will need to examine the
packed stone better.*

"You mean—"

You will have to climb up to it, the old man said, a slight
impatience in his voice.

The wanderer sighed. He had expected as much, of course, but
he'd hoped to be wrong.

He regarded that great weight of stone packed between the
two chasm walls and, as he did, contemplated the turns a man's
life took him through, wondering what he'd done—or who he'd
pissed off—to find himself here.

When he had traveled through the pass with the villagers, that
crushing weight of stone had felt as if it were just over their heads,
so close that, had he stood on his tiptoes, he might have almost
reached it. But now that he was set on climbing up to it, it seemed
much farther away. Too far?

There was only one way to know for sure.

True, he did not know if he would be able to finish the climb,
but another of Soldier's favorite sayings came to him then, one the
man had shared when the wanderer had been complaining about

another day of training when his body was already sore and bruised from the last.

I can't, he'd said to Soldier, and the older man had only given him a smile.

Maybe you can and maybe you can't, lad, he'd said. *Fact is, the world, life, being what it is, a man never knows if he'll be able to finish anything he starts. So he just starts on faith and hopes for the best, hopes he can see it through.*

And so, left with no choice, the wanderer dismounted Veikr and gave his friend a soft pat on the muzzle. And then, after seeing that Veikr obeyed—albeit reluctantly—his request to wait for him at the far end, beyond the great ceiling of rock, the wanderer moved to the stone wall and began to climb, hoping that he could see it through.

***

He had thought, staring up at those great walls of stone that seemed to reach to the sky, their surfaces pocked from the attentions of time and weather, that the climb would be difficult. After about fifteen minutes he realized that he had grossly underestimated the task he'd set himself.

The massive wall was not completely sheer, but it was closer than any mountain he'd ever seen, the available handholds sometimes so small that he was forced to hang from his fingers and nothing else. When he was low to the ground this was an annoyance, but as he grew higher—high enough to die horribly, should he fall—annoyance gave way to a creeping fear.

What handholds he did find seemed to be made of nothing but edges so sharp that as he climbed, he began to think someone had come along and sharpened them the way a veteran soldier might sharpen his blade each night. His hands were scraped and bloody in minutes.

Worse than the sharp edges, though, was that many of the handholds he made use of were damp, the stone so slick that on more than one occasion, his hand nearly came free. Accumulated water from the rain, he supposed, water that had not found its way out of the small gouges in the rock. The thought of that, of rain in such a confined space and what that might mean for him and the villagers, was a fresh worry to add to the list, but he forced it out of his mind.

It was hard going, and soon his entire body ached from the effort. His legs burned, his arms, too, and his hands and fingers hurt from the many fresh scrapes and abrasions they'd endured. The worst pain, though, was in his shoulders, a burning so strong that it felt as if someone had placed a flaming brand between them.

He continued until he discovered hand and foot holds that, compared to the others, felt relatively stable, then he paused to rest, his breath rasping in his lungs. The wanderer was in good shape, with little excess fat on his body—a hundred years of running didn't leave a man much time to put on fat—yet he was shocked by how difficult the task was. He hurt all over, was exhausted all over. He'd heard of people climbing mountains for enjoyment, and he thought that surely such tales must be bard fictions. And if by some incredible stretch such people *did* exist, he decided, as he clutched against that great stone edifice like an ant along a castle wall, that he did not want to meet them.

After all, if a man—or woman—was willing to put themselves through such torture when their most likely reward was to fall to a painful, though admittedly not for long, death, then to his mind there was really no telling what they might do.

Such thoughts were only distractions, a way for his mind to cast about for something, *anything* to think about besides how much his body ached, not to mention the danger and difficulty of what he was doing. When his breathing was as under control as it was likely to get, the wanderer glanced up above him. He did not bother biting back the curse that came, for the great packed in stone above his head seemed no closer than it had when he'd been standing on the ground.

That prompted him to glance back down at the chasm below him—an action he immediately regretted as a wave of vertigo swept over him. He quickly pulled his gaze away. While the stone packed between the two walls of the chasm might not seem any closer than it had when he'd started out, the ground beneath him had certainly gotten farther away. Plenty far enough that should he fall, it would be the last thing he ever did.

But while fear and pain were both useful mechanisms of the body—or so Healer had taught him—neither would serve him now. He balled up his fear and tucked it into a deep corner of his mind and, doing his very best to ignore the complaints of his sore fingers and arms, the wanderer began his ascent once more.

He did not look up again for some time, for he had been taught that when a man has a long, painful path ahead of him, it does not serve him to focus on how many steps he has remaining to him before he reaches its end. Instead, he can only focus on each step as he takes it—it is the only way to get it done.

As sweat poured from him, the wanderer was reminded of a joke he'd been told long ago, one that Veikr, when he'd repeated it, had not enjoyed nearly as much as he had. *How does a man eat an entire horse?* The joker—a bartender in some village, the name of which he'd forgotten—had asked. *One bite at a time.*

And so the wanderer did not think of how far he had gone nor of how far he had left to go. Instead, he only focused on taking one handhold after the other, one placement of his foot after the other. Doing so, he fell into a sort of rhythm. His back and arms, legs and shoulders seemed to hurt less. Or, perhaps, they were simply biding their time so that they might make their complaints known all the more forcefully soon. Either way, the going seemed to grow a little easier. The wanderer did not spend much thought on the reason why, superstitiously confident that doing so would break the effect as if it were a spell.

Instead, he climbed.

A light breeze had begun to pass through the gorge, and it felt good on his hot skin, refreshing. As he climbed, the wanderer felt a small smile creep onto his face. Crazy, perhaps, but there it was. He was happy. Things were simple, here. For the moment, he was not worried about the cursed blade or the enemy, nor about Dekker and his family or the villagers of Alhs, not even the Wizard of the South or the man's obvious hatred for him. Here, on the side of the mountain, all his other worries and concerns seemed to fall away, for it was all his mind could do to focus on the task at hand.

Silly, maybe, for those problems still existed, whether he thought of them or not, and the lion tamer who thought that turning his back on the creature under his charge would keep him safe was in for a rude awakening. But silly or not, the wanderer felt good, comforted.

At least, that was, until something struck the stone about a dozen feet above him and to his right with a loud *pinging* sound. Loose scree rained down on him from overhead, nearly causing him to lose his handhold.

The wanderer hissed as several small stones struck him, some hitting his arm and drawing blood. He looked to where the sound had come from but saw nothing. He was just preparing to start up again when there was another *pinging,* perhaps twenty feet to his left and he paused, holding himself tightly against the wall as the sound and vibrations caused more loose stone and dust to rain down from overhead.

Confused, the wanderer looked along the wall, trying to discover what had caused the sound, and was still doing so when something flew up, about ten feet from him, and the wall was struck a third time, only this time he saw what had caused the sound. Or, at least, thought he had.

It had been a blur, moving fast, but it had looked nothing like so much as an arrow. Only, that was impossible. Unless…

A feeling of trepidation growing in his gut, the wanderer made sure his hold on the stone was secure then craned his neck, peering at the ground beneath him. It seemed very far away, so far that it seemed to him that should he fall he would fall forever. But that was a fleeting thought, for in another moment he noticed something that caused his breath to catch in his throat. Figures standing at the base of the gorge, dozens, hundreds of them. And at their front, bow raised with an arrow nocked to it, was a figure he recognized, and why not? After all, he had trained under him.

He would not say that Ranger had been his friend, not in the way that Soldier had, at least, for Ranger had had very little time for people, preferring instead to spend his time among the trees and valleys, rivers and mountains. Yet he thought that the man had cared for him, at least in as much as he cared for anyone.

The creature far below though, while it might have worn his face, might have, by the unknown, dreaded magic of the enemy, stolen his talents, clearly did not share Ranger's feelings, for in another moment he let the bowstring loose again. From this distance, the arrow seemed to leap from the bow, and the wanderer tensed, fully aware of Ranger's skill with the weapon. For any other bowman, the shot would have been an impossible one, but Ranger was no normal bowman, and the wanderer tensed as the missile seemed to hurtle directly toward him.

But then, perhaps struck by the breeze or simply losing momentum due to the great distance between them, the arrow flew wide, striking the rock face half a dozen feet to the wanderer's right. It didn't hit him, which was good, but the wanderer was all too aware of the fact that it was the closet yet. The man below him was judging his shots, getting closer each time, which was bad. Worse was that the wanderer noted movement among the Revenant ranks and as he watched two dozen of them started forward toward the wall.

In another moment the Revenants began to climb. The wanderer needed no more motivation than that. He turned away from the sight of the Revenants—moving surprisingly fast, with no care for self-preservation. He turned, also, away from Ranger's impostor as he began to nock another arrow.

Then he began up the mountainside once more, trading some of the caution he'd used thus far for speed, for it was not enough that he reach the packed stone before the Revenants. He had to reach it and then perform the tasks that Scholar had told him about as he climbed, to search for those parts of the packed stone which anchored the rest. Destabilize these stones which served as linchpins for the entire thing, and it would all come crashing down. Or so Scholar had told him, but that problem, at least, the wanderer put away for now.

He would deal with the stacked stone soon enough—he had to reach it first. The ache was back in his shoulders, the needling pain in his fingers where the skin on his knuckles had been rubbed raw during the climb. Whatever rhythm, whatever peace had come over the wanderer when he'd climbed before was gone now, and so he gritted his teeth as he dragged his weary body up the cliff-face.

He glanced back from time to time and saw that, despite his efforts, the Revenants were catching up to him. At least those who remained on the rockface. While their total disregard for their own safety might have allowed them to move at incredible speeds, it also meant that not all those who ventured up the cliff-face *stayed* on the cliff-face. Even as he watched, one of the Revenants reached for a handhold only to have some of the stone come loose and crumble in his hands. The creature lost its balance and a moment later fell, its hand reaching out toward him, not an indication that it was trying to hold onto its pseudo-life, but only that even as it plummeted to certain death it was reaching for him, trying to finish the command its master had given it.

The creature did not make a sound before it crashed on the chasm floor far below. The wanderer turned away, looking up above at the packed stone. He did some quick calculations—something Scholar had taken time to train him at—and decided that, at this rate, he would make it to the piled rock before the Revenants reached him, but only just. Which meant he needed to buy more time, moving fast enough to put some distance between himself and creatures who cared nothing about their own safety and were completely willing to risk death if it meant going even a fraction faster.

Not a good way to be getting on, then, but it wasn't as if he had any choice in the matter. He continued upward at dangerous speeds until, suddenly, he couldn't any longer. For looking above him, he saw that there were no handholds within reach. This had happened to him several times on his ascent and, each time, he had backtracked, moving down and then to the left or right until he found another way up the cliff face.

This time, though, he knew that there wasn't the time, not if he wanted to reach the piled rock before the Revenants caught up to him. Biting back a curse—he simply didn't have the breath to utter it just then—his arms and shoulders burning, the wanderer craned his head backward and examined the area around him. There was no hole within reach, but he did see one, perhaps two arms' lengths up. And near to it and slightly above it was another. Two handholds that he might use, then, but to do so would require giving up his current grip on the side of the mountain and leaping upward.

It was a terrible idea, but it was his only one and a quick glance down showed the wanderer that the Revenants were coming on with a will, at least those who had not yet fallen. But for each one that *did* plummet to its silent doom, more and more were coming up the mountainside, swarming it like ants. A terrible idea, terrible choice, but when a man's choices were to die horribly or *probably* die horribly...well, that was the kind of choice that made itself.

The wanderer crouched as low as his footholds on the mountainside would allow, bending his knees. Then he took a deep breath, let go of the handholds and, in the same moment, he leapt.

For an instant, he was completely free of the cliff face as he was propelled upward by the force of his jump without even so much as a finger touching the stone in front of him. A terrible sense of vertigo, of weightlessness, and a powerful certainly that he was a complete fool overcame him then, and he was sure, in that moment that he wasn't going to make it, that his hands would fall short.

As it turned out, undershooting his mark wasn't the problem. What *was* was that, in his rush and fear he had jumped harder than he'd needed to which meant two things, neither of them good. The first was that he flew past the handholds he'd spotted, carried by his momentum. The second was that he had leapt *out,* away from the cliff-face far more than he'd intended.

Had he been a normal man, he would have died then. Or, technically, he would have died a few seconds later, after his momentum had carried him beyond reach of the rock wall and he then proceeded to plummet to his death. As it was, his reactions, honed by years of training and a century of surviving where being too slow to react would ensure certain death, meant that his body reacted before his mind had fully processed the danger.

He reached out desperately, his already raw hands and fingers scraping roughly against the stone cliff face as he lunged for some nook or divot that he might grab. For a moment he was sure he wouldn't find it, that this would be the end of it all.

But just then his left hand caught on a small lip of stone. Not much, but enough to grasp and grasp he did, ignoring the pain in his fingers. He hissed in agony as the entire weight of his body jerked against his hand, and he felt as if his shoulder were being ripped out of its socket.

He didn't take time to breathe a sigh of relief, though, for his grip was already beginning to falter, so instead he cast about in search of another handhold—but saw nothing. His feet began to scrape against the wall as his fingers slipped further and then he froze as he felt something stable beneath his right foot. Glancing down, he saw that, in his panicked scrambling, his foot had alighted on a small hole that he had not noticed.

That allowed him to get a better grip with his left hand while he put the palm of his right against the cliff face, the side of his face pressed against it as well as he sought to gain control of his rapid breathing. It would have been nice to have had a moment to relax then, to appreciate just how close he'd come to death. The problem, of course, was that he did not have the time, for a glance below him showed that the Revenants were still coming on.

And so the wanderer started climbing again, moving as fast as he could. He was growing closer to the piled stone—and closer to the actual problem of how to move it—feeling that he would have ten minutes, perhaps a little more, to figure it out.

That was when he heard it.

A strange, scraping, clicking sort of sound. It was faint, faint enough that the wanderer only just made it out over the sound of his heart hammering in his chest. It was an odd sound, a sort of rasping *honk* that was impossible to ignore.

Frowning, the wanderer turned in the direction of the sound and felt his breath catch in his throat. He had been warned of the Untamed Lands by the other Eternals, warned that there were creatures within it that were unlike anything he had ever seen, *deadlier* than he had ever seen. Even the wizard had warned him of dangers and creatures that called the chasm home.

And while he could not speak to the deadliness of the creature clinging to the cliffside, the wanderer could certainly agree that it was unusual. It was like a spider, if a spider was the size of a large dog and possessed of what appeared to be a hard armored shell similar to that of a crab.

But neither of those things were what struck the wanderer as strangest. That dubious honor belonged to the creature's face. It possessed two eyes, much like a human's, but they were completely black. Its mouth was a jagged slash that formed into a sort of macabre smile, the effect of which was made worse by the serrated mandible sticking out from it, one that put the wanderer in mind of an ant.

The creature was twenty-five feet away from him, studying the wanderer with its head cocked to the side as if trying to decide what he was. The wanderer saw that it clung to the side of the mountain with widespread "feet," underneath which he could see some sort of dark ooze coming out.

The wanderer was aware of the Revenants approaching from beneath him, yet he remained still, watching the creature. It made no move toward him, but he could not help but notice that the mandibles sticking from its dagger-slash of a mouth looked sharp and strong, as if they could snap through rock without difficulty. He didn't care to contemplate what they might do to an arm or a leg.

He waited, hoping that the creature would lose interest and move away. Only, it continued to study him, its head cocked, its too-human eyes watching him with what almost appeared to be sadness. As if the wanderer had just suffered some great loss, and the creature sought to console him with its gaze.

The wanderer could not deny that he might have used some consolation just then, but he did not think he would find it from the strange creature with the giant, sharp mandibles who was studying him so intently.

Or, at least, it had been.

There was a sound from below them, and the creature, who had been so still to that point, suddenly spun with a swiftness that was shocking, to stare farther down the cliffside. The wanderer followed its gaze to see that, while he had been waiting for the creature to lose interest in him, the Revenants had not been idle.

Indeed, he was surprised by just how much those in the lead had managed to close the distance, the nearest of which was no more than fifty feet below him, staring up at him with a face that was, while considerably more mortal than the creature's, possessed none of the emotion that seemed to lurk in the creature's alien gaze.

But while the Revenant might have shown no expression, its intent was clear enough, for in his teeth was a wicked-looking knife which, judging by the bleeding cuts at either side of the Revenant's mouth—cuts of which it seemed completely oblivious—was sharp. The creature watched him as it came on, intent on fulfilling the task its master had set it.

The armored spider-like creature skittered along the cliff-face, moving with an agility and ease far greater than that of the wanderer or those chasing him. It moved to above the climbing

Revenant, cocking its head to study him curiously the way it had studied the wanderer moments ago. The Revenant, true to form, didn't let the obstacle give it pause, instead continuing forward until the creature was within reach. Then it took the knife from its teeth and swiped at the spider-like creature with a blow that appeared casual but, the wanderer knew from experience, would have considerable force behind it.

Not that it mattered, for the strike never landed. The creature skittered to the side, seeming to easily avoid the blow before coming back to cling to the mountainside over the Revenant's head once more, studying him with its doleful eyes.

But Revenants were nothing if not determined—it gave a second swipe. Again the creature skittered away again, only this time it did not go as far, apparently having judged the Revenant's reach. And then, with a casualness to match that of the Revenant, its mandible jaw shot forward with a deceptive speed. The pincers snapped shut, and the next thing the wanderer knew half of the Revenants arm was gone. The creature's mandibles gave its grisly prize a shake and the knife fell free. Then the mandibles retracted, pulling the severed hand and arm into the creature's mouth.

The Revenant, though, barely seemed to notice. Now that the creature was out of its way it had all but forgotten it, reaching up to grab the next handhold that would bring it closer to the wanderer and the cursed blade which its master sought. Or, at least, it *tried* to grab it. The thing about handholds was that, in order for them to be useful, a person had to have hands, and after the alien creature's attentions the Revenant was somewhat lacking in that department. A fact it no doubt realized a moment later as it attempted to use the nub that was all that remained of its forearm to grab the cliff-face and instead lost its balance and fell, plummeting to its silent doom far, far below.

Whatever relief the wanderer might have felt at seeing one of his hunters defeated was short lived, however, as following the Revenant's descent he saw dozens more of its kind not far behind, making their way up the mountainside.

Which was bad. What was worse, though, was that the lone, spiderlike creature finished its meal and let out a loud, trumpeting sound, almost like a child's hoot of pleasure and then it was not alone anymore. More of its kind, a dozen at least, skittered along the cliff face toward the climbing Revenants, stopping in front of them.

The wanderer, who had been taught that while sometimes caution was called for, hesitation caused more deaths in battle than any weapon ever could, took this opportunity to resume his climb up the mountain. Let the Revenants and the creatures introduce themselves, if they'd like—preferably to death.

He had business to be about, and he could only hope that the two groups kept each other busy while he went about it.

He made it half-a-dozen or so handholds up the cliff-face before he heard another trumpeting call, only this one did not sound like the happy honking of a child. Instead, it sounded like the call of an angry or frightened goose, and the wanderer paused in his ascent to glance below him.

It did not take long to discover the source of the sound. Two Revenants had surrounded one of the spiderlike creatures. Each of the Revenants held onto the wall with one hand but, with their other, they had grabbed hold of two of the creature's legs. The creature continued to let out that strange, pained honk, so incongruous with its appearance, shaking and trying to pull itself free but without success, for while the Revenants might not have been as agile as the creatures on the mountainside, they were incredibly strong.

The creature let out a terrible wail as the Revenants holding it gave savage jerks, ripping the two legs they held from the creature's body in a spray of ichor that matched, in ruddy brown color, the ooze staining the mountainside.

The creature tried to skitter away on its remaining six legs, but one of the Revenants grabbed hold, stopping it. The other, meanwhile, ripped and tore at the armored carapace covering its head until it finally ripped it free with an accompanying, pitiable wail from the creature that ended abruptly as the Revenant slammed his hand into the soft tissue that had been revealed.

The Revenant moved his hand around like a man searching for something he'd dropped in bath water, and the creature's body gave several terrible jittering shakes until it was finally still. Then the Revenant removed his hand and he and the one on the creature's other side ripped it free of the wall and tossed it away to fall to the chasm floor far below.

That was when the wanderer noticed two things. First was that, even with the creature's body being cast aside, one of its legs remained attached to the rockface, the ooze that slowly seeped from it acting like an adhesive to hold it there.

The second thing he noticed—and one which took all his attention away from the first—was another honk. But this one was far, far different from the ones which had come before it. Not a high, cheerful honk like that of a child playing nor the pained, terrified, goose-like honks the creature had let out while the Revenants had savaged it.

This sound was far deeper than the others had been, not really a honk at all so much as it was a roar of fury. A roar that seemed to shake the very cliffside, causing stone dust to shower around the wanderer who found himself gazing up at the distant ceiling of piled stone—not so distant now as it had been—holding his breath, sure that it was all about to collapse. Which, of course, was his plan, only he had no intention of being underneath it when it did, at least not if he could help it.

The piled rock trembled, and the wanderer tensed as a stone as large as his head came loose, falling past him, close enough that, had he wanted, he thought he could have reached out and touched it as it passed.

There was another honking roar then, and the stone wall shook more. It was all the wanderer could do to hold on, and he was thankful that the handholds he was currently using were deep and allowed a good grip. Some of the Revenants below him were not so lucky, losing their balance from the shaking and falling to their deaths far below.

The gorge wall continued to be shaken with tremors beneath the wanderer, which was bad, but what was worse was that, in another moment, something enormous skittered down from above. This creature looked, in appearance, much the same as the others, but where it differed dramatically was its size. While the other creatures had been of sizes ranging from a cat to a large dog, this creature was the size of a wagon, its mandibles the length of two swords extending wickedly from its mouth.

The wanderer had thought the smaller spiderlike creatures terrible enough but he realized now why their honking had reminded him of the sounds a child might make. It was because they *were* children. And here, then, was their mother or father, come at the sound of one of its brood in distress. Its giant eyes, the size of saucers, did not look sad as the one the wanderer had studied. Instead, they looked angry, filled with a fury to match the roar that had nearly shaken the wanderer loose of the mountainside.

The creature studied the wanderer for a moment before there was another high-pitched, terrified call, and it turned to regard a Revenant who was currently holding onto the cliff face and battering one of its honking young with his other hand, leaving huge dents in its carapace with each blow.

The Revenant, focused on the task of beating the spider-like creature to death, was oblivious of its parent's furious regard. At least, that was, until the giant creature rushed forward in a shocking burst of speed, its eight giant legs moving so fast that they were little more than a blur. The creature was a hundred feet away, likely more, but it covered the distance before the Revenant could strike its hapless spawn three more times.

Indeed, the Revenant was rearing back for its third strike when the creature was upon it, reaching out with one of its legs and flicking the Revenant off the cliffside the way a man might flick away a troublesome bug.

The Revenant sailed through the air, knocked free of his perch, but the giant creature was not finished. Before the Revenant had traveled more than a few feet through open space the creature caught it in its giant mandibles. With seemingly no effort at all the mandibles closed, splitting the Revenant in two halves, both of which plummeted down toward the chasm floor. Perhaps, in another time, the creature might have eaten its victim the way its child had eaten the arm and hand of the other Revenant. But based on the way it spun to the next closest Revenant, its alien eyes dancing with an all-too-human fury, the wanderer did not think it was interested in eating, not then.

It was interested in vengeance, vengeance for the spawn the Revenants had killed, vengeance for those which the Revenants were currently fighting. The creature charged toward the nearest Revenant, and the wanderer gritted his teeth as he struggled to keep his grip on the wall.

Thankfully, the giant creature's onslaught on the Revenants carried it away from the wanderer so that the trembling of the stone lessened. Knowing that time was running out, the wanderer started upward again. Dangerous, given that the stone still shook beneath his fingers, but he knew he had to take advantage of the brief reprieve from the Revenants' pursuit while he could. Either they would defeat the giant armored spider—in which case they would no doubt immediately resume chasing him—or the creature and its spawn would win, and somehow he doubted that it would listen to any explanation he might give about how he hadn't been the one to hurt its children.

Besides, he wasn't sure that was going to remain the case for much longer anyway, for several of the creature's children, those nearest him, seemed to have taken an interest in his movements and were moving forward, likely intent on a meal.

They were moving slowly at the moment, creeping toward him the way people might move slowly toward a frightened child, not wanting to scare him further.

Or the way a lion moves toward a rabbit. Quietly, stealthily also, but with very different reasons, lad. This from Soldier.

He's right, Youngest, Ranger said. *They might be inquisitive for a time, but do not doubt their motives. Animals, unlike people, are predictable. They are hungry, and you are food. Best not stick around for them to decide as much.*

All that talk of loving nature, of how pure as the driven snow it is, Tactician said. *I wonder, Ranger, do those evil little bastards change your mind?*

There is no such thing as evil in nature, Ranger answered. *Evil, good, they are human conceits and why not, for humans are the only creatures capable of either, in truth. Some might look at a storm and say that it is evil, for it knocks down houses, floods rivers, but that same storm also renews the world. Its terrible, driving rain sustains the plants which, in turn, sustain animals, including us. And the same rough winds that force people to seek shelter in their homes also carry seedlings that will be spread across the land, continuing the cycle of growth that sustains the entire world.*

Nature isn't evil, Tactician repeated. *An easy thing to say, I suppose, just so long as one of those damned monstrosities doesn't decide to eat your arm.*

They devolved into an argument then, others joining in. The wanderer considered telling them to be silent, that there were more important things to worry about at the moment than whether civilization and nature were good or bad. Things like him surviving the next five minutes. In the end, though, he said nothing, partly because he doubted they would listen even if he did but mostly because he didn't have the breath to argue. He was tired, exhausted in truth, and he needed to reach the piled rock as quickly as he could if he was going to have any hope of causing the collapse he intended before either the Revenants or the creatures interfered.

The giant creature gave another honking call somewhere below him, and while it still sounded furious, the wanderer thought he heard something else in its voice, something that sounded a lot like a sort of panic. He knew time was of the essence, but his curiosity got the better of him, and he glanced down, immediately seeing what had made the creature's call sound the way it had. The Revenants, as heedless to their own safety now as ever, had flocked toward the creature, likely determining that the only way to finish their mission and kill the wanderer was to deal with this latest arrival first.

The creature trumpeted its anger as the Revenants swarmed over it, climbing above it so that they might leap down on it. Some of them fell to their deaths. Most didn't. Soon, the giant armored spider was covered in Revenants, all of them punching and hacking at its thick carapace. The creature fought desperately, flinging them away, but it seemed that for every Revenant it knocked loose there were two to replace it.

The wanderer left them to killing each other, wishing both groups luck. Then he was climbing again, taking the handholds as quickly as he could, ignoring the burning, rubbery feel of his muscles. The great ceiling of stone loomed over him. He was close now, so close that he was suddenly overcome by the certainty that it would fall, that it had only been waiting for him to draw close so that he might see his doom. Somewhere on the mountainside below him the giant creature and its spawn continued to fight the Revenants, their battle shaking loose several small stones and showers of rock dust as he continued his ascent.

Suddenly there was a great trembling, shaking, *shifting* sound, and the wanderer froze, looking up. Above him, the packed stone began to tremble, and suddenly one stone fell loose. Falling away from that massive line of stacked stone. At a distance, it seemed small at first, little more than a pebble, but as it hurled toward him, the wanderer realized that it was far, far larger than he'd first taken it to be. As big as the giant creature fighting the Revenants below him, in fact. Which was bad. What was worse, far worse, was that he was directly in its path.

In seconds he would be crushed like a bug beneath a bootheel, and dead as he would be, thoroughly unable to appreciate the irony with giant insects crawling along the mountain a short distance below him. Left with no choice, the wanderer braced himself on the footholds he was currently using and leapt to the side as far as he could, desperately scanning the mountainside for somewhere he might hold on as he did.

He saw one at the last moment and just managed to catch it with his right hand, finding a small divot for his foot as well. No sooner had he managed this than a falling rock struck him in the arm. Not the giant stone he'd leapt to avoid—evidence of this could be found in the fact that his arm was still attached—but one large enough that he cried out as it hit, his forearm, where it had struck him, immediately going numb.

The wanderer hissed in pain, glancing at his left arm where it hung limp and saw a knot there, an ugly bruise already beginning to form. He tried to flex feeling back into his fingers and hissed again as the effort produced no more result than a wave of sickening pain and dizziness. For a moment, it was all he could do to hold on as pain lanced up his arm.

When the pain had subsided from an all-consuming storm of agony to a not-quite-all-consuming storm of agony the wanderer craned his neck downward and saw that the giant boulder had hit the chasm floor far, far below and exploded. Among the wreckage he could just make out the forms of several Revenants whose pseudo-lives had been brought to an abrupt end by the tons of falling stone, though nowhere near enough as far as the wanderer was concerned, for there were plenty more where they came from, still swarming over the beleaguered giant creature as it and its offspring continued the battle.

The wanderer left them to it, starting his ascent once more, though moving far slower than he had. For the moment, his left arm was all but useless, and anytime he tried to put any amount of weight on it he was overcome with terrible, sickening pain, and so he was forced to climb one handed, a task that made each transfer from one handhold to the next like a magic trick performed by an amateur magician—with far too great a chance of failure, so far as he was concerned.

But then, it wasn't as if he had a choice, so he continued to climb, hissing and gritting and cursing with each grueling foot that he traveled further up the mountainside. It was one of the hardest things he'd ever done in his life, a test of his strength, his will that he would have failed, had he not led the life that he had.

But the last century, while it had stolen much from him, such as his hope and his joy, had not stolen his will. Indeed, it had left little else, stripping the rest away like a man whittling away the excess of the wood upon which he worked. Even still, he thought he might have failed, for will without hope is a fickle thing. Yet meeting Dekker and his family, speaking with Felden Ruitt, with Clint and the others, had restored his hope to him, and so while his will drove him upward, toward the great stone ceiling, it was his hope that made him believe he would reach it.

Which, in an interminable amount of time, one that he could judge not by minutes but only by degrees of suffering, the way a man running a great distance might, he did. Or, at least, nearly so. Glancing up the wanderer saw that the piled stone was no more than twenty feet above him.

He might have grinned then, for a part of him—a very large part—had not thought that he would ever make it. The truth, though, was that his left arm still pained him terribly, and he was using every bit of his flagging strength to keep himself from falling off the cliffside. He barely had the energy to breathe, much less smile.

Well done, Youngest, Scholar said in his mind, the ghosts having been silent for some time—likely realizing that to distract him would have risked his death and, of course, banishing themselves to an eternity of existence in the massive chasm. *Now for the hard part,* the old, wizened voice finished.

The wanderer blinked at that, finding enough energy to croak a curse.

Now, now, Youngest, this was your idea after all, Scholar said.

That was true, but the wanderer still thought it best that Scholar was only a ghost in an amulet and not a corporeal presence near him, for he thought it likely that, had he been, the wanderer would have left go of the mountainside and strangled him. Since that was not a possibility, however, he did the only thing he could do—he climbed.

It couldn't have taken him more than a few minutes to reach the packed stone, but it felt as if it were an eternity.

Eventually, though, he managed to work his way to where he hung on the stone wall beside the tightly-packed rock. The wanderer stared at it, taking in the enormity of it, and began to think that he had been a fool. How could one man hope to move so much stone? Stone that looked as if it had set there for centuries and would sit there for centuries more. Uncountable tons of rock. A man might as well try to move a mountain.

Thankfully, the ghosts were with him, and so he did not have to count on his own expertise—or complete lack thereof. "Scholar?" he croaked, his mouth dry from exertion and stone dust. "What now?"

Ah, that is simple, the ghost said. *Bounce on it.*

The wanderer frowned. "What?"

Forgive me, just a joke, the ghost said, *in order to lighten the mood.*

The wanderer thought that, given the circumstances, he couldn't have been a poorer audience for a joke, but he supposed the one benefit of not really being alive, like Scholar and the other ghosts, was that you couldn't really die, a fact that likely took some of the ghost's stress away. "Hilarious," he managed, thinking he could give the ghost a real piece of his mind later, assuming he lived that long.

Very well, the ghost said, sounding disappointed, *I see you're not in the mood. Well, in that case, we must closely examine the mass—there will be weaknesses within it, ones that we might exploit to cause it to fall in sections. Should we find the correct flaw to target it should cause a domino effect that may send the entire mass crashing down.*

Might. Should. May. They were words that engendered little confidence in the wanderer, but he saw no other way, so he nodded. "How long will it take?"

It...is not an easy thing at which one might guess, Scholar replied slowly.

"Try," the wanderer said.

Not so very long, Scholar said. *A few hours, perhaps. No more than a day, certainly.*

Scornful laughter from Tactician at that. *A few hours? A day? Why not make it a week? A month?*

Look here, Scholar began. *To be thorou—*

No, you look here, you daft fool, Tactician interrupted, *he'll be dead in hours. Surely there's got to be a better way than that.*

Oh? Scholar asked archly, an arrogance to his voice. *And tell me, Tactician, what ideas do you have?*

My idea, he said after a hesitation, *was not to climb up the side of damned gorge in the first place! If Youngest had listened to me he wouldn't even be here!*

Yes, Soldier said, *and all those villagers would be dead.*

They're going to be dead soon enough anyway! Tactician countered. *Unless that creature taking Ranger's place intends to sit and wait for a day or so while Youngest plays with some rocks and somehow I doubt that.*

Perhaps, but at least he tried.

What of you, Alchemist? Leader asked. *Any ideas?*

If you mean are there mixtures that might cause an explosion capable of causing all the rocks to fall, absolutely, a young, energetic woman's voice answered.

Great, Leader began, *then—*

The problem, Alchemist went on, *is that the necessary ingredients aren't going to be found simply hanging from the side of a mountain.*

The ghosts started to speak then, each of them putting forth ideas, including Shaman, but each idea, the wanderer knew, would simply take too much time, time he did not have. Time the *villagers* did not have.

They were still engaged in trying to find some solution when there was a loud, trumpeting sound that was somehow a mixture of anger, pain, and exhaustion. The wanderer might not have let himself be distracted by it—after all, he'd heard quite a few similar calls while the creature and the Revenants had fought, except for one thing. This call did not sound as if it came from below him.

He turned, his gaze traveling in the direction from which the sound had come and saw that the giant armored spider was a hundred or so feet away from him at roughly the same height as he and the rock shelf was. The distance might have been comforting except for the fact that the wanderer had seen the creature move and was well aware of how quickly it could close the distance between itself and the object it wished to attack, a fact the split-in-half Revenant might have attested to were he still alive to attest to anything.

The wanderer glanced down and saw that the nearer part of the cliff face was clear of the Revenants with which the creature had done battle, though there were more, dozens of them, making their way up the mountainside. They were not moving particularly fast, but they were coming. A problem, then, but a second trumpet from the creature reminded the wanderer—not that he needed it—that the Revenants were not the most pressing issue he faced.

He looked back at the creature. It had defeated the Revenants it had fought, but the creature had not walked away unscathed. It'd had eight legs before, but somehow during its fight with the Revenants one of its limbs had been cut in half and was slowly dripping ooze. A second leg, on the other side, was missing entirely. Its armored carapace was battered and cracked in at least a dozen places, also slowly oozing a thick substance from it. The worst injury the creature had taken, though, was neither of these. Instead, it was that where it'd had two eyes before, now it was only one. Where one had been there was now a shattered ruin that oozed a viscous greenish liquid from it.

The creature was wounded, then, perhaps even dying, but the wanderer needed only to glance at its remaining eye—an eye filled with an insane rage and hate—to see that it was not ready to retreat and lick it wounds quite yet. The creature's offspring gathered around it, more and more by the moment, and the wanderer watched with a mixture of disgust and fascination as some began to crawl along the creature, pressing their ooze-covered appendages against the cracks and dents in its carapace.

They're healing it, Healer said with an amazement that the wanderer found difficult to share, given the circumstances.

He didn't dare move for fear that he would provoke the creature, barely dared even to breathe. Instead he only continued to hang on the wall, doing his best to ignore the complaints of his aching arms and calves, watching it watch him. As he did, he thought of how the mountainside trembled beneath the creature's movements, and a thought occurred to him. A dangerous, likely suicidal thought.

"I have an idea," he muttered as he and the creature studied each other across the intervening space, as dozens, what must have been hundreds of its offspring continued to appear on the mountainside around it, crawling up from hidden crevices and cracks in the wall.

*What do you—*Tactician paused. *Please, Youngest, tell me you're not so big a fool as that.*

"I think you're grossly underestimating me," the wanderer said as he continued to study the distant creature, noting that a few of its offspring were scurrying toward him. Not moving as fast as they were capable of, but not showing the same reticence that they had up to that point, either.

The wanderer shot a quick glance behind him at the long line of packed rock that began about ten feet to the side and a few feet above him.

It's impossible, Tactician said. *If you were looking for a way to commit suicide, Youngest, you might have said as much. There are far easier ways for a man to kill himself than this. Berserker's method of chopping himself to pieces with that great axe of his comes to mind.*

Ain't often I find myself in agreement with him, lad, Soldier said. *But the nobleman's right. That giant spider's lookin' the worse for wear, I'll grant you that, but that damned mandible still looks sharp enough. Better to run, to leave it. Maybe that fella, Dekker, has managed to get the rock blocking the pass clear—he seems capable enough.*

"And if he hasn't?" the wanderer asked quietly as he watched the nearest of the dog-sized armored spiders crawling closer along the mountainside.

A hesitation, one that was long enough for him to know that Soldier knew the truth as well as he did. *You and the villagers could...could hold them off, maybe. It wouldn't be long, I'm sure, until the path was clear, and—*

"It wouldn't take long," the wanderer said, thinking of how poorly the Perishables had fared the last time they'd encountered the Revenants. It was not their fault, of course. Even trained troops would not have stood long against such creatures, and the Perishables had largely consisted of farmers and clerks, most of which had never raised a weapon in anger. "Besides," he went on, "even if the path *is* clear, with them this close they cannot help but catch up to us." He shook his head slowly. "No. This is not the best way—it is the only way."

Tactician hissed in frustration. *Even if you do somehow manage to bait the damned thing, and even if, by some miracle, you manage not to get split in half like that witless Revenant, you don't know if the creature possesses the necessary mass to cause the rockfall you're looking for.*

Perhaps not, but then it is possible, Leader said before the wanderer could speak, and he was shocked to hear the ghost coming in on his side, likely realizing that his mind was set. *Scholar? What do you think?*

The wizened ghost made a contemplative sound. *The creature is large, but there is no way of knowing specifically how much weight it possesses. Considering their agility while clinging to the side of the rockface, I would think that they would not be terribly heavy but then that might not necessarily be true. After all, the viscous substance which their appendages seem to secrete is surprisingly powerful. I wonder—*

So you don't know, Tactician snapped. *What he means is he doesn't know.*

I...I cannot be sure, Scholar admitted, clearly reluctantly. *I...I am afraid to say that there is no way to know for sure whether it will work or not.*

"Oh, that's not quite true," the wanderer said quietly. "There is one way."

And if the creature does not possess the mass to make the rock fall? Leader asked.

"Then the rock will not fall, and likely I will be eaten," the wanderer said.

And if you succeed and the rock does *begin to fall,* Leader said, *how then will you escape?*

"I don't know," the wanderer answered honestly. "Now quiet, please," he said.

The ghosts complied for once, likely all too aware that, should the wanderer fall here, they'd spend the rest of eternity—or at least the time it took Oracle's spell to fade—trapped at the bottom of a ravine. At best, the amulet in which they resided would be buried under tons of rubble and, at worst, it would be taken by the enemy. The wanderer did not know if the ghosts could be hurt, but he thought that, if anyone might discover a way to do so, it was the enemy, for they were nothing if not versed in cruelty and the causing of pain.

The closest of the spider-like creatures was only feet away now. The wanderer watched as it drew closer, slowing now, its too-human eyes studying him, its head cocked to the side. With its doleful gaze, it almost looked innocent, like a small puppy investigating a new toy, but the wanderer did not let himself be fooled, for he had marked well what the creatures' mandibles had done to the Revenants during their battle, slicing through flesh and bone as easily as a blade.

The creature approached warily, coming within reach, its ant-like mandible slowly opening and closing. An innocuous gesture, the wanderer thought, or its equivalent of licking its lips? The wanderer, though, while he was aware of the creature, was also aware of the giant parent, as well as the now hundreds of spawn, further away on the cliffside, all of them watching him with their human eyes.

Curious or, more likely, he thought, waiting to decide if he was going to act out or be a good meal and wait patiently for the small creature to devour him.

As if the thought had been a cue, the creature suddenly lunged forward, its mandible snapping open and closed again. The wanderer had been waiting for just such an attack. He kicked off the rock wall, swinging himself away from the creature. But he had underestimated its speed, and while the ant-like mandible did not manage to get a complete hold on his arm, he hissed as the dagger-sharp ends of it traced a shallow cut across his forearm before his swing carried him out of reach.

Before his swing carried him back to the creature whose mandibles were snapping shut hungrily now, the wanderer drew his blade from where it was secure at his back. A moment later his swing carried him to the creature once more, and the wanderer took advantage of his sword's greater reach, swinging it at the creature's eight armored legs. His blade was sharp—he kept it so—yet he was shocked by the amount of resistance the armored carapace covering the creature's legs provided, so much that he was only able to cut through four of the creature's appendages before the blade became stuck halfway through the fifth.

The creature let out an agonized honk and, its remaining legs no longer able to support it along the mountainside, it came free. Which would have been a good thing—certainly it had been what the wanderer had been trying for—only, his sword was still stuck halfway into one of its legs. The creature came free, falling until its weight gave a savage jerk at the wanderer's shoulder, and even though he'd tensed in preparation, he was shocked by just how heavy the thing was.

So heavy that he was very nearly pulled free of the stone wall himself and only just managed to hold on with his now only slightly-numb left hand. The creature, wounded and panicked, flailed about wildly, and with its weight on his sword the wanderer felt as if his shoulder was being dislocated from its socket. Growling and cursing, the wanderer gave the creature a panicked kick, then another. It felt like his foot struck a stone wall but on the third kick it came free of his blade and let out one final, trumpeting honk before it fell.

Gasping, his shoulder aching, the wanderer watched its descent for a moment until another honk, this one like nearby thunder, drew his attention back to the parent of the creature currently falling to its death. The giant creature's remaining eye danced with madness born of rage, and it started forward. Several of the creatures offspring, not expecting the abrupt motion, were knocked loose of their perches to fall to their deaths but in its fury the creature did not seem to notice.

Having seen just how quickly the creature could move the wanderer knew he had very little time. He slid his sword back into its sheath and started climbing, trying to come parallel with the stacked stone before the creature was on him.

He was still slightly below it, but nearly within reach, when another trumpet, so close it seemed to come from inside his own head, alerted him to the creature's presence. He shot a look behind him to see that it was less than ten feet away, charging at him madly, its giant mandible opening and closing, not looking like it meant to stop until it had gone through him like a hammer through glass.

There was no swinging away from this creature, for even if he did he would have been easily within reach of its deadly mandible, so the wanderer did the only thing he could think to do—he braced his feet and then, calling on as much strength as he had left, he leapt in the opposite direction of the creature. His jump carried him up and in the direction of the long line of packed stone. The wanderer hit it chest first, and the air exploded out of his lungs as he clawed desperately at the rocks, searching for purchase. Finally he managed it then, knowing that the creature would be on him in an instant, he hauled himself over the lip of packed stone so that his weight was completely on it.

He thought for sure that it would fall, the whole thing collapsing and taking him with it, but it appeared that it would take more than that to cause the rocks to crumble, a fact that at once relieved and disappointed him.

He'd barely had the thought when the creature slammed into the rock shelf in an effort to get at him. The tightly-packed stone beneath the wanderer's feet gave a terrible shake, and the wanderer lurched as the ground seemed to come alive beneath him. He stumbled and only managed to keep his feet by catching hold of one of the gorge walls.

The creature, though, seemed undaunted by ramming headlong into the packed stone. It scurried over the top with its familiar shocking speed, rushing toward him. He was forced to jump, planting his feet on the wall and then leapt, sailing over the creature as it rushed toward him.

Or, at least, meaning to. He nearly made it, but in such things nearly was all the difference in the world. His left foot, which he hadn't been able to tuck in quickly enough as he leapt and rolled into a ball, struck the creature's back as it charged beneath him. It was a glancing blow, but given the creature's size and momentum, was enough to alter the trajectory of his leap so that his controlled flip turned, instead, into a haphazard tumble that ended with him striking the tightly-packed stone hard. He was sent into a bone-jarring roll that only ended when his back fetched up against the rock wall of the gorge.

It isn't enough, lad, Soldier said, stating the obvious as the wanderer laboriously made his way to his feet, and the creature appeared to be slightly stunned from its impact on the wall. *The stone's not giving way. You need to think of something else.*

The wanderer glanced over and saw the smaller spiderlike creatures rushing across the chasm wall, eager to help their parent, and an idea occurred to him. It was a bad idea, sure, but then people who were prone to good ideas didn't tend to find themselves on the side of a giant gorge fighting enormous armored spider-like creatures.

He gave another quick glance at the creature. It was still stunned, but he did not doubt that it would pull itself together soon enough and, when it did, would no doubt resume its attempts at trying to pull *him* apart. So the wanderer turned back to the stone wall and began to climb. His back ached where he'd struck the wall, another pain to add to the plethora plaguing him, and his breath came in ragged wheezes, but the wanderer did what he had always done—he endured.

He went up the wall as fast as he could—which wasn't very fast at all, truth be told—getting as high above the packed stone shelf as he could manage. A skittering from above him warned him, and he looked up in time to see an armored creature flying at him.

The wanderer growled a curse then flung himself to the side so that his back was against the rock wall, the only thing keeping him from falling was his left foot and left hand where they were tucked into a hand and foothold. The creature flew past him but managed, in its flailing, to catch the side of the wall with one oozing foot which was enough to stop its descent, the viscous adhesive like fluid they secreted, even from a single appendage, proving enough to halt its fall.

The wanderer marveled at this even as he drew his sword and hacked through the single leg before the creature could find purchase with its others, and it let out a squawking, pained honk as it fell to the stacked stone below.

At least, most of it. It left behind its leg, still stuck to the wall. That gave the wanderer another idea, and he reached out and pulled at the leg. It didn't want to come free, and he was forced to wiggle it back and forth before it finally, reluctantly, came loose of the wall.

No sooner had the wanderer done so, than he heard another roar from below and saw that the sire had righted itself and was now gazing up at him. He thought, in the moment it took the creature to scurry to the wall and start toward him with shocking swiftness, that it said a lot about his plan—and probably a lot about him as well—that this had been what he'd been hoping for. And likely none of what it said was good.

Still, he was already clinging to the wall high above the stone, the creature rushing toward him, as fast on the side of the gorge as a grown man would have been sprinting along the ground, and it was too late to second guess himself. Too late to do anything, in truth, except slide the severed leg of the giant creature's offspring into his belt.

He'd barely done so before the creature was on him. It came at him from the side, its giant mandible flashing forward, lightning quick, the pincers opening in preparation.

Hanging from the mountainside with his left hand, the wanderer used his right to bring his sword around, striking the mandible. He'd hoped to do some damage to the creature's primary method of attack, but while his strike did deflect the mandible from its lunge, it otherwise seemed to do no damage to the armored appendage itself. The main result, so far as the wanderer could see, was for his arm and shoulder to ache, feeling as if he'd just struck a boulder with his blade.

The creature, on the other hand, didn't seem bothered in the slightest. No sooner had the wanderer batted the mandible away than it was coming at him again. He didn't have time to bring his sword back around, at least not with enough momentum to cause the armored mandible to deviate from its path, so he did the only thing he could do and gave it a kick instead, knocking it out of its deadly path.

A jolt of pain shot up his leg followed by a tingle of numbness, but he didn't have time to think about it, for the creature wasn't finished, not yet. The mandible came a third time, flashing forward with deadly promise. The wanderer brought his blade back around, swinging it desperately. But in his haste the blow was only a glancing one, enough to knock the mandible away from his dangling legs but also enough to cause his sword to come free of his grip and fall to the stone wedged in the chasm beneath him.

The creature didn't continue the attack but instead turned to regard the blade's descent before turning back to the wanderer, its single remaining eye seeming to dance with malevolent glee, and why not? If the creature possessed any intelligence at all then it knew that the wanderer had just lost the only means he'd possessed of keeping the deadly mandible at bay, of defending himself.

It took its time then, slowly circling around him, its mandible stretching outward only to retract again, as if it were teasing him. It did a semi-circle around him, moving over his head until it was at his other side when it performed another feinting lunge with its mandible. Only, the wanderer realized, too late, that it wasn't a feint after all, not this time. Hanging from his single hand, he kicked off the wall and swung, but was too late to completely avoid the creature's lunging attack. Its pincers were unable to find purchase around his torso the way it had attempted, but one of them scraped along his side, and he cried out as a line of white hot agony traced along his flesh.

The wanderer glance down, sure that he was going to find his torso opened up by the razor-sharp pincer. But when he looked he was relieved to see that while the cut the creature had given him was long, over a foot down his side, and while it was incredibly painful, it was also shallow. If he died in the next seconds or minutes, it would not be from the cut. Which didn't say as much as it might have considering its stiff competition.

The creature might have continued the attack then and finished it, for it was all the wanderer could do to keep hold of the mountainside. It didn't, though, clearly intent on toying with him a bit longer. It circled until it was at a downward angle to his right side. Exhausted and bleeding, the wanderer watched it, waiting for what it would do even as his brain tried—and failed—to come up with some solution to his plight.

The creature watched him, too, its saucer-sized, humanlike eye seeming to twinkle with dark joy as its mandible, dripping fat red drops of his blood, slowly eased forward then retracted.

The wanderer tensed, preparing himself, trying to anticipate the creature's speed where he couldn't counter it. He failed. The creature's mandible flashed forward again, toward his leg. The wanderer pulled his legs up, bringing his knees to his chest, but not quite quickly enough, and he cried out as he suffered a cut along his right thigh.

The creature still refused to press the attack though, only watching him as fresh drops of blood, *his* blood, dripped from its armored, razor-sharp appendage. It moved along the cliff side until it was beneath him, looking up at him, blood dripping from his wounded leg and wounded side onto its armored carapace.

Another idea came to the wanderer then, perhaps the worst he'd had yet. But then it wasn't as if he had a lot of options.

Don't, Tactician said. *You'll die, you fool.*

"Maybe," the wanderer admitted through teeth clenched against the pain.

Maybe? What if that damned thing falls on top of you?

The wanderer didn't bother talking anymore though, for he knew that this was the best chance he was going to get—likely the only one. He'd climbed up here with the intention, after all, of trying to make the creature fall, hoping that its great weight would be enough to cause the packed stone to come loose and begin to tumble. True, he'd had no intention of falling with it, but then what was life if not full of surprises?

So, fully aware that Dekker and his family's life, that the lives of every villager of Alhs, rested on what happened next, the wanderer did not hesitate as he might have—as he probably should have. Instead, he drew the knife he always kept sheathed at his belt and let go of the mountainside.

He had the dark satisfaction of seeing the creature's eye widen in surprise as he plummeted toward it. It happened in an instant. So fast that while the creature's great physical speed might have been enough to avoid its fate, its mental ability to comprehend and react to what he'd done—the last thing anyone would have expected—took too long, and the wanderer's fall took him directly into it.

Which, as he'd planned, took his knife directly into its remaining eye. The wanderer struck the creature's armored carapace hard, and the breath was knocked from his lungs. Meanwhile, the creature, its lone remaining eye pierced by his blade, bellowed a terrible, earth-rattling honk. And then, in its agony, it did exactly what the wanderer had hoped it would—it let loose its grip on the wall. At which point the wanderer, who had been unsure of the plan, felt a great, heady sense of relief. One that lasted for only a moment before he realized that he was falling at least thirty feet down onto hard-packed stone, the only thing that might soften his blow a giant armored spider that, while blinded, was also intent on killing him.

They fell.

The creature lashed out with its legs and its mandibles, and the wanderer did his best not to die in those first few seconds, not to be torn apart by its flashing mandible or crushed by its flailing, armored limbs. Meanwhile, he also tried to keep track of their descent, to judge the exact moment when they would strike the packed stone.

The wanderer suffered half a dozen more minor cuts from the creature's armored carapace that only seemed to be made out of hard edges and sharp angles. Then, catching a flash of the hard packed stone rushing toward them, the wanderer braced, and the instant they struck he leapt, pushing off the creature's armored body with both legs.

Several things happened at once then. There was a great *crash* as the creature's incredibly heavy body struck the wedged stone, followed by a great, painful crash as the wanderer's own body struck it. He hit the ground in a roll in an effort to absorb most of the shock, tumbling across the stone shelf for nearly a dozen feet, each jarring, rattling bump across the jagged rock giving him a fresh scrape or bruise.

By the time he came to a stop, his body was a mass of aches and pains, cuts and bruises, so many that it was nearly impossible to separate one from the other or decide just how badly he was wounded. Certainly there was plenty of blood, but he had no time to delve further, for the shifting, grating noises all around him alerted him that if he hadn't already suffered a wound that would prove fatal he soon would, if he tarried.

He stumbled to his feet, a task made more difficult by the fact that the ground was shaking and trembling beneath him as if it were some great beast coming awake. A particularly vicious heave threatened to steal his balance, and he caught himself on the rock wall of the gorge noting, as he did, that the pinky of his left hand was bent at an unnatural angle. As if waiting for him to notice it, his finger suddenly hurt terribly, its agonized voice rising above the tumultuous tempest of pain roaring inside him.

He did his best to ignore it—after all, if a broken finger was the worst thing he got out of this he'd count himself lucky. But then...he didn't think it would be. He turned quickly, glancing at where he and the armored spider had fallen, half-expecting the creature to be rushing toward him. After all, over the increasingly loud thunder of the rocks shaking and trembling he doubted if he'd have heard its approach.

But as his eyes settled on the spot where they'd fallen, he saw that this worry, at least, was not one he needed to entertain. The creature, already wounded, had hit the packed rock hard, and he saw several of its armored legs lying scattered about it, broken off during the fall. The creature moved weakly, a sort of slow-motion thrashing. Even as he watched its struggles began to slow as the life faded from it.

But while the giant creature might be done for, its offspring were still very much alive. The creatures appeared from behind it, swarming over their sire's body. Some, the wanderer saw with a certain degree of sick fascination, began to eat it.

Damned monsters, Tactician thought.

Nature does not waste, Ranger said.

The wanderer didn't care much about the constant, ongoing argument between the two, one that had been decades old even when they'd been alive. What he *did* care about though was that while some few of the creatures stopped and began to feast on their late sire, others swarmed toward him, their dewy, humanlike eyes fixed on him as they rushed forward, their intent clear enough by the eager opening and closing of their mandibles.

The wanderer turned and started in the opposite direction in a sort of shuffling, limping run, his left hand trailing along the gorge wall the only thing managing to keep him upright.

He tripped several times, falling to his knees and adding fresh bruises to the assortment of aches and pains dotting his entire body, and each time it was harder and harder to rise.

He had only just managed to climb his way to his feet once more when suddenly the sound of rocks shifting beneath him changed from a distant thunder, like the warning sounds of an approaching storm, to the storm itself, a great, final heaving, scraping *shift*.

The wanderer glanced behind him and his fears were confirmed as he saw that, at the other end of the packed rock, the "domino" effect that Scholar had spoken of had begun. The tightly-packed rock had begun to fall, the bridge it formed between the gorge collapsing on itself in a wave, one that was quickly approaching him. Even as he watched, that wave of destruction overtook the armored spiders at the back of those rushing toward him, and they vanished in tons of falling rock.

The wanderer hissed and started away in his limping, dragging run again, forcing his exhausted, battered body forward.

The roar of the falling rock grew louder and louder, so loud that there seemed as if there was nothing else in all the world except the sound of its fall, as if the giant stone walls on either side were falling too, as if the entire world were collapsing on itself.

The wanderer didn't look back, focusing all his energy on moving forward, on keeping his feet on the shaking, rumbling ground beneath him, the rocks seeming intent on throwing him and making him fall. A fall from which he was confident he would never rise.

Finally, though, as the ground beneath him bucked and heaved, and it was all he could do to stand on the stones that rippled beneath him like water, he *did* look back.

And immediately regretted it.

The falling stones had continued, the wave approaching at an incredible pace, one that would overtake him in seconds.

It's useless, Youngest, Tactician said, his voice grim, resigned. *You are not fast enough.*

The wanderer knew that the ghost was right, and he racked his brains for some means of escape. It came to him then, and the cursed blade seemed to thrum on his back. "Not alone, perhaps," he grated, hacking and coughing out a gobbet of blood.

You cannot mean to use the enemy's weapon, not again, Healer said. *It wounds in a way you do not understand, Youngest, cannot, understand—*

"Perhaps not," he said, reaching for it, "but I understand being crushed by tons of rock well enough."

Then you trade one doom for another, this from Oracle, her voice resigned, a desperate note to it.

The wanderer, though, said nothing, for he was out of time. He reached for the blade. It almost seemed to him that it leapt from the scabbard into his hand. No sooner had his fingers wrapped around its hilt than an alien, fey energy rushed through him. He felt stronger, faster, but at the same time his skin felt feverish hot, sickly, and it seemed to him that darkness itself spread inside him.

He almost thought he heard a pleased sort of sound, though whether it might have come from the blade, a weapon of potent magics even Oracle had only guessed at, or from some dark, hidden part of himself, he did not know. Was not sure that he wanted to know.

There was no time to ponder it in any case, for the avalanche of rock was approaching. In moments, it would be on him, and he, like the dozens of armored offspring of the giant spider, would be sent plummeting to his doom, his remains to be buried under uncountable tons of stone.

He ran.

It was not the shuffling, awkward, pained run of a wounded man now, though. With the cursed blade's fey energy filling him, the wanderer ran faster than he could ever remember running. Yet despite his great speed, the wave of falling rock was faster still, and it caught him in moments.

Yet it was not speed only that the cursed blade's dark magic imbued him with. It was strength and agility too. And so, as the rocks began to fall, the wanderer did not fall with them. Instead, he used his newfound reaction time and grace to leap from falling rock to falling rock like a child skipping their way across a stream by leaping from one stepping stone to the next.

He continued this, the roar of the falling rock reverberating inside his head, until he went to leap only to see that there was no rock to leap *to*, at least not one within reach. So instead he jumped to the side, planting his feet on the wall of the gorge itself before crouching and, in an instant, using all his newfound strength to explode off the stone, propelling himself toward a falling piece of rock the size of a small house.

The boulder was spinning slowly as it descended, and the wanderer was forced to half-run, half-climb up its surface until he reached the top. Then he leapt to another piece of rock, and another. And on and on it went, the wanderer so focused on his task that he did not realize he'd reached the end of the line of packed stone until he leapt high into the sky and saw, beneath him, nothing save for the chasm floor far, far below him, a promise of his waiting doom, a doom which even the strength and vitality given him by the cursed blade would not protect him from.

Before he had completely lost the momentum his leap had given him, before his jump turned into a fall, the wanderer spun in midair, drawing the armored leg of the spiderling he'd tucked into his belt and slamming the oozing end of the appendage into the gorge wall.

He was not sure if it would work, was uncertain if the adhesive properties of the ooze would persist long after the leg was severed from the creature's body. Nor was he sure that the secreted ooze would be strong enough to stop his rapid descent even if it did.

He was somewhat surprised, then, when his downward plunge turned into a sudden, abrupt halt, one so jarring that he cried out as he felt as if the tendons in his shoulder ripped and tore even through the feeling of invincibility given to him by the cursed blade.

He hung there as the roar of the collapsing stone filled his mind, vibrating the mountainside around him, the sound so loud, so all-consuming that it felt as if he were being shaken apart.

Eventually, the deafening roar of falling rock ended and stone dust rose in a great cloud, obscuring the world from view, and the wanderer hung there, his breath rasping in his lungs. As he did, a voice spoke in his mind.

It is done, the voice hissed. At first, the wanderer thought it was one of the ghosts, but he knew their voices as well as he knew his own and he did not recognize this one.

The wanderer frowned. The voice did not belong to the ghosts—he was sure of it.

What is it, Youngest? Leader asked. *Why do you hesitate?*

It is the weapon, the doom, this from Oracle. *It works at him, even now. Sheathe it, Youngest. Quickly, lest it overtake you.*

Warily, he lifted the cursed blade and began to slide it back into its sheathe.

They lie, the voice said. A deep voice, one that somehow made him think of caves hidden far beneath the earth, caverns in which no mortal man had ever trod, caverns so deep that they had never felt the touch of the light and knew only darkness. *It is not doom, Youngest of the Eternals, once known as Gabriel. It is power—power that I promise, and you need only—*

The wanderer slammed the sword back into its scabbard and the voice cut off. Someone watching might have thought he did so with more force than was necessary, but they would have been wrong. He'd *needed* to do it. He knew well the dangers of the blade—after all, it was why his life's mission had been to keep it from the enemy, and while he had not thought that it might speak to him, as it had, that the magic within it would take such a shape, still he knew that the voice did not change that danger. In fact, he thought it made the danger all the greater, for while he knew well the dangers of the cursed blade, part of him had *wanted* to listen to that voice, to hear what it might say.

Part of him had been *drawn* to it, the way, he thought, some insects were drawn to the flames, and never mind that reaching the target of their desire ensured their own destruction. It was not only insects, after all, that acted so—men were little better. Worse, perhaps.

Still, he pushed the unsettled feeling aside. He was alive, against all odds. Which was good. Unexpected but good. It would have been easy to have fallen down, carried to his doom among the tumbling stones, but he had managed to avoid that. It was good, but it also meant that he had a lot of mountainside to climb down and, with the cursed blade in its sheath once more, the many aches and pains he'd sustained over the last hours came back full force, as if they had been biding their time, waiting impatiently for him to put it away.

The effect was incredibly powerful, sweeping over him in a great wave, one that was very nearly strong enough to send him hurtling from the mountainside. Instead, he gritted his teeth and, blind with agony, clutched at the mountainside with his free hand, his other still clinging to the armored leg attached to the chasm wall.

He didn't know how long he hung there, his eyes squeezed shut as he waited for the worst of the agony to subside. Eventually, though, the pain lessened to a degree that made it at least bearable, if only just, and the wanderer opened his eyes again to find—unsurprisingly but plenty depressingly—that the chasm floor was just as far below him as he remembered it being.

Then, his body trembling with a mixture of pain, exhaustion, and overwork, the wanderer did the only thing he could do—he began his descent.

CHAPTER SIX

It felt as if he climbed forever, as if he had died after all, somewhere along the chasm wall and had been banished to a purgatory in which he would spend eternity grasping for one handhold then another, growing a little more exhausted with each minute, each hour.

It was a ridiculous thought, but one that grew harder to ignore as he continued to climb and never felt as if the chasm floor drew any closer until, eventually, he began to think that maybe he hadn't died on the gorge wall after all. Perhaps he had died long before that, and everything that had transpired since, all the many travails and trials that he had gone through, all the pains, emotional and physical, that he had suffered, had been no more than part of the punishment—likely earned—that he would be forced to endure in the afterlife.

But despite his growing certainty that he would spend the rest of eternity on the chasm wall, in time he reached the bottom of the gorge. He'd stopped checking his progress an hour ago, for each time he had only been reminded of how far he had left to go, a reminder that had seemed to steal the strength from his limbs and the will from his mind.

Instead, he had focused only on moving a little farther down at a time, taking one halting, careful step after the other as his feet and hands quested for a new divot or small outcrop in the stone that might serve as a means of him continuing his interminable climb.

He was so engaged in the effort, that and nothing else, that when his foot touched something beneath him, he jerked it back, confident that one of the armored spider creatures—that he hadn't seen since he'd escaped the tumbling rock—had come upon him from below and was preparing to do to his leg what he had seen its kin do to the Revenant's arm what felt like a lifetime ago.

He spun, preparing to draw his blade in what, considering his exhaustion, would likely be a vain effort to defend himself and was shocked to see that what he had felt had not been an armored spider after all but was, instead, the ground. The ground that he had sought for the last hours, the ground that he had never thought to feel again.

The wanderer was exhausted, in body and mind, and so he stared dumbly for several seconds before it finally registered.

He'd done it.

He'd made it down the chasm.

Still, he reached his foot out tentatively, half convinced that as soon as he put his weight on it the ground would fall away, and then *he* would fall. It didn't though, and in another moment he was standing, one hand still clutching at the last handhold he'd used just in case it decided to change its mind.

He flexed his shoulders, stretched his legs, in an effort to work some of the stiffness out, then turned to regard the path behind him. Not that there *was* a path anymore. The ceiling of packed rock had seen to that, as he'd hoped it would. Now, the enormity of stone that had been trapped halfway up the gorge was at its bottom, stacked twenty feet high, at least. The wanderer thought that the hard-packed stone should prove a hindrance even to Ranger and his Revenants. He caught sight of a metallic shimmer at the edge of the rock and moved forward.

He picked up several of the rocks there, tossing them out of the way to reveal his sword. An exhausted smile came to the wanderer's face, for he had thought the weapon lost, and it had served him well for a very long time. He grabbed the blade, wiping it on his trousers before sheathing it.

That done, he glanced back at the fallen rock, thinking. He might have climbed up and checked, but he simply didn't have the energy and the thought of anymore climbing sent cramping spasms through his legs and shoulders.

No, he was confident that the rock would block the way for several hundred feet, what had been the length of the hard-packed stone. Confident enough that he didn't think he needed to do anymore climbing.

Not that he was capable of anymore just then anyway. He turned back to the trail. Veikr would be waiting somewhere up ahead, he knew, at a safe distance. And, beyond him, Dekker and his family, along with the Perishables and the villagers of Alhs. They were waiting and, for once, the news he would bring them would be good.

Well done, Youngest, Leader said with a mixture of pride and reluctance. *I admit that I did not think it was possible, but you succeeded. The way is blocked, and you have bought your villagers time.*

Yes, but at what cost? Oracle asked quietly, not sounding scornful or angry, only sad. Worried. *The cursed blade is not something to be trifled with, Youngest. Its magic is ancient, its power timeless. I do not know how the enemy harnessed it, but what I do know is that its magic presents a danger to everyone, even—perhaps particularly—he who wields it. It is like some great, sleeping beast, one which you have woken. It is awake, and its eyes are trained on you. You feel it, don't you? Hear it?*

"I'm fine," the wanderer said quickly, perhaps too quickly, eager to convince them that it was the truth. Eager to convince himself. For there was something, a sort of strange tickling at his mind. He found that his fingers were flexing, the way they sometimes did before a fight, and that his lip was pulled back from his teeth in a silent snarl.

He gave himself a shake. "I'm fine," he said again.

We all are, Youngest, Tactician said carefully. *Until we're not.*

You did what you had to do, lad., Soldier said. *Oracle's right, the blade's dangerous, but then any blade is to a man who wields it carelessly. You did well—take the win.*

The wanderer gave a smile he didn't feel, for that tickling was still there, a sort of scrabbling against his mind, one that somehow reminded him of the sound of skittering in the dark of some deep, unknown cave. He gave his head another shake. "Tha—" He cut off at a sound from behind him, back in the direction of the blocked path.

His fear was that he would see one of the Revenants, somehow having overtaken the barrier of stone. It wasn't, yet what it was gave him little relief. It was one of the dog-sized armored spiders, perched atop the rock barrier and staring down at him with its sad, human eyes.

The wanderer frowned. All the creatures he'd seen had been sent plummeting to the bottom of the gorge, but as was always the case with bugs, it seemed that there were more. At least one, anyway, and...that thought came to an abrupt halt as he saw several more skitter atop the pile beside their companion, all of them studying him.

The wanderer's frown deepened, and suddenly the skittering seemed to be coming from everywhere as more of the creatures climbed down either side of the rock gorge around him onto the pile. Dozens more. Plenty enough to get the job done and then some, if he tried to fight them, though the truth was he didn't have much more fight left in him just then.

So instead, the wanderer continued to watch the creatures as he took a step back. They remained still, only watching, so he took another. Then another. On the third, they all skittered forward then stopped, as if meaning to maintain the distance between them.

He took another step and, this time, they skittered closer, closing the space of two steps, at least.

He frowned as they continued to study him. They were toying with him. Like a kitten who has caught a mouse in its paws and, thrilled at the sudden fun to be had, means to stretch out the encounter as long as possible. A fun enough game, perhaps, if you're the cat, but somehow the wanderer doubted that the mouse would agree. Not that it was ever able to, of course, for the game always ended the same way, and the mouse was never there for it.

There were too many to fight, even if he'd been in perfect condition, and he was far from that, so the wanderer backed up another step, then another. The creatures followed, coming a little closer each time.

At their current rate, they would be on him in a few minutes, and while the wanderer's mentors and teachers had never accused him of having too much imagination, it didn't take a whole lot to guess at what would happen then. The wanderer drew his blade as he continued to back down the path. He doubted it would help much if they caught him, but at least swinging it would give him something to do while they went to work on him with those razor-sharp pincers.

He continued to slowly shuffle backward, letting his sword hang at his side, conserving what little strength he had. After all, soon—very soon—he would need it. His gaze traveled up to the walls of the gorge on either side of him, where dozens of the creatures swarmed along the walls, all of them watching him with their sad eyes, and he decided that it was unlikely it would do much good, not anymore than the mouse's strength did it against the kitten.

Still, he intended to take as many of the damned things with him as he could. He was still thinking as much when suddenly his back fetched up against something, and he grunted in surprise, turning to see that a stone the size of a carriage had fallen and blocked the path. It must have come loose and been thrown free to roll or land here. The wanderer looked back to the creatures and saw them slowly creeping up.

Somehow, he doubted that they meant to sit back and watch as he climbed over.

This is it then, he thought. He was going to die. Not at the hands of some near-invincible creatures or their experiments but instead at the hands of giant armored spiders. Not the way he would have guessed, but then death, he knew, came upon men out of the shadows like an assassin, and rare indeed were those who saw its approach.

"Come on then," he panted, and the creatures, as if they understood, obliged, moving forward. Still slow, but not stopping now, easing toward him in a wave of razor-sharp mandibles that opened and closed in eager anticipation.

He was still standing there when he heard a familiar squeal from somewhere on the other side of the boulder. *"Veikr?"* he asked in disbelief.

The horse's answering neigh came a moment later. Veikr was waiting, and with his great speed the horse would have no problem outrunning the creatures. The wanderer only needed to make it over the boulder, and he was free. But then, that was an easier thought than it was a task. Still, the wanderer decided that some hope was better than none, and he slid his sword back into the sheath at his back. Then, doing his best to ignore the aches and pains in his muscles, the wanderer started up the boulder.

It was a simple enough task, one that would have given him little difficulty under normal circumstances, but he'd left "normal" behind somewhere at giant armored spiders, and the wanderer's entire body complained as he continued up the boulder.

He was nearing the top when he felt something on his leg and looked down to see that it was one of the creatures. The wanderer grunted in fear and disgust and gave a frantic kick. Pain shot through his shin where he struck the creature's armored carapace, but his blow sent it hurling through the air into the horde of its fellows that were coming toward him.

The wanderer turned and started back to the boulder, finishing the climb up it. Veikr waited a few feet away. Aware of the creatures coming after him, the wanderer half jumped half fell off the boulder. He hit the ground of the path hard, rolling to absorb the shock and coming to his feet. He stumbled, his exhausted legs threatening to give way beneath him, and only managed to keep his balance by catching himself on the gorge wall.

"I told you not to wait for me," he said as he limped toward Veikr.

He made his way to the horse's side and climbed up. He took the saddle like an amateur with none of his usual grace or poise, but he at least made it up. A wave of dizziness swept over him at the exertion, and he nearly fell over, but he managed to catch himself. Then, easing up into a sitting position, the wanderer glanced back to see that the creatures, apparently realizing that they were in danger of losing their meal, had started forward in earnest now, moving with surprising quickness.

"Whenever you're ready," the wanderer panted.

Veikr needed no more urging than that. The horse gave another shake of his head and spun in the direction of the villagers, starting away at a gallop.

The creatures, though, were not yet prepared to accept the loss of their plaything. Dozens skittered along behind them, while others swarmed along the walls, more appearing all the time out of the cracks and crevices of the gorge.

But whether they traveled on the ground or the walls, the armored creatures could not hope to match Veikr's speed, and so the wanderer was not overly concerned. At least, that was, until they began to leap from the walls, throwing themselves at the speeding horse and its beleaguered rider like dozens of giant ticks leaping from tree branches to land on their unsuspecting prey.

The wanderer kicked the first away with a jolt of pain that went up his entire leg. The second landed on Veikr's side, and the horse cried out as its mandible scratched it before the wanderer grabbed it by one of its spindly, armored legs and with a growl of anger and disgust threw it off.

But there were more coming all the time. Most missed their target but others were more accurate, and the wanderer pulled the sheathed blade from his back, batting the creatures away as they leapt at him and the horse.

He wasn't sure how long they suffered underneath that deadly rain of homicidal armored spiders—it might have been seconds or minutes or hours. All the wanderer knew for sure was that, by the time Veikr's far greater speed had carried them away his arms burned as if on fire from swinging his sheathed blade two-handed, and Veikr had suffered several shallow cuts along his flanks.

The wanderer continued to scan the gorge walls for anymore of the creatures, and when he was satisfied that he and Veikr were beyond them he replaced the sheathed blade at his back. Then, exhausted both inside and out, he leaned over Veikr, his friend, putting his arms on either side of the great horse's neck and allowing himself, finally, to rest.

It is no time to close your eyes to the world, Youngest, Tactician snapped. *One danger is gone, but do not think that there are not others.*

Yes, Oracle agreed, *like the cursed blade. Youngest, I fear that—*

Leave him be, Soldier said. *Can't you see he has nothing left? Can't you see that he's given everything that he has?*

The voices said nothing at that, and the wanderer took their silence as the gift that it was, closing his eyes to the world as Veikr, his friend, traveled toward the morning sun.

CHAPTER SEVEN

The wanderer came awake to the sound of Veikr's soft whinny and rose from where he'd lain with his arms wrapped around the great beast's neck. He blinked his eyes in a vain effort to rid them of the grainy, dry feeling that told him that however much sleep he'd gotten, it had not been enough, then scanned the area around them. Thankfully, he saw no more armored spiders or any pursuing Revenants.

Then, as his eyes settled to the trail in front of them, he saw, through his blurry, exhausted vision, why the horse had woken him.

Ahead of them, in the distance, he could make out the tail end of the procession of villagers. In another few minutes they arrived at the back of the group. As he drew near, the wanderer noted the villagers whispering amongst themselves, staring at him with shocked expressions. He could not hear what they said, but he could feel the weight of their gazes on him as they separated on either side of the path, opening a space between them through which Veikr walked.

In many ways the wanderer felt more uncomfortable beneath those gazes—the meanings of which he could not imagine—than he had facing the Revenants and the armored spiders. Say this for the Revenants—their intentions were never hard to guess at, for they only ever wanted one thing. The same thing.

Beneath the weight of the villagers' gazes it felt as if it took an eternity to reach the front of the line where Dekker, Clint, and

Sheriff Fred stood with the wizard. All of the men, save the old, robed figure, were covered in dust and sweat, as were many of the other nearby villagers. They were passing a couple of waterskins between them, drinking greedily. As the wanderer rode up, Dekker, who'd been tilting his head back and taking a long pull from a waterskin, noted the wanderer and sputtered in shock. "Son of a bitch," the big man said.

"I've been called worse," the wanderer said tiredly as he half-climbed half-fell from Veikr's saddle.

The big man handed the skin off to Clint who was grinning like a child, then started forward. Dekker had taken his shirt off during his labors, as many of the men had. The difference, though, was that the big man was twice as large as any of the others and as that mountain of muscle stomped toward the wanderer, his expression intense but unreadable beyond that, several of the nearest villagers flinched away as if afraid. The wanderer could not blame them, for he was tempted to shy away himself, only he knew the man did not mean him violence. Though one might have been fooled by the pressure of the hug as he wrapped his arms around the wanderer and pulled him from his feet, patting him on the back with blows that, from another man, might have been considered a physical attack.

"Son of a bitch," Dekker said again, as the wanderer fought for breath.

"So you've said," the wanderer managed.

"Let him go, Dek, before you kill him," came Ella's voice.

Dekker did, his sheepish grin turning to a frown as his gaze traveled over the wanderer. "Looks like somethin' already gave that a shot. Run into trouble?"

"Just a bit," the wanderer said.

The big man grunted. "We all heard a crash—loudest thing I could imagine. Figured the whole world was gettin' ready to drop on our heads. That your doin'?"

"Yes," the wanderer said.

Dekker shook his head slowly. "I'll tell ya, Ungr, you—"

"Chose not to flee after all, Eternal?"

The wanderer turned, along with Dekker and those nearby, to regard the wizard as he walked up, scowling.

"Flee?" Dekker said. "Are you out of your mi—"

"It's okay, Dekker," the wanderer said, watching the wizard.

"I cannot help but notice, Eternal," the wizard said with a frown, "that you have returned just as we are finished clearing away the stone blocking the path."

"Good timing, I suppose," the wanderer said, giving the wizard a smile that he did not return. "Anyway," he went on, "I can see from all the dust on you that you've been hard at it." The wizard's frown deepened at that, as well it might, for it was obvious to everyone present that the man was pretty much the only one whose clothes *weren't* stained with stone dust.

"Someone had to keep watch, in case those things caught up with us," the wizard growled.

"No doubt," the wanderer agreed.

"And what exactly have you been doing?"

"Slowing them down," the wanderer said.

"I see," the wizard said. "And the ichor staining your clothes and skin?" he asked. " Or do you mean to suggest that those Revenants bleed in such a way?"

"I do not," the wanderer said. "There were...others."

"Others," the wizard repeated. "And I am to assume by the ichor staining you that, when you encountered these 'others' you chose violence?" He sneered. "An Eternal indeed."

"I wouldn't say I chose it," the wanderer said. "The creatures seemed capable of that easily enough.

The wizard snorted. "So *you* say, but then you Eternals have always proved more than willing to destroy anything or anyone who becomes an inconvenience to you."

"Look here now," Clint said, "I'm not gonna stand here and—"

"It is okay, Clint," the wanderer said. "He is allowed his opinion, as are we all."

"Sure he is," Clint agreed, watching the man angrily, "and he's allowed to get a black eye for it, too. Where I come from, a fella's held accountable for the shit that comes out of his mouth."

"Funny," Dekker said, his own voice full of menace as he also eyed the wizard angrily, "I didn't know we grew up on the same street, Clint."

"Enough," the wanderer said. "We all have the same goal—" He paused as the wizard snorted again, then continued. "And it will serve none of our purposes to fight amongst ourselves. Now—"

He cut off at a woman's scream. More screams and shouts rose up behind them, and the wanderer spun to see something barreling toward him. He had only enough time to realize that it was one of the creatures from the gorge wall, no more than that, before it was on him, leaping forward, its mandible opening in preparation. His body reacted before his mind had fully caught up, stepping to the side and out of the way of the creature even as his hand went for the sword sheathed at his back.

Clint also stumbled out of the way, as did Dekker, and the wizard let out a cry that was a mixture of shock and terror as the creature flew at his face, its mandible clicking open and shut. The wanderer started forward, but Clint was in the way, and he knew, even as he did, that there was not enough time for him to reach it before the creature's mandible did to the wizard what he had seen it do to the Revenant in such gory detail.

Before it could, though, Dekker's hand shot out with a speed that the wanderer would not have credited him had he not seen the big man employ it before. Dekker caught hold of one of the creature's leg's and slammed the creature against the wall. The creature fell, stunned, but Dekker wasn't finished. Before it could regain its composure, he picked it up by its armored shell, his great muscles thrumming with the effort of lifting it. The creature's legs and mandible clicked crazily, and the big man grunted.

"Yeah, musta been Ungr here that chose violence," he growled, his muscles tensing with the effort of keeping hold of the writhing creature. "This fella here, he's just tryin' to live his life, ain't that right?" He looked at the wizard who, along with everyone else, was staring at the armored spider with pale-faced shock.

The wizard's mouth worked but it was several seconds before he managed to speak. "I-I take your point," he managed in a breathy voice. "P-please, d-do something with it."

"Do somethin'?" Dekker asked. "Like what? I mean, I'd hate to be accused of, you know, *destroying* something on account of you found it inconvenient. Maybe we could, I don't know, talk to it, you know, about our feelings, and—"

"*Dekker.*" It was Ella's voice, and the wanderer heard a warning tone in it. Dekker must have heard it as well, for he gave a nod, bearing his teeth at the wizard in what might have loosely been called a smile.

"Alright, hon," he said. "I was just jokin', that's all." The big man watched the wizard for another moment, then still holding the creature whose legs and mandible were clicking and thrashing wildly, he moved to the gorge wall.

With a great heave, Dekker slammed the creature into the gorge wall. Ichor sprayed, covering the big man's chest and arms.

"Dekker—" the wanderer began, stepping forward.

"Just a moment, Ungr," the big man said. "I'm a bit busy." Then, before the wanderer could speak, the big man lifted the creature back over one shoulder and, his entire body flexing, brought its relatively soft underside crashing into the chasm wall again, then again.

Ichor sprayed with each blow, until it coated the big man and struck several of the nearest, including the wizard, who watched with a sick sort of fascination, seemingly completely oblivious of the ichor dripping from his face.

On the fifth blow there was a distinct *crack,* similar to the sound of an egg cracking, and a terrible smell, like the giant armored spider had given off when it had been wounded, filled the air. Dekker lifted the creature again, eyeing it, then satisfied that what the hard shell covered was little more than a sickening, ichor-coated paste, he tossed it aside where it lay unmoving on the ground.

As everyone stared in shock at the creature, the big man turned to the wanderer. "Now then, Ungr, what was it you had to say?"

"I was just going to say that I could stab it."

Dekker blinked, then a moment later, tilted back his head and roared with laughter. Shirtless, his thick muscles on display, covered in ichor—the blood of his enemies, even if it wasn't exactly blood—the wanderer thought that the big man looked as if he would have been at home on some ancient field of battle, roaring his victory among the slaughter.

But then there was much more to Dekker than that, much more than some mindless creature of violence, and he showed that a moment later, giving the wanderer a wink. "Maybe next time, I can keep clean, if you learn not to bring your work home with you." He raised an eyebrow, glancing at the creature—as thoroughly dead as anything the wanderer had ever seen. "Anyway, should we go?" He glanced over at the wizard who was still staring wide-eyed at the creature's corpse. "Unless the wizard has an objection. Seem to be pretty full of those. Who knows, we wait around long enough, maybe some of this little bastard's family'll come along, and we can all appreciate nature in all its glory while they give us a good chewin', how'd that be?"

"*No*," the wizard said, the word coming out in a sound that was somewhere between a shout and a croak. He paused, taking a deep breath. "No," he said again, his voice more controlled this time but still betraying his fear and disgust, "that will not be necessary."

"You sure?" Dekker asked. "I wouldn't want us not to give nature its due."

"I'm quite sure," the wizard said.

Dekker grunted, giving a shrug and glancing at the wanderer. "Lead the way," he said.

The wanderer glanced at the wizard, expecting protest, but the man did not seem prepared to protest just then. Instead, he was once more staring at the dead creature, or at least what Dekker's attentions had left, of it which wasn't all that much.

The wanderer nodded, walking forward and pausing at Clint. "Good to see you," the Perishable's leader said. "Heard that great commotion hours back, got to thinkin' maybe you might not make it."

"Funny," the wanderer said. "I thought something similar." He gave the man another smile before moving past him to where the sheriff stood, staring at the armored spider. "Damn," the man said.

"Yes."

"Ran into one of those back when you were doin' what you were doin'?"

"One or two."

"Imagine that was a good time."

"It was a blast," the wanderer agreed.

"And the Revenants?" the sheriff asked, pulling his gaze away from the creature with obvious effort to meet the wanderer's eyes.

"Still coming," the wanderer said, "but there are quite a few tons of rock in between us and them."

The sheriff nodded. "Seems like you got a habit of riskin' your life for us," he said. "Maybe he won't say it," he went on, jerking his chin in the wizard's direction, "but I will. Thanks."

The wanderer gave the man a smile. "That's why we do it," he said.

The sheriff laughed.

Dekker and Clint, nearby, also laughed.

The wanderer laughed.

Then he passed out.

CHAPTER EIGHT

The wanderer woke to Dekker's face looming over him. There was a frown on the big man's face. "Hi," the wanderer croaked.

The frown faded as Dekker's mouth turned up into a wide grin. "Told that old hag you'd wake up," he said.

"Old hag?"

"It's my husband's foolish pet name for Clara, the herbwoman."

"Clara the witch, maybe," the big man said. "That woman'd sour spoiled milk."

The wanderer glanced over at Ella and raised an eyebrow—he felt tired, exhausted really, numb all over, and he didn't think he was capable of much more just then.

"The herbwoman of Alhs, it seems, is one of the few who is completely immune to my husband's...charms. Such as they are," Ella explained. "Anyway, I'm glad to see you awake, Ungr, though I imagine there are better ways to wake up than to my husband looming over you."

Dekker frowned, opening his mouth to speak, but the wanderer beat him to it. "Anytime I wake I find that I'm grateful."

"See there," Dekker began, but the wanderer went on as if he hadn't spoken.

"Though I admit that sometimes I am more grateful than others."

Dekker frowned at that. "For someone who could have died accordin' to the hag, you got enough energy left to be an asshole, it seems."

"I always keep some spare lying around," the wanderer said, managing a tired grin. "Just in case. But sorry...where am I?"

"Damn," Dekker said, letting out a low whistle. "Seems she wasn't just spoutin' nonsense after all when she talked about you bein' in a bad way. You're in the wagon, at the back of the procession."

The wanderer blinked, thinking back. "And the wizard?"

Dekker grinned. "Wasn't too keen on givin' up his ride, truth to tell—I don't know if you've noticed, but he ain't all that fond of you. He's up front now, just about as far away from you as he can get, I reckon."

The wanderer nodded slowly. "I see."

A few seconds passed in silence, then the big man shrugged. "Well," he said. "Now you're awake, I'd best get the old ha—"

"That won't be necessary," a voice came from somewhere beyond the wanderer's sight. "The hag is here."

Dekker winced at that, clearing his throat. "I'll be seein' you later, Ungr." He glanced away then back at the wanderer, speaking in a whisper. "Try to stay alive, eh?" he asked in a mumble. "The hag seems more like a murderer than a healer if you ask me. Murders my patience anyway."

"The hag is old, not deaf," the voice came. "Now, will you move your far-too-large body out of my way and let me do my job or not?"

Dekker glanced back at the wanderer with an expression as if to say "do you see what I have to deal with?" then gave him a pat that was surprisingly gentle before turning and leaving. The pat, more than anything else, let the wanderer know just how close it had been, and he began to think that perhaps he'd suffered worse wounds than he'd realized during his fight with the Revenants and spiders, and the subsequent part-climb part-fall down the ravine wall. Which, he supposed, shouldn't have been all that surprising—the surprising part was that he'd survived at all.

A moment later, the familiar face of Clara, the herbwoman of Alhs, appeared over him. The woman frowned at him the way one might frown at a misbehaving child. She said nothing, and the wanderer blinked, clearing his throat. "Nice to see you again," the wanderer told the scowling old woman.

The woman snorted. "Don't try to flatter me," she said. "I was no treat for the eyes in my youth, and I've long since left that behind. Though, considering how close you were to death—more dead than alive, I'd say—I imagine being able to see anything feels like a pleasure. All men are born with the talent of dying, Ungr, but it seems to me that you've made a study of it."

The wanderer winced. "If that's true, then it's a study I didn't intend."

"Didn't you?" the woman asked, raising an eyebrow. "Or did I misunderstand the situation? Because, from what I heard, you volunteered to go back toward that army chasing us to, what, exactly? Cause an avalanche?"

"Well," the wanderer said, trying a smile, "when you say it like that..."

The woman did not return the gesture, instead only shook her head wearily. "There is nothing charming about courting death, Ungr. Or, at least, if there is a charm, then it is one that is lost on me."

"I understand," the wanderer said.

"I don't mean to be rude, ma'am," Ella said, "but Ungr did what he did to keep us safe, to slow down the Revenant army. If he hadn't, they would have already caught us by now. He is a good man."

"And very nearly a dead one," the woman countered, turning. "The graveyards of the world are full of good men, Ella. Imagine, then, the frustration of one who has dedicated her life to healing, to helping the wounded, when she finds herself confronted with a man who seems to have made it *his* life's mission to get wounded as much as possible."

"That isn't fair," Ella began, "Ungr didn't go out looking to get hurt, he—"

"Leave us, if you please," Clara said softly, and Ella paused.

Dekker's wife opened her mouth as if she might say something, but the herbwoman beat her to it. "Now."

Ella tensed, then, after a moment, she gave the wanderer an apologetic look before climbing out of the wagon. The herbwoman did not speak again until she was gone, then she turned to regard the wanderer. "They care for you," she said.

"Dekker and Ella?" the wanderer said. "They are good people—the best."

"Not just them, you fool," the woman said. "Everyone—the entire village."

The wanderer frowned, thinking of the way they'd looked at him, the way they'd whispered when he returned from his battle with the Revenants and the armored spiders. "I'm not so sure about that," he said.

"Then I'm even more sure that you are a complete fool," she said. "They were all afraid while you were gone. Why, I've never seen Sheriff Fred pace so much—risk your life much more and he'll lose that belly that he's so proud of. Not that his wife'd mind, of course."

"I...he didn't say anything," the wanderer said.

"Before you passed out, you mean?" the woman said, arching an eyebrow.

The wanderer winced. "Yes."

She grunted softly. "I don't tend to suffer fools, Ungr, but I suppose that, in your case, I'll have to make an exception, won't I? Seeing as you're the only one likely to get us out of this mess. Why, I reckon if I let you die they'd all string me up and never mind the chamomile teas I make for wives for their stress or the gingko powders I mix for the husbands so they stop forgetting so much—particularly those things their wives tell them." She glanced at him knowingly. "Sometimes, I almost get the feeling that the husbands don't *want* to remember, but there's no herb that can fix that."

"String you up?" the wanderer asked surprised. "But...I'm sure you're exaggerating. I mean...there's the wizard, too. He might well have ways of getting you all out of here."

"The wizard didn't lead us through the Death Whisperers," the woman said pointedly. "Neither did he kill a giant snake or save us from those damned Accursed. It wasn't the wizard who risked his life to buy us more time. It was you, Ungr." She leaned closer. "I know it, and the villagers know it. Now, why don't you just hush and let me take a look at you—as I said, I'd rather not be the one responsible for you dying. I've seen corpses that looked more alive than you."

"Sure," the wanderer said, "but could they do this?" He held up one hand meaningfully, snapping his fingers.

She frowned. "Dekker and Clint, from what they say, you've lived for a hundred years and more, that right?"

He winced. He'd spent a hundred years hiding his true identity, an outcast, an exile on the run, and someone knowing who he was gave him a queasy feeling. "That's right," he said.

She nodded slowly, thoughtfully. "And in all that time, all that walkin' around, you never, not once, stumbled over a sense of humor?"

"Stumbled over a lot of things," the wanderer admitted. "If a sense of humor was one of them I must not have noticed."

"I mean, you would think that, in a hundred years, you would have had enough practice to at least have something with a passing resemblance to one."

"I spent a lot of time alone."

"It shows," she assured him. "Now, lie back and let me do my work."

The wanderer did as he was ordered, lying back while she saw to his wounds, applying an acrid-smelling poultice. And as he lay there, he drifted, treading the line between sleeping and waking the way a performer of a mummer's troupe might tread a tight-rope. And soon the wanderer had closed his eyes and was carried away by thoughts that were as much dream as conscious reflection.

And within those thoughts, those dreams, was Joan. With her bright red hair, and her bright red spirit, a light shining in the darkness of the world. He thought, too, of Anne. A softness to her that gave answer to all the hard, sharp edges of a man's life. Even her voice a balm for the inevitable cuts he received as he stumbled his way through it.

He thought of the Eternals, too. Most he'd had the privilege to call friend, in his time, but all of them he had learned from, listened to. They had helped him, on the mountainside, and he had not even gone so far as to thank them. He reached for the locket at his neck, meaning to open it, to speak with them, and felt a thrill of panic rush through him as he realized it wasn't there. It was a shock no less than if he had reached up to his face only to find that his nose was gone, in its place nothing but unmarked skin. Had he lost it, somewhere? In the climb down the gorge wall or, perhaps, in his wild ride with Veikr as he made his way back to the others?

Normally, he would have never allowed such a thing to happen, would have noticed the moment the amulet's familiar weight left his neck, but he had been half-delirious from pain and exhaustion, and he thought maybe it was possible. It was a terrifying thought, one that sent a cold shiver of dread up his spine. As annoying as the ghosts sometimes were, he had long since lost count of the times he had leaned on them over the years, the number of times they had helped him, saved him. It was only with their help that he had survived this long, only with their help that he had been able to keep Dekker and Ella and Sarah and all the rest *alive* this long.

He continued to paw at his neck, hoping, praying, that perhaps the amulet had fallen to the side, or he had only missed it. But it was not there. No matter how many times he checked.

"Everything alright?" Clara asked, clearly picking up on some of his stress.

"*A-an amulet,*" the wanderer croaked. "There was an amulet—"

"Ah, sure, that thing," the woman said. "I took it off while I worked—kept gettin' in the way. Now just where did I put that?" she continued, more to herself than him, as she turned away.

The wanderer waited, his breath caught in his chest, until she made a satisfied sound. "Ah, there it is," she said, and when she turned back to him she was holding the amulet. The wanderer let out the breath he'd been holding, doing his best not to snatch it out of her hands as he took the offered locket, sliding it back onto his neck.

From her face, he apparently failed. "Important, is it?"

"Yes," he said simply. "To me it is."

She nodded slowly. "As I said, I took it off while I was seein' to you. Took your pants off too, in case you care."

The wanderer knew she was joking, but the truth was that he didn't care. He had the amulet. For the moment, that was all he cared about, all he *could* care about. The herbwoman was looking at him strangely, he knew that, but for the moment he couldn't think on it. Instead, he did the only thing he could do—he opened the locket.

Hello? he thought.

There was no answer. At first, he had the thought that it must be the wrong locket, that somehow the woman had got it confused with another, but as soon as he lifted it, he realized that was not the case. He knew well the weight of the locket, knew every inch of it, for he had felt it against his skin for the last century.

He found himself thinking of the way the ghosts had acted before, of the way they had not known who the wizard was, of how disoriented and confused they had been.

Hello? he thought again, only barely aware of the herbwoman giving a grunt before going back to her work. While he waited for a reply, the wanderer's mind raced. There was no answer, and he thought of what that might mean. Were the ghosts...dying? Could ghosts die? Or was something else at work?

Are you there? he asked, trying a third time.

Youngest?

It was Leader's voice, a voice he knew well but now, like before, it sounded disoriented, confused, unsure in a way that the man had never seemed in life.

The wanderer felt his breath go out in a heavy sigh of relief. *I'm here,* he thought.

Is...are...is everything alright?

We've...been sleeping again, Oracle said, her voice sounding drowsy, muddled with sleep.

Again? This from Tactician, sounding worried.

But why? Alchemist asked. *How?*

Something is at work, Healer said slowly, thoughtfully.

What something? Charmer snapped. *Care to be a bit more specific? Are we dying? Is that it?*

What is dead cannot die, Healer said, not angrily but simply as a statement of fact.

And yet...something is happening, Scholar said.

What...what's the last thing you remember? The wanderer asked.

You fleeing from those damned things atop your mount's back is what, Tactician said.

*No...*Soldier countered thoughtfully. *No, not that. I...I remember you coming upon the villagers, remember them waiting in line for you, but...*

And me speaking to Dekker? To the wizard?

What is this talk of this damned wizard again? Tactician asked, clearly agitated.

The wanderer frowned at that. They didn't know the man. They knew Dekker and Clint, the sheriff and everyone else the wanderer had met but, for some reason, they did not know the wizard. And as he thought of that, another realization came to his mind. The first time he'd noticed any issue in the ghosts' perception was when he'd met the wizard back in that snow-blasted landscape.

Some might have called it a coincidence, but the wanderer did not. *Coincidences,* Scholar had told him again and again, *are only the method by which the ignorant attempt to excuse their ignorance.*

No, not a coincidence, but if not, then what? An idea began to form in his mind. The wizard had made no secret about the fact that he had come to the Untamed Lands to avoid the Eternals, to get as far away from them as he could. The wanderer did not know the reason for that self-imposed exile, but that it was true he did not doubt. And what methods might the man have employed to ensure that he remained undiscovered? After all, when the wanderer first met found him, the man had claimed that it should not be possible. The wanderer had assumed, at the time, that the man meant because of his isolation so deep in the Untamed Lands. But what if he'd been wrong, what if the wizard had been referring to something else? Something like a spell meant to keep the Eternals from recognizing him, one that would completely block the man from their sight or minds?

The wanderer had never demonstrated much of an aptitude for the Art, but he thought it was possible. He considered asking Oracle or Shaman, but in the end he decided against it. Perhaps later he might change his mind on that. For now, the wizard had done whatever he had in an effort to maintain his anonymity from the Eternals, and the wanderer saw no reason to steal that from him. The man might not have been the most pleasant of people, but a person who spends years, perhaps centuries, creating and maintaining a barrier—and, it seemed, likely more than one—so that those within it remained safe couldn't be all bad.

But then as he considered it further, he was no longer sure. After all, if some spell the wizard had cast, a sort of avoidance or forgetting spell, was responsible for the ghosts' confusion, for their silence, then why were they able to speak now?

It came to him a moment later, and he decided that Clara was right—he was a fool. The ghosts could speak because he was in the wagon, of course, while the wizard, by Dekker's words, was at the opposite end of the procession, as far away from the wanderer as possible. Far enough, apparently, for the effects of his spell to be minimalized.

What is it, Youngest? Oracle asked, and there was a note of what might have been almost suspicion in her voice. *What is it you're thinking?*

Nothing, he thought back, perhaps too quickly.

Do you know something of this, Youngest? Leader asked. *Something of why we sleep?*

"Nothing," the wanderer said, then snapped the locket closed.

"What's that?" the herbwoman asked. "Or is it that you speak of what my reward will surely be for stitching you back together?"

The wanderer winced. "Sorry I was...thinking."

The woman looked up from her work, raising an eyebrow. "Thinking, huh? Well, I s'pose now's as good a time to start as any. Who knows? Maybe you'll live another century."

The wanderer considered the last hundred years of his life. *I hope not,* he thought, but he only gave the woman a small smile. He had met such healers before, over the years, ones who took the wounds and sicknesses of their patients as a personal affront, and he supposed he understood that. It was, to their way of thinking, as if they were building a house for someone but before it could ever be finished, be whole, that same someone kept coming along and tearing it down.

He could tell her that he didn't mean to, but he didn't think he could do so truthfully, and so he said nothing.

After all, he had chosen the life he had long ago. Back when he had not been Youngest of the Eternals, not Ungr, or the wanderer. Back when he had been Gabriel and that only, a young man from a small village, one who, in the normal course of events, would have likely been a farmer, perhaps a town guardsman. Young Gabriel, known for being a bit brash, a bit of a dreamer—not that he had many dreams now. For the dreams he'd had—of becoming a great warrior, an Eternal—he had largely achieved, but in achieving them, had found them of little value. Like a man who covets a sack which he thinks is full of gold only to find, once he's finally acquired it, that it's empty.

Gabriel the Dreamer, the other kids and teens of the village had called him mockingly. His mother had called him the same, but she had not been mocking. She, like most mothers, had found only good in him, had loved him and his quirks. She, like most mothers, had told him that he was special, that his would be a charmed life.

And certainly, he thought that it had been, at least for a time. He'd met Anne, after all. Met her when they were kids and they had been friends. And then, when they'd grown older, they had found their love for one another. Found it so easily that they might have been forgiven for thinking such a thing easy to find and never mind that most people spent their entire lives questing for it and, in the end, settled for something less.

"Or maybe you just like to suffer," Clara said, half-teasing. "Some people do, after all."

"Maybe," the wanderer said distractedly, still lost in the memory of Anne, of the smell of her hair, the way her smile had warmed something in him, something that had long since frozen over.

They had fallen into their love so easily that the wanderer had not known, in truth, what he was giving up when he'd gone off to chase his dream of joining the illustrious rank of the Eternals. Not to help others, as he'd said at the time, but for his own glory. And in seeking his glory, he had lost his love, and he had *not* forgiven himself.

He had achieved the glory he'd sought, at least for a time— recognition above all his peers. Yet while love, he'd discovered young, was a meal that filled one up to bursting, glory and self-aggrandizement were empty fare that left one hungry, unsatisfied. And by the time he'd realized as much, it had been too late. She was gone, and he was alone.

"Ungr? Everything alright?"

The wanderer blinked, looking up at the herbwoman to find that she had paused in her ministrations and was now staring at him with an unmistakable expression of compassion.

The wanderer was just about to say that he was fine—a lie, but one he'd long since grown good at telling, even to himself—but then he felt something wet on his face. He brought his fingers up to his cheek and realized that there was a tear there. He blinked in surprise. "I'm...I'm alright," he said. He had cried over what he'd lost before, but not in a very long time. It was as if, somehow, the meeting with the Whisperer's, when they had taken the guise of his lost love in an attempt to lure him to his demise, had awakened something in him. Some wound that he had thought long since turned into a scar. He'd been wrong, though. What had covered that wound had been, it seemed, no more than a scab, and now that it had been pulled away, he found that the wound, the *hurt* beneath was just as fresh as it had ever been.

"I've seen alright, Ungr," the herbwoman said, not admonishing now but soft, gentle, and in that moment she reminded him of Healer. "I've seen it—and you ain't it."

"I'm f—"

"Fine," the woman said. "Sure you are. I've seen fine, too. When I was young—yes, such a time existed, though it might be hard to believe—I had a cousin who lost his wife to a tragic accident after only being married a year. Me and the rest of the family, we checked in on him as much as we could in the days following the tragedy. He was fine too, or so he said. And we all believed him. *Wanted* to believe him, I guess, the way people do. Tellin' ourselves the lie he was tellin' us so that we could excuse ourselves to go back to our own lives instead of worryin' over his. Sure," she went on, nodding grimly, "he was fine. Right up until he walked out of his house one day and stumbled over a cliff, fallin' to his death. Only..." She paused, leaning in. "Only that cliff, Ungr, was several hundred feet from his home and the fella that found him said that there weren't no way he'd have gone so great a distance from the cliff's end. That is, not unless he jumped. In my experience, Ungr, people are always fine. Right up until they ain't."

The wanderer opened his mouth to speak, but she held up a hand, silencing him. "You're hurtin', Ungr. That's plain enough to see for someone's been trained to see hurt and fix it where she can. But I'm no fool to think I can cure all the hurt of the world. I was once, but then the world's got a way of dispellin' such foolish notions, don't it? All I'll say is this: sometimes, what ails us'll go away on its own, given time enough. And sometimes it won't. Sometimes, the only way to heal is to dig into the wound, scrape the infection out. It hurts, hurts more'n we think we can bear—and sometimes we're right. But with some hurts, Ungr, with some wounds, there just isn't any other way. So you don't have to talk to me, but for what it's worth, I think you might ought to talk to someone."

The wanderer opened his mouth, meaning to argue, to tell her that she was wrong, but he knew it to be a lie, and she knew it too, so he only nodded. "Thanks," he said.

She shrugged, sitting back with a sigh. "Anyway, you're all patched up—as good as I can make you, given what I started with. You ought to live a while yet." She raised an eyebrow. "Just so long as you don't go fallin' off any cliffs."

"I'll do my best."

She nodded, rising. "Well. I'll leave you to your rest. But don't rest *too* long," she said. "Best to move, if you think you're up to it. Otherwise, the body gets stiff, and it'll be that much harder when you try."

The wanderer inclined his head. "I will. And...thank you," he said. "For everything."

The woman nodded again and then turned, climbing out of the wagon. She'd been gone less than five minutes when Dekker poked his head through the back of the wagon. "I talked to the old hag as she was leavin'," the big man said, his expression and voice grim. "I'm sorry to say, she seems to think there ain't no cure."

"Cure?" the wanderer asked, confused.

"Yeah," he said, nodding solemnly. "She says some folks are born ugly, that's all. Ain't nothin' she can do about it."

"*Dekker,*" came Ella's outraged voice from somewhere outside the wagon, and the big man gave an expression that was caught somewhere between a wince, as if he expected a blow, and a self-satisfied grin.

The wanderer laughed. A good, true laugh, one that went a long way to banishing the thoughts of Anne, of what he'd lost.

He started to rise, and Dekker's grin faded as he held out a hand. "Hold on there," the big man said. "Don't you think you ought to rest?"

"I've rested plenty," the wanderer said. "It's about time I got back to it."

The big man frowned. "You sure about that?"

"Hag's orders," the wanderer said, giving him a small smile.

"Alright," Dekker said with obvious reluctance, eyeing the wanderer as if he was ready to leap forward and catch him, as if he were made of glass. Which, of course, with all the aches and pains in his body, was just about what he felt like.

He rose and slowly made his way to the wagon's exit. His body was stiff, as Clara has told him it would be, and so it took what felt like an inordinate amount of time to make his way out of the wagon.

Still, eventually he did, climbing out of the wagon and standing, blinking in the sunlight. Dekker, Ella, and their daughter, Sarah, were all watching him. "Okay?" the big man asked.

The wanderer allowed himself a few seconds to take stock. He was sore pretty much all over—fighting giant armored spiders and half-climbing, half-falling down a mountain would do that to a man—but considering what he'd been through that was pretty much the best-case scenario. "Okay," he agreed. "Best we go talk to the wizard."

The big man blinked. "You really are a glutton for punishment, aren't you?"

The wanderer looked around him. "Veikr?" he asked.

"A little ways ahead," Ella said. "Sarah and some of the other children have been riding on him...I hope that's okay."

The wanderer remembered the last time he'd seen the horse, his mane covered in ribbons the village children had tied into them, and he grinned. "It's fine." He turned to Dekker. "Ready?"

"To talk to that old bastard?" the big man said. "Sure. I was considerin' slammin' my head into the gorge wall a few times, but I suppose this'll work just as well."

Then they were moving, making their way through the procession of villagers. As they did, the wanderer was surprised to see several of them wave and smile, nodding at him as if he were an old friend, and surprised also by just how much those small gestures meant to him. He'd been alone a long time, a hundred years and more, and he had thought he'd come to terms with it, had found himself being far more frightened of being around others than by himself. But he was beginning to discover that a man never really grew used to being alone. He tolerated it, no more than that.

"When they saw you pass out the way you did...well. Lot of folks thought you were goin' to die," the big man said.

"Thought it myself a few times," the wanderer admitted.

"Seems the world ain't so kind," the big man offered with a grin.

"Seems not. Still, give it time," he said, returning the smile. "In my experience, the world doesn't give up easily."

Soon they reached the front of the procession. The wizard walked a short distance ahead of the others, his walking stick—that resembled nothing so much as a wizard's staff from a bard's tale—held in one hand. Clint and the sheriff, along with the Perishables, walked behind him, and they all grinned as they saw the wanderer walk up.

"Some of the lads were scared you wouldn't make it," Clint said. "But I told 'em they had nothin' to worry about. After all, for you, somethin' like climbin' and causin' an avalanche, well that's a slow day, ain't it?"

The wanderer winced, for that was a truth he was not all that comfortable with. "It's good to see you, Clint," he said. "How's everything?"

"Everything's just fine," the sheriff answered for the man. "Or, at least, as fine as it can be when you're travelin' through a monster-infested wilderness through a narrow chasm—" he paused, glancing at the walls and paling slightly as if he expected them to crush him at any moment. The man cleared his throat, rallying. "Anyway, it's good to see you up and about, Ungr, and not just because we're all pretty much relyin' on you to keep us alive." He laughed, shaking his head. "Ah, all I mean is, we're glad you're okay."

The wanderer smiled in answer then glanced up at the wizard who hadn't so much as turned, though there was no way he couldn't have heard Clint's happy shout as the wanderer had approached. "Not everyone, it seems."

The sheriff grunted, following the wanderer's gaze to the wizard's back. "Well, I'll admit some folks are a bit gladder than others. A quiet one, is our wizard. Still, my ma always used to say that still waters run deep."

"Sure," Dekker said, scowling at the wizard's back, "and some faces are just made for punchin'. That one's from an old friend of mine."

"Friend?" the wanderer asked.

Dekker grunted. "Well. Acquaintance, then. Not that the fella does much talkin' anymore."

"No?"

"Got punched one too many times," Dekker said with obvious reluctance. "Mostly just sits around droolin' on himself now."

"Had a dog like that once," the sheriff said. "Worst damn sheep dog I ever had, though that mighta been on account of I didn't have any sheep."

The wanderer blinked then found himself grinning as Dekker tilted his head back and roared with laughter. The big man was many things but subtle was not one of them, and the loud roaring laughter was enough to cause even the sullen wizard to turn and regard them.

Slowly, the wizard walked back to them, a grim expression on his face that might have looked more at home on a man trudging to his own execution. "It seems that you have survived," the man said, staring at the wanderer with an expression that made it all too clear that, had the wanderer succumbed to his wounds, here was one person, at least, who would not have been overly distraught.

"For now," the wanderer agreed.

"Well," the wizard said with obvious reluctance. "I imagine, based on the fact that we are not dead at the hand of an army of Revenants that you succeeded in your attempts to bring the piled stone down?"

"I did."

The wizard nodded slowly. Then, with even more reluctance, each word coming with as much effort as if he'd had to dig it out of the ground with a shovel, "I suppose some might say thank you for that."

"And I suppose some might say you're welcome," the wanderer countered.

The wizard nodded, his mouth working, his entire face twisted as if he'd just eaten something sour. Then he turned and walked back to the front of the line.

"Well son of a bitch," Clint said.

"Ain't you two a pair," Dekker said.

The wanderer turned to regard the big man. "What's that?"

"Aw, nothin'," Dekker said. "Just, with the way you two were carryin' on, I'm just wonderin' how long it'll be 'fore you're exchanging letters, maybe comin' up with nicknames for one another."

"Sendin' out holiday cards," Clint said grinning.

"Finishing each other's sentences," the sheriff said, joining in with a wide smile.

The wanderer shook his head, smiling despite himself. "You're all bastards, you know that?"

"Wonder if your new best friend'd say as much," Dekker said.

The wanderer glanced at the wizard where he was at the front of the procession once more then back to Dekker. "I think maybe I'll wait to ask him."

Dekker laughed. "Can't say I blame you there. No reason to push your luck."

"So what now?" Clint asked.

The wanderer shrugged. "We keep going. I don't know how long we have left in this chasm, but hopefully we'll soo—"

"Two days," Dekker said. The wanderer looked at him, surprised, and the big man shrugged. "I asked the wizard, you know, while you were takin' your beauty sleep. Turns out that when you're not around he isn't all that bad."

"Good to know I bring out the best in him," the wanderer said, but the truth was he was barely paying attention. Instead, he was thinking about the time they had left in the chasm. Two days. He thought that would probably be alright. After all, he didn't doubt that the creature posing as Ranger had immediately set his troops to clearing the path as soon as it had become blocked but even with the Revenants who cared nothing for their own safety, such an undertaking would require no small amount of time.

Time enough for him and the others to lengthen their lead, perhaps time enough for them even to reach the end of the gorge before Ranger and the Revenants were finished.

"Anyway, I imagine the worst is behind us," Clint said, his voice sounding like that of a child seeking comfort, and the wanderer was aware of the way the three men were watching him, waiting for what he might say.

The worst is behind us. The wanderer had heard people say as much over the years, but he had never found it to be true. The worst, he'd found, was always somewhere up ahead, waiting for a man. And how could it not be so? After all, tragedies were rarely as bad in memory as they were in the moment. If the world—or the gods who'd made it—had ever shown a kindness, it was that time, while it did not heal all wounds, did help a man to forget at least the worst of the pain that wounding caused.

The problem with this, of course, was that a man experienced each new pain, each new tragedy afresh, for he had been allowed to forget just how terrible life can be until the moment in which the world chose, once more, to remind him.

"I hope so," the wanderer said finally. The men looked unsatisfied as they nodded, and he knew that they had expected more, just as he knew that he could not give it to them. They set off after the wizard then, and as they did the wanderer found himself looking around them. The world was, in some ways, predictable. It would see their hope and, seeing it, begin its attempts to destroy it. His job, then, was not to hope but to stand ready for when that attempt came. And so, as they walked, he took nothing for granted, studying the area around them, trying to find from where the threat would come, for living as long as he had, he knew enough to know that it *would* come.

***

They'd been traveling for several hours, the wanderer just beginning to feel a little like himself again, the worst of the stiffness working its way out of his muscles, when the world made its first attempt.

And despite the wanderer's effort to stay prepared, despite his vigilance, when that attempt came, he was not ready for it. For it did not come in the form of the Revenants, soulless, emotionless creations of the enemy. Neither did it come in the form of the giant armored spiderlike creatures or some other mysterious, terrifying beast of the Untamed Lands. The gorge walls, which pressed so close on either side, did not creep inward to smash him and the others between them—a ridiculous possibility that seemed to grow less and less ridiculous as time wore on.

When their doom came, it did not come with the metallic *whisper* of swords leaving scabbards or in the roar of some primordial beast. Instead, it came in silence, or nearly so. It came in the soft, patting, almost non-existent sound of a raindrop striking the wanderer's forearm.

The water felt nice and cool against his exertion-warmed skin, but that gave the wanderer no comfort. After all, many things which felt good spelled a man's doom, in the end, and he felt a shiver of fear run up his spine as he stared at that small drop of water, watched it trace its way down his skin.

Rain was an innocuous thing, most of the time, something that might, at worst, prove inconvenient for a man or woman caught in it. But when you were traveling through a narrow gorge cut into a mountain it was much more than that.

The wanderer glanced around as they continued to walk and noted, once more, the small pieces of dried sea-weed littering the ground here and there. He had noticed it before, when they'd first entered the ravine, but he had been too busy trying to survive and keep the others alive to give it much thought. He thought of it now. There was little to no vegetation down here in the chasm, only a few tiny, dried, gnarled bushes, no more than a few inches high. He had made out some few scraggly, largely leafless trees peeking over the top of the chasm in the time they'd been walking through it, but they had been few and far between.

Another thing the wanderer had noted when they'd first stepped into the chasm was how smooth the gorge floor and wall was. He had not given this much thought either, not at the time, but as he felt another drop of rain strike him, then another, he began to.

He paused, glancing up at the sky, and judging by the way the others stopped to gaze over their heads as well, he was not the only one who was beginning to ask himself a question. Namely, in such a place as the chasm with the great sheer walls on either side, where would the rain go? It was a question, the answer of which he thought they would discover all too soon, and he was quite certain it was one they would not like.

But even as he had the thought, the wanderer frowned, noting the way the wind began to pick up and tousle his clothes. That wasn't what bothered him the most, though, at least not for the moment. The sky which, moments ago, had been completely clear of even a wisp of a cloud, the sun shining bright, was now beginning to fill with midnight-dark clouds, filling with a speed and completeness that was far from natural.

Something was happening. Something was wrong. And going by the troubled whispers and moans of the villagers and Perishables around him, he was not the only one who sensed that something was amiss.

Dekker and Clint walked up to him, shooting nervous glances at the sky even as more rain began to fall. "Ungr. How bad is it?"

The wanderer shook his head slowly as he gazed up at the sky, full of clouds now, all of them shifting and roiling. "I don't know," he admitted. "I've never seen anything like it. Not good, though, that's for sure."

"If that's a joke, it's an ill-timed one, Ungr," the big man said.

The wanderer frowned. "Joke?"

"Yeah," Clint said. "He says that because *we* have both seen something like this before. Back on the mountain—when you went away. When the storm came. Remember?"

The wanderer blinked as realization struck. The man meant when the wanderer had Sojourned with Shaman, and the ghost had called down nature's wrath, killing some of the Revenants chasing them and slowing others. The wanderer had not noticed much of the effects of the storm, at least not in the beginning, for he had been too focused on using the Art. And later he had been mostly unconscious and not capable of judging the effects his efforts had produced in anything but a very immediate, very intimate sense.

"Shit," he said.

"Guessing you're not behind this one, then?" Clint asked.

"No," the wanderer said. "No, I am not, but then I think I might know who is," he finished grimly. After all, just because the enemy posing as Ranger was chasing them, that didn't mean he was the only one. The creature who'd taken Shaman's place had, it seemed, entered the fray. Until that moment, he suspected that the enemy had been confident enough in the ability of Ranger and his Revenant army to catch them. But now that the wanderer had blocked their path, slowing them, they had chosen to try another tactic. After all, it wasn't as if the wanderer needed to be alive for them to do what they intended, and it was far easier to catch a dead man than a live one, just as it would be far easier to take the cursed blade from a corpse.

"Anything you can do?" Dekker asked.

The wanderer frowned, wishing he could speak to the ghosts, but they had gone silent since he'd returned to the villagers and come too close to the wizard. But then, he thought he knew well enough what their answer would be, should he ask them the question Dekker had posed. After all, Shaman, the *real* one, would be available to him, but the man was about allowing nature to do what it did, to working within it. To learn to understand and therefore use the chaos of nature to one's advantage—it was most certainly *not* to attempt to impose some sort of artificial order upon that nature.

No, the storm was coming, that was all, and he was confident that there was nothing he or any of the ghosts could do about it, even if he had been able to speak to them. Which left one other option. "We need to speak to the wizard," he said. No sooner had he said as much then, as if to accentuate his point, thunder cracked the sky as if it were made of glass, and the light rain turned into a driving storm, immediately soaking the wanderer through.

"If we're goin' to do it," Dekker said grimly as he stared up at the sky, blinking as water fell on him, "we'd best do it soon."

The wanderer had no intention of arguing with that and so, without another word, the three men started toward where the wizard had gazed up at the sky with a scowl from beneath his wide-brimmed hat as if the storm was a personal affront meant for him and him alone.

"Eternal," the wizard said as he approached. "Why am I not surprised? Since this is your fault and all."

"His fault?" Clint asked. "You think he made this rain?"

"Someone did, didn't they?" the wizard asked, studying the wanderer.

"I believe so, yes," the wanderer answered.

The other man sneered. "I suspected as much. One of your friends?"

"I don't have many friends that want to kill me, do you?"

"Doubt the bastard has many friends at all," Dekker muttered but loud enough for the wizard to hear.

The wizard opened his mouth to speak, but the wanderer, knowing that they were running out of time, spoke first. "Do you have any means of stopping the storm?"

The wizard sneered again, opening his mouth to respond in what was clearly going to be mocking but, apparently realizing, as the wanderer had, that time was of the essence, he settled for an annoyed shake of his head instead. "No."

The wanderer nodded grimly—he had been afraid of as much. "How long until we reach the end of the chasm?"

The wizard shook his head again, clearly frustrated and, more than that, afraid. "A day? Perhaps a little more."

"A day?" Clint demanded, having to shout to be heard, for the rain had picked up again and it was coming down in sheets, thundering down on them as if they were a stain that it meant to wash away. "We'll be swimming by then!"

"Don't blame me," the wizard snapped. "I'm not the one who broke the barrier protecting the village, am I? Neither am I the one—"

"Look here, now," Dekker began, "I don't—"

"*Enough,*" the wanderer growled, and the two squabbling men grew silent. "Blame me later, if you want," the wanderer told the wizard. "*Hate* me, if you want—it makes little difference to me. But for now, let's focus on finding a way out of this, so that you can be *alive* to hate me. How does that sound?"

The wizard frowned, but, finally, he gave a reluctant nod. "Fine, but I don't know what you expect me to do. I cannot stop this storm—it is not how my magic works."

"Very well," the wanderer said. "Then we walk on, as quickly as we can."

"And if the gorge fills with water?" Clint asked, glancing down at the ground where a thin layer of water already sat.

"Then we swim," he said.

"There...might be another way."

They all turned to the wizard then. "If you've got an idea, I'd love to hear it," Dekker said. "I never have been that good of a swimmer."

The wizard frowned. "If memory serves—and if it doesn't we're all dead anyway—there is a switchback trail leading up the gorge a few hours ahead."

"And this trail," Dekker said slowly, picking up on the wizard's grim mood despite the fact that he was announcing what might have been their salvation. "It leads to the top of the gorge?"

"I don't know," the wizard said.

The big man blinked. "You don't know?"

"Of course not, and how would I?" the wizard demanded. "I have been through here only once, and I did not take it. It seemed too dangerous, even then." He frowned. "I do not do well with heights, and it is a thin trail, one that a person might easily fall from."

Dekker grunted. "So let me get this straight—your plan, such as it is, is for all of us to go climbing up a trail that you thought was too dangerous in *normal* weather, with no idea if it actually *leads* anywhere."

"And what if it doesn't?" Clint asked. "We'll all drown."

"Which is *exactly* what we'll do if we remain down here," the wizard hissed.

"You must be out of your damned mind," Dekker said.

"No, he's right," the wanderer said, and they all turned to him, the wizard with a look of shock on his face, no doubt surprised to find the wanderer supporting him. "Maybe the trail continues, maybe it doesn't," the wanderer said to Dekker. "Maybe it is dangerous and maybe it is not—the truth is we simply don't know. What we *do* know, however, is that we cannot stay here."

"But you heard him," Dekker said. "Another day, a little more, and we'll be out of here. Just a little time and—"

"It is time we do not have," the wanderer said.

The big man sighed, nodding. "As you say, Ungr."

The wanderer glanced at Clint, and the Perishables' leader inclined his head in a nod. "We're with you, Ungr."

The wanderer stared between the two men, at once touched by their faith in him and also terrified by it. "Very well," he said, praying that he only imagined the sense of impending doom that came over him as he turned back to the trail. "We continue on."

***

The next few hours were some of the most miserable of the wanderer's life, and that with no small competition.

The rain continued, pelting them with water that felt like thousands of tiny rocks when it struck exposed flesh. Worse, water would gather from time to time at the top of the gorge and sluice down on them in sheets so that, one moment, he'd be walking, shoulders hunched against the storm, soaked all the way through, and the next the wanderer was struck with water that, having fallen so far and in such a great quantity, nearly knocked him from his feet.

Overhead, the sky roiled with clouds as dark as night, some seething maelstrom constantly illuminated by sporadic bolts of lightning. A powerful, buffeting wind howled through the chasm like some wild demon, pushing against them as if it had a mind of its own, a mind that was set on slowing them as much as possible, on ensuring that they did not reach the trail the wizard had spoken of before the water slowly filling the gorge built up high enough to drown them all.

An event which the wanderer did not think would take long. They had only walked for a touch over an hour and a half and already the water level had risen to above their ankles, and the rain showed no signs of stopping anytime soon.

No one spoke as they traveled, each of them entertaining their own fears, their own worries, each of them marking every inch that the water level rose. Not that they could have talked, even had they wanted to, for the constant roaring thunder and howling wind would have made conversation all but impossible anyway.

And so the wanderer and those with him did the only thing they could do—they hunched their shoulders against the wind and the rain, and they continued.

The water had risen to around the middle of the wanderer's calf when they finally reached the thin trail cut into the gorge that the wizard had told them about. The wanderer turned and glanced back at Dekker who, like many of the other parents, had his child, Sarah, on his shoulders, for the water was too deep for the young to move easily.

The big man stared at the small path as rainwater sluiced down his face and gave a slight shrug at the wanderer as if to say that however bad the trail might prove, it could not be much worse than this. A sentiment the wanderer could not believe, no matter how much he might have wished to. After all, he had traveled the world for a very long time and if there was anything he had learned from that traveling it was this—things could always get worse.

Still, aware that many of the villagers standing nearby were watching him, gauging how frightened they should be by his reaction to the situation, the wanderer nodded, looking as confident as he was able.

They had to leave the wagon behind them, for the trail up the ravine side would not accommodate it, but before they did they took the rope from it that they had used when going through the Whisperer's territory. All too aware of the dangers of falling, a danger that would only increase as they traveled farther up the mountain slope, the wanderer and the others used the rope to tie around the old and the very young, then passed it down the line so that each person held it. That way, if one person should fall, they might be saved by the others.

The wanderer moved to take the lead and the normally argumentative wizard seemed all too willing to give up the spot. Then they began their ascent.

The trail was thin, as the wizard had said, no more than five feet wide, and slippery from the storm. Worse, the wind continued to buffet them as they moved, like invisible hands trying their best to shove the wanderer and those making their way behind him off the mountainside. The wanderer did his best to thread the fine line between moving fast enough that they would stay ahead of the water—rising steadily now beneath them as it filled the gorge—but not so fast that he or one of the others slipped.

Despite his efforts, several people slipped and would have fallen from the side of the gorge had it not been for the rope. Worse, their progress up the mountainside was brought to a complete standstill several times as they came upon piles of rock blocking the path. Rock that they were forced to move before continuing.

After the third such pile, the wanderer glanced down at the gorge and saw that already it was at least six feet high. Had they remained below, they would all now be in water over their heads. Which was bad. Worse was that, try as they might, the rising water was growing closer and closer. It was a slow sort of race as they moved up the mountainside, as the water filled the gorge, but one that the wanderer thought they were losing.

They traveled for several hours and were about halfway up the gorge when they came to a gap in the path. The wanderer was so distracted by his grim thoughts, by trying to keep his feet amid the roaring wind and pelting rain, that he nearly stepped right into it.

He stopped, staring in shock. One moment, the path was there, five feet wide, a little more at some places, a little less at others, and the next, it was simply gone as if some giant had taken a hammer to it.

There were three feet of emptiness before the trail resumed, continuing up the mountain. The wanderer hissed a curse, glancing down. Their journey had taken them far up the gorge side. The water filling the ravine had not been idle in the meantime and was now less than twenty feet below them. But while that meant that anyone that might fall trying to clear the gap in the trail might not die on impact, he did not think that would prove much of a comfort. For in that roiling water, shifting tumultuously under the grip of the storm, even the best swimmer could not help but drown.

"*What is i—*" Dekker began in a shout to be heard over the roaring storm, but as he stepped beside the wanderer he cut off, not needing to finish the question.

"*Damnit,*" the big man said, echoing the wanderer's own thoughts from a moment before. He glanced at the wanderer. "What do we do?"

"We go over it," the wanderer said, knowing that there was no choice. Then he glanced down at the steadily rising water filling the gorge. "And we do it quickly. There is little time."

Three feet.

It was not so much, under normal circumstances. A jump that most people could have made and that with little effort. The problem, though, was that these were far from normal circumstances. The trail was inclined, so that the jumper would have to move not just forward but *upward*. Worse, the stone path was slick with water, and the wind seemed all too eager to pluck the climbers off the trail and toss them away the way a man might rid himself of a troublesome nettle in his clothes.

The wanderer, Dekker, Clint, and Sheriff Fred met at the front of the procession and spoke briefly before deciding on their course of action. The wanderer leapt across first, then turned and nodded to the next men in line, two Perishables. The men looked nervous, afraid, but to their credit they hesitated only a moment before following after him. Meanwhile Dekker stayed on the other side of the gorge. Clint and the other Perishables helped organize a line that made sure that the women and children were sent forward first.

Dekker made use of his seemingly limitless strength, grabbing one child, then another, and tossing them across the intervening space to the wanderer who caught them and handed them off to the two Perishables.

On and on it went until all the children were safely across. Then came the women. Most were able to make the jump without incident, the wanderer catching them as they came across and helping to steady them. There was one, a young woman in her early twenties, though, who balked at it, terrified and screaming, screaming that did not lessen as Dekker did the only thing he could do, lifting her up and tossing her across to the wanderer.

The wanderer caught her, handing her over to the Perishables and preparing for the next in line. They continued, the wanderer glancing occasionally at the rising water level, until only Dekker and Veikr were left. The big man looked exhausted. Unsurprising, perhaps, considering the dozens he'd helped across in the near half hour it took them all to bridge the gap, but he stepped forward without hesitating, aware, as was the wanderer, of what was at stake.

The big man jumped, but weary as he was, his feet landed on the very edge of the gap. His eyes went wide as he started to tip back, his fall quickly halted by the wanderer who reached out and grabbed him, pulling him forward until he got his balance.

"Thanks," Dekker grunted, glancing down and swallowing hard.

"No problem," the wanderer said. "You're an alright guy, and I haven't got that many friends—seemed a shame to let you drown."

Dekker snorted, giving a grin that was belied by his pale expression. Then he turned back to regard Veikr who stood on the other side. "What about your horse?"

The wanderer raised an eyebrow. "There's no need to worry about Veikr. He could do such a jump in his sleep, far easier than you or I. Still, best we give him some room."

They did, moving forward, and with a casual leap that made the danger almost seem non-existent, Veikr came across, landing easily on the path and looking at them with a gaze that seemed to say that, next time, they should actually give him a challenge. Which, of course, was one suggestion that the wanderer hoped to avoid—if he had his way, everything going forward would be easy. The problem, of course, was that he so very rarely got it his way.

Many of them were shaken after bridging the gap, but there was no time to rest, for the water did not pause as a courtesy while they worked their way across. It continued to rise. By the time they were all past the gap it shifted and roiled hungrily no more than ten feet below them. The wanderer worked his way back to the front of the line and they started forward once more.

As they walked, the trail leading them around the mountain, the wanderer found himself growing more and more tense. One of his worries was that they would come upon another gap like the first, and that they would lose even more time trying to cross it. His greatest fear, though, was that they would come across a gap wider than the first. One too wide to cross. What would they do then? What would they do should they come upon a ten-foot or twenty-foot section of the trail that was simply gone? He thought the answer to that question was all too simple, but that made it no easier to accept.

They would die, that was all. There was no time to turn back, no time to do anything but move forward, and should their way forward be blocked, they would be left with nowhere to go, left with no choice but to stand upon the mountainside and hope that the waters would recede. A hope that he did not doubt would be in vain.

As they continued on, they began to see some vegetation growing on the side of the mountain, small bushes clinging to the rock. They also began to encounter pieces of driftwood that had been carried down into the chasm at some point by the rain. These might have been comforting signs—after all, it meant that however high the waters tended to rise, they did not reach this point. If they had, they would have swept away the driftwood and any signs of vegetation. The problem, of course, was that the storm raging all around them was no ordinary storm, was almost certainly unlike any storm that this part of the world had ever seen. And so the wanderer continued on, checking the rising water level from time to time, finding himself holding his breath each time they came around a bend in the trail, expecting to see that it was too blocked to clear in time or else that there was a giant hole in it that would not let them journey onward.

But despite his fears, the path remained before them for another hour, then another and they came upon no more gaps in the trail. They were nearing the top, no more than an hour away from it, the wanderer judged, when trouble came.

He turned another bend in the trail and his fears were confirmed as he saw that, indeed, their path was blocked. Only, it was not blocked by piled stone, nor was their path forward hindered by a gap in the mountain pass. Instead, it was something altogether different, something he never would have expected.

Less than a hundred feet up the path stood a creature that anyone from the "civilized" world outside the Untamed Lands would have thought no more than fiction. But it was real, all too real, the wanderer thought, for standing directly in their way, blocking the path, was a giant cat, one that was bigger than a wagon with paws bigger than dinner platters.

The creature did not seem to notice them for the moment. Instead, its attention was trained on the cliff edge—or more particularly, on a huge piece of driftwood that had once been a large tree but was now stripped of any leaf or branch and had somehow become wedged into the cliffside underneath an outcropping.

At first, owing to the bend in the path, the wanderer couldn't see what it was about the driftwood that had drawn the great cat's attention, or why it paced back and forth, its eyes on the outstretched driftwood as it growled and mewed. But as he leaned out, peering closer at the driftwood, he realized what it was. For there was another great cat, clearly of the same line, though this one was much smaller, which meant only that it was larger and far more deadly looking than any lion he'd ever heard of—not that the creature, who by its color was clearly the child of the giant cat on the cliffside, seemed all that menacing just then.

It had likely been swept off the cliffside by the storm, or perhaps it and its mother had traveled down here in an effort to avoid the storm in the first place. However they had come to be there, though, was not what was important just then. What mattered was that the cub was currently hanging from the driftwood tree, clawing and desperately trying to right itself but unable to gain purchase amid the driving rain and roaring wind.

Meanwhile, the mother could not go to her cub, for while the piece of driftwood might have been large it was certainly not so large as to support her weight, and she seemed to know this as she paced back and forth, clawing at the air and hissing in obvious terror at her cub's plight.

There was no way for the wanderer and those with him to make it past, for the creature's massive frame did a thorough job of blocking the trail. He glanced back at the cub and frowned. He knew, given time enough, how the thing would end, for the cub could not hold on forever, and there was no way the mother would be able to get to it, nor could she reach it from her spot on the cliff. The problem, at least so far as the villagers and everyone with him were concerned, however, was that however much time it took for the cub to fall and the mother cat to leave was too much time. The water was rising by the moment, so high now that the giant cub's back feet were kicking it as it struggled vainly to right itself on the protruding driftwood.

"Damn."

The wanderer turned to see that Dekker had moved up beside him, along with Clint, the sheriff, and the wizard.

"Yes," the wanderer said.

"Reckon that's the same one that we saw before?" Dekker asked.

The wanderer considered that. He knew that such beasts were often territorial, having a general area in which they hunted and lived. Given that, he thought it unlikely that it would have traveled this far under normal circumstances. Of course, these hadn't been normal circumstances, for a predator, while it was reluctant to give up its territory, would do so if something more dangerous invaded it. Something such as an army of Revenants led by the most dangerous and capable woodsman in the world. The cat might have abandoned its regular hunting grounds in such a case, particularly if it had a cub to protect.

"Maybe," he said finally.

"You saw that damned thing before?" This was from the sheriff, and the wanderer turned and nodded.

"Yes."

"Don't s'pose you made friends, did you?"

The wanderer thought of the last time he'd seen the giant beast, when he, Dekker, and Clint had gone back to check on the progress of the Revenant army, before he and the others had braved the Whisperers. He remembered the way it had chased an equally abnormally giant deer and had paused in its hunt to stare at them, remembered thinking that in those eyes it had seemed to communicate the fact that, had it not been previously engaged, they would have served as its dinner.

"Not quite," he said finally.

"Great," the sheriff said dryly. "We're all going to get eaten because you're bad at making friends."

"I'd relax, Sheriff," Dekker offered. "After all, it's unlikely the giant beastie would be able to eat all of us, even if it is bigger than some houses I've seen. It'd have to get full some time or another, wouldn't it?"

"That ain't as much of a comfort as you might imagine," the sheriff said.

"No," Dekker agreed. "No, it ain't."

The wanderer, though, was barely listening to the exchange. Instead, he was staring at the giant cat, at its cub struggling to keep hold of the dead wood as the storm raged around it. Some might have called them monsters. Perhaps they would have been right. But even monsters felt fear—in fact he thought they felt it more than anyone. He knew that better than most, for in the last hundred years he had been considered a monster, a traitor of the worst kind. And he thought that, to some degree or another, he had *been* one. The story of him betraying the Eternals had been a lie, it was true, but to survive for a hundred years, to keep the cursed blade out of the enemy's' hands for so long, he'd had to become hard. To learn to ignore the pain and suffering of others, telling himself each time that the blade was more important, that it had to take precedence. Yes, he had been a monster. A monster who had been created by his attempts at doing good, but then wasn't that how most monsters came to be?

Had he not met Dekker and his family, had he not met Felden Ruitt, he would be that monster still. A shade of a man traveling the face of the world, barely more alive than those creatures which the enemy sent after him. He had been saved, but he had not saved himself, could not have. Just as the cub could not save itself. It would fall, soon, as he might have.

Unless someone helped it.

"What do you think, Ungr?" Dekker asked beside him. "We all rush it at once, try to knock it in the chasm?"

"Maybe we could grab some of the deadwood," Clint offered, "use it as spears..."

"Or *perhaps* we could let it alone," a new voice said, and the wanderer turned to see that the wizard had walked up.

"Hey, I'm all for live and let live," the sheriff said. "The problem is that if we let this fella live, we're gonna drown." He paused, glancing down at the rushing water steadily rising beneath them. "And that soon enough."

The wizard sneered. "And so you judge the creature's life of less worth than your own," he said, not to the sheriff but to the wanderer.

"Sure," the sheriff offered, and never mind the fact that the wizard was only staring at the wanderer. "On account of it doesn't have thumbs. All the best creatures do."

The wizard did round on the sheriff then. "And if I were to chop off your thumbs?"

The sheriff considered that. "It'd be a challenge openin' doors, that's for sure."

The two began arguing quietly then, Dekker and Clint joining in. The wanderer was barely listening, though. He was all too aware of the tragedy playing out in front of him, all too aware, also, of the villagers and other Perishables watching them squabble. And he could see by the looks on their faces that they were not comforted.

Perhaps they might have rushed the creature while it was distracted and managed to knock it over the edge, as Dekker had suggested. Perhaps they might have used driftwood spears to do it, as Clint had said. Yet those ideas did not sit well with him. It was a monster, it was true, but even monsters might be saved.

The wanderer started forward.

The men cut off their argument when they noticed.

"Ungr?" Dekker's voice, worried, and the wanderer could hear the frown in it without turning.

"Something has to be done," the wanderer said, turning to regard the big man.

"Right," Dekker said. "That's what we're sayin'."

"And I will do it," the wanderer said.

"Alone?" Dekker said.

"Yes," the wanderer said. "And there is no use arguing," he continued before the big man could say something, "we cannot all come upon it at once—the path would not accommodate so many. Only two might approach it at the same time and then they would not have room to move around, if moving was needed."

"So you mean to take it on alone?" Clint asked.

"Something like that," the wanderer said. He started to turn away then paused when the wizard spoke.

"Just like an Eternal," the man said, his voice bitter. "Destroying anything or anyone whose existence is inconvenient for you. It is only trying to protect its family, Eternal. Can you not see that?"

The wanderer glanced at Dekker and Clint, then beyond them at the villagers. He saw Ella and Sarah among them, all of them watching him and the others, seeing what they would do. Then he turned back to the wizard. "So am I," he said. Then, before anyone could say anything more, he turned and started forward.

He did not know how the creature became aware of his presence, for he could hear nothing over the storm, smell nothing besides the scent of the rain and the wet. But the creature *did* become aware of him, turning away from its endangered cub long enough to regard him with its luminous yellow eyes. The giant cat opened its mouth, baring fangs as long as a small child, conveying, in that gesture, a message as clear as if it had spoken to him in the common tongue.

Do not come any closer, it told him.

But the creature spared him only a moment of its attention before its child let out another panicked cry, then the giant cat's gaze began to shift, almost frantically, between the wanderer and its cub.

Perhaps there was a better way to get the thing done. He suspected there was, for one of the things that Ranger had taught him—the real Ranger, not the impostor currently doing his level best to kill him—was the correct way to treat animals, both domesticated and wild. He'd taught him how to approach them, the different ways to earn their trust. The problem, of course, was that all of those ways took time and time was one thing he and the villagers—and the cub—simply did not have.

The wanderer took a step toward the creature, then another. Somehow making use of its heightened senses, the creature spun, regarding him where he stood less than fifteen feet away, baring its teeth once more.

No closer, it told him, more clearly than if it had said the words.

But the storm raged, the water rose, and there was no time. The wanderer raised his hands, another gesture that, he hoped, was as clear as the giant cat's own as he kept moving forward.

The cat watched him approach, tilting its head as if it could not believe the audacity—which he understood. He suspected that, had he looked behind him, he would have seen the villagers of Alhs, as well as Dekker and Clint and all the rest, studying him with looks of disbelief to match.

He moved forward until he was ten feet in front of the giant cat, able to make out the squalling cries of the cub as it clawed desperately at the driftwood log for purchase it could not find. Then closer still, until he was eight feet away, then seven, close enough that he could hear the rumbling, warning growl issuing from the giant mother like nearby thunder.

Five feet, close enough that the creature could have lunged out and clamped its fangs around him with little effort. No sooner had he the thought than the giant cat moved. He saw the blow coming before it did. He might have drawn his sword—the creature was fast, but so was he—but he did not. He only stood, his hands still raised, and so the creature's giant paw struck his shoulder like a smith's hammer. Pain roared through the wanderer, and he collapsed to one knee under the force of the blow.

Still, he was glad to find that the creature had not chosen to use its claws, for if it might have easily split him in two. He knew he should be grateful for that much at least, but it was difficult to be grateful for anything with the terrible pain in his shoulder. If he lived past the next few minutes, he knew he'd have a large, ugly bruise come morning.

It took all the wanderer's will power not to draw his sword, to fight or retreat, but he had been taught many things at the hands of the wisest, most powerful people in the world and one of those things, taught him by Soldier, was that, sometimes, the right thing to do was nothing. Of course, it was also usually the hardest thing. Certainly it felt that way now as the wanderer resisted the urge to draw his blade. Instead, he rose to his feet once more, lifting his hands up again in a gesture to indicate he meant no harm, doing his best to ignore the throbbing pain in his shoulder as he did. The wanderer met the giant cat's eyes then moved his gaze to its struggling cub. The creature followed his gaze then slowly turned back to regard him.

The wanderer waited for a moment, but the creature made no other move toward him. Then, satisfied that they understood each other, the wanderer started forward again, his hands still raised.

The creature watched him, moving away from the edge to give him room to approach where the driftwood was stuck. Then, just as he reached it, the giant cat lunged out, opening its jaws wide, turning its head to the side, and the wanderer tensed in expectation of terrible pain and a quick death.

But the creature paused with its teeth on either side of his torso, and the wanderer froze as the yellow eye that he could see regarded him. And the message here, too, was clear. *Do you see how easy it would be?* the creature seemed to say.

And the wanderer did, for the creature had moved far faster than he'd given it credit for. Even now, its teeth were only inches away from him, and he knew it would only take an instant of choice and the creature's razor sharp fangs would settle the matter definitively.

The creature remained that way for a second, then another, letting the reality of his situation sink into him. Then its cub squalled again, the loudest cry yet, and the wanderer tensed, sure that the giant cat's claws would close around him, if only in reaction to its cub's screams. They didn't, though. Instead it pulled away from him, moving toward its cub again and letting out a pitiable growl that was far more terror than anger as it paced back and forth.

Watching its distress, the distress of this creature that would be considered a monster by pretty much any being that could consider anything at all, watching its desperation to save its youngling, the wanderer decided that the wizard was right. Men often believed that because things were different they were also evil, but then men believed a lot of things, *feared* a lot of things— that did not mean that any of those things were true. Fear, after all, Scholar had often told the wanderer in his studies, was not the path to knowledge but the trap lying in the way, all too ready to snare the unwary.

The wanderer did not know much about the creature besides the length of its fangs and the crushing strength it held in its paws. But he knew one other thing, too. Knew it in those moments that he watched it pace back and forth frantically, desperate to get at its cub. It loved. And if there was one thing that could be said about love, it was that nothing that loved could be wholly evil.

The wanderer felt a pang of sympathetic sadness and fear for the creature, for the cub, too, so desperately clawing at the driftwood, seeking purchase, fighting the inevitable as all living creatures did, for it was clear that it would not manage to get atop the log. Worse, the log was slowly shifting. Only just noticeable, but inexorable as the wind and the rain and the cub's weight combined to begin to free it from where it had been stuck fast in the cliffside.

"I will help him, if I can," the wanderer told the giant cat, and the creature turned to look at him, its yellow eyes shining dangerously. "But you must let me," he finished.

The creature watched him for several seconds, as if it understood, then, slowly, it backed away from the edge, its eyes never leaving him. The wanderer nodded, then carefully, all too aware of the still throbbing ache in his shoulder where the great beast had struck him, he started toward the now open space.

He reached the edge with all his pieces in their proper places, so he knelt, examining the driftwood log. It was still jammed into the cliffside, but it had begun to shift slightly. Worse, the water level was rising. There was little time. He might have used the rope they'd brought, the one keeping the villagers secured together, but there was no time to retrieve it even if he would have felt okay about leaving them without it, and he did not.

He might have consulted the ghosts, but he knew well enough what they would say, what they would call him. They would say he would fail. They would say he was a fool. And likely, they would be right. There was no other choice. No good choices then, only bad ones, and in such circumstances, when a man was faced with only bad choices, he'd been taught that the best thing was to pick one and to move forward.

So he did.

The wanderer knelt and eased himself onto the log. The surface, devoid of any bark or branch, was slick, and beneath the driving rain and roaring wind he began to slip almost instantly. He was forced to hug the log to keep hold of it. He began to ease himself forward slowly, aware that time was running out, confident that, at any moment, the driftwood would give way beneath him, and he and the beleaguered cub would plummet into the tumultuous waters filling the chasm. And there was no need in guessing what might happen then—they would, the both of them, drown.

He continued forward.

The cub was young, but even still he saw, as he approached, that its claws had dug great furrows into the tree. In its panicked efforts to save itself, it doomed itself, clawing away at the very thing keeping it alive. Another way, then, in which the creatures were like men.

The wanderer was within five feet of the cub when its struggles caused the tree to shift, and suddenly the wanderer was hanging upside down from the driftwood, his arms and legs wrapped around it, the rain pelting his face, the wind pushing at him, as if both wished for nothing more than to drop him into the roiling waters below.

Knowing that each second brought him closer to that exact eventuality, the wanderer began to shimmy closer to the cub until he was only a foot away. And then, for a moment, he was at a loss of what to do. He had been taking this one step at a time, had been so focused on getting past the giant cat, on getting *to* the cub, that he'd given very little thought to what he'd do once he actually got there.

He decided, in that moment, that the ghosts would have been right to call him a fool. But a moment later he heard a muffled shout and raised his head, looking back toward the cliff face to see Dekker and Clint, along with the sheriff, standing near the cat. The men were clearly uncomfortable; being within spitting distance of a creature large enough to swallow you in one bite—or perhaps, in Dekker's case, two—would do that to a man. But they were also holding a rope. The wanderer knew what they meant to do in an instant, and he gave a nod—the most he was capable of with the water pelting his face.

Not much, but Dekker clearly noticed it, for he began to swing the rope around in a circle and, in another moment, it was flying toward the wanderer. It came up short, but he was able to throw his leg out, hooking the lassoed end that Dekker had tied with his foot. Then, hissing with the effort of holding himself there, particularly with his aching shoulder, the wanderer brought his foot up until he was able to grasp the lasso with his left hand.

He tried to call to the cub, to use soft words of comfort the way a man might calm a frightened horse, but the animal was fully given to its terror now, its eyes wide and wild as it clawed desperately at the driftwood, digging fresh furrows into it. The wanderer knew it wouldn't be long before those furrows were enough to cause the driftwood to break apart altogether. Already he could hear it splintering.

So hanging from one arm, he used his other to spread the lasso wide and then tried to swing it so that it came over the creature's hindquarters and wrapped around its waist. But with the wind and the rain and the creature's struggles, he missed. He tried a second time and, again, he failed.

Knowing that the time left them could be measured in moments, the wanderer reluctantly let go of the driftwood with his other hand, hanging on only by his legs as he grabbed either side of the lasso. Then, swinging himself toward the cub, he threw the lasso up and felt a great sense of relief as it went around the cat's hind legs.

With a growl of effort the wanderer pulled the lasso tight, and it caught hold of the cub's waist.

That, of course, was when the cub finally lost its battle with the driftwood and plummeted toward the water. The wanderer, had he been given a moment to think, might have let it go, deciding that he had done all he could. But there was no time to contemplate, to plan, and he reacted instantly, grabbing the rope and looping it once, then twice around his arm even as the cub crashed into the roiling water.

The slack on the rope vanished in a moment, and the wanderer cried out in agony as the rope slashed into his arm like a knife, coiling around his forearm like a snake, and the full weight of the cub jerked at his shoulder, threatening to rip him—or at least his arm—off the driftwood log.

The cub was thrashing wildly in the water, and each panicked movement sent a fresh wave of agony through the wanderer, pain so terrible he felt as if he might black out at any moment, which of course would mean death not just for the cub but for him as well, and likely for those he meant to protect.

Hissing through gritted teeth, he reached out with his other hand, taking hold of the rope and easing some of the pressure off his arm. Some, but nowhere near enough. Then he did the only thing he could do: he began to swing the cub. Slowly at first, the pendulum movement bringing it back and forth, fighting its great weight. But then it began to swing more, increasing the pain in the wanderer's shoulder, doubling then trebling it until spots danced in his eyes.

Then, with a final roar, a last effort that made his back feel as if it would snap in half, the wanderer swung himself outward from the driftwood, creating a pendulum that lifted the heavy cub up high into the air and dropped it onto the chasm ledge in front of its mother. The wanderer felt a heavy sense of relief as the mother came forward, gripping her cub in her mouth and lifting it easily. Then the creature gazed at him, and he thought he saw unmistakable gratitude in its eyes.

Gratitude that warmed some deep part of him. He had a moment to appreciate it, no more, before the driftwood log to which he still clung gave one final creak, then snapped in half.

And he fell.

The water seemed to rise up hungrily to meet him, swallowing him and bringing him down into its churning depths. The wanderer was disoriented almost immediately. He spun and fought desperately, trying to right himself, to face himself upward so that he might escape the crushing waters.

He managed it once, his head bobbing above the surface for an instant before watery hands seemed to reach out and jerk him downward once more. He tried to right himself again but soon he lost all sense of direction, all sense of where up *was*. Yet he struggled on, fighting as useless a fight as the cub had fought as the water pushed in all around him, knowing it was pointless but struggling as all the living did against the inevitable.

His chest and lungs burned like fire as he thrashed and fought and then, despite his efforts, despite his willing it otherwise, his throat opened and water rushed inside.

Water and darkness and death.

CHAPTER NINE

He woke to a scarred face looming over him, one he recognized at once as belonging to one of the Accursed. He did not stop to contemplate how he had survived the water or why the creature hadn't killed him while he was unconscious. He caught the creature by the throat with a snarl.

He was disoriented, confused, but he promised himself that if the creature meant to eat him, at least it would have to fight for its meal. But he was weak from his ordeal, and the creature demonstrated the incredible strength of its kind, breaking free of his grip and leaping away onto all fours like a monkey.

The wanderer rolled to his side, knocking over what appeared to be a small table and scattering several items he didn't take time to identify as he came to his feet in a fighting crouch, ignoring the stiffness in his muscles. The light was dim, and he realized in a moment that he was inside a cave. He cast his gaze about for his swords but did not find them. Instead, he saw a six-inch length of bone that had been sharpened and shaped to appear almost like a long needle lying on the floor. It was different than the boneshard weapons he'd seen the Accursed use to such great effect, hardly a weapon at all, but he decided it was better than nothing. He scooped it up, growling as he brandished it in the direction of the Accursed that was watching him as it shifted on its hands and feet like an animal.

"What in damnation is going on here?" a voice demanded, and the wanderer turned, wincing at the sudden appearance of light to see the Wizard of the South stepping through what he took to be the cave mouth, a candle in his hand.

"Careful," the wanderer said. "They are dangerous."

The wizard snorted. "The only dangerous one here, *Eternal,*" he said, making of the word a curse, "is you. Why, if Phelda wanted you dead you'd be dead. Now put that damned needle down. It'd be a cruel way to repay Phelda's kindness by stabbing her with the very tool she used to save your life."

"Phelda?" the wanderer said confused, glancing at the Accursed. "It has a name?"

"*She* has a name," the wizard snapped. "I swear, you Eternals. As soon as I begin to think you're different you go and prove you are no better than the others."

"She saved me?"

"Didn't sew yourself up, did you?" the wizard said, sounding more tired than angry now. "You took a nasty hit somewhere under the water, before that friend of yours got you out. We bandaged it as best we could, but it was Phelda here who sewed it up. And she and the others didn't just save you—they saved all of us. They found us on that ridge, got us here to the caves, to safety. And then, by way of thanks, you *attack* her."

"I...I'm sorry," the wanderer said to the Accursed. "I...I did not know. I thought..."

"Thought what, exactly?" the wizard demanded. "That she was going to eat you? Is that it?"

"Yes," the wanderer said simply. "The others of her kind I've met would have, and so I have been taught of all Accursed."

"*Accursed,*" the wizard sneered. "The names you Eternals give to those things which you do not understand. They are the Free, and not all Free are the same, Eternal, not anymore than every man is the same as every other."

The wanderer considered that then winced. "You are right," he said. "I was wrong," he told the woman. "I'm sorry." He bowed his head to her, and she only continued to watch him.

"She does not understand your tongue," the wizard said, but he sighed, and spoke in a guttural, clicking sort of language to the woman who turned to him, listening silently as he spoke. Then she bobbed her head in a nod before glancing at the wanderer and inclining her head. And with that, she turned and loped out of the cavern on all fours.

"An Eternal who apologizes and admits that he's wrong," the wizard said when she was gone, watching him. "One who risks his life to save a cub...what many would consider a dumb beast. You are a complex creature, Eternal."

"I've been called many things," the wanderer said, offering the man a smile before he sat down, glancing at his leg to see that his thigh had been bandaged, a poultice applied. "But never that."

The wizard watched him for a moment, and the wanderer thought he could almost see the hint of a smile on his face, but then the man grunted. "Your friends will want to know you're awake," he said, then hurried, almost seemed to flee, for the cave exit.

Alone, the wanderer glanced around and saw that the cave he was in was small, no more than fifteen feet across. He flexed his leg and was surprised to find that, while it was stiff, it did not hurt overly much. Whatever the Accursed had done, it had clearly worked wonders. He was trying to put weight on the leg—finding that he was capable of it and that, while it ached, it was far from unbearable—when he heard voices at the cave mouth.

He turned to see Dekker file in, along with Ella and Sarah. More people came after but the wanderer barely noticed as Sarah let out a shout and barreled toward him, wrapping her arms around him in a tight hug. Despite all that he'd been through, despite the ache in his leg from a wound he didn't remember getting, the wanderer found a grin spreading across his face.

"Mister Ungr, you're okay," the girl said.

"I've been worse," the wanderer agreed. "And how are you?"

He felt a stab of regret as she pulled away from the embrace, staring up at him with a solemn expression. "I'm okay," she said. "But Daddy says my ears are getting bigger by the day."

The wanderer, who knew well Dekker's sense of humor, laughed. "Well. At least you'll be able to hear better."

"That's true," she said, smiling.

"Go on then, floppy," Dekker said, "back to your mother."

"*Dekker,*" Ella said admonishingly, but the big man only grinned in response.

"How's the leg?" Dekker asked.

"It works," the wanderer said. "After a fashion."

The big man grunted. "Back on the ridge...that was just about the dumbest thing I ever saw."

"Stick around."

Dekker shook his head in wonder. "But you saved us—all of us." He glanced over at Clint and Sheriff Fred and, the wanderer was surprised to see, Daggett, little Johnny's father.

"From what I hear," the wanderer said, turning back to Dekker, "you saved me."

The big man raised an eyebrow. "What's that?"

"The wizard told me," he said. "He said that you dove into the water. It seems I'm not the only one capable of doing dumb things."

Dekker winced. "Yeah, about that," the big man said. "That uh...that wasn't me. I meant to, sure, but truth to tell, Ungr, I ain't all that much of a swimmer. Far better drowner, I find."

"You and I both," the wanderer said, "but if it wasn't you..." He paused, glancing at Clint, and the Perishables' leader shook his head.

"Me and some of the boys, we tried using the rope," he said. "But the waters were so rough, and we...we couldn't get to you."

"It was Daggett here who pulled you out," Dekker said, nodding his head at the man who stood in the corner looking decidedly uncomfortable. "Man swims like a fish."

"Funny," the sheriff said, "Daggett here and some of his buddies used to always go swimmin' in the mountain pond when they were kids. Long since lost count of the times I ran 'em off." He shook his head. "Never did stop 'em though."

"Liked to swim is all," Daggett said, avoiding the wanderer's gaze.

The wanderer thought of the Accursed woman—Phelda, the wizard had said—and then thought of Daggett. Sometimes, most times, perhaps, the thing that saved a man was never what he thought. "Thank you, Daggett," he said. "I...I don't know how to repay you."

"You paid any debt you might ever owe me and then some when you brought my boy back," the man said.

"Still," the wanderer said. "Thank you."

The man nodded and there came several seconds of uncomfortable silence. Then Dekker grunted. "Anyway, now that the niceties are out of the way, I figure you might have a few questions."

"Yes," the wanderer said.

Dekker nodded. "Well. Once you saved her cub, that giant she-cat took it in her mouth and left. Then once Daggett here fished you out we got movin'. Didn't make it far before the Free found us, helped us along and brought us here. Saved us, if you want to know the truth of it. Then Phelda took a look at your leg. Clara likely would've but she caught a chill durin' the storm as did a few others. They'll all be okay or so Phelda—as close to a village herbwoman as they have here—assures us. Or at least assures the wizard in her tongue who then assures us."

"Are you...are you saying you stopped for me? But our lead—"

"Won't matter for shit if you die," Dekker said.

"But—"

"But nothin'. Look, Ungr, I know you ain't accustomed to havin' friends—at least those not of the equine variety—so let me fill you in on a little secret. Friends don't leave friends to drown or die from a leg wound on a mountainside when they might have helped."

The wanderer winced. "But the Revenant army is coming...I can't imagine the wizard was all that thrilled at the idea of stopping."

Dekker gave him a small smile. "It was his idea. He said if we didn't get somewhere to rest soon, you'd die. A short time later, Phelda and her people showed up, brought us here. I don't know how he done it but, you ask me, he called to 'em somehow. Anyway, that's when they brought us here, to these caves." He leaned forward, speaking in a whisper. "I know they look...well, like the others, but I'll tell you, Ungr, these here are a lot nicer than their cousins we met back at Alhs."

"You'll get no disagreement there," the wanderer said, blinking. His eyes felt terribly heavy, and he thought that whatever the woman, Phelda, had given him to help him recover it had also served to make him exhausted. Which, he knew from his time with Healer, many such medicines did. After all, there were few things better for a man than sleep—he'd spent enough sleepless nights to know it.

"Well," a voice said from the cave entrance, and the wanderer turned to see that the wizard had returned, "if you're all done chatting, best leave the Eternal here to get some rest."

"Thank you again, Ungr," Ella said. "For saving us."

He smiled, nodding, for he found it difficult to say much then, the exhaustion seeping through his body with surprising speed.

When they were alone, the wizard glanced at the cave opening then back to the wanderer. "They care for you," he said.

"More than I deserve."

"That I do not doubt," the wizard said, but the words lacked much of his usual anger and scorn. In fact, more than anything, he sounded sad.

"Is everything alright?" the wanderer asked.

"Is anything ever?" the wizard countered, then sighed. "These caves...Phelda and her ancestors have lived here for generations. It will be hard on them, leaving them behind."

"But...why will they leave them?" the wanderer asked, giving his head a shake in a vain effort to rid himself of the weariness settling over him like a thick blanket.

"Because you are here," the wizard said simply. "You see, Eternal, the Free, or the Accursed, as your kind call them, have many talents. They are strong, fast, possessing a cleverness and a grace that are more akin to animals than men. Yet for all their many gifts, they will not be able to stand long against the army that follows you. Make no mistake, they would fight, if I asked it of them, for courage is another of their talents. But no matter their bravery, they would lose, in the end. And in that end, the creature, Ranger, and his ilk would no doubt begin to experiment on them. So that, in a decade, perhaps two, they would have creatures like those that chase us, but ones that, forged not from a mortal but from a Free, would be far stronger and far faster. Almost impossible to stop. Can you imagine it, Eternal?"

"I can..." the wanderer said slowly. "It's terrifying."

"Yes," the wizard said. "It is."

"Such a force...it would be nearly impossible to beat."

"Yes. It is why it has been tried before."

"You mean...the enemy...they tried to take over the Acc—sorry, the Free, before?"

"*An* enemy, yes," the wizard said, watching him. He opened his mouth as if to speak then closed it again and seemed to change what he meant to say. "You had best sleep, Eternal. Phelda said it is necessary, and in such matters she is far wiser than I."

"But...we need to get going. Any time we waste, Ranger and his army, they'll get closer and—"

"You need not worry on that score," the wizard said. "This cave network is vast—even now, after all these years, I do not think Phelda and her people have explored half of it—but the entrance is well hidden. I do not doubt that those chasing us will find it in time, but no matter how good of a tracker he is, it *will* take him time. Phelda and the others know how to cover their tracks well. Now rest—we are safe...for now."

For now. Those two words rang loudly in his mind, and the wanderer knew that, despite the wizard's reassurances, he should get up. They'd gained a hard-won lead, some of which they had lost during the storm with the giant beast, and it was foolish to squander it. He knew that, yet his eyes felt impossibly heavy, and there was a not-unpleasant numbness spreading through his body. The wanderer meant to rise, truly he did, tried to do exactly that. He was still trying when, in less than a minute after the wizard's departure, he fell asleep.

CHAPTER TEN

"Ungr."

It was a voice he knew, but that was not what pulled him so quickly from his sleep. Instead, it was a certain note he heard in the voice, one of concern, a tenseness to it he did not like.

"Clint," he said, coming awake in a moment and finding the Perishables' leader's face looming over him. He did not miss the tense set of the man's jaw or the slightly too-wide cast of his eyes. "What's happened?"

"They've found us," the man said grimly.

The wanderer needed no more urging than that. He rose to his feet, ignoring the stiffness that had set into his body as it healed. He was relieved, at least, to find that whatever the woman, Phelda, had done, it had worked wonders. It seemed that the wizard was right about this much, at least—the Accursed...*No, that's not right. They call themselves the Free.* The *Free* were good at more than just killing. "How long do we have?"

The Perishables' leader shook his head. "Half a day, no more."

The wanderer wasn't sure how to feel about that. At first, when Clint had woken him, he'd been sure that Ranger and his Revenant army had somehow caught them or, at best, that some other terrible danger had presented itself. Now, part of him felt relief at the realization that they still had a twelve-hour lead. Mostly, though, it was not reassuring. After all, he'd hoped his actions in the chasm would have bought them more time than that. Besides, if what Clint and the wizard had said was true then even had they somehow managed to move all the stones so quickly—a task that beggared the imagination—that didn't explain how Ranger and his troops had *found* them as fast as they had.

"How do we know?" the wanderer asked as a thought struck him. "That they're close, I mean."

"Phelda's people, the Free," Clint said. "They set watches—a precaution they take living where they do. Not that I blame them, understand. Anyway, one of their scouts saw and reported back."

The wanderer nodded slowly, thinking. "Dekker and the sheriff?"

"Waiting for you," the Perishables' leader said. "I can lead you to them, if you're ready."

The wanderer glanced around and caught sight of his pack, along with his two sheathed blades sitting in the corner. He retrieved them, strapping the blades back into place and resettling his pack, then nodded. "Ready."

***

Dekker and the others waited in a large cavern which had at least a dozen exits where the caves branched off into other directions. People, villagers and a few hundred Free, moved here and there, and there was an almost frantic energy to all of it.

The villagers, the wanderer saw, appeared to be packing, receiving supplies from the Free and stowing them in their bags. The wanderer watched it all for a moment, then he and Clint started toward where Dekker waited with the sheriff and the wizard, overseeing the process.

Veikr stood a short distance away from the men, Sarah patting his muzzle and rubbing him while Ella replaced his saddle. Meanwhile, a dozen of the Free looked on from their low crouches, their heads cocked as they stared at Veikr in open wonder. The wanderer paused for a moment, watching them.

The wanderer might have thought it was odd that these creatures who lived in a land full of monsters and nightmare beasts would be so impressed with a simple horse, but then Veikr was far from a simple horse. He was of the greatest line of horses that had ever existed, one which existed no more. And, at least so far as the wanderer was concerned, Veikr was the greatest of that line.

The wanderer watched for a minute and, deciding that Veikr was in good hands, at least for the moment, he moved to where Dekker and the others waited. "Ungr," Dekker said. "You know?"

"Clint filled me in," the wanderer said with a nod. "Twelve hours, he said?"

"Give or take," the sheriff said. "It depends on just how much he knows about where we are. The entrance is well-hidden and even if he and that army of his do find their way inside, these caverns are vast." The man shook his head and gave a low whistle. "You wouldn't believe just how vast. With any luck, that army'll get lost in here and never find their way out."

The wanderer took in the man's expression as he said it, then he glanced at Clint and Dekker and saw grim looks to match the man's. Apparently none of them, including the sheriff himself, held out much hope for that.

"You don't think that will be the case," he said.

It wasn't really a question, but the sheriff chose to answer it anyway. He shrugged. "Seems to me that the bastard isn't havin' all that hard of a time trackin' us, and I don't see any reason to think that might change."

"If you do not see it, then you are not looking closely enough."

They all turned to the wizard to see the man giving them a small, humorless smile. "You said, before, Sheriff, that the caverns of the Free are vast—you have no idea. You have only glimpsed the barest fraction of the intricate network of tunnels and caves that surround us. It is enough that a dozen men might be lost for a week, traveling independently of one another and yet each of them could easily starve to death without ever seeing another."

"Truly, they are that large?" the sheriff said, licking his lips, and the wanderer remembered that the man did not care for enclosed spaces, and the thought of spending a week working their way through caves was clearly not a pleasant idea for him.

"Truly," the wizard said. "An entire world exists around us," he went on, glancing around the caverns with something like appreciation, oblivious to the squeamish, slightly sick look that came over the sheriff as he did the same. "It is, after all, why I brought the Free here, in the first place."

"You brought them here?" Clint asked.

"Does that surprise you?" the wizard said, scowling. "Oh, because they are not mortal, as you are? I suppose you think it would have been better to have killed them all? Or perhaps put them in cages, is that it? Cages so you and others you deem *superior* to the rest of the world might, for the price of only a few coins, gawk at them, maybe poke them with sticks?"

The Perishables' leader blinked. "I was just gonna say that was nice of you."

Dekker snorted, and the sheriff let out a strangled gasp of laughter, quickly cut off. Even the wanderer could not stop the smile that crept on his face. The wizard scowled at each of them. "Make ready—we will be leaving shortly. Prepare yourselves."

"You mean like...stretch?" Dekker asked.

There was another snort of laughter, this time from Clint, and the wizard's upper lip peeled back from his teeth in a sneer before he turned and walked away.

***

Five hours later, they were still making their way through the caves, led by what the wanderer had taken to be the leader of the Free, an old, scarred creature who, despite his obvious age, was possessed of a wiry muscle and a cleverness in his gaze that was unmistakable.

Others of the Free moved around them, and it was a tense group that made their way through the caves. At least tense on the side of the villagers of Alhs who shot suspicious, nervous glances at the Free, not surprising, perhaps, considering that their village had recently been attacked by creatures that looked pretty much identical to them. Thankfully, the Free did not seem to take offense at the villagers' regard. In fact, they largely seemed to ignore the villagers altogether.

Or so it seemed, though the wanderer couldn't be sure. After all, he knew little of the Free, except that they were far stronger and faster than normal mortals. More, they were able to see in the darkness of the caverns and those torches which had been lit were only for the villagers' benefit. The Free's lack of regard for the villagers—if indeed it was—might have meant nothing or meant everything; there was just no way to know. Stranger still, when the Free *did* look at the villagers, the expressions on their faces almost seemed to be ones of pity, the way a fully-grown adult might look at a child.

But then the wanderer supposed he understood that. The people of the civilized world, while they had many failings, also had many talents. Talents for creating infrastructure, a society, a code of laws. They were creative and intelligent and goal-oriented, but it had to be said that here, in the Untamed Lands, those strengths were of little use.

But the awkwardness between the Free and the villagers was not the only issue at hand, nor even the most pressing. That distinction instead went to the caves themselves. They were vast—the wanderer had decided after an hour's travel that what the wizard had said was nothing short of the truth. But what the man had failed to mention was that, at times, they were not caverns at all. Sometimes those vast, spacious caverns gave way to tunnels and, sometimes, those tunnels to spaces that were barely six feet tall and four feet across, spaces so tight that they were only barely able to accommodate Veikr.

Not that the horse seemed to mind. Veikr accepted this latest trial the same way he had always accepted all of those difficulties which he and the wanderer had faced over the years—with a comforting sort of equanimity and acceptance. One which the villagers of Alhs, who stared about the tunnels with pale, grim expressions, did not share.

The tight, confined spaces were enough to make even the wanderer, who had never had an issue with such places, feel claustrophobic. He had thought the gorge before had felt suffocating, but he realized now that he'd had no idea what the word meant.

He was learning, though. With each minute that passed within the confines of the tunnels, he was learning. Yet as bad as it was for the wanderer and the others—Dekker was currently hunched, his head ducked low like a turtle trying to retreat into its shell—it was worse for Sheriff Fred. The sheriff was struggling—that much was obvious, for he walked with his teeth clenched, his jaw set, not studying the way ahead but instead only marking his feet as he moved.

The wanderer checked on him from time to time as they walked, but he thought that the man would be okay. Many might not have been, when forced to confront their worst fears in such a way, but the sheriff was made of sterner stuff than most. That was a truth the wanderer had already learned, so after a time he told himself to stop worrying about the man.

And that was alright. After all, there were plenty of other worries to concern himself with, such as how Ranger and the army he led was tracking them, if indeed they had been as concealed as the wizard and the others had said. Ranger had been an unparalleled tracker, it was true, and the wanderer had seen enough of the enemy to make him confident that the creature who had taken the Eternal's place shared that talent.

Yet no amount of training and natural talent could help a man track another along solid rock like the mountain, rock that made no footprints and held no vegetation that might betray a person's passage. Despite this, though, they seemed to be having no problem tracking the wanderer and the others.

The wanderer might have asked the ghosts about it, about how they thought such a thing was possible, for if there was anyone who might have shed some light on it, it would have been Ranger himself. The problem, of course, was that he had tried the amulet multiple times, had tried speaking to the ghosts, and despite his efforts he had received no response.

He told himself that was just further proof—if any were needed—that the Wizard of the South had indeed cast some sort of spell so that he might be invisible to the Eternals, so that even if their eyes had seen him and their ears heard them, their minds would have skirted by this information, blocking it out the same way a survivor of some terrible tragedy might avoid the memory of it.

And so the wanderer was left to puzzle out the problem alone. But then...he thought that, perhaps, that didn't need to be true. The next time the tunnel through which they traveled opened wider, the wanderer moved past the other villagers to the front of the line where the wizard walked, accompanied by the leader of the Free whose name the wanderer did not know.

The two spoke in a language of clicks and guttural sounds. The wanderer had traveled through much of the world, heard many tongues, but never one that sounded like the language the two spoke. When the wizard noted the wanderer he scowled and said something more to the leader of the Free who regarded the wanderer for a moment before moving away.

The wizard glanced at him before looking back to the trail. "What do you want, Eternal? To mock me, perhaps, or to make light of my opinion as you and your friends seem to so enjoy?"

"No," the wanderer said. "In fact, I came to ask it—your opinion, that is."

The wizard frowned, as if he thought the wanderer was laying some sort of trap for him. "You want my opinion?"

"I do."

This admission only made the wizard look even more suspicious. "What game are you playing at, Eternal?"

"No game," the wanderer said. "Or, at least, if it is one, then it is the same one we're all playing—a game of survival, with stakes as high as they come."

The wizard watched him for another moment, then finally he sighed. "Very well, Eternal. What is it you would like my opinion on?"

"The army—the one following us—they seem to know every move we're going to make before we make it, every direction we're going to go. I wondered if you had any idea, with your magic, I mean, about how that might be?"

The wizard frowned. "Do you mean to ask me if the creatures following us are making use of the Art in some way to track us?"

"Yes," the wanderer said.

"No."

"No?" the wanderer said. "So quickly?"

The wizard gave him a sidelong glance. "You are not the only one capable of thought, Eternal. I, too, have noted how they found the cave entrance so quickly, and, for that matter, how they tracked us through the wilderness of the Untamed Lands so easily. But if there is some sort of enchantment upon us, then it is one that has eluded my attention, and that is exceedingly unlikely."

The wanderer nodded slowly. "So what, then?"

The wizard watched him for a minute then let out a sour grunt. "As much as I enjoy watching an Eternal admit to not knowing something and asking for advice...the truth is, I have no idea. Short of actually seeing us with their own eyes or there being a traitor in the group, one who's letting them know where we go, I have no idea."

"Is that the reason you have kept so quiet about our destination? That you believe there might be a traitor?"

The wizard raised an eyebrow. "What do you think?"

The wanderer watched the man for a moment then nodded. "I see," he said. "But you are wrong—there is no one here who is a traitor. These are good people."

"How can you be so sure?" the wizard said. "You only just met them, what, a month or two ago?"

The wanderer considered that question for a time then, finally spoke. "I don't *know,*" he said. "I choose to believe." He smiled, glancing back at where Dekker walked with his wife and daughter, remembering what Sarah had told him when Veikr had gone missing. "I choose to believe because I have to believe in something, and so I choose to believe in them."

The wizard gave him a strange look at that, as if he were a puzzle he was trying to figure out. "You are very odd, Eternal," he said finally.

The wanderer saw no point in arguing with that, so he didn't try. They continued in something that quite nearly approached companionable silence, at least to the wanderer, until they reached an intersection in the caverns, and the leader of the Free loped up.

"Serack and I need to speak," the wizard said. "If you'll excuse us."

"Of course," the wanderer said, and in another moment the two walked toward the intersection, speaking in the alien language of the Free.

He stared after them. The creature called Serack might have been the leader of his people, yet the wanderer did not miss the way he treated the wizard—with obvious respect, even deference, almost like some famous personage that had come among them. The other Free treated him much the same. The wanderer thought it said a lot about the wizard that he spoke their language instead of expecting them—considering the high regard in which they clearly held him—to speak his.

The man, for reasons the wanderer still didn't understand, might hate the Eternals, but it was clear that, in the other aspects of his life, he was not foolish or cruel. Which made the wanderer think, once more, of the man's words concerning how Ranger and his army were able to track them. He did not believe the idea that there was a traitor among them. First, he was confident that, had there been someone sneaking way or leaving intentional evidence of their passage he would have noticed. More than that, though, he had come to know something of the villagers of Alhs during their travels together, something of their tenacity, their loyalty to each other, and he did not believe any of them capable of such duplicity.

Which only left one other option, at least according to the wizard. *Either there is a traitor,* he'd said, *or they are watching us with their own eyes.*

But then that, too, was impossible. After all, if they had been being shadowed, he'd have known that, too, would have seen whatever creature Ranger would have set to do such a task.

No sooner had he had the thought than realization struck the wanderer, and he winced. *Fool,* he told himself. His first thought had been right—had something been following them, marking their progress, he would have seen it.

Unless, of course, it was invisible.

***

They continued on for another two hours until the wanderer began to make out light up ahead in the distance. Or, more specifically, a warm, steady, soft ambience that was far different than the flickering, ruddy red glow of the torches some of the villagers carried.

The others, he knew, not gifted with eyes like his own, did not notice it, though he thought that the Free did. Still, he moved to the sheriff who was nearly bent double now in an effort to look at nothing but his feet to forget the tons and tons of stone hemming them in on all sides. The wanderer gave a small smile to the sheriff's wife, the woman walking beside him, studying her husband with a mixture of love and worry. "We're almost out," the wanderer said.

The sheriff looked up at him, and the wanderer saw in his pale expression, in the lines on his face, what traveling through the tunnels had cost the man. There was a common saying that claimed that whatever didn't kill a man made him stronger. The wanderer understood what was meant by it, but he understood, also, that it was wrong. What didn't kill a man sometimes weakened him sufficiently that the next thing would. But he thought the sheriff would be alright. He *hoped* that he would. "How are you?" he asked.

"Me?" the man said, trying for casual and not even coming close. "I'm f-fine," he said. "Shit, I could do this all day. Who needs the sun or fresh air, open spaces? Who needs to breathe?" he finished in a sort of gasp, and the wanderer nodded.

"You're doing well," he said.

The man snorted. "If this is well I'd hate to see what bad looks like."

"Just the same," the wanderer said. "I thought you should know that we are very nearly finished with the tunnels. A half hour, an hour at most. No more than that."

"Really?" the sheriff asked, a childlike hope in his voice. "Are you sure?"

"I'm sure," the wanderer agreed.

"Well then," the sheriff said, nodding, his back straightening. "Reckon if I've spent years listening to Deputy Ward's particular brand of belly-aching and bullshit I s'pose I can survive a few minutes of this."

The wanderer grinned. "I suppose you can."

Satisfied that the sheriff would be alright, the wanderer moved to where Dekker walked with his family.

"Ungr," Dekker said, nodding. "Everything alright?"

The wanderer glanced at Sarah and Ella, then back to Dekker. "I don't think so," he said honestly. "I wonder, can you gather up Clint and the Perishables?"

Dekker raised an eyebrow. "A job to do, is it?"

"Maybe," the wanderer said. "But let's keep it quiet, please," he said. "I don't want to alarm anyone."

Dekker frowned. "Whatever it is you're thinkin', Ungr, I'd be lyin' if I didn't tell you I ain't exactly comforted by it."

"Neither am I," the wanderer said. "Will you gather them?"

"Of course," Dekker said, "though, if it's trouble that needs lookin' into, we might be able to get some more men, if that's what's called for. Plenty of the villagers I think'd be willin' to help."

The wanderer considered that. "Very well," he said, "but no more than a half dozen or so. For what I have planned, more isn't necessarily better. When you've gathered them, will you meet me with the wizard and the sheriff at the front?"

"Will do," Dekker said. He started away, pausing at the sound of his wife's voice.

"What can I do?"

Dekker glanced at the wanderer, and he looked at the woman. "Keep everyone calm," he said. "Let them know there's nothing to worry about—we need everyone acting normal."

Ella frowned but, to her credit, she didn't ask any questions, only nodded. She and Dekker shared a look then. It only lasted for a moment, but in that instant the wanderer saw, once more, the love they held for each other and, once more, he was humbled by it.

Then the moment passed, and Dekker turned to him, giving him a nod before walking away to find Clint and the others.

When the big man was gone, the wanderer gave Ella a smile and a nod then started away.

"Ungr?"

He turned back and saw clearly the worry in her eyes. "Yes?" he asked, knowing full well what she meant to say, what she *needed* to say.

"You'll..." she paused, glancing after her husband. "You'll look after him?"

"With my life," he told her, meaning it.

She gave him a small, timid, fragile smile. "Thank you."

He inclined his head to her then, well aware that time was of the essence, turned and walked away to speak to the wizard and the others.

CHAPTER ELEVEN

The wanderer sat with his sword lying across his lap, the blade bared. And he waited. He had sat so before, countless times on countless nights, waiting to discover if the fate he had run from his whole life would finally find him. This time, though, was not like all the others, for this time he did not want to avoid that fate—he welcomed it.

He had run long enough. It felt good to sit and wait, to run no longer.

He crouched on an overturned, flat rock, and waited for five minutes.

Then ten.

And nothing happened.

Nothing except that the late afternoon sun, already sank low on the horizon, sank a little lower. It was quiet here, outside the cave, with all the villagers gone on farther along the trail and only Veikr to keep him company where the horse stood a short distance away.

Ten minutes gave way to fifteen, and still the wanderer did not stir. He only sat, listening, watching, soaking in that brief moment of peace, peace that could only be found in the waiting before blood was shed. But then he thought that was nearly always the case.

It seemed to him that it had been decades since he'd last been alone. True, he had been alone when he'd climbed the ravine just as he'd been alone when he, with Shaman's help, had called a storm down upon his enemies, but both times he had been driven by purpose and had been left no time to appreciate the quiet. The stillness.

He appreciated it now. His thoughts wanted to drift as he waited, but he kept a tight rein on them. Drifting thoughts, carried on the flotsam of a man's consciousness, almost always fetched up against something, like twigs caught in a river current, and that something was distraction.

He could not afford to be distracted, not now. The ghosts of his past, of those he had loved and those he had hated, drifted into his mind's eye, and he ignored them. It was not easy, but it was something at which he'd had plenty of practice—after all, he had lived for many years, and there were many ghosts.

He sat in the stillness, the stillness without and the stillness within, and he waited for what would come. But as fifteen minutes drew on to half an hour and more, he found himself shifting, beginning to think that, perhaps, he had been wrong after all. Despite his best efforts, his thoughts began to drift, the phantoms of his past growing louder in their murmuring. And so, deciding that if he were going to be haunted by ghosts then he at least meant for them to be ghosts of his own choosing, the wanderer opened the locket.

He had not heard from the ghosts in some time, not since he'd reunited with the wizard and the villagers, and some part of him feared that their silence would be permanent this time. He was relieved, then, when he heard Tactician speak in his normal tone, one that was his own personal mixture of condescension and scorn. *This is a foolish plan, Youngest, if plan it can even be called.*

Reckless, Alchemist said, her bubbly, energetic voice sounding almost frantic. *A deadly mixture this, and with such ingredients as you have added, Youngest, how can it be anything but?*

You should run, Tactician said, as close to agreement with Alchemist as the ghost ever got with anyone. *It has kept you and those with you alive so far—why stop now?*

The wanderer had been silent so far, but he chose to answer that, felt almost compelled to. "Because I am sick of running," he said quietly. "Now, I will stand."

Said as if you think it noble, Tactician said, the sneer clear in his voice. *But there is nothing noble about standing and watching as the storm comes, waiting for it to destroy you.*

"I do not mean to let it," the wanderer said quietly.

Alchemist is right, Youngest, a new voice, this one belonging to Oracle, said. *This is reckless, and while you have been many things over the years, you have rarely, if ever, been that. Do you not see? It is the weapon, the blade of the enemy. It works at you, Youngest. It is subtle, the weapon, so subtle that it might make its voice sound like your own, so that you might listen. And, in listening, be doomed.*

"You're wrong," the wanderer said. Or, at least, he meant to say it. Instead, the words came out in an angry growl, one that surprised him and, judging by the silence that followed, surprised the ghosts as well.

Do you not feel it, Youngest? Oracle asked softly. *Working at you? Corrupting you? Spreading through your body like a plague so that, in time, it will—*

The wanderer snapped the locket shut.

He felt his heart hammering in his chest like some tribal drum as he stared down at the locket. He had not meant to be rude, had certainly not set out to be so. It had just been that Oracle's words, in that moment, had seemed unbearable, each of them somehow feeling like the agonizing prick of a knife or dagger.

Or a sword, part of him thought, and he felt his attention going to the cursed blade, sheathed at his back. In that moment, he was very aware of its presence, for it seemed almost to thrum against him with some malevolent energy. His imagination, stirred to life by Oracle's words, or something more?

The thought spawned a feeling of cold dread in him, but he forced it back. No. It was his imagination, that was all. He felt the sword no less—and certainly no more—than normal. Oracle was wrong about the blade, just as the others were wrong about his plan. He knew that, just as he knew that he had *meant* to close the locket and never mind the fact that he did not remember making the conscious decision to do so.

He was sure he had. Of course he had. Only...he did not remember it. He was still trying when he heard a *crunch* from ahead of him, and he pushed away the thought, the worry, raising his eyes to regard the cave opening, the one through which he and the others had exited the caverns a little over two hours ago.

He stared at that apparently empty cave opening, where he and some others had spent a few minutes littering the ground with small dried twigs they'd found, and gave a grim smile at the shadows gathered there. "I've been waiting for you," he told the shadows. "I knew you would come, in time."

The shadows said nothing. Or, at least, nearly so. The answer that came was not one of words but instead another *snap* as a second twig broke. The wanderer rose slowly to his feet, finding that part of him—a small part, but not too small—was excited for what was to come. He told himself that was normal, as he let his sword hang out to one side, at an angle to the ground. After all, any man who had spent so long running would be glad to finally stop and face his foe. He told himself that was all, that it was natural, not some bloodlust brought on by the cursed blade. He told himself that...but he did not wholly believe it.

Another *snap.* Another *crunch.*

The wanderer found his mouth spreading into a wide grin. "You have come in service to death," he told the shadows. "Have been bent to that end and no other. You have come searching for it, for death, and you have found it. Come then—come and claim it." Then, the wanderer turned to the side of the cave, regarding the shadows pooled there and what he knew lay within them. *"Now!"* he roared.

No sooner were the words out of his mouth than men stepped forward from both sides of the cave. Men holding buckets full of a mixture of crushed mountain flowers and rainwater he and the others had made while they waited. The men, mostly the Perishables but some few villagers among them as well as Dekker, slung their buckets forward and out came the water. Mixed as it had been with the mountain flowers and herbs, the water was all manner of colors, and where it struck the apparent emptiness of the cave mouth it splattered on four figures standing there, dyeing them various shades of color.

The wanderer gazed at the four Unseen, now visible from the colored water staining them, and as the men retreated he felt a moment of panic, thinking that Oracle had perhaps been right and that he had acted in haste, recklessly. Two he had expected. Not four. But while some of him felt nervous, mostly for the villagers in his care, there was another part, a dark part, that rejoiced. He took in their too-long, too-thin arms, with those great talons on the end of them, took in their elongated, monstrous faces, and found his upper lip peeling back from his teeth in a silent snarl.

How long had these creatures or those like them chased him? And how many innocents had died in that pursuit? Innocents like Felden Ruitt. Innocents like Joan and those villagers of Alhs whose names the wanderer had never even known. Many of the Perishables, too. He found that he was gripping the handle of his sword so hard his fingers ached, but he did not mind. It was a good pain, a promise of things to come. "You have tracked us," he told the creatures, "have come meaning to keep an eye on us in service to your master. Well, you have found us. You *see* us." He paused, grinning wider. "And we see you."

With that, the wanderer let out a roar and charged toward the creatures who were still standing, unmoving, in the cave mouth. The Unseen's greatest strength was their ability to remain invisible, undetected and he had stolen that from them. But while it was their greatest strength, it was not their *only* one. Another of the dark gifts their masters had given them was a speed unrivaled even by the wanderer himself.

So despite the fact that he'd rushed toward the cave mouth before the creatures had moved, when two of them burst into action they covered well over half the distance to him in what felt like a heartbeat.

The dyed water had not completely covered the creatures and so the wanderer caught sight only of bits and pieces as they hurled themselves at him, their dagger-sharp talons flashing. The wanderer, though, knew well their tactics, how they used their great speed to fling themselves past their prey even as their talons ripped into them. He knew, and so he was ready, moving to the side so that he was not in between the two. Then his sword flashed out as the one nearest him passed him, and instead of the talon finding purchase in his flesh it was his sword that connected, and with a spurt of ichor the creature's arm flew free.

The wanderer aimed his backswing for the creature's neck, but it was already out of his reach, and he spun, holding his ichor-stained sword two-handed. The two Unseen stopped a short distance away, turning to regard him. One was nearly completely still, the other, whose arm lay near the wanderer's feet, slumped and wavering. He risked a quick glance behind him at the other two, expecting them to rush forward any moment.

Likely they would have, only before they did there was a shout and more men rose on either side of the mountain trail from where they'd hidden on the slope brandishing bows and crossbows and slings. In another moment missiles filled the air, sailing toward the Unseen who staggered as bolts and arrows embedded themselves in their flesh, stumbled as stones and rocks pelted them.

There was a great roar and a boulder large enough to crush a man flew out from Dekker's hands and struck one of the two who collapsed to the ground underneath the great weight as if struck down by the fist of some angry god. The massive boulder smashed the creature and ichor sprayed.

The second, though, seemed to rally, and although wounded and bleeding ichor from a dozen wounds, it spun, flashing forward, and a man cried out as its claws dug deep into his flesh. The wanderer started forward, meaning to help, but before he could he felt, more than heard, the other Unseen coming at him again.

He ducked, giving a roar as he brought his blade around in a two-handed grip and, as he'd expected, he caught one of the creatures moving past him. The blade's sharpness, coupled with the Unseen's momentum, was enough to cleave through the creature's legs just below the knees.

The Unseen wailed as the top half of its body flew through the air, leaving its legs—or most of them—behind. The wanderer, though, paid it no more attention. Instead, his focus was on the second creature, the one missing a hand, that had turned to regard him, its head cocked to the side. "Come on then," he told it, aware of the shouts of the Perishables and villagers as they fought the remaining Unseen.

The creature needed no more urging than that, rushing forward in a blur. The wanderer did not dodge this time. Instead, he waited for it to come, his teeth bared. He pivoted, lunging away from the creature's strike but not away from the creature itself. Instead, his movement brought him inside its guard, and its momentum brought its body onto the tip of his sword, impaling it.

The force was so great, that the wanderer staggered. His sword was nearly ripped from his hands, but he managed to keep hold of it.

The creature let out a guttural wail, struggling against the sword. Before it thought to strike him with its remaining talon, the wanderer took one hand from his sword, withdrawing the knife he always kept at his waist and using it to dig a bloody furrow in the creature's throat.

Ichor sprayed along his face, his chest and hands. The wanderer watched the creature as it died, watched it fade into existence even as its life faded out of it, whatever magic had concealed it dissipating in its death.

The wanderer gave the creature a kick, ripping his blade free and it collapsed at his feet. Then he stalked to the legless Unseen, the creature clawing at the rocky ground in an effort to get toward him as it regarded his approach with hate-filled eyes. The wanderer stopped in front of it, watching its struggles, some part of him finding a dark contentment at the creature's struggle. "The world is full of many truths, and this is only one," the wanderer told the dying creature. "He who goes out seeking blood and death will always find it."

He brought his blade down into the creature's back and through it, driving into the ground and pinning it there. He might have stood and watched it, as he had the first, but there was a shout from nearby, a man's voice, raised in pain.

The wanderer blinked, feeling as if he were waking from a dream, or perhaps a trance of the kind Shaman and Oracle had sometimes put him under during his training. He turned and saw that Dekker and the Perishables were busily fighting the final Unseen. The creature was full of bolts and arrows, its body leaking ichor from seemingly everywhere, surrounded by a dozen Perishables and villagers, yet it was not finished.

Even as the wanderer turned to regard it, the creature's talon lashed out, and a Perishable screamed as the claws, sharp as daggers, ripped into his stomach, opening it. The man collapsed to the ground, blood and worse coming out of the wound. The wanderer was rushing forward even before the man hit the ground. Dekker was closer, though, and he beat him to it, roaring and charging into the creature from behind, wrapping his muscular arms around it in a tight bearhug.

"Dekker, watch its talons!" the wanderer shouted, but he was too late.

He was just reaching the group when the creature made use of its far-too-long arms, flexing its talons and cutting a line down the big man's leg.

Dekker roared in pain, losing his grip and stumbling away, turning before the wanderer could see how bad the wound was. But then the wanderer was there and for the moment he pushed his worry for Dekker away.

He shouldered his way between two of the Perishables, only realizing in that moment his sword was still stuck in the creature he'd pinned to the ground.

He transferred his knife to his right hand as he stepped up behind the creature bringing his left hand over its head and forehead, jerking it back as he drove his blade underneath its elongated chin.

The creature's entire body tensed as the knife went in, but the wanderer wasn't finished. He ripped the blade free and shoved it to the ground onto its back.

The creature tried to move but it was sluggish from its injury, and in another moment he was straddling it, bringing the knife down, two-handed, into the creature's chest. Then again and again.

He did not know how many times he stabbed it, knew only that the image of Dekker stumbling away, blood spurting, filled his every thought, and he was somehow possessed of the feeling, irrational though it was, that if he kept going, if he stabbed again, and again, then he could take it back, could make the big man okay again.

He roared his anger, his defiance, as he brought the blade down again and again and for a time he knew nothing but the feel of the creature's body at each thudding impact.

Then he felt something on his shoulder, and he spun with a snarl, his blade flashing out to take the creature who'd attacked him. He realized, at the last moment, that it was not a creature at all, but was instead Dekker.

The knife came to rest inches from the big man's chest, and the wanderer blinked. "You're...you're alright? I thought, the creature, it struck you."

"Sure," Dekker said, glancing down at his leg. "Just a glancin' blow, though that bastard's claws are sharp, that's for damn sure," he went on as the wanderer breathed a heavy sigh of relief, realizing that it was only a shallow cut and one that was no real danger. "Anyway...how about you? Are...that is...are you alright?"

The wanderer wasn't sure what the big man meant at first, for he'd taken no wound in the battle. But he saw the worry in Dekker's face and it came to him a moment later. He winced, aware that the Perishables and the villagers who'd accompanied them were all staring at him, looks of shock on their face.

He glanced down at his arm, now hanging at his side, at the ichor-covered knife held in an ichor-covered hand. He wiped the blade on ichor-covered trousers then slid it back into its sheath at his waist.

There were several awkward seconds of silence as the gathered men studied the wanderer as if they thought he might attack them at any moment before the stillness was broken by a pained moan.

The wanderer turned and saw that two Perishables were lying on the ground. One's throat had been opened, and he lay unmoving, no life left in him. The other was the one the wanderer had seen wounded, and he lay moaning and writhing, his hands pressed tightly against the rent in his stomach in an effort to keep everything inside.

The wanderer moved toward him, kneeling beside him.

"H-how bad is it?" the man asked, and the wanderer saw, looking at him, that he appeared to be in his early twenties, certainly no older than twenty-five years. Just then, though, his pain made his voice sound even younger, like that of a child.

"Hold him," the wanderer said. Two men came forward, kneeling on either side of the wounded man, taking his arms.

As soon as the man's hands were out of the way the wanderer saw just how bad, how *final* the man's wound was. The Unseen's talons had done their work, ripping three jagged rents into the man's stomach, through which could be seen several of his organs.

"*P-please,*" the young man said. "H-how bad is it?"

As bad as it can be, the wanderer thought, *and the only consolation is that you will not have to feel the pain of it, at least not for long.*

He felt a rush of shame and self-recrimination fill him. If he'd been faster, if he hadn't gloried in the creatures' deaths, he might have made it in time, and the man might not have been wounded at all.

No, he thought. *No.* The man would not die—he would not allow it. "A needle or a knife. Thread. Hot water and bandages. Now."

"But how do we get the water hot?" someone asked. "By the time—"

"Just get it!" the wanderer roared, spinning on the man who'd spoken so fiercely that the Perishable took a step back, his eyes wide, his hands going up to say that he meant no harm.

Several men rushed away then. Meanwhile, the wounded man moaned again, and the wanderer pushed his hands against the rent in his stomach, trying, in vain, to keep his blood from leaking out of him.

"How...bad?" the man asked again, this time in a throaty whisper, barely loud enough to hear.

"It's fine," the wanderer told the dying man. "You're fine. We're fine."

But they were lies, all of them. He knew it, yet as the wounded man continued to squirm, as his struggles lessened, the wanderer continued to press his wound together, pressed it so tightly that the man moaned in pain.

"We have to keep the blood in," the wanderer told the man. And he pressed harder. The man did not moan, not this time, and the wanderer continued to hold the wound together. *"Where is that water?"* he yelled. *"I need the thread and—"*

"Ungr."

It was Dekker's voice, but the wanderer didn't turn to him. He shook his head, pressing tighter. "I need the water, Dekker, quickly. He's in serious da—"

"He's dead, Ungr," the big man said, his voice soft.

"What?" the wanderer said, turning to Dekker, seeing the truth of it in the man's face even before he turned and looked at the Perishable.

"No," the wanderer said, shaking his head at Dekker, at the dead man. "No, he can make it." He bent back, closing the wound again, redoubling his efforts. "*Water,*" he yelled, his voice hoarse, raw. "*Please, damnit, bring the water!*"

"Ungr, it's too late. You tried."

The wanderer thought of the way he'd hesitated, enjoying watching the Unseen die. Only moments squandered, but then they were moments that might have made all the difference. "No, Dekker," the wanderer said. "I can save him. I...I *need* to save him."

He started to turn back to him, but the big man put a hand on his shoulder, turning him, pulling him away. "Let it go, Ungr. You tried."

The wanderer stared at the big man, feeling hollowed out, empty. Then, finally, he rose, looking around at the Perishables and villagers, at their faces, studying him. They appeared, at first glance, to be full of compassion for him, but another part of him thought that he saw recrimination in their gazes. Perhaps even hate. "I'm...I'm sorry," he told them.

"No one blames you, Ungr. You did what you could—we all did," Dekker said, and several of the Perishables nodded their agreement. "Now come on—the others are waiting."

Feeling empty, as lifeless as the dead man lying at his feet, the wanderer only nodded, allowing himself to be led away.

And then, like so many other times in his life, the wanderer did the only thing he could—he walked on, leaving the dead behind him. But not too far, he knew, for he had suffered enough, lost enough, that he knew the dead man's ghost would come back to haunt him in the days to come. And if there was any consolation to be had, it was this and this alone—the young man's ghost would have plenty of company.

CHAPTER TWELVE

Night fell as they followed after the others, a starless darkness to match the darkness the wanderer felt within himself. Two men were dead, and it was his fault. His fault because he had been more focused, in that moment during which he'd fought the Unseen, on killing, not saving. Two men were dead because they had done what he'd asked, because they had trusted him. Two men whose faces would forever be engraved upon his mind, faces which would rise in the still, quiet moments, to remind him, should he ever think to forget, of how he had failed.

He was well aware, as he walked, of the cursed blade at his back, seeming to hum with dark promise. He had carried the blade for a hundred years and more. After so long, it had lost much of its menace, becoming just another *thing* in his mind when, in fact, it was *the* thing, the weapon that, should it fall into the enemy's hands, would be instrumental in destroying the entire world.

He had forgotten that somewhere along the way. Had told himself, in those moments when he had seen cause to draw it, that he was doing so out of necessity, that he had no choice. That surviving, that saving those he meant to protect, was worth the cost. But that was an easy thing to think when the cost was some nebulous uncertainty. It was far harder to justify drawing the sword, even in defense of himself or those he'd come to love, when the cost was finally come due.

The beginning of that cost he'd paid already, in being too slow to save the Perishables while he'd been focused on reveling in the deaths of his enemies. But he thought the cost was far from paid. He felt as if some part of him had been ripped away. But no...no, that wasn't quite right. It, whatever *it* had been, had not been ripped away—it had been stolen. It was as if he stood in a library, one with books stacked on shelves from the floor to the ceiling. Many books, each of which was some small part of who he was. He had closed his eyes, only for a moment, and one of those books had been taken. There were so many that he could not remember which book it had been, but he could see the empty place in the shelves where it had once stood, could see the shadowed proof of its absence. More than that, he could *feel* that absence. Could feel it the way a man who has recently lost a tooth might run his tongue along the spot where it had been. The man might not have thought much of the tooth when he'd had it, but now that it was gone, he could think of little else.

And so part of him was missing. Gone. Likely gone beyond retrieval. He could blame the cursed blade, perhaps, the instrument of the enemy, or he could blame simple time—a hundred years was a very long time to carry a burden. He could blame circumstance or chance, as men so often did, but the truth was that while men often complained about their situations in life, they were situations they had created themselves. And if the paths they walked were inimical to them, then they were at least *known,* and how not? They were the ones who had started down them, after all.

So he could blame no one and nothing but himself. Perhaps those moments when he'd drawn the cursed blade had felt necessary, but then the poor choices of a man's life often did. It wasn't as if people woke up and decided that they would try to make terrible decisions. It just happened—a consequence of life, maybe, and while those decisions were often understandable, they were very rarely excusable—particularly when they involved a weapon that could destroy the world.

They reached the spot where the wizard, the sheriff and the others were waiting about an hour later. Those who had accompanied the wanderer on his mission moved forward, sharing words with family and friends relieved to find them returned and alive. Dekker also moved forward to where Sarah and Ella stood.

But not everyone moved forward, for there were two who would not be celebrating, not today. Not ever again.

The wanderer stood beside Veikr, his silent companion, and watched that reunion, thinking thoughts about himself that were particularly uncharitable.

"You don't look like a man who has won a victory."

The wanderer turned and was surprised to see that the wizard had walked up. "Because I am not," he said.

"Entertaining dark thoughts, then?"

"Dark thoughts for a dark night," the wanderer said. "One without victory."

The wizard frowned, turning to regard those who had returned as they talked excitedly with their friends and family. "It seems they, at least, would disagree with that."

A response did not seem required to that, so the wanderer gave none.

"And the others?" the wizard asked after a time. "There were two more who went with you, were there not?"

The wandered nodded grimly. "There were."

The wizard watched him for several seconds then, slowly nodded. "You know what your problem is, Eternal?" he said after a moment.

"Please," the wanderer said, the word coming out harsher than he'd meant it to. "Not now. Later, if you wish, you can regale me with my faults and failings—most of which, I assure you, I am more than aware of. But please...just leave me in peace. If only for a little while."

The wizard watched him for several seconds, and had the wanderer not known better he would have said there was something almost like compassion in the man's gaze. "Your problem," the wizard went on, "is that you think too much of yourself."

The wanderer sighed. "Very well," he said, "tell me why I am evil, but I warn you, if it is disagreement you're looking for, you are likely to be disappointed."

"You think, for example," the wizard went on as if he hadn't spoken, "that you have the power of life and death over others, that they are like children that you are meant to protect, that you are *supposed* to protect."

The wanderer frowned. "I didn't—"

"But they aren't," the wizard said. "They are, all of them, grown men and women," he went on, glancing at the villagers. "Plenty capable of making their own decisions, for good or ill. Decisions which you cannot be held accountable for."

The wanderer frowned deeper. "It was my plan, and—"

"And did you force anyone to go?"

"No, but—"

"But some who went did not make it back," the wizard said. "The same could be said for any man or woman who wakes up in the morning, Eternal, for any person who dares to leave their bed, and even those who do not."

"But if I'd have been faster or—"

"Sure," the wizard agreed, nodding. "If you'd have been faster. Or stronger. Or smarter, maybe. Or if he'd been faster or stronger or smarter. Or if the world were all blushing maidens smiling as they refilled our wine...but it isn't. Placing blame is never hard, Eternal. But unless you are the one that killed those men..." He paused, glancing at the wanderer who sighed and shook his head. "Then you are not responsible for their deaths."

"But—"

"People die, Eternal," the wizard said, and there was something strange about his voice, about the faraway look in his eyes, something that let the wanderer know he was thinking about some memory. "It is what we are best at. And if there is an answer to that inevitable truth, it is not to spend our lives in fear or regret or shame. Instead, it is to live them as fully and wholly and as well as we can. That is how we honor the dead. Do you understand?"

He finished the last gravely, his voice full of emotion, more forceful than the wanderer had heard him speak so far. "I understand," the wanderer said.

The wizard watched him for a moment, seeming to brim with intensity, as if that memory whatever it was, were threatening to overtake him. Then, in another instant, the look vanished, and he sighed, seeming to deflate, seeming, in that moment, very tired. "Good. Because while self-recrimination and moping are a favorite of many men, you simply do not have the luxury right now. Some are lost, it is true, and we can grieve for them. Later. For now, there are those who might yet be saved."

The wanderer nodded. "Okay."

The wizard raised an eyebrow, as if surprised to hear him say as much. "Okay," he said uncertainly. Then gave a nod of his own. "Good. That's good because these people need a leader, and in case you haven't noticed, I am not particularly good with people."

"Oh?" the wanderer asked, a small smile coming to his face. "I never would have guessed."

The wizard gave a snort. "Alright, alright. Laugh it up, you bastard. Better that than more moping."

Bastard. It was the first time, to the wanderer's recollection, that the wizard had called him anything besides "Eternal." Not a great improvement, maybe, but he thought that it was one just the same.

"Very well," he said. "No more moping."

"Good," the wizard said. "That's good, because we've only got room for one antisocial asshole on this journey." He started away then paused, glancing back at the wanderer. "Those men chose to help," he said quietly, "chose to risk sacrificing themselves to save others, and they did. Do not tarnish that sacrifice by making it about you. You do not deserve that—*they* do not deserve that." And then, before the wanderer could say anything, the wizard turned and walked away which was just as well as the wanderer had no idea what he might have said.

"Everything alright?"

The wanderer turned to see that Dekker had moved up beside him and was currently scowling at the departing wizard's back.

The wanderer considered that then slowly shook his head. "No, not yet," he said, regarding the wizard then turning to look at the Perishables and villagers as they celebrated their small victory. "But I think maybe it will be."

CHAPTER THIRTEEN

They traveled on through the night, the villagers of Alhs and the Perishables carrying torches in order to see. Meanwhile, the Free demonstrated their greater night vision by traveling on the outside edges of the torchlight in their loping, ape-like movements.

The wizard led them down the mountainside to a flat plain from where, a short distance ahead, the wanderer could see forest. Forest much like those he and the villagers had traveled through before reaching the Whisperers, dense and thick and untamed.

Here, the wizard and the leader of the Free paused, speaking in that clicking, guttural language of theirs. They exchanged a few words and then the leader of the Free moved away, calling out in words the wanderer did not know but the meaning of which he learned soon enough as the other Free that had accompanied them separated themselves from the group of confused-looking villagers and moved to stand beside him.

"What's happening there, you reckon?" the sheriff asked from beside the wanderer.

The wanderer shook his head. He glanced at the wizard, saw the man looking after them with obvious sadness in his gaze then, suddenly, realization dawned. "They're leaving."

"Leaving?" the sheriff asked. "To go where?"

"I...don't know," the wanderer said. Then he moved forward to where the wizard stood looking after the Free. By the time he reached the man, the Free had begun to walk away, the leader pausing to cast one more glance back at the wizard who held his hand up in farewell, unshed tears shimmering in his eyes.

"Is everything alright?"

The wizard started, glancing at him and clearing his throat, running an arm brusquely across his eyes. "Everything's fine. The Free are leaving."

"I saw as much," the wanderer noted. "Are...are you sure that's wise?"

"Wise?" the wizard asked.

"I mean...for them to venture out on their own?"

The wizard shook his head slowly. "The Free, Eternal, are more than capable of taking care of themselves against most threats. Besides, the Untamed Lands are their home. They will be fine."

"And yet you seem sad."

"I *am* sad, damnit," the wizard said, "but not for them. I am sad for myself, for it is unlikely I will see them again."

"But...why?" the wanderer asked.

The wizard turned to regard him, his expression not angry, only sad. "Because you wanted to save your friends. And so I have lost mine."

The wanderer blinked. "I...I didn't mean—"

"I know," the wizard said. "You did what you thought was right, as all men must. And, like all men, you must suffer the consequences." He sighed, glancing once more at the departing Free as the last of them faded into the distant tree line. "As we all must. Now," he went on, sounding very tired, "if you have no more questions, I would like to continue on. We are close now, but I am not as young as I once was, and I would save my breath for the journey."

The wanderer understood that the man wanted some time alone, so he nodded. "Of course," he said.

The wizard inclined his head as if in thanks then turned and started away. The wanderer glanced at the departing Free, wishing them well, then followed the wizard.

***

The wizard led them into the woods of the Untamed Lands, and they traveled on for several hours, the wanderer's eyes scanning the trees around them for any tell-tale sign that might give away someone watching them. He thought they had taken care of all the Unseen following them, but he knew that had only bought them some time, little more. After all, there was nothing stopping Ranger or the enemy from sending more of the creatures to track them down.

Still, he saw no sign that they were being followed, and they continued trudging wearily onward as night gave way to morning. As they walked, the wanderer became aware of a sound, distant at first, but growing louder as they walked. It was the rushing sound of a river. He walked up to where the wizard trudged, alone, at the front of the procession.

The man's expression was grim, and when he turned the wanderer saw unshed tears in the wizard's eyes, ones that he quickly wiped away with an arm. "What is it, Eternal? Everything okay?"

"I'm...I'm certain they'll be okay," the wanderer offered, not sure what to say, what comfort he might give.

The wizard watched him for a moment, raising an eyebrow. "An Eternal offering comfort. You really are full of surprises. Anyway, is that what you wished to speak to me about?"

The wanderer shook his head. "There's a river close, I think."

"Yes."

"I was thinking perhaps it might be a good time to refill our waterskins, take a short rest. They could all use it."

The wizard shook his head. "Not here."

"But—"

The other man sighed, stopping and holding up a hand to call for a halt. The sheriff walked up as the villagers stopped. "Everything okay?" he asked.

"No, but that's another story," the wizard said. "I wonder, Sheriff, if you wouldn't mind keeping an eye on everyone for a few minutes, while I speak privately with the Eternal here."

The sheriff glanced between the two of them then shrugged. "Fine with me," he said.

"Good," the wizard said, then he glanced at the wanderer and, without another word, turned and started into the trees.

The wanderer and the sheriff shared a look, then the wanderer set off after the wizard. He led them toward the sound of the rushing water, and the wanderer followed after. It did not take them long to come upon the source of the sounds, a river that was thirty feet across with rapid currents—always a good sign when looking for drinkable water.

The wizard stopped a short distance from the shore, and the wanderer started past him, meaning to check the water. The wizard, though, caught him by the shoulder before he'd taken more than a couple of steps. "I wouldn't," the wizard said.

"I...don't understand."

"No," the wizard said, "but if you dipped your hands in that water you would soon enough," he said. The wanderer opened his mouth to ask what he meant by that and the wizard held up a hand, silencing him. Then, the hand still raised, he reached in his belt, withdrawing a small knife he kept there, and poked himself in the finger, hissing as blood began to gather at the small point. Then, watching the wanderer, he knelt and picked up a stone, smearing the blood on it before throwing it into the water with a grunt.

A moment passed, then another, and the wanderer was just about to ask what the man was trying to show him, when suddenly sleek, scaled forms erupted out of the water. They were fish, but larger than any the wanderer had ever seen—five and six feet long—with rows of long, serrated teeth. The fish flashed out of the water in great leaps, their teeth snapping at air before they fell back in.

It went on for thirty seconds or so, then the river was still again save for the current. The wanderer found himself taking a step back, and the wizard grunted what might have been a laugh. "Not everything, Eternal, is as it seems, a notion that is truer nowhere than here, in the Untamed Lands."

"So I see," the wanderer said.

"The blood calls them," the wizard said, "but they would come anyway, if one were to make enough noise, to disturb the water enough."

The wanderer nodded. "Thanks."

The wizard blinked as if it had been the last thing he'd expected him to say. "Things are not as they seem indeed. You are one, and that sword at your back another."

The wanderer found his hand going protectively to the cursed blade on instinct. The wizard gave him a small smile. "You need not worry, Eternal—I have no interest in magic weapons, nor weapons of any kind. I did not come to the Untamed Lands for war but for peace."

The wanderer nodded. "The blade...it's cursed. A burden I would not wish on you at any rate."

The wizard frowned. "Cursed, is it?"

"Yes."

"May I see it?"

The wanderer tensed at that. "It must not be taken from its sheath, for to do so would warn the e—"

"I assure you, I have no plans of removing it from its sheath."

The wanderer could not remember the last time anyone had held the cursed blade save him. Except, of course, when the bandits had tried to take it from him, but it had been years before then, perhaps decades. He felt a strange sort of jealousy overcome him, jealousy like a child might feel when another child asked to play with his favorite toy. Still, he removed the sheathed blade, offering it over.

The wizard took it, holding it up almost like an offering in both hands, then closed his eyes, murmuring some words that were too low for the wanderer to hear. After a moment, he opened them again and handed the blade back. "It is indeed a powerful weapon, full of more potent magicks than any I have ever seen."

"I told you. It—"

"But not cursed."

The wanderer frowned. "What?"

"I only mean that there is no 'curse' on it. Though it is true that it is imbued with powerful sorcery, sorcery far beyond that of which I'm capable. And yes, you are correct, there is a sort of tracking spell on it, one that would alert its master to its whereabouts."

The wanderer nodded, not really understanding the distinction, for it sounded cursed enough to him. He was about to ask the wizard more when the other man shrugged. "Anyway," the wizard said, "perhaps it is best we get going—we cannot afford to tarry, and there is not far left to go."

The wanderer didn't argue, following the man back to where the villagers waited and then they began moving again.

Several hours later, the dense trees through which they'd walked were interrupted by a sheer rock wall that appeared, to the wanderer at least, uncomfortably similar to the chasm they'd left behind. And, judging by the expressions on many of the villagers— and the sick look on the sheriff's face—he didn't think he was alone in this.

The wizard, though, ignored their questioning glances, leading them along the rock wall until he came to a gap in it, one that seemed to justify the wanderer's fears. The wizard turned then, motioning the wanderer forward.

"I wanted to speak with you, Eternal, before we get where we are going."

"Alright," the wanderer said, all too aware of the formal sound of the man's voice, all too aware that, once more, he had called him "Eternal."

"I know that circumstances, when you arrived at Alhs's barrier, made you feel as if you were left with no choice but to put a hole in it to enter. I have come to believe, over our association, that you did not intend for that hole to spread as it did, destroying the barrier. But we can agree, intentional or not, that the result of that action is that many of the villagers lost their lives and that the others have been forced to endure a grueling journey for a chance to be safe again, yes?"

"Yes," the wanderer said.

"Then I ask for your word," the wizard said, "that when we arrive at this new place, you do nothing to in any way threaten or weaken the barrier. I ask that you take no action against it without consulting me first."

"You have my word," the wanderer said, then glanced at the gap in the stone wall. "Is it somewhere through that gap? I must admit no one seems all that thrilled about the idea of traveling through another chasm."

"They will like this chasm more than the last, I think," the wizard said. "Now, your word—you are sure I have it?"

"I am sure," the wanderer said.

The wizard watched him for a moment, as if searching for something. Then, finally, he nodded. "Good, because we are here."

"I...don't understand."

The wizard smiled. "I'll never tire of hearing an Eternal say that. Go on," he said, waving to the gap. "Have a look."

Frowning, the wanderer moved toward the gap, then stepped through. The path took a sharp turn as soon as he stepped inside, and he had thought it must continue on for some time, but he was wrong. In fact, it continued for no more than ten feet and then came out onto a ledge. And beneath that ledge, far below him, stretched out a long, wide valley that was surrounded on all sides by great walls of stone. The grass seemed greener than any the wanderer had seen, and he felt as if he was gazing at some place of magic and wonder, one created by the gods themselves as a sanctuary away from the dangers of the Untamed Lands. Trees ringed the valley, fetching up against the stone walls. A river ran through the valley's center and near it was a small village one that, the wanderer would have guessed, was nearly the same size as Alhs though it looked tiny and insignificant in the sprawling valley.

The wanderer found himself reluctant to pull away from the sight of the beautiful valley, finding it difficult to believe that such a perfect place existed at all beyond, perhaps, a master artist's canvas. But he knew that time was of the essence, so he forced his gaze away, turning to walk back to where the wizard waited beyond the gap. Something of his thoughts must have shown on his face for the wizard grunted what might have been a laugh. "Well?" the wizard asked. "What do you think?"

"It...it's beautiful," the wanderer said.

"Yes," the wizard said, smiling. "So it is, and let's hope the villagers think as much, for it is to be their new home."

The wanderer frowned. "I understand that the rock walls would serve as protection against many mundane threats, but what is to keep Ranger and his army away?"

"Had you started down that trail toward the valley floor you would have had your answer quickly enough," the wizard said, "for you would have encountered a barrier much like that which protected the village of Alhs."

The wanderer nodded. "I see. So...what do we do?"

"*We* don't do anything," the wizard said. "At least not so far as it concerns the barrier. I will work on opening a *temporary* gap in it, so that the villagers might be moved through it to safety, but it will take time."

"How much time?" the wanderer asked, aware that while they had put some distance between themselves and Ranger and his army, they would still be coming.

The wizard shook his head, a frustrated expression on his face. "I don't know. I have never tried to move so many all at once. Perhaps...three quarters of a day? Certainly no more."

Eighteen hours. The wanderer winced. "It cannot be done any quicker?"

"If I could, I would," the wizard said. "There are many things to consider when working with the Art on so large a scale. And if I want to ensure that the barrier isn't, you know, *destroyed* in the process of creating an opening, then it will take time."

"I see," the wanderer said, not bothering to pay any attention to the anger in the man's tone for he knew that it was not directed at him. Instead, it was directed at a fact that they both knew well—they did not have enough time.

Even being optimistic and assuming that the Unseen they had killed had been the only ones tracking their progress—unlikely—and assuming that others which had no doubt been sent hadn't yet found them—unlikelier still, when one considered the speed at which they moved, they simply did not have enough time. Ranger and his army would reach them in half a day, no more than that.

The two men stood in brooding silence for several seconds then, both of them thinking about the dire situation in which they found themselves. "Well," the wanderer said finally, "you had best be getting started."

"And what will you do?" the wizard said.

"I mean to meet with Dekker and Clint and the sheriff, tell them what's happening."

The wizard nodded. "Very well. It is my hope that they have some solution."

"Mine as well," the wanderer said, then he inclined his head in a bow. "Good luck," he said.

"And to you," the wizard said, heaving a deep breath. "My guess is that, in the coming hours, we'll both need as much luck as we can get."

Fifteen minutes later, the wanderer sat around a small fire with the sheriff, Clint, and Dekker. Meanwhile, the villagers of Alhs set about making camp, starting fires and laying out their bedrolls. They all looked excited, eager to relax and have an opportunity to rest after their long journey and joyful at the knowledge that safety—true, permanent safety—lay so close

The men sharing the wanderer's own fire, though, looked far grimmer, as well they should, for they alone knew the truth of what they faced. The wanderer had considered sharing it with the other villagers but, in the end, had decided against it, at least until he'd spoken with Dekker and the others.

The wanderer had just finished telling them the bits he had left out when speaking to the villagers, and now he sat in silence, waiting as each man digested the news. The sheriff's face had grown pale, and Clint's brow was furrowed in concentration, looking at it like a puzzle in need of solving. Which, of course, it was.

Dekker, meanwhile, sat with his fists clenched where they were propped on his knees, his mouth working as if he were chewing on something.

It was over a minute before anyone spoke. When they did, it was Clint who managed it. "Are...are you sure?"

The wanderer might have lied then, or at least have done as many did, covering the truth in fictional frills and pandering platitudes, as if by doing so made it easier to swallow. And maybe it even did, but that didn't mean it would sit well once digested, so he only nodded. "I am sure."

Dekker grunted. "Well. Shit."

"Just about sums up my feelings precisely," the sheriff said. He turned to the wanderer. "And this wizard. He can't...I don't know, hurry it along? Like...maybe if we help?"

"I don't know much about casting spells," the wanderer said. "Do you?"

The sheriff sighed. "Only magic I know is how to go to sleep and wake up sore from doin' nothin' but lyin' there. I don't think that'll serve here."

"No," the wanderer said, giving the man a small smile. "No, I do not believe it will."

"So what then?" Dekker asked. "What's the plan?"

"I was hoping you could tell me," the wanderer said honestly, looking at the three men.

They glanced at each other then Dekker sighed. "Look, Ungr, I've never been all that clever," he said, words the wanderer had cause to know were completely false. "Not the plannin' type, really. You, though, well you always seem to have one. Granted a lot of 'em are shit and involve a man riskin' his life way more than he ought, but they're plans anyway. Unless either of you's got somethin' to say on it?" he asked, glancing at the other two men.

The sheriff shook his head. Clint, though, was staring at the gap in the stone wall. "A small gap," he said. "One or two men might hold out, at least for a time."

"Yes," the wanderer said.

"Long enough?" Clint asked, glancing at him.

The wanderer winced, shaking his head. "No."

The Perishables' leader frowned. "Thought as much."

The men sat in silence for another few seconds, thinking it over, before Dekker spoke. "Well, go on then, you bastard," he told the wanderer. "I'm sure you've got some solution."

The wanderer shrugged. "I was hoping one of you would have a better one but yes, I have a solution...of sorts."

"Well?"

"You're not going to like it," the wanderer said.

"'Course I'm not gonna like it," the big man said. "Shit, Ungr, I'd be shocked if I did. Still, best tell us."

"Ranger and his Revenants are, as near as I can tell, perhaps twelve hours behind us. The wizard claims that creating a break in the barrier will take six hours longer than that, give or take."

"Which means we need to buy six hours," Dekker said slowly. "Six hours against creatures that do not feel pain or fear."

"That's right," the wanderer said.

"Do you think...that is..." the sheriff said. "Well, you and those others, you took care of the creatures trackin' us, didn't you?" He paused, glancing at the stone wall. "It's a pretty small gap and a pretty big wall. A pretty big *forest*, so far as that goes. Maybe they won't find us at all."

"Maybe," the wanderer said slowly, "but I doubt it. We have gotten rid of their scouts, true, and so they have lost our trail, but if the creature posing as Ranger has even a fraction of the real man's woodcraft, it will not take him long to pick it up again. After all, a village of people moving through a forest can't help but leave tracks."

"I see," Dekker said. "And how long, do you think, it'll take him? To find our trail, I mean?"

The wanderer considered that. "It is possible that they lost time in the caves, and then there is the forest to think of...an hour? Maybe two?"

"Which leaves five, maybe four hours to account for before the wizard gets the barrier open," Dekker said.

"Yes."

"And how long do you think we'd be able to hold them here?" this from Clint, glancing again at the gap in the wall.

"Another hour?" the wanderer asked, wincing. "Maybe less. It is true that the small entry will not allow many of them to come at us at once, but they will not stop, will do anything to push through, including giving their lives without hesitation. It is...difficult to fight a creature who cares nothing for its own preservation."

The grim looks on Dekker and Clint's faces showed that they knew that well enough. The big man sighed. "So, what, then? Three, four hours before the wizard's got the barrier open, you're sayin' that we'll all be fertilizer?"

"Not...necessarily," the wanderer said.

"So? What have you got in mind?"

"As I said, you won't like it," the wanderer warned.

"Well, Ungr," Dekker said, "considerin' that the other option is a horrible death at the hands of creatures who have no mercy or compassion, I'd say I'm willin' to entertain some alternatives."

"They will find you," the wanderer said. "Before the wizard is finished. Unless—"

"Can't help but notice that you said 'you,' not 'us,'" Dekker said, frowning.

"They will find you," the wanderer repeated, meeting each man's gaze, "so long as Ranger is alive to track you. That is a fact."

"Hold on a damn minute," Dekker said. "You mean to go take that bastard on by yourself."

"Yes."

The men were shaking their heads immediately. "Not a chance," Dekker said.

"Not alone," Clint said.

"Listen, Ungr," the sheriff said, "I appreciate all that you've done for us, all that you've tried to do, but...this fella, Ranger. Didn't you say that he's the best at woodcraft in the world?"

"That's right."

"So what would you say your chances are, you know, of beatin' him?"

Dekker snorted, opening his mouth to speak, but the wanderer beat him to it.

"Not great," he admitted, "but our chances of surviving, if I do this, are infinitely better than if I don't."

"You really think you can beat 'em?" the sheriff asked.

"I think there's a chance."

"And this chance," Dekker said, "would it be better if there were more than just you?"

The wanderer had known it would come to this, but he acted as if he had not, frowning. "I don't know what you—"

"I mean," Dekker interrupted, "would you have a better chance of succeeding in beating Ranger if some folks went with you?"

The wanderer shook his head. "My plan is to sneak past the Revenants and the Unseen, if there still are any, and make it to Ranger himself. Too many people would be impossible to hide, and we'd be—"

"Three then," Dekker said.

The wanderer frowned. "What?"

"Three'd be easy enough to hide," Dekker said. "After all, you thought it a good number back when we went to check on the army, before the Whisperers, when you, myself, and Clint went, didn't you?"

"This isn't the same—"

"Isn't it?" Dekker pressed. "What of you, Clint? You willin' to go?"

"Wouldn't be anywhere else," the Perishables' leader said, watching the wanderer.

"Thought as much," Dekker said. "Then it's settled," he finished, glancing at the wanderer in challenge.

"Dekker, this...what of your family?"

"I'm doin' this for my family," the big man said.

The wanderer shook his head, opening his mouth to speak but before he could the big man held up a hand. "Tell me true, Ungr, does this plan of yours have a better chance of success if you have a couple of us along with you?"

The wanderer sighed, nodding. "Yes."

"Thought as much," Dekker said. "Good. Then, as I said, it's settled." He started to rise. "Best I go tell Ella."

"Wait," the wanderer said.

The big man looked at him, as did Clint, and the wanderer saw in both their gazes that they would not be talked out of it. "If you insist on going," the wanderer said, "then let us at least wait a few hours, until night is fully on us. The darkness will help cover our tracks. In the meantime, you should get some rest, restore your strength. You will need it."

"And you?" Dekker asked, his eyes narrowed in suspicion.

"I will rest as well," the wanderer said, "I'm exhausted," he finished and that much, at least, was the truth. It had been a long, grueling journey, a long grueling flight from Ranger and his army, and his one consolation, if it could be said to *be* a consolation was that that journey was very nearly over. One way or the other.

Dekker grunted, glancing at Clint who shrugged. "I could use a bit of a rest," the Perishables' leader said, then gave a small smile. "I'd hate to show up in the afterlife with bags under my eyes."

Dekker snorted. "Got a grim sense of humor on you, Clint. Damn if you don't."

"Given what we face," the Perishables' leader said, "is there any other kind?"

The big man considered that then nodded. "I'm off then to speak to Ella, get my ass chewed off, like as not. See you in a few hours."

With that, Dekker turned and left, then Clint nodded. "A few hours rest sounds like just the thing," he said, then turned and walked off.

The wanderer watched the two men leave, was still watching when the sheriff spoke. "It ain't an easy thing, is it? Watchin' good men risk their lives."

"No," the wanderer agreed. "No, it isn't."

"Watched you do it half a dozen times since I met you, I reckon," the sheriff said.

The wanderer gave the man a small smile. "I know what you're trying to say, Sheriff, and I thank you for it. But whatever I am, I am not a good man."

The man grunted. "Can't say I agree with that. Not considerin' that there's plenty of folks breathin' now that wouldn't be if it weren't for you. Particularly since I'm one of those folks."

The wanderer found himself feeling uncomfortable, unsure of what to say, and the sheriff barked a laugh. "Relax, Ungr. Talk about traipsin' through woods full of monsters and soldiers huntin' you and you're fine. Try to pay you a compliment, and you shift like a child caught at mischief. Anyway, I'd go with you if I could, only I'm afraid I'd just slow you down." He glanced down at his ample stomach, sighing. "Ain't exactly as light on my feet as I used to be, though truth to tell I wasn't ever all *that* light in the first place."

"It's better if you stay," the wanderer said. "If the worst happens, the villagers will need your leadership to keep it together."

The other man frowned at that. "Sounds like you don't plan on you all making it back."

"It isn't that I don't plan on it—I do," the wanderer said. "It's just that, in my experience, the world couldn't care less about a man's plans. Goodnight, Sheriff," he said. "And, in case I don't see you...it has been an honor."

"That goes both ways," the man said, his voice sounding strange, hoarse. He cleared his throat and nodded. "You're a good man, Ungr."

"A good man who has managed to find himself in this situation?" the wanderer asked, giving the man a small smile.

"I said good," the sheriff said, giving him a wink. "Never said smart."

With that, the man turned and walked away. The wanderer checked on Veikr, making sure the horse had all that he needed, then laid out his bedroll a short distance away from the rest of the camp.

As the villagers of Alhs and the Perishables went to sleep, the wanderer lay and closed his eyes. But he did not let sleep claim him. He knew how to meditate—Shaman had taught him. A way to give the mind and body rest without losing consciousness completely, a peace, the Eternal had told him, that a man could find within the storm of his own life. And so the wanderer found it.

He waited an hour, then another, until the camp was silent, until he judged that everyone was asleep. Then, he rose and quietly made his way to where Veikr lay. The horse was asleep and, for a few minutes, the wanderer only stood and watched him. Then, a smile that was equal parts sadness and happiness on his face, the wanderer turned and started away. He moved stealthily, making note of the sleeping forms of the villagers and Dekker specifically as he made his way past. He hoped that the man would understand, him and Clint too. He suspected that they would be angry, but he thought he could live—or die—with that, just so long as they were alive to *be* angry.

He reached the edge of the camp, moving away from the wall and toward the woods, and was just beginning to think he was in the clear when a form appeared out of the shadows of the trees in front of him.

He thought at first that it must be Dekker, but as the figure moved closer he realized that it wasn't the big man at all but the Wizard of the South.

"Shouldn't you be working on the spell?" the wanderer asked.

"Do you mean to teach me about wizarding now?" the other man countered. The wanderer winced, saying nothing, and the wizard looked him up and down before raising an eyebrow. "Going somewhere?"

"Yes."

The other man nodded, rubbing at his chin. "Your friend, Dekker, he asked me to watch for something like this, to wake him if you tried to leave on your own."

The wanderer tensed, wondering if he could reach the man, could silence him, knock him out, perhaps, before he could raise an alarm. He doubted it, but he tensed, preparing to try anyway. "And do you mean to? Wake him, I mean?"

"Not sure yet," the wizard said. "First, why don't you tell me why you're sneakin' off like a thief in the night?"

The wanderer considered that, then glanced at the villagers, at Dekker and his family, at Clint and the Perishables. "Because I want to save them," he said finally.

"Your friend, the abnormally large man and his family?"

"All of them," the wanderer corrected.

"I see," the wizard said. "And you do not wish to take them with you?"

"No."

"Because you think you are better alone?"

"The answer to that would have been yes, once," the wanderer said thoughtfully, "but not anymore. I met a man, one I'd like to consider a friend, and he taught me that no one is better alone, that people need people."

"Why go alone, then?"

"Because...because I would protect them, if I could," the wanderer said. "Because it is my fault they are all here, and I would not ask them to sacrifice themselves for my mistake."

The wizard watched him for several seconds. "You are not like the others of your kind," he said finally.

The wanderer didn't know what to say to that, so he said nothing, and the wizard nodded, continuing. "You admit when you are wrong—"

"Blame it on plenty of practice."

The wizard gave him a small smile then continued as if he hadn't spoken. "You try to do the right thing, without assuming that you always know what that is." He took a slow, deep breath. "You remind me of my son."

The wanderer blinked. "You have a son?"

The wizard smirked. "Surprised that an exile, a hermit like myself might have a family?"

"Yes," the wanderer answered honestly.

The man nodded. "Well, I suppose that's warranted." His smile faded, slowly turning into a sad frown. "To answer your question, I *had* a son. I will not go into the details, but it is enough to say that he died doing what he thought was right, died in service of the Eternals, long ago, serving in the army that pushed back the 'Untamed Lands,' as you call them."

"And that...that's why you hate them."

"Yes," the wizard said. "I hate them because they took my son from me, used him in an unjust campaign to conquer creatures and beings solely because they were different. Used him until there was nothing left to use."

The man's voice was raw, hoarse with emotion, and the wanderer noted unshed tears shimmering in his eyes. He realized then, that he had always thought of the Eternals as gods—just like everyone else did—gods who were infallible, incapable of making mistakes. Even when he'd become an Eternal himself, that had not changed. Even their being defeated had largely left that feeling, that reverence, unchanged. Now, though, he was forced to confront the fact that the Eternals, however powerful, had just been men and women like any other. And *like* any other capable of evil as well as good. "I am sorry," he told the wizard, meaning it. "For your son."

The wizard took a slow, ragged breath. "Thank you," he managed. Slowly, he raised his gaze from his feet, meeting the wanderer's eyes. "I will not tell your friends, if you do not wish it, and for what it's worth, I hope that you survive. Good luck...Ungr. I wish you well."

The wanderer was surprised by how touched he was to hear the man use his real name. "Thank you...wizard. Good luck to you as well."

The man gave him another smile then turned and started away. The wanderer did the same, pausing as the wizard spoke. "Ungr?"

"Yes?" he asked, turning back to regard the man.

The wizard seemed to consider for a moment then, finally, let out a soft sigh. "It's Earl. My name."

The wanderer stared for a moment, did his best to conceal his surprise but was unable to completely keep the grin from his face.

The wizard sighed. "I know. Not a very wizardly name, but there it is."

The wanderer nodded, still grinning. "It's nice to meet you, Earl."

"And you, Ungr," the wizard said. "Anyway, try to stay alive, won't you? Seems to me that the world is a little bit of a better place with you in it."

"I could say the same," the wanderer said.

"I'd just as soon you didn't," the wizard said, then he gave him a wink, turned, and walked away.

The wanderer watched him go, wondering if he would ever see him again, doubting it. Then, when the man was gone, he turned and moved away from the camp, into the waiting darkness.

CHAPTER FOURTEEN

The wanderer's eyes were better than a mortal man's, able to pick up even the smallest shred of ambient light, yet that did nothing to illuminate the darkness through which he walked as he left the camp, leaving behind everyone that meant anything to him.

He had done it once before, long ago, leaving Anne standing by their tree, and it had been terrible. This time, though, was worse, for now, unlike then, he knew well what it was he left behind, what he was giving up.

He walked on grimly, wishing that there were some other way and scolding himself for his weakness. After all, there *was* no other way. Ranger was coming, he and his army, and if they were not slowed down, they would be on him and the others before the wizard could alter the barrier. He needed to buy time, that was all, and *this* time, there was no giant stacked rock he might use to bar their way.

There was only him.

But then, he realized, even as he had the thought, that it wasn't quite true. He reached for the locket and snapped it open, tensing in expectation of a barrage of scolding as the ghosts recounted, as they so often did, all the ways in which he had disappointed them.

Instead, he was greeted with only silence. At first, that silence was a relief, but as it stretched from an instant to two, then three, it was no longer relief the wanderer felt but worry. He was all but certain that he knew the source of the ghost's "sleeping," was confident that it was due to some sort of avoidance spell the wizard had cast, but he had no idea what prolonged exposure to the spell might do. "Hello?" he said, and although he spoke softly, his voice seemed to echo strangely in the forest.

No answer, and the wanderer's heart began to speed up in his chest. The ghosts had woken from their "sleep" the other times, but that was no assurance that they would do so now. He wished, then, that he knew more of the Art, that he had listened more carefully when Oracle and Shaman had spoken, but his had always been a mind of muscle and metal not spells and sorcery.

Perhaps they would never come back. Perhaps he truly was alone. "Hello?" he asked once more, not really expecting an answer.

He was surprised, then, when one came.

We're...we're here, Youngest.

Leader's voice, sounding sleepy and confused.

Damn this spell of yours, Tactician snapped.

It isn't my fault, Oracle said defensively. *In fact, it shouldn't be happening at all. Unless, perhaps there is some sort of interference, or maybe a flaw in the weaving, I can—*

The spell can wait, Leader said. *I do not think that is why Youngest has called on us. Am I correct in that much?*

"Yes."

Very well, then it would be best if you caught us up with current events, Leader said.

And for the next few minutes, the wanderer did, recounting all that had happened since he'd reunited with the wizard and the others after causing the rockfall in the chasm, for they had no memory of any of it.

This wizard, Oracle said musingly when he was finished, *he sounds...powerful. And one of such power...I should know him. Tell me, Youngest, did you happen to get his name?*

The wanderer considered that, remembering the wizard telling him, and he shook his head slowly. "Sorry," he said.

Well, Oracle said, *perhaps you might describe him, that might—*

Who gives a shit who the wizard is? Tactician snapped and for once the wanderer was glad of the man's snappiness, for he had never lied to the Eternals before, and he found that it did not sit well with him. Yet neither did the idea of giving up the wizard's identity after the man had trusted him with it. *What matters isn't what's happened or who did it but what is* going *to happen. You mean to take him on, don't you?* There was no need asking who he meant. "Yes."

Tactician let out a derisory snort, but it was Soldier who spoke. *You sure you thought this through, lad? Seems pretty desperate to me.*

"I *am* desperate," the wanderer admitted. "They need more time."

And you think that the way of buying them that time, Healer said, *is to take him on?*

"Can you think of another?" the wanderer asked, not a challenge but a desperate hope, for he did not like his chances against Ranger and an army of Revenants, had only resigned himself to it because he could think of no other alternative.

I'm...afraid I cannot, Healer said after a moment, and the wanderer nodded. He had expected as much.

Taking on the greatest woodsman of all time and an army of creatures who feel no fear or pain? Alchemist said. *That sounds like a recipe for disaster, Youngest.*

The wanderer did not disagree.

How do you mean to do it? Soldier said after a moment.

"I...don't know," he answered honestly, ignoring Tactician's frustrated hiss. "I was hoping that you all might have some idea."

Several seconds passed then as the ghosts talked it over, debating the different avenues they might take, many ideas of which the wanderer did not care for at all. The sort of ideas one would only come up with if the person suggesting them had no risk of being the one who actually had to enact them.

While he waited, the wanderer busied himself with searching the surrounding woods. After a few minutes, he found a long branch of an oak tree that he thought would serve his purposes well. He would have preferred yew or ash, but as he had told the ghosts, he was desperate, so while the Eternals continued their debate, he sat on a fallen log, pulled out the knife he kept at his waist, and began to whittle away at the branch, cutting away the bark and branching growths.

He enjoyed the work, for it was something he could do, a problem he might solve. And now, as always, performing a relatively simple, well-practiced task went a long way to soothing his nerves. When he was finished and the branch was smoothed, he rose, running his hand along it and finding the natural curve. He searched for where the bow was flexible, shaving off the unyielding parts as the ghosts continued their increasingly heated—and largely depressing, for the wanderer at least—discussion.

It was not lost on him, as he worked at shaping the bow and arrows that he might use with it, that he was applying lessons given him by Ranger to shape a weapon with which he meant to take on the same man—or at least, an impostor whose impersonation of him was so complete that it was impossible to tell one from the other.

Still, he continued the work, remembering a lesson that Soldier had taught him often—when it came to war, a man rarely regretted preparing too much, but nearly always regretted preparing too little. So as the night wore on and the ghosts talked, he prepared the best way he knew how. He shaped the wood as he'd been taught, that of the bow and half a dozen arrows, too.

Then there was the task of finding a material suitable for a string—always the hardest part. Animal hide or sinew might have served, but he did not have the time to wait for day when they might dry in the sun. In the end, he settled on a thick vine from a nearby tree, one that, when he hung from it, easily took his weight. He then set about the job of thinning it, peeling away the fibers so that he was left with a piece thin enough to serve as a string. Such a string would not last for long, but then he did not think that would be a problem, considering what he faced. Whatever happened, he thought it was likely that it would happen quickly.

As the wanderer worked, the voices of the ghosts became little more than a steady susurration like that a man might hear when standing on the beach and watching the tide come in, and he let them debate, largely not listening as he sought and found the simple peace of doing a job and doing it well.

Do you want *to get him killed, you damned fool?* Tactician growled, the ghost's raised voice drawing the wanderer's full attention.

It might work, Scholar mumbled, and Tactician gave a disgusted snort. One that the wanderer found he agreed with, for from what he'd heard of Scholar's plan it had involved a lot of theory and conjecture and was far too complicated.

If your goal is to kill him, there are easier ways, Tactician said, not sounding angry now but exhausted. *What of you, Ranger? This thing, it has taken your form, after all. How would you beat you?*

Ranger, who had yet to speak, made a thoughtful sound, and they all remained silent as he considered the problem. The wanderer, too, waited silently, unmoving, for he thought that if there was anyone who might know a way of defeating the creature he faced it would be the man whose place it had taken.

I am sorry, Youngest, the ghost said after a time, *it cannot be done. You face the greatest woodsman who has ever lived.* Not a boast, the wanderer knew, only the simple truth.

Only a copy, Tactician countered, *and he has the* actual *greatest woodsman in his mind.*

A copy, perhaps, Ranger allowed, *but close enough, from what I've seen, as to make little difference. And while I will, of course, help Youngest in any way I can, such decisions as he will face in the coming encounter will need to be made instantly, without hesitation. Even the time it would take me to suggest his course would be too much, for he faces a master woodsman in his own environment.*

The ghost made the pronouncement without joy, but the wanderer knew that now, as in life, Ranger did not believe in falsehood. A grim truth, then, but a truth just the same.

"Anyone else have any ideas?" the wanderer asked without much hope.

Silence then, a silence that spoke louder than any words might. *Sorry, lad,* Soldier said after a moment. *If there is a way forward, I don't see it.*

Of course you don't, Tactician said. *Ever the grunt, the good soldier, a man whose mind only moves in straight lines. But the world is not straight—the old bastard, Scholar, might tell you as much, if you asked. The world is curved, and so we must curve with it.*

"What do you mean?" the wanderer asked.

You face the world's greatest woodsman, Tactician said, *everyone is agreed on that much.*

"Yes."

So how, then, Youngest, might you defeat the greatest living woodsman?

"That is the question we've been asking," he said, frowning.

An annoyed sigh. It seems that you did not listen to my lessons nearly well enough, Youngest. A man avoids losing battles by refusing to fight battles he can only lose.

A nice sentiment, Soldier said slowly, *but I do not see how it helps him here.*

Nor would you, Tactician said, his tone thick with condescension. *Isn't it obvious?* The ghost went on. When no one answered, the ghost spoke on. *My, what it must be like to possess such simple minds. Boring, I suspe—*

Tactician, Leader said in a warning tone.

Very well, Tactician said. *The question we have posed is, how does a man defeat the world's greatest woodsman? The answer is simple—you don't.*

"That...isn't as helpful as you seem to think it is," the wanderer said slowly.

The problem isn't with the answer, Youngest—it's with the question. We have been asking how you defeat this creature, but you do not need *to defeat him—you need only buy this wizard of yours time, isn't that right?*

The wanderer frowned, impressed, as always, by the way Tactician's mind worked. "You have an idea, then?"

Plenty, Tactician said, *now listen close, Youngest, and see if this lesson, at least, you might learn.*

And as the ghost spoke, condescending but clever nonetheless, the wanderer did what he had to do—he listened.

***

A short time later, they were done discussing everything that might be discussed, finished preparing everything that might be prepared, and the wanderer started forward into the darkness once more. The night was still, as quiet as an indrawn breath, and just as tense, as if the world were waiting on something. His death, perhaps.

Or perhaps it was just his own fears which he was projecting on the world around him. Certainly, he had enough to be fearful about. It was not often a man found himself stalking through the woods, pitted against the world's greatest tracker, its most accomplished hunter. Perhaps it was only his fear that made the darkness seem deeper, that made the shadows look like demonic figures capering around him as he passed, but he did not think so.

Evil stalked these woods. It drew closer with each breath he took, each moment that passed, and instead of running away from it—as any sane man ought to do—the wanderer found himself moving toward it. No, he did not think he imagined the feeling of impending and unavoidable doom. He could almost feel them creeping closer, Ranger and his army of Revenants. Could feel them like a blight on the land, like a parasite scurrying along the body of its unintentional host.

The only sound to break the silence as the wanderer moved through the woods, back in the direction of the mountainside they'd left behind, was the sound of the river off to his right side, the sight of it blocked by the thick trees all around him.

The wanderer soon broke into a run, eager to cover as much ground as possible. He continued that way until he saw, in the distance, the edge of the forest where the trees gave way to the mountainside that he and the others had walked down when they'd left the caves of the Free.

He slowed then, examining the forest around him, first for any sign of a threat. He did not think that the Revenants would have made it so far so quickly, but then people rarely died for overestimating their enemies, whereas untold corpses sat in their graves for underestimating them. Despite his concerns, though, the woods remained empty, and the path which led off the mountainside, that path which the wanderer, along with the villagers and Perishables, had taken hours ago was still clear.

The wanderer looked around. He took his time, considering, as he did, the path that the approaching army would likely take, making use of the knowledge Ranger had shared with him long ago. In a hurry as they were he suspected the Revenants, like most creatures, would take the path of least resistance, funneling through the cleared path and avoiding the snarls and tangles of undergrowth around it. As he looked, the wanderer also constructed his own path in his mind, imagining each step he would take, how he would do it.

When he was satisfied that he knew the best route, he began to walk along it. At intervals, he grabbed one of the recently carved arrows from where he'd stuck them in his belt and intermittently pushed them gently into the ground until five were spaced along the path he would take. The sixth he kept.

When he was finished, the wanderer moved off to the right side of the road to a large oak. After a quick inspection he decided that it would serve his purpose as well as any. He made sure his makeshift bow was secure across his back then grabbed hold of the tree's lowest branch and hoisted himself up. He climbed until he was a good twenty feet above the ground and found a branch that he was confident would hold his weight and that was also facing in the direction of the forest path.

He settled himself on the branch, withdrawing the bow from his back and loosely nocking his last remaining arrow. Then, with everything as ready as he could make it, the wanderer sat and waited for what would come.

He did not have to wait long.

Even his most pessimistic estimation put the Revenant army, along with Ranger, at least another hour, perhaps two out from his current location. It was with some surprise, then, that he watched the first of their kind step into the distant tree line, its dead-eyed stare scanning the forest, its sword held in a loose grip.

More followed along behind it. In moments, the woods were filled with them, all of them moving at a steady, inexorable walk. The wanderer continued to wait, barely daring even to breathe, watching as more and more filtered into the trees. Most, as he'd suspected, traveled along the forest path, but not all. Some braved the tangles of bushes, slashing away at the viny obstacles with their swords, showing no reaction to the thorns that pricked their skin as they ensured that no one lay in ambush along the path.

The wanderer tracked their movements, until he saw a familiar figure appear within the forest. It was a face he had seen many times, often hovering over him when Ranger woke him for a new lesson. A lesson that usually involved a day of biting insects and wearing clothes soaked through with sweat, of learning about this plant or that flower, about this animal or that beast.

He had never been as close to Ranger as he had been to Soldier—he didn't think Ranger could have been said to be close to *anyone,* at least not any mortal—but he had still admired the man, and he thought that Ranger had respected him. At least as much as the man had respected anyone or anything that walked on two legs.

It was a face he'd come to associate with an earthy wisdom, a clever mind honed razor sharp in one survival situation after another, a man who did not *think* like a man but, in turns, like a predator or prey—both, he'd assured the wanderer, essential to survival in the wild. It was the face of a man who'd taught him much, who he'd come to respect and, in many ways, to love, one that he had missed over the years, along with the others. The wanderer looked at that face, the mouth in a small, arrogant smile that the real Ranger had never had, for he had not been arrogant. He watched the graceful, predatory walk that had always put him in mind of some jungle cat stalking its prey.

A familiar face, one that was known to him, that he had counted on in days spent in the wild, days when he would have died had it not been for the man walking in the distance. He looked at that face as he raised his bow, along with the nocked arrow, regarded that face as he focused on controlling his breathing.

In and out. In and out.

Then he fired an arrow directly at it.

The recently made arrow sailed through the air and struck the creature posing as Ranger in the eye, driving through the socket and out the back of his skull with an accuracy that the wanderer had not expected, given the poor materials from which it had been fashioned and its lack of fletching. Luck more than skill in truth, but either way the wanderer watched in shocked relief as the impostor's head rocked back with such force that it threw him backward, and he collapsed on the forest path.

The wanderer felt his breath catch in his own throat as he stared at the distant figure, vaguely aware of the Revenants in the woods around it, all of which had frozen the moment the arrow had struck and were now studying the unmoving figure lying on the forest path with emotionless expressions.

In that moment, despite all that he had learned of the world, despite all it had taken from him, the wanderer acted against his nature—he hoped. He hoped that it might all be done so easily. That the figure lying on the path unmoving, an arrow through its eye, might remain unmoving, and that the Revenants surrounding it might continue to regard it on into eternity, puppets as lifeless as the creature who had held their strings.

But a moment later, that hope faded, blown apart like a pile of leaves in a high wind, as the figure of Ranger's impostor sat up, a smile on its face and never mind the arrow still protruding from its right eye. The figure ripped the arrow free then turned, seeming to look directly at the wanderer over the intervening distance, a thought that was confirmed a moment later as he thrust his finger out, pointing at the tree in which the wanderer had taken shelter and barking a command that sent all the Revenants in sight rushing forward.

The wanderer didn't waste a moment in disappointment that the creature had not died, for in truth he had none to waste, not if he intended to survive the next hour. He slung the bow over his back and climbed down the tree as quickly as he was able, half-falling half-jumping from one branch to the next until, in the space of a few heartbeats, he was on the ground again.

The figures were rushing toward him, not moving as fast as their Unseen counterparts, perhaps, but certainly moving fast enough. The wanderer ensured his bow was secure over his back then turned and rushed into the woods, following the path he'd chosen an hour before. He reached the first arrow sticking out of the ground and pulled it free, removing the bow from his back, knocking the arrow, turning and firing it in one smooth motion the way he'd been taught.

The arrow struck the nearest Revenant, about fifty feet away, in the heart, and it collapsed. The wanderer was already resettling his bow along his back and running again before the body hit the ground.

He stopped twice more along his path, firing an arrow into the Revenants, taking two more down. He was drawing closer to the river, the sound of its rushing water growing louder and louder, but the river itself still invisible through the trees, when he felt more than saw something hurling toward him from the side.

He was in the middle of a sprint when he saw it, the distinct blur rushing toward him out of the greenery, and he planted his front foot, pushing off it and abruptly changing his direction, though not abruptly enough to avoid a clawed talon slicing across his arm.

He cried out at the pain, his graceful leap, turned by the Unseen's momentum, causing him to spin. He struck the ground hard, and he took control of the roll, coming to his feet in time to see that blur rushing toward him again. He could not easily get at his sword with the makeshift bow hanging from his back, so he drew it instead, brandishing it in a parry guided more by instinct than sight and knocking aside the creature's next attack.

Then, as it was still off balance, he dropped the bow, drawing his knife in the same moment and burying it in the blurred form before him. He was not sure what he struck, but he didn't take time to think about it, ripping the knife free and plunging it in again and again and again until the figure collapsed at his feet.

He moved toward the bow, bending and meaning to pick it up, but he was then, quite forcefully, reminded of one simple fact—the Unseen hunted in pairs. He heard a slight rustle behind him, was given no more warning than that. He reacted instantly, knowing that to do anything else meant a quick and definite death. He tossed the bow aside and threw himself forward, striking the ground and turning it into a roll that brought him to his feet, drawing his sword as he did. Knowing that the creature would push the attack, he spun, bringing the sword around two-handed and hissing in satisfaction as it struck something solid.

The creature let out a wail, its great speed carrying it past him to crash at the ground at his feet. The wanderer moved forward, plunging his blade down until the creature's struggles ceased. The he turned and saw that, in the time it had taken him to deal with the two Unseen, the Revenants and Ranger had closed the distance to him.

He glanced back at his bow, lying between him and the approaching army, and calculated that there was no time to retrieve it. He let out a curse and then, with no other option, left the bow behind, turning and sprinting in the direction of the river.

He had hoped to take out a few more, to slow them, but as was so often the case, hope withered in the face of brutal reality. Still, they were chasing him, and that was something, for he had meant for them to. This way, at least, they were not moving toward the villagers, toward Dekker and his family.

The problem, of course, was that they were all moving toward *him.* His arm burned where the Unseen had struck him, but he did his best to ignore it—pain, at least, like fear, was a companion he knew well. He rushed through the trees, following a path toward the river, his eyes scanning the area around him as he did in search of any Unseen.

He was still running when something struck him in the lower back, and he grunted, his run suddenly turning into a fall as he struck the ground on his knees, hard. He hissed as pain lanced through him, his hand going down to his lower back where an arrow stuck through his side. He spun to see the Revenants rushing toward him through the wood and the creature posing as Ranger standing in the path fifty feet away, his bow still in hand, the string still pulled back from the shot, a grim smile on his face.

Ranger reached for another arrow from the quiver at his back, and the wanderer staggered to his feet, one hand pressed against the wound where the arrow stuck out of his side. Not a fatal shot, he knew, but a painful one nevertheless and one that sent agonizing shocks through him with each footfall he took as he sprinted at a diagonal, keeping as many trees as possible between him and his pursuers as he made his winding way toward the river.

It felt as if it took forever, though he knew in truth that less than fifteen minutes passed before he stumbled out of the trees and saw the rushing river in front of him. He glanced behind him at his bloody trail and saw flickerings of movement in the shadows beneath the trees where the Revenants and their master were coming for him.

One hand cupped to his side, blood leaking through his fingers, he moved toward the river—or, more specifically, toward a large tree he had felled hours ago that currently spanned the river. As he drew close to the river the wanderer studied the water carefully, all too aware of the creatures lurking beneath it. He frowned down at his side, stained crimson. He had not meant to be wounded when he came, and it was a problem, for the wizard had shown him how the creatures responded to the scent of blood in the water. He took a moment to rip the arrow free, hissing as sharp, hot agony roiled through him, then tore off a piece of his shirt and tied it around his waist as a makeshift bandage, grunting as he pulled it tight. He studied his work for a moment, seeing if any blood dripped from the wound. When he was satisfied that it was as covered as he could make it, he stepped up to the fallen tree.

The wanderer had a moment of doubt, as he stared at that tree, one in which he questioned his entire plan. What if some blood slipped past the bandage? Or what if the creatures attacked anyway? He allowed himself a moment of fear, of doubt, but no more than that. Then he shoved that doubt away, for it would not serve him here, not now. He was committed. For better or worse.

He stepped onto the tree. He watched the water warily, his entire body tense, but nothing happened. Then he took another step and another, speeding up with each one, no longer hesitating. After all, the choice had been made, and there was no time to make another. He paused halfway across the river, the water rushing beneath him, the spatters of it soaking his boots and trousers, and turned to regard the shore as he drew his sword.

As he watched, Revenants seemed to pour out of the woods. A few at first, then more and more until there were at least thirty of the creatures standing still and silent, regarding him. Then, seconds later, Ranger's impostor walked out of the woods, seemingly not bothered in the slightest by the arrow still protruding from his eye.

"*It is over, Youngest,*" the creature called in a voice that was indistinguishable from that of his old teacher. "*Why not give up now? You know that you cannot outrun me nor lose me, not here.*"

"*I don't intend to,*" the wanderer yelled back.

The creature grinned, then motioned, and a dozen Revenants started forward. The wanderer watched them come, noting that they did not move quietly as he had but walked without a care, without fear, as he had known they would. He focused on remaining still, silent, not moving the half-submerged giant tree beneath his feet.

The Revenants, though, didn't hesitate. They stepped onto the fallen tree without thought, their steps vibrating the log. The wanderer glanced at the bloody arrow he still held in his left hand then, saying a silent prayer, he threw it so that it landed in the river beside the closest Revenant. He did not have to wait long to see if his plan would work for, in seconds, great forms suddenly leapt out of the churning water. Creatures like the one the wizard had shown him, fish as long as a man was tall with jagged, razor-sharp teeth.

They flashed through the air, leaping from one side of the fallen tree to the other in graceful jumps. But it was not art they were after, only slaughter. Blood. As they sailed through the air past the Revenants their elongated maws of jagged teeth flashed out, tearing into the creatures' flesh like a knife through paper. In moments, there was nothing left of the dozen Revenants but a few dismembered body parts lying on the tree. The rest, the creatures had taken.

The wanderer watched it all tensely, remaining as still as he could, regarding Ranger and the twenty or so Revenants remaining on the shoreline with him as the giant fish continued to leap and finally stopped, going back into the water as if they had only been a dream or, perhaps, a nightmare. The creature posing as the Eternal was not smiling now but baring its teeth in an angry, silent snarl. It nocked the arrow it held in one hand to its bow and let loose the missile. The wanderer was watching this time, though, and, his free hand pressed to the wound in his side, he deflected the arrow with his sword.

The creature growled in fury and tried again and again the wanderer knocked the missile aside. The wanderer waited for the impostor to order more of its troops forward, but instead it only stood there, watching him, a cleverness in its remaining eye that seemed to match Ranger's own and sending waves of anxiety through the wanderer's stomach.

Finally, the creature smiled. *"A neatly placed trap,"* he called. *"But sometimes, Eternal, we fall victim to the traps we set for others. I am surprised you have not learned that by now."*

The wanderer took them as idle threats and said nothing, conserving his strength.

The creature continued to smile. *"Perhaps you are safe, for you need only to cross the river and move the log to bar our way, buying yourself hours."*

"Maybe we ought to just call the whole thing off then," the wanderer called.

"Funny," the creature called. *"I wonder, will your friends, the villagers, find it as funny when they are being tortured to death?"*

The wanderer frowned. *"They have nothing to do with this."*

"Oh, but they do," the creature shouted. "After all, you made sure of it. Now, enjoy your freedom while you can, Eternal. When I am finished with them, I will come for you."

With that, the creature turned, along with the Revenants, and began moving south, in the direction of Dekker and the others.

It was a trap, the wanderer knew that as much as he knew anything, but in the end he thought that made little difference. The best traps, after all, were those a man could not help but step into, and there was no one better in the world at laying them than Ranger.

The wanderer glanced at the water around him, then he looked at the shore where the impostor had now paused, along with twenty Revenants. The creature was smiling, for it knew it had him, knew it as certainly as the fisherman when he feels the hook set and knows that his prey is caught fast.

The wanderer walked to the shore.

They spread out as he came, surrounding him in a half-circle as they waited. The wanderer moved to stand on the shore, regarding the circle of twenty Revenants spread out around him and, beyond them, the creature who had taken Ranger's place. The enemy.

The creature smiled as it regarded him, and although it looked identical to the way Ranger had, there was something alien in its gaze, something inhuman. "And so here we are," the creature said. "All of your running, your years spent fleeing across the world, and what good any of it, if it has brought you to this?"

"A man's path is never over until he draws his last breath," the wanderer said quietly. "My teacher, the one who you can only ever pretend at being, taught me that."

The creature pulled its upper lip back from its teeth, ripping the arrow out of its eye and examining it with its remaining good one before tossing it away and turning to regard him with its glistening bloody socket on full display. "It will take time to produce a new eye," it said. "Time and pain beyond what you can imagine. I will make sure that you suffer for that."

"And here I was thinking you meant to take it easy on me."

The creature gave him a humorless smile. "Know this, Eternal. You will die here. And when I am finished with you, when I have carved all possible pain and agony from the sack of flesh you call

241

your body, carved until there is nothing left, I will go and find your friends. And when I have them, I will exact from them the price of a century of your crimes."

"My crimes? Do you mean staying alive?"

"Where your kind are concerned, there can be no greater," the creature hissed. "Death is the only answer for such grotesqueness."

"Very well," the wanderer said, standing up straight and doing his best to ignore the pain in his side where the arrow had pierced him. "If death is the only answer, then perhaps it is best you stop talking and come and ask the question."

"As you wish," the creature hissed. It motioned, and the Revenants started forward. The wanderer, though, knowing full well that he would be finished in moments if they all got within reach of him at once, did not wait. He charged the creature on his left. It slashed out with its blade, and the wanderer, still coming on, caught the blade in a full parry, knocking it away with a blow that sent a jolt of shock traveling all the way to his shoulder.

Then, the creature's strike thrown wide, the wanderer pivoted, spinning and bringing his blade around in a low blow that caught the creature behind one knee, severing it. The now one-legged Revenant wobbled and collapsed onto its back. The wanderer rose from his crouch and buried his blade in the creature's heart before ripping it free and charging through the gap his attack had created.

He moved to the next who only just managed to turn in time for the wanderer's upward blow to take it in the stomach, driving up and out of its back with such force that it lifted the creature from its feet. He followed it down, pulling his blade free and sliding it across the creature's neck, separating its head from its shoulders.

No sooner had he done this than he heard a step behind him, alerting him to the approach of another Revenant, and he turned on one knee, bringing his sword up in a parry that was far more guesswork than he liked. He managed to block the sword, but he was off-balance, the parry a poor one, and his weapon was knocked wide as he fell on the ground. The Revenant began to raise its sword again and from his position in what was quickly becoming mud on the shore of the river the wanderer lashed out with his leg, sweeping the creature's feet out from under it. It fell to the ground, and he rolled until he was above it, bringing his sword down two-handed and plunging it into the creature's chest.

The Revenant struggled for a moment then went still. All the movement had aggravated the wound in the wanderer's side, and he winced, clapping one hand over it as he staggered to his feet, turning to regard the remaining Revenants, as well as the creature posing as Ranger.

The creature sneered, clearly frustrated that he wasn't dead yet, but the wanderer thought it would not be frustrated for much longer. He was exhausted, hurt, and there far too many of the Revenants left to face, even if he didn't have to worry about fighting Ranger as well. Still, if he was going to die, he decided he was going to die standing. And he had always been taught that if a man had a tough job ahead of him, the best thing he could do was to get on with it, so he did, roaring his defiance and sprinting toward the next-closest Revenant.

The creature swung its sword as he approached, but the wanderer stepped to the side, bringing his own blade down and severing its hands at the wrists. He was just raising his sword for another stroke that would have taken the Revenant's head, but he saw the flash of steel and pivoted instead, bringing his blade around in a close guard as he turned. Metal *rang* as he only just managed to stop a downward stroke that might have easily cleaved his own head from his shoulders.

Even still, the force of the blow, powered by the Revenant's unnatural strength, was enough to drive him down to one knee and send a shock through the wanderer's arms and shoulders. He was still struggling to push the blade away when something hit him in the back, hard, and he was sent hurling across the muddy ground.

He rolled for several feet, a terrible ache in his back where he'd been struck. It took an effort to lift himself up on his hands enough to glance over and see that what had struck him had been the handless Revenant, who was clearly unconcerned with the fact that both of its hands had been lopped off at the wrist.

The wanderer watched the Revenants encircling him where he lay on the ground and part of him, the part that was tired of running, tired of being afraid, wanted nothing but to lie there and let his fate come to him. It had been coming for a long time, after all, and he was so very, very tired.

But there were the others to think of, Dekker and Ella and Clint and Sarah most of all. He may have earned his fate, but they did not deserve to share it. He could not die. Not yet. They needed more time.

The wanderer staggered to his feet, his back aching as if he'd been struck by a blacksmith's hammer, his side, where the arrow had taken him burning as if it were on fire.

In his pain it took him a moment to realize that he was no longer holding his sword. He cast his gaze about in the churned mud around him and saw it lying at the feet of one of the Revenants.

"Do you see, Eternal?" the creature posing as Ranger asked as the semi-circle of Revenants hemming the wanderer in separated to show the familiar figure. "You did nothing but extend your own anguish by running, for this was always how it would end—how it *must* end. You and your kind are the old way, and there is a new one, a better one. You have no place in this world, and it has no place for you."

The wanderer reached into his belt and drew the small knife there. "Are you finished?"

"No, Eternal," the creature said, its lips curling into a big smile. "You are. And, with you, all of your kind. I do not see the cursed blade on you, but it matters not—I will find it. *We* will find it, for it calls to us."

The wanderer had left the cursed blade hidden in the hollow of a tree, not daring to bring its very real curse on Dekker or the villagers of Alhs by leaving it with them, so he could only hope that the creature's words were a boast. Either way, though, he didn't see any point in answering, so he chose to save his breath instead. After a moment, when the creature realized its taunting would get no reaction, it gave a sour expression and motioned to the Revenants. "Finish it," Ranger told them. "We must go and retrieve the weapon." It gave the wanderer another smile. "And exact our revenge on those who dared aid this fool."

The wanderer snarled at that and then he was rushing forward without ever making the conscious decision to do so. The first Revenant was caught off-guard by the abrupt charge and didn't manage to raise its blade before the wanderer was on him, charging into it and sending it sprawling into several of its fellows.

That opened a gap and, for a moment, the wanderer felt a flash of hope. The Revenants were many things, but they were not fast. If he could break free, he might yet stall a bit longer, might buy the wizard and all the others more time.

He lunged for the opening, was through it, or at least thought he was, when suddenly something caught him by the ankle, closing around his leg like a vice. The wanderer hissed, turning to see that the Revenant he had knocked down held him. He kicked it in the face, hard. Such a blow would have caused any normal person to release their grip as the creature's nose broke, its lip busted. But the Revenant held on grimly, showing no reaction as the wanderer kicked it again and again, making a bloody ruin of its features.

The wanderer growled in anger, kneeling and swiping at the creature's wrist with his knife again and again, trying to weaken its grasp and get away. He was still trying when something struck him in the side of the head and stars exploded in his vision.

The next thing he knew, he was being pulled to his feet. He groaned, opening his eyes and saw the creature who'd taken Ranger's place standing in front of him, regarding him. The wanderer tried to move, to lash out, but nothing happened, and he realized a moment later that he was being restrained by two Revenants, one on either side.

"You poor, pathetic little creature," the impostor said, eyeing him. "How weak and fragile you all are. Even the strongest of you are as nothing to us." It paused, smiling. "That is why it was so easy to defeat you and the other *Eternals.*" It gave a cruel laugh. "How very presumptuous of you all, to name yourselves so. And how very, very wrong. Nothing in this world is eternal, Eternal. Not even the world itself. That is a fact all your kind will come to know very, very soon. Just as soon as the weapon is returned to its rightful place."

The wanderer said nothing, but he noted movement in the shadows of the woods off to his left. His first instinct was to turn and see what had caused it, but he resisted the urge, instead continuing to regard the figure.

"Oh, how I wish you could be there to see it," the creature said. "To see all of your effort come to naught but blood and ash. Tell me, Eternal, how does it feel to know that you have failed? That all those who looked to you for protection will suffer and die for their misplaced trust?"

The wanderer said nothing, gritting his teeth, as he caught sight of more movement in the woods to his left. None of the others saw it, for they were all of them, Revenant and impostor, watching the wanderer. Perhaps the one posing as Ranger *would* have seen it, had his right eye been working. But it was not, was not there at all after the arrow the wanderer had put through it, and so was completely unaware of the giant figure stepping silently out of the nearby wood.

"Oh, well," the creature said, shrugging. "I suppose it is time to have it done." It lifted its hand, and the wanderer saw that, clasped within it, was his sword. But before the creature could complete the killing stroke, the figure which had now fully emerged from the nearby trees rushed forward, charging into him, and in another moment the impostor was hurtling through the air end over end until he struck a tree hard enough that the wanderer heard the trunk *crack*.

The giant cat paused, turning to regard the wanderer before its claws lashed out, neatly severing the heads from the bodies of the two Revenants holding him and managing, by some miracle, to avoid doing the same to him.

The moment their grips fell away the wanderer moved forward, away from the group of Revenants. He scooped up his sword as he did, spinning and meaning to fend off their attacks, but he needn't have bothered. The giant cat leapt among them, its razor-sharp claws lashing out again and again and with each blow Revenants fell. The creatures were strong, and the wanderer did not doubt that had they managed some blows on the creature, it would be hurt. Only, the giant cat never gave them the chance, making use of its incredible agility to dance out of the way of their strikes, each time pivoting and returning with shocking speed to continue its bloody harvest.

The wanderer was confident, after a few seconds of watching, that the creature had the fight well in hand. Which left one thing to do.

He turned to gaze at the tree where the creature known as Ranger was slowly trying to work its way to its feet and stalked forward, one hand on his wounded side, each step bringing a fresh wave of pain and dizziness.

He came upon the creature in another few moments. He gazed down at the visage that had been menacing him for weeks since fleeing Alhs. It was not menacing now.

The creature's back had been broken by the blow—that much was clear by the unnatural way that it lay. One of its legs, also broken, sat at nearly a right angle. It stared at him with alien eyes dancing with fury. *"This...is not over,"* it croaked, bloody froth leaking from its mouth as it did.

"For you it is," the wanderer said.

"The others...they will come for you, for all *of you,"* it said, trying a bloody smile. *"Your suffering will be a thing of legend. Run while you can, Eternal, but know that your death comes for you. I am nothing compared to what comes, to what will be unleashed against you."*

"No," the wanderer said. "I'm done running. It's your kind's turn to run. It's your turn to be afraid."

The creature opened its mouth as if it meant to say something else, but it never got the chance. The wanderer's blade flashed out, cleanly severing its head from its shoulders.

The wanderer stared at the dead thing for a moment, then turned back to see the giant cat finishing up with the last of the Revenants. He moved forward as the cat turned to regard him.

"Thank you," he said in a hoarse whisper.

The cat, unsurprisingly, did not answer. Instead it only studied him with its large, luminous eyes.

"Well," the wanderer said. "I must be going—the others, my friends, are waiting." He started away then staggered, nearly falling. The cat stepped in front of him and gave him a look before it lowered itself to the ground. The wanderer glanced at its back, then at its eyes, hoping he didn't misunderstand, for he had so recently seen what the great beast's claws were capable of doing to mortal flesh.

Then, when the creature didn't move, the wanderer crawled onto its back, half-expecting to be killed for his presumptuousness. The creature didn't throw him off, though, instead it only rose to its feet, surprisingly gently, and glanced back at him with a look that seemed to say that this was a one-time thing.

"They're that way," he said, pointing, and the creature seemed to give him a look that said he was a fool—a fact he'd long since come to accept—and that it knew exactly where the others were.

Then, before he could do or say anything else, the creature bounded into the woods, and for the next few minutes it was all the wanderer could do to not fall off.

CHAPTER FIFTEEN

Riding atop the giant beast, who was able to leap and lunge around any obstacles such as trees or bushes without slowing its pace in the slightest , it took very little time to reach the spot where the wanderer had left his friends what felt like a lifetime ago. They were delayed only long enough to retrieve the cursed blade from where he stashed it and, in short order, caught up to the others.

There were shouts of panic and warning as the giant cat appeared out of the woods and villager and Perishable alike brandished weapons to defend themselves—an effort that the wanderer knew, after watching the creature battle the Revenants, would have been in vain.

"It's okay," he called. "It's alright."

Dekker, who'd been standing at the front and center of the group, stepped forward. "Ungr?" he said in a shocked voice. "That you?"

"Most of me," the wanderer agreed. The cat eased itself down and the wanderer stepped off, staggering and barely managing to catch his balance with legs that had gone numb sometime during the ride.

There were several gasps from the crowd as they took in the wanderer's blood-stained clothes.

"Damn, Ungr," Dekker said as he walked up.

"It isn't as bad as it looks."

"That right?" the big man said. "Because you *look* like shit."

"Well. Maybe it is as bad as it looks."

"I ought to kick the shit out of you for sneakin' off, you know."

"I know."

Dekker watched him for several tense seconds where the wanderer thought he might do just that. Then, finally, the big man snorted, coming forward, pausing only long enough to cast a nervous glance at the giant cat that regarded them silently. "The army?"

"Gone," the wanderer said.

The big man grunted, nodding. "And the creature, the one that took Ranger's place?"

"Dead."

The big man grunted. "Can't say I'll mourn him."

"Me neither."

There was a snort, and the wanderer turned to see Veikr approach and pause, staring at the giant cat not in fear—no surprise, that, for the wanderer had never seen the horse afraid of anything—but instead with a sort of frowning distrust. Then he glanced at the wanderer, his meaning clear.

"Don't worry," the wanderer said, giving a soft, hoarse laugh. "You aren't being replaced. After all, just imagine how much the saddle would cost."

Veikr snorted at that, and Dekker grunted. "Come on then, you hilarious bastard. Let's let Clara take a look at you."

***

Two hours later they all stood in a crowd, Perishable and villager and Eternal alike, watching as the wizard muttered words too low to hear, gesticulating as he stared at the gap in the mountain beyond which the valley lay.

The wanderer could feel the man's use of the Art, the growing power in the air. His hair stood on end and a shiver ran up his spine. Then, all that power reached a crescendo, and abruptly the wanderer felt as if he'd been struck by a strong wind, one that came from inside him and was gone an instant later. The wizard turned back to regard them. "It is done," he said, giving a small, tired smile. "Welcome, all of you, to your new home." He gestured at the chasm and the villagers, laughing and talking excitedly with each other, started to file through.

The wanderer watched them pass, a smile of his own coming to his face. They were safe. He realized, as he watched them file through to their new home, that part of him—a very large part—had never thought they'd succeed.

A familiar figure stopped in front of the wanderer, and he saw that it was Daggett, carrying his son. "Just wanted to say," the man said in a grumbling, uncomfortable voice, "I 'preciate all you done for us, me and my boy and all the village. You're alright, Ungr."

"So are you," the wanderer said, taking the man's offered hand and giving it a shake.

Daggett watched him for a moment, as if he might say more, but in the end he only gave a nod and turned and walked toward the gap in the mountain.

"You're alright," a voice said, and the wanderer turned to see Sheriff Fred standing beside him. "That's high praise comin' from Daggett."

The wanderer smiled. "I'll take it."

The sheriff nodded. "So...will you be comin' to stay with us? You and that horse of yours?"

The wanderer blinked. The truth was he hadn't even considered that possibility. He glanced at the wizard, standing nearby, and the man nodded to say that, if that was what he wanted, he could do so.

The wanderer considered that, *really* considered it, for several seconds. Could it be so easy? To step into that barrier, to let it come up again, and let his burdens go? To be free of the worry and the fear that had followed in his wake for the last hundred years?

But should he do so, should he hide away with the cursed blade then he was confident that the enemy would bring all their considerable power to bear on the wizard's shield, would not rest until it was destroyed. And while the wanderer did not doubt the man's skill in the Art, he doubted if even his barrier would stand against such opposition indefinitely.

And even if somehow the villagers and the rest of them *would* remain safe, even if somehow *he* would remain safe, the barrier impossible for the creatures to break, still the enemy would be out there, wreaking havoc on the rest of the world, bringing pain and despair to all its people. The wanderer realized something, then. He had meant what he'd said to the creature posing as Ranger. He was done running from evil, done hiding from it. It was their turn to run. Their turn to be afraid.

"I...I cannot," he said.

The sheriff nodded slowly. "You sure, then? We still got that drinkin' contest I promised you back in Alhs." He paused, glancing at the chasm, beyond which lay the valley and the village. "Don't know much about those folks livin' there already, not yet, but if they're breathin' I imagine they've found a way to make alcohol."

The wanderer smiled. "Maybe another time."

The sheriff watched him for a moment then nodded. "Alright. I'll be hopin' for it." He offered his hand. "Good luck, Ungr. And thanks. For everything."

The wanderer took the man's hand. "And you."

The sheriff gave him a wink then turned and walked away.

"Well. Where are we off to now?"

The wanderer turned to see Dekker and his family standing with Clint and eleven Perishables. Some few others, the wanderer had seen earlier, had chosen to start their lives over here, far away from their grievances and the civilized world. "Sorry, Dekker," the wanderer said, "but the village will be safe. I had thought—"

"Then you're a fool." This was snot from the big man but from Ella, his wife, frowning at the wanderer who blinked.

"I didn't—"

"You're a fool," the woman went on, "if you think we'll let you go off alone to face the others."

"But...what about Sarah? She—"

"Sarah's the whole reason we're doing it," Ella said. "The world should be better. It *deserves* to be better, and we won't stand by and ignore the evil in it, not anymore than you will. Unless, of course, you've changed your mind and plan to settle down in this new place with the others?"

"I...don't. I can't," the wanderer said.

Ella glanced at Dekker and Clint, and he, as well as the Perishables, gave a nod as if to say they agreed. Even little Sarah gave a nod, her face scrunched up in her best attempt at a grave expression. "Then we can't either," Ella said.

The wanderer winced. "If...if you're all sure."

"Sure we're sure," Dekker said, giving him a smile. "We're with you, Ungr. On whatever road you choose, to wherever that road takes us. We're with you."

The wanderer felt overcome with a powerful emotion then, and it was all he could do to nod as he turned to the wizard. "I guess…I guess that's everyone."

The man watched him for a moment. "You're sure?"

"Yes."

"Very well." The wizard turned to start away then paused, glancing back. "I will pray for your good fortune, Ungr the Eternal. And I will pray that you conquer the world's evil." He met the wanderer's gaze, then his eyes traveled down to the amulet at the wanderer's neck then back up to his eyes. "Wherever you find it."

And with that, the wizard turned and walked toward the gap in the mountain. The wanderer watched him go, wondering if he would see him again and doubting it.

"Well," Dekker said, drawing his attention. "We're with you, Ungr, but…what do we do now?"

"We leave the Untamed Lands in peace," the wanderer said.

"In peace…" the big man said slowly, frowning. "Didn't feel a whole lot of peace on the way here. How you reckon to get that done?"

"Oh," the wanderer said, smiling as he glanced at the woods where a large, furry form waited, eyeing him with yellow, luminous eyes. "I do not think it will be so bad. After all, it may be that we'll have help."

And now, dear reader, we have reached the end of A Ranger's Journey. I hope you enjoyed this latest adventure with the wanderer and Dekker, Clint and the Perishables and, of course, Earl the wizard. If you did enjoy the read, I'd really appreciate you taking a moment to leave a review

The next book in The Last Eternal is coming soon. In the meantime while you wait, I've got some other books you might want to give a shot.

Want another story of an anti-hero in a grimdark setting where a jaded sellsword is forced into a fight he doesn't want between forces he doesn't understand?
Get started on the bestselling seven book series, The Seven Virtues.

Interested in a story where the gods choose their champions in a war with the darkness that will determine the fate of the world itself?
Check out The Nightfall Wars, a complete six book, epic fantasy series.

Or how about something a little lighter? Do you like laughs with your sword slinging and magical mayhem? All the world's heroes are dead and so it is up to the antiheroes to save the day. An overweight swordsman, a mage who thinks magic is for sissies, an assassin who gets sick at the sight of the blood, and a man who can speak to animals...maybe.
The world needed heroes—it got them instead.
Start your journey with The Antiheroes!

If you'd like to reach out and chat, you can email me at JacobPeppersAuthor@gmail.com or visit my website at JacobPeppersAuthor.com.
You can also give me a shout on Facebook or on Twitter. I'm looking forward to hearing from you!

Turn the page for a limited time free offer!

Sign up for my VIP New Releases mailing list and get a free copy of *The Silent Blade: A Seven Virtues novella* as well as receive exclusive promotions and other bonuses!

Go to JacobPeppersAuthor.com to claim your free book!

NOTE FROM THE AUTHOR

And so, dear reader, *A Ranger's Journey* has come to an end and so, too, has our journey together. At least for the moment. I hope you have enjoyed this latest entry in *The Last Eternal*, this latest adventure with the wanderer, Dekker, Clint and all the rest. We faced many trials together, threats known and unknown, but that part of our adventure is done now and Ranger's impostor lies dead.

The villagers of Alhs, thankfully, have found a place where they might be safe, where they might mourn their losses in peace and, in time, rebuild. They are as safe as the wanderer can make them, but now it is time to move on.

He has spent the last century running, but he will run no longer. Now, it is time to fight. Now it is time to hunt the enemy, to make them feel the fear that has been his constant companion for the last hundred years and more.

And in this, at least, he will not be alone, for he has friends to help him. But the path the wanderer has chosen is a dangerous one with many twistings and turnings, many ways in which a man might become lost or find himself falling into a pit from which he cannot climb out.

The running is done, one way or the other.

The battle has begun.

So stick around, won't you?

We're just getting started...

I want to take this opportunity to thank everyone who has been instrumental in making this book what it is.

As always, thanks first and foremost to my wife, Andrea, for your constant support and for at least feigning interest when I describe a plot point for the hundredth time. It's a tough job being married to a writer—an even tougher one being married to this *particular* writer—but you do it with a grace and patience that is nothing short of amazing.

Thank you, also, to my family and friends, particularly my children. No fantasy world, however detailed, however caringly and meticulously created could ever be half as rich as the world in which I live, the *life* I live with the three of you and your mother.

Thank you, next to all of those beta readers who sacrifice their time and energy to make sure that the book is as good as it can be. I sometimes feel that I hand you all a great lump of misshapen coal and somehow you manage to hand me back a diamond. An acknowledgment in the back of the book doesn't seem like much repayment for all that you do, but I want you to know that I am very grateful nevertheless.

Thank you, lastly, to you, dear reader. It is your support, your reviews and emails, that make all the grumbling and cursing worthwhile. It's also what keeps the lights on, and I cannot thank you enough. I can only promise you that I will continue to write the best books that I can as quickly as I can, and it is my sincere hope that you will find your time with them worthwhile.

Until next time,

Happy Reading,

Jacob Peppers

ABOUT THE AUTHOR

Jacob Peppers lives in Georgia with his wife, his son, Gabriel, daughter, Norah, and newborn son, Declan, as well as their three dogs. He is an avid reader and writer and when he's not exploring the worlds of others, he's creating his own. His short fiction has been published in various markets, and his short story, "The Lies of Autumn," was a finalist for the 2013 Eric Hoffer Award for Short Prose. He is the author of the bestselling epic fantasy series *The Seven Virtues* and *The Nightfall Wars.*

Made in United States
Troutdale, OR
05/17/2024